JENNIFER PROBST

any time, any place

POCKET BOOKS

New York   London   Toronto   Sydney   New Delhi

The sale of this book without its cover is unauthorized. If you purchased this book without a cover, you should be aware that it was reported to the publisher as "unsold and destroyed." Neither the author nor the publisher has received payment for the sale of this "stripped book."

Pocket Books
An Imprint of Simon & Schuster, Inc.
1230 Avenue of the Americas
New York, NY 10020

This book is a work of fiction. Any references to historical events, real people, or real places are used fictitiously. Other names, characters, places, and events are products of the author's imagination, and any resemblance to actual events or places or persons, living or dead, is entirely coincidental.

Copyright © 2017 by Jennifer Probst

All rights reserved, including the right to reproduce this book or portions thereof in any form whatsoever. For information, address Gallery Books Subsidiary Rights Department, 1230 Avenue of the Americas, New York, NY 10020.

First Pocket Books paperback edition February 2017

POCKET and colophon are registered trademarks of Simon & Schuster, Inc.

For information about special discounts for bulk purchases, please contact Simon & Schuster Special Sales at 1-866-506-1949 or business@simonandschuster.com.

The Simon & Schuster Speakers Bureau can bring authors to your live event. For more information or to book an event, contact the Simon & Schuster Speakers Bureau at 1-866-248-3049 or visit our website at www.simonspeakers.com.

Manufactured in the United States of America

10 9 8 7 6 5 4 3 2 1

ISBN 978-1-5011-2428-0
ISBN 978-1-5011-2427-3 (ebook)

Redford Township District Library

3 9009 0017 5785 1

Forgiveness is the fragrance that the violet sheds on the heel that has crushed it.

—Mark Twain

I wondered if that was how forgiveness budded, not with the fanfare of epiphany, but with pain gathering its things, packing up, and slipping away unannounced in the middle of the night.

—Khaled Hosseini, *The Kite Runner*

———————

To all my beloved readers who have experienced pain, yet are brave enough to offer forgiveness. This world badly needs your strength. Kindness and forgiveness will always triumph in the end because both require one mighty thing: love.

And to my family who give me such strength every day.

I love you.

prologue

Raven Bella Hawthorne watched the casket drop into the ground. The rain caused the hole to look slippery, almost like a mud hill. When she was younger, she probably would've looked at the slope as a great adventure, letting out a big war-type chant while she hurled herself down over the edge as if it were a giant Slip 'N Slide. She'd climb out with a big grin, mud crusted on every part of her body, and her father would shake his head and try to scold her. Meanwhile, his dark eyes would glint with laughter, and Raven would know she wasn't really in trouble.

But now, her father was in the hole. She'd never see that sparkling humor, or hear his deep belly laugh, or listen to one of his lectures in that gravelly voice that reminded her of a big papa bear.

Because her father was dead.

Aunt Penny squeezed her hand, but Raven hardly felt it. The cold chill of rainwater seeped into her skin and her soul, burrowing deep inside and making a permanent home to rest. The crew of men in black suits with bowed heads recited a prayer as the casket disappeared for good.

People threw roses in the hole. One weeping woman clutched her rosary. The priest concluded the prayer service, telling Raven and everyone else not to grieve, because Matthew Albert Hawthorne was in heaven with the angels and was finally, mercifully at peace.

Raven stared at the priest. At the mishmash of distant relatives she barely knew and friends who seemed more focused on the scandal surrounding her father's death than on her. No, other than Aunt Penny, she was truly alone. And she didn't feel grateful, or happy, or humbled her father was with God.

Instead, Raven was filled with rage.

Her beloved father, who had been her entire world, was a liar and a cheat. The man who dragged her to church on Sundays and lectured her on saving her body for love and being kind to others and always believing she'd accomplish great things in this world had abandoned his only daughter to run away with another woman. A stranger.

If it hadn't been for the red light, her father and that woman would be in Paris, building a new life away from their children. Instead, they were both dead, lying in the cold, damp ground while she dealt with the stinging slap of betrayal. For the first time, Raven knew what it was to hate.

She hated her father. She hated the woman who had stolen him away. She hated the three sons the woman had left behind, sons who spread evil words about Matthew luring their innocent mother away, painting him as a charming manipulator who cared nothing about the bonds of family.

Her father's once spotless reputation now lay in tatters around her. People gossiped and stared and whispered behind raised hands about the single father who'd ruined two families by seducing the matriarch of Pierce Brothers Construction. Somehow, some way, Diane Pierce had become a martyr. Which made Matthew Hawthorne the only villain of the story.

So Raven hated and burned for revenge while she stood in the rain, nodding at well-wishers. She listened to Aunt Penny thank the endless line of people for offerings of food, prayers, and help in their effort to feel validated during someone else's tragedy. Finally Raven walked to the limousine and slid onto the smooth leather seat. As they pulled away toward her new life, Raven had only one thought:

Payback was going to be a bitch.

chapter one

> ✦ <

Dalton looked at the table in front of him and frowned.

It was all wrong.

Frustration nipped at his nerves. Sweat dripped down his chest, and the familiar scents of varnish and sawdust rose to his nostrils. He rubbed his head, staring at the sharp curves and clawed feet of the dining room table he was restoring for the Ryans. The lines were right. His hands trailed lightly and lovingly over the top and down each leg, sensing the quality wasn't the problem. Dropping to his knees, he crawled underneath to check further, but there were no skips and the grains were full and smooth. The shape was perfect. Then what was niggling at his gut that something was completely off?

He rolled to his feet, backed up, and looked at the table in the light.

Too dark. The Brazilian walnut finish blended into blackish tones.

All wrong.

The voice whispered from within, and as usual, he didn't question where the answers came from. He just followed where they led. His clients had insisted on the darkest finish possible for their new antique find, and if he rebelled against those instructions he'd be taking some heat.

From both the Ryans and his brothers.

And as usual, he ignored the warning, choosing to follow his gut.

It needed a softer finish. Brazilian chestnut would work. The color was fuller, which would round out the angles to illuminate the gorgeous curves and elegant dignity of the antique. They'd chosen wrong, but if he did it the right way, they'd agree.

Maybe.

He pushed away the doubt, grabbing the towel to wipe his stained hands and guzzle some water. The low hum of the central air wrapped him in the perfect temperature. He didn't mind the cloying humidity outside, since he was used to some sticky Northeast summers. But his precious wood needed care, and it did best under steady conditions. Humidity was known to warp grains.

Sometimes he needed to protect the raw materials from Mother Nature's occasional temper, and he had no problem embracing artificial environments.

His brothers would make fun of him for that thought, so he'd never shared it. Just like he'd be taking their shit when he called the Ryans to tack on an extra day to deliver the table. Too often they perceived him as flighty and irresponsible. The three of them might co-own Pierce Brothers Construction, but it was obvious Caleb and Tristan still didn't believe Dalton could handle his part in the business. The past year had been rough, and they'd all grown much closer, yet Dalton noticed Cal and Tristan still treated him like an annoying younger brother. Sure, they respected his talent with woodworking, but they still refused to acknowledge his contribution to the bottom line.

They drove him batshit crazy.

He shook his head and trudged over to the workbench. He began cleaning up his tools, kicking up another cloud of sawdust. Dalton thought over the past year and how far they'd all come. When he'd first learned of his father's death and the will that forced him to move back to Harrington, Connecticut, to run the family business with his two older brothers, he'd been pissed off and betrayed. He'd been happy in California, starting up his own business and free from his father's brutal ways. Christian Pierce had ruled his family like an old Roman king—his way or no way at all. He'd refused to allow any changes in the business, and the only softness in the boys' lives had been their beloved mother, who'd kept the family together.

Until the fatal car crash that not only took her life, but broke Dalton's heart and shattered his hope that anything would ever be okay again.

Everything he'd believed in crumbled and left him in ruins. Diane Pierce had been the force that made them whole. Learning she'd run away with a strange man, leaving her family behind, crippled them all. The two one-way tickets to Paris confirmed the betrayal. The only way to get through it was to imagine she'd been conned by the man who'd burned in the car beside her. Of course, he'd never get the answers he sought. They had all died with her, as had everything good and gentle and pure in his life.

After that, a perfect storm of horrific events tore them all at the seams until there was nothing left but anger and pain between them. Dalton fled to California, Tristan settled in New York, and Caleb remained behind to work with their father.

He tightened his grip on his saw. Five years and they'd barely spoken. Once so close to them, Dalton had lived in a void, as if he didn't have a family, until he got the news that Christian Pierce had died of a heart attack. When he'd returned for his father's funeral, the will had made fools of them all. Christian's will decreed all three of them needed to run Pierce Brothers at a profit for one year, or the business would be sold off. When Cal begged Dalton and Tristan to help, they reluctantly agreed, but it was a rough year, full of painful revelations and lingering resentment. They'd somehow managed to slowly rebuild until they'd become a family again.

When the year was up, Dalton made his choice to stay. His vision of running Pierce Brothers as a full partner filled him with pride and ambition. Now he was able to stand proudly next to Caleb and Tristan and call it a real family business. Caleb oversaw the new builds as the main contractor. Tristan dealt with real estate, design, and flipping houses. And Dalton was lucky enough to do what his life calling had always been: work with wood. Building pieces from scratch into treasured and beautiful objects soothed something within his soul. His hands were an extension of creativity and nurturing, and each piece was unique and special, as if he'd just stepped away from the wood to allow it to reveal the heart. The brothers had finally found their rhythm, and Pierce Brothers Construction had leapt to stellar status once again.

He just wished his brothers would stop shutting him out of the big decisions.

Dalton stored his tools carefully and straightened up his workshop. The large shedlike structure looked plain on the outside, but inside, it was his own personal paradise. Set back by the woods on the family mansion's property, it was completely private, surrounded by thick brush like a hidden fairy-tale house no one could find. Shelves covered the walls and were filled with various tools and scrap pieces. Each piece told a particular story Dalton treasured. His saw collection was legendary, and if anyone got too close, he actually felt a growl rumble from his chest. He might not be possessive of women, but grubby fingers better stay the hell away from his power tools.

Band saws, circular saws, and panel saws were his livelihood. Over the years, he'd added to his collection of lathes, planers, sanders, jointers, and routers. His machines were top-of-the-line and lovingly cared for. An extension of his fingers, the right tool could make or break a job. A large multifunction worktable sat at the center of the room, with numerous drawers neatly labeled and tagged. He knew exactly how many drill bits lay within each compartment, and their sizes.

Cal had once "borrowed" a bit and forgotten to return it. After Dalton "mistakenly" shipped all the wood for a project to the wrong place in retaliation, his precious shed had never been touched again.

His favorite music was always at hand with his Amazon Echo; its digital voice assistant, Alexa, had lately become his favorite girlfriend of all time.

Dalton finished clearing his work space and glanced at his phone. He thought of his plans for the evening, which included picking up the new varnish for the Ryans and little else. Caleb and Morgan were going out. Tristan was away for a few days on a business trip. Maybe he'd call that pretty little blonde, Avery, and take her to dinner? His lackluster response told him it wouldn't be a good move. On their last date, he'd noticed she'd gotten that moony look in her blue eyes and had casually mentioned her sister coming to visit. Like she wanted him to meet her.

He fought back a shudder. Meeting any type of family was a danger. Connections were made, and women got false ideas of where a couple of nights out could lead. Dalton hated hurting anyone, so he made sure the rules were laid out plainly for the women he dated so they knew where he stood. Unfortunately, too much time together equaled greater expectations.

That's when it was time to move on.

His gut burned with a strange hollowness that had never been there before. What he needed was a project all for himself. Too often he was doing cabinetry and decks for the specific houses being built, but they weren't his choices. Back in California, he'd been able to pick and choose the jobs he was passionate about. He was starting to feel like a factory worker rather than a woodworking artist. Sure, he knew it was part of being in the family business, and he prided himself on delivering pristine work. Though his brothers bitched about him not meeting his clients' demands, they grudgingly admitted that 99 percent of the time, the clients agreed Dalton was right and loved the outcome.

Yes, that was it. He'd keep his attention cocked for a special project that really meant something to him. That would take care of the itch and soothe the restless beast within.

He grabbed his shirt, took one last look around, and shut the door behind him.

chapter two

Raven breathed hard, sweat pouring down her back, wet strands of hair falling in her eyes. She pushed it all down and focused, gritting her teeth against the pain of strained muscles and threatening exhaustion.

She bent down to connect with more power, then launched herself through the air.

Her foot hit the target dead center. Without losing her balance, she shifted her weight and delivered the crushing left hook, sending the dummy toppling to the ground.

"Nice work." The voice was full of respect and the teasing edge that solidified Xavier's status as her favorite trainer. "For a girl."

She wiped her stinging eyes and began to unlace her boxing gloves. "Cute. How about you take me on and I show you how to scream like a girl?"

He flashed her a grin. White teeth blinded her, drawing a few more onlookers their way. With his rippling muscles and gorgeous coffee-bean skin, Xavier was not only one of the most sought-after trainers in the state but one of the most eligible bachelors in Harrington. He'd been training her for almost a year now, and they'd formed a solid connection as friends. Sure, they'd flirted with the idea of trying to be more, but it was obvious to both of them they didn't experience the chemistry needed to take it to the next level. His past was still a bit of a mystery. He'd come on the scene as a contestant for *American Ninja Warrior*, gone viral by getting close to the end, then dropped out to train clients at the local gym.

Raven could tell there was more to the story, but she never asked. Raven had learned to respect people's secrets. After all, he never probed for hers.

Xavier retrieved the toppled dummy and shook his head. "No, thanks. I've got enough women in my life kicking my ass. I don't need a new one."

She laughed and grabbed the water he handed her. "At least you're smart."

"Been trying to tell you, sugar. The fight is usually won in the first few moments. Keep your mind clear to see all angles of the situation. Then decide whether to attack or retreat. Neither one is the wrong choice."

"Yes, my enlightened one." Her words teased him back, but Raven knew each piece of advice he gave her was crucial. Since she'd started training in boxing and karate, she'd learned to tap into parts of herself that could scare her.

Unconsciously, her fingers touched the tattoo on her shoulder in memory. The sword tipped with blood reminded her every day of her promise. But over the past year, she'd been tugged in a new direction, and she wasn't sure which would finally win out. She wondered when she'd finally have to make the choice.

"I'll see you Wednesday?" he asked.

She shook herself out of her trance. "Definitely. Hey, when are you going to swing by for a drink? I'll mix up a specialty cocktail just for you."

"They already have one named after me. It's called the Orgasm."

She rolled her eyes. "I'll make you a better one. It's called Overrated."

His laughter followed her down the short hall toward the locker room. It was easy to banter with Xavier. She admired his male beauty but didn't crave being in his bed. From her past, she'd learned sex could be a dangerous tool that destroyed relationships, even the ones that were the most precious. She had no intention of going down that bumpy road. No, when she was ready, she'd look for a man who was mature, loving, and

kind. She was done with all the bad boys and se-
rial bedders who had no interest in a real relationship.

Not anymore.

Raven showered and changed into her street
clothes. The humidity hit her as she opened the
door, wrapping its cloak around her head and trying to smother her. She'd heard people in Arizona
called the heat dry, but here in Connecticut,
it was a wretched, clogged invasion that drove
people indoors to their beloved air conditioners.
And it was only June.

Her designer sneakers were black and silver
with a high wedge, but they were comfortable
enough to accommodate her long legs and rapid
pace without a hitch. She jumped into her Jeep
and drove the short distance to the demanding
lover in her life that greedily took all her time and
energy.

My Place.

Her soul practically sighed with contentment
when she pulled into the graveled lot. The restaurant was simple on the outside. Dark wood and
a big front porch. The lighted sign was hitched
a bit askew and slanted toward the right. Once
she unlocked the main doors with the dead bolt,
another set of old saloon-style doors came into
view, giving the place a fun feel. She left the main
doors ajar when the bar was open, but for now,

she locked them again behind her and stepped into her pub.

An automatic smile curved her lips. The smells of lemony polish, lingering garlic and grease, and a hint of old wood and must rose to her nostrils in a symphony. Her gaze took in the high raftered ceilings with thick beams, noting the small circle of water damage that would eventually force her to replace the roof. She'd need to invest before winter. Scarred plank floors and large booths with red vinyl seating gave off a comfortable aura. She made sure there was plenty of activity for the regular bar crowd—two large television screens, a pool table, a dartboard, and a working jukebox screamed old school. Shelves held various knick-knacks like bobbleheads, sports memorabilia, and the occasional antique mirror. Signs hung on the walls, shouting familiar catchphrases such as RULE NUMBER 1: THE BARTENDER IS ALWAYS RIGHT. RULE NUMBER 2: IF THE BARTENDER IS WRONG, GO BACK TO RULE NUMBER 1. Yosemite Sam held a smoking pistol with a MOST WANTED placard over his head. A vintage *Cheers* sign—WHERE EVERYBODY KNOWS YOUR NAME—was one of her favorites.

But the main feature was the bar.

It was another antique, and she bet in its heyday it had been a glorious piece of art. The dull mahogany wood set off the brick wall behind, along with her fully stocked collection of liquor bottles, the taps, and her cocktail-creating section. The length and width were massive, allowing her to seat over a dozen people.

Raven loved stuff. She might not know how to restore or decorate properly, and she couldn't care less about frilly curtains or bedding or sofa pillows, but a good, solid antique spoke to her. She enjoyed spending some free time roaming at the local vintage store, the Barn, and seeing what else she could pick up.

Pride flowed rich in her veins. When she'd decided to buy the bar, it had been almost unsalvageable from a previous fire and was dirt cheap. After years of refusing to touch her father's life insurance money, Raven decided it was the only way to buy the pub. After restoration, she was even able to reopen the restaurant. At first, she kept the menu simple but satisfying, featuring her famous sweet potato fries. But when she snagged her real live culinary chef, they decided to step it up and give the cornerstone restaurants in town competition. The burgers were gourmet, with specialized toppings the locals flocked in for. The steaks were oversize and thick, and the few vegetarian dishes offered were creative and satisfying, not the usual rabbit food most thought of. Her staff was well trained, well treated, and always backed up. But what kept the crowds booming was the best damn cocktails imaginable. She'd finally made a name for herself, and she intended to keep growing doing what she did best.

Working her ass off.

Yeah. Things were good.

The past surged up and tried to sucker punch her, but she stepped neatly away and allowed herself to let it go. Hadn't she learned her lesson? Steeping herself in a world that could only provide bitterness and regret wasn't something she did anymore. As long as she moved forward, there was enough to make her happy.

She had a few more hours till opening and a lot to do. Besides a brief staff session and a meeting with Al to go over the menu, she'd been playing with a new cocktail idea that combined fresh raspberries and mint, which were in season.

Raven headed behind the bar and got to work.

chapter three

Dalton walked through the saloon doors and took in the scene.

My Place was becoming *the* place to hang out, which was surprising since it was located just outside of Harrington, away from the popularity of Main Street. Harrington was a well-known town that drew tourists by the busload to explore the marina and artsy shops and seafood restaurants. Nestled close to Greenwich, it was also a town that boasted pure money, and many celebrities resided behind its exclusive gates. It was an easy commute to Manhattan, and was featured in some highbrow magazines as the best hidden secret in the Northeast. Dalton had been sad when he'd seen how much the town had grown. He missed the purity of the place he'd grown up in. But the locals had claimed My Place for themselves, preferring to leave Main Street and all its pretty trappings for amazing pub food, cocktails, and a pool table.

The place was packed, and classic Michael Jackson blared from the jukebox in the corner. Four guys were playing a lively game of pool, and a baseball game flickered on the dual televisions. The Mets were on. He'd actually become a Dodgers fan during his time in California, but he wouldn't admit it here. A group of young women took up the far right side of the bar, giggling and sipping some type of frothy pink cocktail that gave him a toothache just looking at it. The scents of sweet potato fries, grilled meat, and draft beer drifted in the air.

Finally he allowed his gaze to narrow in on the two things he was becoming obsessed with.

Raven.

And her bar.

The latter lay before him in tired, battered glory. The brick wall behind set off the massive high-topped bar that desperately needed restoring. Dents and chips marred the wood, and cheap gold foot bars and handrails seemed stuck on without thought as to aesthetics. His fingers itched with the need to touch the magnificent mahogany and bring it back to its original condition. In his head, he saw pictures of how he'd piece it back together and replace the gold trims. Take off the awful glass top and install hand-carved shelves to properly show off the array of liquor bottles and glasses that could stun an onlooker. The stools were structured of cheap, old oak that actually detracted from the main focus of the bar.

Oh, how badly he wanted to get his hands on her. Show her some tenderness and stroke her back to beauty. It would change the entire look of the restaurant and restore the bar to the queen she should be. This was a project that excited him.

Almost as much as the owner did.

Unfortunately, he didn't think Raven would let him get his hands on her body, or her bar.

She was talking with a bunch of guys, and by the looks of it, they were desperately trying to flirt with her. He already knew they'd strike out. He'd been trying for months to get her attention, and she still treated him with a chilling politeness that froze his balls right in place. Her attitude completely contradicted her appearance, which screamed *SEX* from the high heavens and left a trail of men panting in her wake.

Her hair was long, coal-black, and wild. She wore it back in a clip when she was serving food, and loose when just serving drinks. She didn't seem to care about forcing the strands to behave, which only made her sexier. Her eyes slanted up at the sides like a cat's; they were the color of soot with a tinge of smoke gray around the rims. Her face was long and lean, with a sharp chin and nose and heavy brows. Her lower lip plumped out; her upper one was defined. She was wicked tall, with small breasts, long arms and legs, and narrow hips. Her uniform consisted of a tank top, dark-washed jeans, and either high-top wedged Skechers or black heeled sandals with crisscross straps. She liked to wear multiple chains around her neck, and a diamond nose ring caught and glimmered under the light. What fascinated Dalton the most was the tattoo on her right shoulder. A sword with a wicked blade, tipped with blood. Not a rose or the scrawl of a phrase with meaning. Instinct told him she'd chosen that tat for a specific reason. He wanted to know what the sword meant. So far, she'd refused to tell him.

From the moment he'd seen her, he'd ached to touch her, but she'd slammed him with her prickly manner and cold gaze. For some strange reason, she didn't like him. It wasn't about his hopeful advances, either. She got hit on multiple times a night, and was well known to give scathing one-liners that guys actually hooted over instead of getting pissed. No, somehow her attitude seemed personal, but Dalton couldn't figure out the mystery. Yet. So he kept showing up at the bar and hoped he'd eventually get her to soften.

So far, no good.

Normally, if a woman wasn't interested, Dalton bided his time. He liked the chase and the lure of a good seduction, but he'd never waited this long, or dealt with so many stinging rejections. He didn't like the phrase *man whore*, either. His brothers drove him crazy with that term. Like calling a woman a slut, it had no purpose other than to accuse, hurt, or judge another person's choices. He had his own code of ethics, and it was his own business.

Bottom line: He loved women. Their scent, their voice, the smooth touch of their skin. Their humor and passion and deep emotion that they had no problem connecting with. Sex was one of the gifts in life, and he took full advantage, yet his pleasure was always wrapped up in his partner's. He loved the sound of a woman groaning in passion or screaming his name. He relished the bite of their nails and the curl of their toes and the way they got all soft and helpless after a few orgasms. He wasn't a chauvinist or an egotist, but he was consistently fascinated with the female sex and didn't see a problem with indulging his cravings. He was always honest and didn't really see himself as ever wanting to settle down. Dalton believed in steeping himself in the experience of a woman's company for however long it felt good, then moving on. Not to hurt them, but just the opposite. He knew he wasn't the marrying type, and he had no desire to offer them false expectations of what he was able to provide. Mostly it worked. Sometimes it didn't.

Dalton walked toward the bar and took a seat. His blood pumped with the sweet lure of the challenge. He'd never run from a fair battle with a woman he wanted. Eventually he'd have her.

And the bar.

He just needed a bit of patience.

"I got a proposition for you, baby. Me. You. And a night you'll never forget. Whatcha say?"

Raven leaned over the bar and pushed out her bottom lip in a sexy pout. Her gaze swept over his figure. Then she smiled real slow. "I got a better proposition. How about you, your hand, and a bottle of lube instead? Baby."

A hoot of male laughter rose to her ears. One of her regular patrons, Dave, reached over to clap his friend on the back, shaking his head. "Dude, I told you, she doesn't play."

The guy who'd taken the hit gave her a grin. "Ruthless, too. Remind me why we came here again?"

Raven winked and pulled back from the bar. With a deft spin on her heel, she grabbed a shot glass and poured two fingers neat of whiskey. "'Cause I serve the best liquor and food in town.

Here, try this. It'll take away the sting." She slid the glass down the bar until it rested in front of him.

Dave threw up his hands. "Hey, what about me?"

"You know the rules. One pickup line. One rejection. One shot. Then you pay."

Dave's friend—was it Mark?—snapped the shot back and gave an appreciative nod. "You're right. That was worth bombing out."

She tossed him a smile and moved down the bar. They were good guys. A little rowdy and immature, but their bar bill was always high, and they were harmless. Each weekend the group recruited another male to pick her up, and failed. The good news was each of them came back the next weekend because My Place was the best damn bar in Harrington.

Sweeping a glance over the crowded pub, she headed back to the kitchen, clicking down her mental list of to-do items. She really needed a full-time assistant, but Raven liked to work alone, and she'd always been known for her temper. No need to start yelling at strangers when she could be happily neurotic all by her lonesome. She dealt well with employees but not partners. Still, she'd managed to grow her profits in the past year and had actual money in the bank. The lesson was simple and proved correct every single time.

Don't count on anyone but yourself.

Leaning on other people was not only dangerous. It was also stupid.

She quickly made her rounds to check on her chef, Al, who was one of the nicest guys she knew. He'd graduated from the Culinary Institute of America near Poughkeepsie, snagged a fancy chef job, and moved in with his girlfriend.

Unfortunately, soon after, his girlfriend left him and hooked up with a guy who liked to slap her around. When she called Al in a panic, he made it his job to show the guy what it felt like to be beaten up.

His second unfortunate circumstance was discovering the asshole was the son of a top prosecutor, and Al soon found himself plea-bargaining and serving three years in prison for assault and battery. His girlfriend lied and swore Al had stalked her in a jealous rage.

When Al turned up on Raven's doorstep asking for a job, sharing his past in clear, emotionless detail, she immediately knew he was a gift. A real CIA chef, and one who wanted to protect the woman he loved. It was a win-win, and she hired him on the spot.

Besides being a talented chef and a hard worker, he always looked after her servers, who were young, single girls who made too many mistakes.

God knows, she'd been one of those. Too bad he hadn't been around back then to save her ass.

Choking heat poured from the stove, and the fryer snapped and sizzled. Her servers hurried back and forth, barking out orders, shuffling trays, and not taking any shit from customers. Raven had learned early to hire experienced waitstaff, pay them well, and back them up when there was a customer problem. They wore a standard uniform of comfortable jeans, T-shirts, and sneakers. Who the hell could work in heels and short, tight skirts? They were loyal, worked their asses off, and were a key ingredient in My Place's success. Turnover of staff was a deadly threat to restaurants, and Raven had no time to deal with such drama.

Even though she frickin' loved watching *Vanderpump Rules* on Bravo.

Al turned, his white uniform already splattered with grease. His shaven head gleamed with sweat. "We're busier than usual tonight," he commented. Meaty biceps flexed with each turn of the spatula. Raven loved to watch him command the kitchen. He reminded her of a dancer with every motion coordinated, multiple burners pumping, a row of tickets in front of him, and a calm, focused energy that was rarely rattled.

"You good?"

He waved a hand in the air, showing off a panel of tats scrolled on his arm. "Course. But I need a cig break soon."

She put her hands on her hips and glared. "You told me you were getting the patch."

"Next week. I promise."

She blew out a breath. "Al, I don't want to lose my best cook to lung cancer. You can quit smoking. Don't be a pussy."

Black brows lowered in a fierce frown. He looked like the Rock ready to punch someone, but Raven knew he was a marshmallow underneath. "Who you callin' a pussy? Just because you take some boxing classes, don't think you're some badass who can threaten me. It's my life. If I wanna die, it's my choice."

"What are you—running for Congress? Screw that. I will kick your ass if I don't see the patch on your arm. You're too old for this crap."

Amanda, one of her servers, bounced over and clipped another ticket to the row. With her blond hair and blue eyes, she was consistently hit on and regularly got high tips. Raven loved her because she always dumped half of her tips in the jar for Al, even though she was paying her way through college. "Yeah, Al, we need you around here. Why don't you try to vape? At least it'll get you off the tobacco."

"I'm not old! Leave me the hell alone so I can cook." He jabbed his finger at Amanda. "Did you study for your damn astronomy test? If you flunk, your GPA will be in the toilet."

Amanda sighed. "Yeah, but I still get the stu-pid stars mixed up. Raven tried to help, but she knows too much. I just want to pass the test, but she gets all excited, and an hour later, she's still lecturing on Orion and Cantis Min something. I think she's a closet scientist."

"Canis Minor," Raven said patiently. "Just trying to help you appreciate the world above, sweets."

Al rolled his eyes. "She just needs to pass the test. Amanda, meet me outside on break and I'll quiz you."

Her smile lit up the room. "Thanks, Al."

He grumbled something foul, then turned back to the grill.

"See? We all love you. Try the vape," Raven said.

"Get out of my kitchen, Raven."

"Leaving." She held back a laugh, enjoying her work family in all its disjointed chaos. Satisfied the kitchen had things under control, she headed back to the bar, where she felt most at home. Music and laughter and chatter soothed her nerves while her mind began to play with new cocktail recipes. Something with mint. Cool and clean, but it needed texture and a bit of a snap. A surprise on the tongue. Cilantro? No, too much. Thyme? She'd never done that before, but maybe it was worth an hour of her time to play. Mixing cocktails was more than her job—it was a creative passion that was a bit of an obsession. She wondered how she'd gotten her strange mix of genes where concocting drinks was her big talent. Aunt Penny had been huge on Broadway, but Raven couldn't carry a tune. Or speak well in public. Her father had painted, of course, until—

Before the pain hit, she tore off the thought like a limb that needed to be quickly amputated. She'd learned to avoid any thoughts of how much her father had meant, and how he'd betrayed her. Much simpler to wipe away her past like a clean, blank slate she could now fill with new memories. Like her bar. And . . .

Well, that was it for now. Still, she'd managed to turn her life around from her disastrous path and become a respected business owner. The pub was all she needed for the moment. Definitely the best relationship she'd ever been in, and the longest. The worst part? She wasn't sorry. And she didn't even miss men. Much.

As if mocking her statement, she heard his voice. Rich like earth and wood. Smooth and hot like whiskey. Tempting like a Red Delicious apple ready to be bitten.

"I'm a thirsty man, darlin'. Got a tall, cool one for me?"

She already knew the man attached to the voice but couldn't believe the punch of heat between them when she turned. Raven had dated a lot of men. Slept with a lot, too. She knew about dating, flirting, and teasing and wasn't scared of anything. She knew about dirty, delicious, mind-blowing sex. She knew about mornings after and speedy Batman disappearances in the ugly dawn light. But this man wiped all her expertise away with one bat of those dark lashes or a tug of those full lips.

Dalton Pierce.

A man she'd vowed to hate and the one man she was crazy attracted to.

A man who held the key to a past she didn't want to unlock.

Raven turned and studied him. Cocky, as always. Charming, as usual. He was a visual feast for the female sex and knew it. Tawny, gold-streaked strands, worn long, framed his face. He liked to tie them back or put them in a man bun, which should look ridiculous but only made him that much hotter 'cause he didn't care. Peacock-blue eyes so bright and so deep, if she stared too long she'd never come back up for air. Square jaw with sexy scruff to keep him from looking too pretty, and actual dimples when he smiled. The sun had turned his skin tan and a bit rough. His hands were calloused, and he always smelled like varnish, lemon, and a faint hint of Hershey's chocolate. Sawdust clung to his black T-shirt, and his jeans had holes in the knees.

Dalton was the ultimate Achilles' heel for any walking, breathing female who'd sworn off men. Thank goodness he'd never be able to bust through her barriers. They were so thick and tall, he'd get bashed in the head each and every time he tried.

Yet the oddest shimmer of connection always sparked to life when they were close. As if the universe was playing the ultimate joke, forcing her to be attracted to the one man she could never be with.

The past surged up like a tsunami and dragged her under.

Eight months ago, on the anniversary of her father's death, Dalton had walked into her bar to join his brothers. She'd served him a bottle of Jack Daniel's and watched them all get trashed. She'd been in a shit mood, trying to wrestle the bad memories. His deprecating charm, even when drunk off his ass, had made her smile. He'd hit on her all evening, and though she gave him a hard time, she kept sneaking glances at him. There'd been an odd pull from her gut, almost as if her body or subconscious mind recognized him. She'd even played with the idea of giving in that night, desperate to bury her own memories in earth-shattering sex and the comfort of a man's arms.

Then she'd heard his last name. *Pierce.* Shocked to the core, frozen in ice, Raven realized his mother was the woman who'd taken her father away. The woman who had gotten him killed in a freak car accident. The woman from her nightmare.

It all happened so fast; she'd told him to get the hell out of her bar, and then he was gone. The pieces suddenly fit together in a lightbulb moment. The brothers were getting drunk because it was the day Diane Pierce was killed. God, she'd felt dirty realizing she'd served them in her bar as they commemorated that fateful day. She swore she'd never allow them back into My Place. Her tat had burned her skin, reminding her of the vow for revenge at her father's funeral. She hated all the brothers for ruining her father's reputation and spinning the story to protect their deceitful mother. The Pierces were a powerful family, with the biggest construction firm in the Northeast, and she'd been . . . nothing. An artist's daughter. Poor but happy. Until they yanked it all away from her without a thought.

Suddenly her father's displays of artwork in the local shops were stripped down and returned to her because they were unsellable. His reputation as a visionary faded under the sting of terms such as *con artist* and *homewrecker*. Gazes were suddenly trained on her with harsh judgment, and whispers rose to her ears in a sickening wave. The place she had once called home turned into a prison, even though Aunt Penny tried hard to comfort and help. Dropping out of the community college, Raven had fled to leave the pain behind, searching desperately for some type of comfort in the expanse of the world beyond.

How many times had she wanted to confront Dalton about the truth? Her father had called her Bella, and she doubted Dalton paid any attention to the remnants of destruction his family had wreaked on a young girl left behind. But each time she opened her mouth to tell him the truth, she stopped. She liked having the secret to herself. She liked being able to study him and his brothers as if they were a key to a puzzle she'd been trying to solve for years. The question still haunted her, no matter how hard she tried to forget.

Why had her father left with Diane Pierce?

Maybe the Pierce brothers knew the truth. If they did, she doubted Dalton would just tell her. No, they wanted to protect their mother, so they'd lie. It'd be easier to find out more if she got closer to them and encouraged them to trust her. Like any good bartender.

So she'd let them back into her bar. She paid attention to their conversations and kept her ears sharp in regard to any mention of their parents or the accident. Raven knew Dalton was her best shot at getting most of the information. He was constantly flirting, and she could easily lead him down the road she needed.

If only she weren't attracted to him.

Dalton had been pushing harder these past few months, demanding more attention. He was flirty, charming, and regularly asked her out. In response, she'd been mean, rude, and regularly said no.

The real problem lay in the treacherous weakness of her body.

Somehow, some way, he lit her up from the inside out. She became more alive around him, whether she was insulting him, teasing him, or serving him drinks. She made up stupid excuses to check on him or hang near his seat. Over the past months, he'd begun to erode her stubbornness with an infinite charm and patience, until it became harder and harder to truly dislike him.

Raven really, really wanted to dislike him.

"I'm flattered to be the target of your attention, but I'm still waiting for my drink."

His teasing, wicked words launched her out of her reverie and made her realize she'd been staring at him this whole time. Fighting a blush, she cocked her hip, narrowed her gaze, and studied him. Deliberately. He looked delighted to have her attention, whether or not it was negative.

"Tall and cool, huh?" She treated him to a dazzling smile, which made his mouth drop open a bit in pure surprise. It was rare that she was nice to him, and a smile was almost an extinct gesture from her. Satisfaction flashed at her ability to throw him off balance, but it was chased with a feminine breathiness she hated. Why did he have to be so damn good-looking? She was twenty-seven, for God's sake. Way past weak-kneed ridiculousness, yet this man got her each time. "I have a better proposition for you. Something I just whipped up that'll rock your world."

"Sounds great. I'd love to try it."

"You got it." She grabbed a glass and went to the mini refrigerator where she kept samples of batches she'd been experimenting with. The giggling group of females taking up the far end of the bar was celebrating an engagement. She'd given them her latest creation and they'd already ordered a second round. Raven bet it would be perfect for the man across from her who was wreaking havoc on her concentration.

She quickly ground some mint, then added it along with simple syrup, a touch of aromatic bitters, and the bright pink mixture to a shaker filled with ice. After a few hard shakes, she strained the liquid into a glass, stuck a froufrou paper umbrella in it, and slid the drink across the bar.

He blinked. "Looks a bit feminine, doesn't it?"

She knew he preferred IPAs, especially Raging Bitch, but she waited him out to see if he'd take the challenge. Already the large, obnoxious pink drink had snagged the attention of some college students, who grinned and snickered under their breath. Raven knew that what a man drank at a bar was sacred. A woman looked for a man who knew how to hold his whiskey, appreciate a good draft beer, and enjoy a cocktail now and then.

As long as it wasn't pink.

"You're secure in your manhood, right?"

She waited for a blustery agreement, but he was smarter than she'd originally thought. His lip twitched and he leaned over, snagging her with that wicked blue gaze, refusing to let go. She fought the urge to fidget under his hot stare, figuring he'd only last a second or two. Instead, he took his time, not afraid to find what he sought, holding his gaze in a patient way that gave her tummy a tug of arousal.

"Why don't you like me?" he asked.

Her breath caught. She allowed him to win and dropped her stare. Bastard. Half of her wanted to scream the truth and let the accusations of pain and betrayal fly loose. The other half knew it was her turf, and she'd promised not to waste her time on regrets from the past. Of course, he knew nothing, and the flash of confusion in those blue eyes almost made her feel sympathy.

Almost.

Raven shrugged. "You're getting way too personal," she said coolly. "I don't like you. I don't *not* like you. You're just . . . there."

"Like an ant?"

"Or a fly."

He nodded, thoughtful. "Bugs are a delicacy in many other countries. Ant eggs are eaten in Mexico. Flies are probably eaten, too."

"You trying to tell me you're an exotic taste that I can get used to?"

He flashed her a brilliant smile, complete with dimples. Her heart gave an extra pump. Damn him for knowing how to use charm to his advantage. "Exactly!"

"We're in the US," she pointed out. "We like simple things. Hamburgers and hot dogs and beer. Are you going to try the drink or not?"

"I can be simple."

"You can't be simple and exotic at the same time."

"I can." His voice dropped to an intimate murmur. "I can be anything you want, Raven." Blistering heat shot from his body in waves. Suddenly the buzzing crowd faded and was replaced by the promise gleaming in his eyes, carved out in the lines of his face. She stilled under the impact of his full masculine power. It had been a long time since she'd been pursued with such focus. Raven had forgotten the adrenaline rush of the mating game and the sweet promise of sexual satisfaction that scented the air with rich pheromones.

She shook her head and forced herself to speak lightly. "You're a master, I'll give you that.

But you're wasting your time. You have nothing I want, or need."

Again he took the jab with charm instead of irritation. "Then I'll have to keep working on finding what you do want. Or need." He paused. "Or crave."

Her brow shot up in warning, but he only laughed. The rich, deep tones stroked her ear in a caress. Damn, he was dangerous. The worst part was he knew it.

"So, what is this drink called?" he finally asked.

She practically purred in response. "Fertility Goddess. It's a drink made to ensure a long life of marriage, children, and commitment. Seems to be popular with the newly engaged crowd."

Raven didn't expect him to drink it. She wanted to make a point.

But Dalton only nodded and lifted the glass high in the air. His blue eyes sparkled with mischief, but underneath was an implacable determination that shook her to the core. "Bottoms up."

He drank the whole glass in one long swallow.

And Raven knew she was in a heap of trouble.

The woman was driving him crazy.

Dalton put down the ridiculous pink cocktail and caught the flicker of wariness crossing her features. Good. Had he finally managed to surprise her? Had he managed to pry loose a tiny chunk of the armor she wore as proudly as a knight? Raven had all the qualities of a modern-day witch: Droolworthy sex appeal. A tiny bit of meanness. Wicked smarts. And cutting humor. The perfect package he'd been trying to tap for months without success.

He watched her flit away from him and head down the bar, refilling beer and wineglasses, tossing out comments or jokes to the regulars. She seemed comfortable talking to a wide array of people and moved in a way that told him she enjoyed her body but wasn't obsessed with it. Women seemed to have so many hang-ups about their physical appearance. When Dalton stared at a naked woman, he didn't see the individual flaws so many of his partners were afraid to expose—he only saw raw beauty as perfect as God made, and he always felt humbled to be chosen to adore such a body. Raven was different. There was an innate sexuality that seeped from her skin, and his instincts told him she'd taken her pleasures on her terms in the past. He loved a woman who owned that power.

"Want another?"

She gestured to his empty glass, but this time there was a gleam of laughter in her dark eyes. Satisfaction speared through him. He'd drink another of those things to keep her amused, but it was time to initiate his plan. One that would hopefully make them both very, very happy.

"I'll let you emasculate me if you listen to my proposal."

She rolled her eyes and wiped a dish towel over the wet bar. "I'll pass on both." Like a perfectly co-ordinated dancer, she swept up a bottle of Raging Bitch, grabbed the opener from her back pocket, scooped off the cap, and had the bottle in front of him in a few seconds. Damn, the woman was hot. "Better?"

"Much. I'm going to give you my offer anyway."

"Have I told you lately I'm a lesbian?"

He grinned. "Cool. I'd just have to work harder to woo you to the other side."

Her lips twitched. When had simple banter been this much fun? His fingers curled with the urge to reach out and touch her hair. Was it as silky as it looked? The glimmer of a black satin bra strap flashed at him from under her skimpy tank. He wondered how she'd react if he bit into that perfect line where her shoulder met her neck. Would she shiver and moan? Arch up for more? Or bite him back?

As if she'd caught his thoughts, her gaze narrowed in suspicion. "Never gonna happen, Slick. Been on the bedpost-notch journey before. I'm done."

He winced at the nickname and the assumption.

"I think you have me confused with someone else. I'm the one who's collected on bedposts. Not looking for a quick score. Not looking for a quick anything."

"Then what do you want?"

He cupped his palms around his beer and leaned in. "I want to get my hands on something you have and make her sing. I want to strip her down, savor every moment, and stroke every corner. I want to break her until there's nothing left, and then I want to build her back up, inch by slow inch, enjoying the smell and feel of her beneath my fingers. I want to look at her naked and beautiful again and know I was the one there for the whole journey. I need it, bad, Raven. And you're the only one who's able to give it to me."

Her pupils dilated. Dalton knew in that instant that she wasn't immune to him or the crackling tension between them. She chose to ignore it, but that didn't make it not real. Her throat worked as she fought to process his statement. Her fingers clenched around the dish towel. Finally she pulled her gaze away and took a deep breath. "A real Don Juan, aren't you? As pretty as those words are, you're not getting me."

"You misunderstand."

She lifted a brow. "Hard to misunderstand that one."

He gave a slow smile. "I want to get my hands

all over your bar, darlin'." He stroked his palm gently over the surface where worn wood was hidden beneath a glass top. "I want to restore it back to its original glory." He paused. "What'd you think I meant?"

Annoyance flickered over her face, along with something else. Dalton hoped it was disappointment, but he figured she'd deny it. "My bar is fine the way it is."

"I disagree. This is an antique, a rare art form." Already he ached to examine the wood, find its strengths and weaknesses, make it great again. "This cheap gold trim was added later. The wood is chipped and peeled, and the glass top surface should be a crime. It's tawdry."

She tilted her head in concentration. "Tawdry? How is a practical glass top tawdry?"

He gave a mock shudder. "Another convenient, cheap addition that takes away the beauty of the piece. I could do amazing things for you. Make this bar the crowning centerpiece of the entire restaurant."

She tapped a finger against the full curve of her lower lip. He fought back the urge to snag her hand, open his mouth, and suck. Nibble. Swirl his tongue around until she looked at him with need and not distance. He shifted on the bar stool and felt his jeans scratch against his erection uncomfortably.

"It would be too expensive," she finally said.

"I'll give you a deal. You can even pay in install-ments. You know I work at Pierce Brothers, and we're the best in the Northeast. You won't regret it."

He thought she'd agree, but a flare of anger lit her eyes and she stepped back. Her voice stabbed at him like icicles, sharp and frozen. "I said no. I don't need your help or your brothers'. With me or my bar."

She walked away with a withering look, and Dalton wondered again what the hell he was missing.

chapter four

———⟩ ⟡ ⟨———

Raven had the dream again.

She was walking down a road, sun drenching her body, a bunch of wildflowers fisted in her hands. Contentment stirred within as she followed the familiar path, listening to the calls of birds and enjoying the light tug of wind in her hair. She was part of her father's paintings, in a still, serene place she liked to visit when life got stressful or she needed clarity.

A squeal of brakes echoed in the air, along with twisting metal crashing into metal. The flowers dropped from her hand and she began running, faster and faster, sensing with every step that she was nearing a terrible truth that would destroy her.

But she couldn't stop. She ran until the breath tore from her lungs in painful gasps, and she skidded to a halt in front of the horrifying scene unfolding before her.

Fire burning bright and melting metal. The explosion of glass and the stench of burnt rubber and oil rising in a fury of smoke. Her father's beloved face appeared through the broken window, screaming her name as the flames ravaged him alive. Raven sobbed and tried to run to him, but her feet were stuck to the ground and she was unable to move. His hands reached out, clawing frantically, and finally she was free and rushing toward him.

Seconds before she reached the car, a woman's face appeared beside her father's, her mouth twisted into a terrible smile. She grabbed Raven's father and dragged him back, screeching like a demon, her words echoing over and over in a terrible mantra that Raven would never forget.

"He belongs to me, not you! He belongs to me! Me, me, me, me . . ."

Then the car exploded, and Raven watched her father burn.

She woke up with her pajamas stuck to her damp skin and her heart beating erratically. Gulping in breaths, she tore off the sheets and jumped out of bed, trying to calm herself. Crap. The nightmare had haunted her after the funeral, until she'd been forced to see a grief counselor by Aunt Penny and given a range of pills to cut her anxiety and help her sleep. She'd literally felt on the brink of a nervous breakdown, unable to process the sudden loss of the one man in the world she loved and trusted. After two years of doctors and burying herself in her room, she'd turned to a different type of distraction to stop the nightmares. A wild ride of destruction that had built like a snowball and morphed into an avalanche. There'd been boys and sex. Drugs and alcohol. She'd dropped out of college, telling Aunt Penny she wanted to see the world, but most of her journeys included bunking with strangers, getting high, and waking up with men she didn't remember.

Until she realized life was whizzing by and she'd done nothing to claim her space.

Her father's words haunted her from beyond the grave.

"Baby girl, always remember we're given a responsibility in this life to claim our space. You can decide to fill the world with beauty and kindness, or laziness and self-destruction. Choose well."

In a matter of weeks, she'd decided to get her shit together. She came home, got a job in a restaurant, rented a studio apartment, and registered for online classes. She mended her relationship with her aunt and swore to beat the demons. She made peace with the past and forgot about solving the endless mystery of why her father ran off with a stranger. And finally, the nightmares stopped.

Until Dalton Pierce appeared.

Raven pushed her hair back and made her way into the kitchen. She wouldn't be going back to sleep for a while, so she might as well make coffee. The silence of night closed around her until each clink of the coffeepot and bang of the cabinet hurt her ears. Maybe she should get a cat. She was used to solitude and usually enjoyed it, but lately she'd gotten itchy. In the past, itchy meant danger, and a downward spiral in the search for an adrenaline rush. Now she had a business of her own and responsibilities. Maybe in the past year, she'd shut herself out of too many possibilities. Like a real relationship, not a quick tumble in the sheets and a wave good-bye in the morning. She was finished with bad boys and charming Peter Pans. She wanted a man who was a fellow business owner, or someone who was getting tired of chasing tail and felt ready to settle down. The idea of doing Match.com made her wince, but she might need to force herself to explore all options. She certainly hadn't met anyone worthy in her bar, since most of her customers treated her like a sex object or a buddy they could confide in. There'd been no time in the past year to think about a relationship, because My Place was an obsessive, jealous lover. Now maybe it was time to widen her scope. Do more than work twenty-four hours per day or collapse on the couch bingeing on Netflix on a day off. Meet someone who could make her laugh, challenge her intellect, and not be a total jerk.

The image of Dalton's bright blue eyes and slow, sexy smile flashed in her mind.

Raven sighed and poured herself a cup of coffee, then sat at the small kitchen nook to watch the sun rise. How long had she been obsessed with the idea of revenge after the funeral? She'd burned with the need to prove that Diane Pierce had seduced her father with wicked lies and sex. That he would have discovered the truth and come back to his daughter, begging her forgiveness, but the crash had occurred before he'd been able. That he'd never have gotten on that plane to Paris and left her.

Over the years, her thirst for vengeance had faded under the need to bury the past and move on. But with Dalton and his brothers visiting her bar on a regular basis, the memories no longer stayed buried. And if she didn't do something about it, maybe the nightmare would keep continuing until she went insane again.

Raven took another sip, enjoying the nip of caffeine in her veins and the slight burn on her tongue. Yeah, that was a problem. She wanted to be able to keep her distance and hopefully gather more information about the brothers, but Dalton threw her off balance. Her body snapped to attention when he walked in the room, and though she was used to dealing with hot men who were bad for her, he made her . . . uneasy. When he'd offered to renovate the bar, she'd been overcome with a surge of pure rage and a sense of shame. Yes, she planned to restore the bar and update the restaurant this upcoming year. She had big plans for My Place. But she refused to allow Dalton to barge into her space. Wasn't she betraying her father's memory just by speaking to him? Her constant seesaw of emotion around Dalton was unnerving. One moment she buckled under the sting of his eyes, and the next she was throwing him the hell out of her bar.

She hadn't changed much.

Her mercurial moods weren't easy to live with, but she accepted them as part of who she was. No wonder she had no long-term relationships to speak of. She doubted any man would be able to handle her past a few weeks, when they learned she was sometimes bitchy, sometimes ridiculously emotional, and always a control freak.

Yeah. A perfect Match.com profile with a high level of desirability.

She groaned into her mug and feasted her gaze on the slope of fields outside her window. She was lucky to own two acres of land, with a perfect view of endless green that spilled out until it disappeared over the horizon. The wrap-around porch was ideal for watching sunsets and sunrises, her favorite thing to do since she rarely slept more than five hours. Poised on the outside edge of Harrington, the small log cabin was right down the road from My Place, and she'd bought and renovated them both. She had a taste for simple, earthy, and strong. The polished wood gave off a rustic appeal, and the decorations reflected a comfortable living environment. The open area between the living room and kitchen boasted leather couches, braided rugs, a stone fireplace, large windows, and little clutter. Large, comfy blankets were scattered about.

She had little patience for big novels, and sought out an array of eclectic magazines with glossy pictures. She also preferred paper to digital. Raven believed in touching and feeling solid items that could give comfort. Her home and bar were reflections of that belief.

She lacked the typical feminine or girly qualities. Maybe from being raised by her dad. Another reason she didn't have many female friends, feeling more comfortable in the company of men.

Her gaze fell on the one corner that held her most precious memories. A few of her father's paintings were propped up against the wall, covered with a canvas cloth. They'd been held for her when she returned home, but Raven hadn't been able to look at them. She'd quickly covered them up, but kept them in her living room so they were always near. It was as if a part of her father's soul was with her, but the idea of looking at his most valued visions broke her apart. His betrayal still seethed through her, raw and overwhelming. One day, maybe she'd be able to reveal them and completely forgive him for leaving.

One day.

The sun crept up, sliver by sliver, bathing the hills in various shades of color. She watched in silence as another day came to be, and wondered if her father would be proud of the woman she'd become.

The pain accompanying the thought made her push the question aside.

Didn't matter. She needed to make a decision on how to deal with the Pierce brothers. Maybe if she had some closure it would help erase the nightmares. Maybe if she dug a bit deeper, she'd be able to restore her father's reputation and ease her own tortured memories.

Maybe Dalton Pierce was the key to it all.

The itch settled between her shoulder blades. She'd been able to retrain it toward more positive outlets, but the lack of physical intimacy was beginning to erode her sanity. She'd always been a woman who craved touch, and it had been way too long since she'd been hugged or stroked. She'd sold her motorcycle to funnel more money into the bar, and stopped having affairs with men who were bad for her. She'd given up smoking and recreational drugs.

Raven sighed, finished her coffee, and went to change. There was only one thing left to do to rid herself of the restlessness.

Go beat the crap out of a punching bag.

chapter five

———— > ✧ < ————

"Y ou need to get me the snakewood."

Dalton jerked back. He stared at the plans for the elaborate chest that would serve as the focal point of the living room and shook his head. "Impossible. Do you think I'm a magician? Plus, it's very difficult to work with, especially with multiple carvings."

Morgan lifted her chin and stared up at him with the familiar stubborn expression that had made his brother Cal fall hard in a tangle of limbs. His future sister-in-law was ruthless when it came to building and decorating houses, and possessed a creative vision that consistently surprised him. They'd gotten close over the past year and spoke the same language of love: wood.

"Of course it's difficult to work with," she retorted. "But you could do it justice. The ripples of red wood with black is stunning. It'll pull the entire room together, and I'll be able to stare at it without ever getting bored."

"I don't know. It's still risky with a large piece like this." They stood on the lot where they'd broken ground on Morgan and Cal's new house. Set atop a high hill overlooking the town of Harrington and the harbor in the distance, it was a beautiful piece of property perfect for starting a life together. Dalton loved being involved in every facet of creating a house that would be their forever home. Morgan gave him a wide range to use his creativity, and he felt this would be one of his masterpieces when it was finished.

Excitement slithered in his blood. He caressed the glossy page she'd ripped out to show him, and he itched to get his hands on the material. Snakewood grew in South America and was pretty damn rare. Plus almost impossible to get ahold of.

Almost.

Her lips curved in a smug smile. "I knew you couldn't say no to the challenge. I have a contact in South America, but I use him sparingly. He's stubborn. Hard to deal with. But I bet you could get him to find it for us."

His mind sifted through a rush of images. He saw a sturdy trunk with individual carvings on the side trim and one perfect symbol on the top. The texture and pattern would demand something simple but powerful. His heart galloped and his head swelled with the rush of adrenaline, and suddenly Dalton knew he needed to have it or die.

"You're right."

Morgan lifted her shoulders in a delicate shrug. "I know. I usually am."

He laughed at her self-assurance, and a wave of affection came over him. He grabbed her into his arms and spun her around, messing up her clean white linen suit and neat bob. She fought him, calling him a Neanderthal like his brother, but she began laughing and hung on hard. He let her down gently on her white kitten heels and gave her a sloppy kiss on the cheek.

She let out a breath, wiping off the sawdust that seemed to cling to him 24/7. "You're impossible."

"But you love me."

"Dude, get your own damn woman." Dalton turned to watch his brother Cal stride across the room, tugging Morgan protectively to his side. She lit up, and her body softened naturally against him, as if they were a complete unit already, better together than apart. Dalton had never seen his brother so in love with a woman, and so comfortable with the emotion. His throat got a bit scratchy when he watched the easy way they dealt with each other, from fighting to cooking to building houses side by side. And Morgan had brought something they'd all been missing into the crew.

A sense of real family.

When Morgan came into their lives as the designer in charge of a celebrity's new house construction, Cal began to change, and by the end of the job, they'd gotten engaged. But Morgan belonged to all of them now. The kitchen that had once been ghostly and silent was filled with cooking, laughing, and joy. She'd welcomed Dalton and Tristan into her heart along with Cal, and Dalton would always love her for that gift she'd bestowed.

He grinned and cocked his head. "I have more than one woman to keep me busy, Cal," he said. "But just remember: if you screw this up, I'll marry Morgan myself."

Cal glowered. "Just keep your dick away from the inspector's daughter and we'll be good to go."

Morgan coughed delicately. "Goodness gracious. Your brother is capable of handling his job. Why don't we leave Dalton to his own business? And his dick."

Dalton hooted with laughter. Morgan was a polite Southern-born charmer with a spitfire living underneath. Hearing her curse in that pretty little accent cracked him up each time. "Glad to know someone around here respects me. Anyway, I have my eye settled on one woman I can't seem to thaw."

"The bartender?" Cal groaned. "I love My Place. Plus, she makes the best damn cocktails. You gonna screw that up for me by getting involved with her?"

Dalton rocked back on his heels. "Always thinking of yourself, big brother?"

Morgan tapped a nail against the curve of her lip, her arm around Cal's waist. "I like Raven. But she's not the type to tangle with, Dalton. There's something about her that tells me she's not as hard as she pretends."

"I just want to get to know her better. She swings hot and cold. Most of the time I get the impression she resents me for some reason. Does she ever talk to you about us, Morgan?"

Her silvery blond bob swished back and forth. "No. I remember when she told us to get out of her bar, but she never mentioned it again. She's always nice to me, but she definitely holds back."

"Maybe no man's ever been her match before," Dalton said thoughtfully. "I don't scare easy."

"Unbelievable," Cal said. "Sure, why find a woman who's willing when it's more fun to find one that hates your guts?"

"Didn't you have that same experience with Morgan?"

Cal glowered. Morgan laughed. "He got you, Charming," she drawled.

"Princess, I knew you were hot for me from day one," he said. "It was just a matter of time."

She jabbed him with her elbow, but Cal didn't even flinch.

Dalton grinned. "I offered my services to renovate her bar. It's a beautiful piece I've been wanting to get my hands on. Could be a great project for Pierce Brothers."

Cal nodded, his face flickering back to business mode. "Hmm. A restored antique bar would be a nice advertisement for the company. Seen by a variety of people, too. What did she say?"

"No." He paused, considering. "But I think she'll change her mind."

"Just make sure to keep business separate from your sex life," Cal said.

"Absolutely. Just like you did with Morgan."

Dalton turned his back and walked away, laughing at his brother's grumblings. Months ago, his sibling's constant ribbing about his sex life would've shot him into a temper with a thirst for a fight. Now he recognized the affection beneath, and the ease they'd had when they were younger had returned. It was nice to have his brothers back on good terms. He'd forgotten how much he enjoyed spending time with them.

He headed down the hill and pulled away in his black Ford Bronco. It was almost lunchtime, and he needed to pick up some supplies close to

My Place. Maybe he'd swing in for a quick lunch and see if he'd be able to persuade Raven to let him touch her bar. Of course, if she was still as prickly as last time, he'd get another pink frou-frou drink and maybe a stinging verbal slap.

The real problem was he liked her attitude. He rarely met a woman who didn't enjoy his company. After the initial surprise, he'd found she intrigued him, seemingly hiding layers beneath the surface. Dalton adored exploring every side of a woman, not just her body. A better sexual experience revealed itself when he got to know not just how she liked to be touched, but what her fears were, her fantasies, her vulnerabilities. He'd refined seduction to a fine art and made damn sure both partners enjoyed the experience. But Raven threw him off guard, and he still hadn't figured out a way to keep his balance.

It was kinda hot.

He pulled into the graveled lot and found the early crowd was just shuffling in. The outside of My Place was simple, with a blinking sign, dark brown shingles, and a saloon-type entrance. Dalton noted the worn condition of the roof. It would need replacing before winter, and the pathway leading up had too many broken cracks for liability purposes. He pushed his way through, enjoying the cool rush of air chasing away the thick humidity. He drew in the smell of frying meat and smiled at the familiar strains of "Piano Man" by Billy Joel. Sliding onto his favorite stool all the way to the left, he watched Raven in action.

Her long hair was caught up in a casual clip, and large gold hoops dangled from her ears. Her black cotton tank top showed off her smooth olive skin, and jeweled letters scrawled out I HAVE NO TIME FOR IDIOTS across her chest. She was multitasking with her usual economical but graceful motions, stacking glasses, tapping at the cash register, checking on the new pot of coffee brewing. He studied her tight ass, cupped perfectly in faded denim, and the lean length of her legs, which would make a Rockette jealous. The image of those legs wrapped around his hips hit him so hard, he skipped a breath. Her diamond nose ring sparkled as she turned her head to say something to a customer, shooting the guy a flirty wink that meant nothing but got Dalton hard, ready to go, and a teensy bit jealous. Damn. He'd been attracted to a thousand women, but there was an extra squeeze in his gut along with the one in his dick that threw him off. Raven pivoted on her heel and snagged him with her gaze.

And just like that, her smile disappeared.

Dalton mourned the loss. With a slight frown, she headed down the bar to stand in front of him. "What are you doing here? It's not even noon."

He threw up his hands in mock defense. "I'm

addicted to the sweet potato fries. Plus, I have a pickup down the road. Figured I'd swing in for lunch."

"Lucky me." She let out an irritated sigh that made him itch to force her to look at him. Really look at him. "Anything else?"

"Coffee."

She didn't respond, just put in his order for the fries, headed to the coffeepot, poured him a large mug, and slid over creamer and sugar. "Here you go."

"Thanks." He ignored the condiments and sipped the steaming black brew. Then coughed, pounding himself on the chest. "Damn, you may want to put a warning on this stuff."

"Too hot for you?"

"Did you grind up the entire Colombian field for this pot? Forget putting hair on my chest. This'll turn me into the yeti."

A gleam of laughter sparked in her dark eyes. "Too manly for you, Slick?"

"This is the third time you've insulted my manhood. Perhaps you're baiting me to prove myself?"

Ah, interesting. She caught her breath, and a flicker of awareness passed over her features. She wasn't immune. She was hiding.

He loved a game of hide-and-go-seek.

"No need. I've heard through the grapevine you're a sure thing."

He almost spluttered the awful brew onto his shirt. "What?"

She ran a towel over the damp bar and shot him a smug look. "Women talk, especially around alcohol. Your name came up a few times."

He cupped his hands around the mug and cocked his head. "Not gonna leave me hanging, are you?"

She played with the chain around her neck, studying him. "Well, you certainly don't leave any of your women hanging, Slick. Don Juan has nada on you. Seems you're amazing in the sack, good company out of it, and always respectful. There's been a line of women through my door, and you seem to have been acquainted with a lot of them. Yet none of them had anything bad to say about you. In fact, most got swoony and said they'd see you again if only you'd ask."

He lifted his brow, waiting for the knockout. "And still you don't like me. Won't go out with me. Why?"

Her smile was luscious and real slow, just the way he liked it. "Because I'm looking for a husband."

Ah, shit.

Raven had trouble keeping a straight face when she caught the flash of horror in those wicked blue eyes. He looked like a trapped animal, growing super still and alert, as if waiting to dodge away at the slightest movement.

She'd thought about her problem with Dalton the past few nights. She desperately needed him to keep his distance due to the intense attraction between them. She was also ready to dig to see what he knew about their parents. If she got to know him better, built up some trust, he might share more. Getting close to him without using sex was an issue, but the perfect solution had finally appeared.

Honesty.

Tell him up front she was the marrying kind. His fear of commitment was stamped on his actions clearer than a tattoo. But Raven sensed the man held a code of honor. Sure, he slept with any female who moved, but they all seemed happy and content with his behavior. A man-whore asshole wouldn't elicit such a reaction from his exes. It would be impossible. That told her he must be up front about his limitations, and charming enough to disengage at the exact right time to minimize casualties of love. Brilliant. But not mean.

Raven could work with that.

Besides, she wouldn't mind finding a deep, meaningful relationship. It was time to meet a man who could get real with her. Handle her past without judgment. Be a partner in business and life, not just for one night.

Her mission was clear. Force him to back off but keep him close enough to spy on.

She tried hard not to smile as the horror on his features morphed into shock. His voice was a delicious growl of sound, mixing velvet with gravel, and it ruffled her nerve endings. "You want a husband?"

She nodded. "I'm twenty-seven. I've done my fooling around, and now I'm looking toward a solid future."

He rubbed his head, mussing up all that thick golden hair. "But, why?"

"Don't you ever get tired of endless affairs and little substance?" she asked curiously.

He blinked. Those thick, dark lashes and the sheer beauty of his face distracted her for a moment. "No. Besides, my affairs have plenty of substance. I'm not a touch-and-go type of guy, no matter what you originally thought."

She nodded. Point taken. "Why do you seem surprised?"

"You don't look like the type to want to settle down."

His stark words stole her breath. Red-hot anger stabbed at her. Yes, she owned a bar, had a tat, and had always been dubbed a sexpot, just from her looks. She dressed like a confident woman, comfortable in her identity. Usually she shrugged off others' opinions like a cheap shawl, but she'd hoped Dalton wouldn't have made such judgments about her. Why was she surprised? He only wanted to seduce her, pat her on the head, and make her feel good about the whole encounter the next day. Or maybe even the whole week. Damn him for assuming she was easy. Time to set him straight.

"You don't look like the type to take anything seriously, especially a business. Do your brothers do all the work and you're the pretty face of Pierce Brothers Construction?"

Missile launched. Hit confirmed.

He jerked back as if her words stung. "No. I pull my own weight, but it's still a struggle to get them to take me seriously. I intend to keep proving my worth, though." Male pride etched his hard tone. Respect flowed through her. He wasn't afraid of real work.

"Exactly. Who are you to judge my wanting to get married? Think I'm too cheap for such lofty standards?"

He slammed the mug down on the bar. Coffee sloshed over the side. "Actually, just the opposite," he said tightly. "I think you're too good for marriage. Besides being gorgeous, you own a business and seem wicked smart. I've seen what happens with marriage. You become unappreciated, bored, unromantic. You lose yourself and get your heart broken. Don't you deserve more?"

Her heart galloped. Was he talking about his own parents? Did he have a messy divorce in his past? He practically bristled with male intensity and an innate raw sex appeal that was part of his nature. A plate of sweet potato fries was plunked down between them, and Raven pulled herself together, grabbing silverware and pushing it in front of him.

"Bad experience?" she asked.

He stiffened. "Just the truth. Don't ever put thoughts in my head that aren't there, Raven. Understood?"

His gaze drilled hers, patient yet determined. She'd never known a man who was so comfortable really looking at a woman, as if he wanted to strip away each layer and find the soft center. She fought a shiver. "Understood."

The tentative truce softened the tension. He nodded and began eating the fries. "What are you going to do while you search for Mr. Right? I can offer a nice distraction."

She rolled her eyes. "Yeah, I bet you can, Slick. Thanks for the offer, but I'll pass."

"You dating someone regularly yet?"

A lie would be easier. Still, she told the truth. "No. But I don't want to be *distracted* if he comes around."

Dalton lifted a fry to his mouth. Strong white teeth opened slowly and then closed around the end. He tugged, and the tip pulled off, disappearing into his mouth. His tongue came out to lick the salt from his lips in a sensual gesture. His gaze swept lazily over her body, as if he was imagining himself licking something else.

"Tastes so good," he murmured.

Arousal dampened her panties. He was a master. She lifted her chin, giving him her iciest stare, and casually crossed her arms in front of her chest to hide her erect nipples. If she was sticking with her plan, she needed to keep her guard up. Evidently her search for a husband gave him pause, but he still considered her fair game.

"You can taste it when you put a ring on it."

He spit out the fry in shock, then burst into laughter. She couldn't help her answering grin at his obvious delight with her banter. Thank goodness the man had a sense of humor.

"Damn, I like you."

"Good to know. I gotta get back to my customers."

She turned, but he raised up his hand to stop her. "Wait. How about a consolation prize?"

"Sorry, the prize bucket is closed."

"Let me get my hands on your bar."

She paused, tapping her foot. Even though it would give her more time with him, there was no way she'd allow him such a gift. He might be the best—but she was positive that when she was ready to renovate, she'd be able to find someone else. Someone less . . . disturbing. "Sorry, Slick. I'm very choosy about who touches my bar. You're not on the list."

A stubborn light shone from his eyes. "Then I'll have to find a way to get on your list, won't I? Because I want it bad, Raven. Real bad."

Holy crap, her body practically wept with the need to shoot over the bar they were talking about, fist his shirt in her hands, and kiss that lush, sinful mouth. His slow, smug smile ramped up her irritation. She hated him knowing she wanted him. At least she could control his inability to do her bar. And do her.

"Take a lesson from the Stones. You can't always get what you want."

He never flinched. "Maybe. But I'm sure I'll eventually get what I need."

Because she couldn't speak, she did the next best thing. Rolled her eyes like she wasn't worried and walked away, pretending to serve another customer.

Unfortunately, Raven had a feeling he knew exactly how worried she was. Because for one tiny moment, she'd dreamed about being the woman who could give him exactly what he needed. In every way possible.

Finally Dalton left, and she steeped herself in prepping for the evening crowd and following the mystery of the new cocktail brewing in her mind. Amanda popped her head out of the kitchen, waving the cordless in her hand. "Phone for you, Raven!"

Wiping off the stray leaves of basil and thyme clinging to her hands, she tucked the phone between her ear and chin. "Hello?"

"Raven Hawthorne?"

"I don't need any more credit cards, thank you."

A chuckle. The woman's voice held a sharp, no-nonsense ring that usually meant city bred. "Nope. I'm Anastasia Duncan, assistant editor from *Good Food and Fine Spirits* magazine. We do articles for restaurants located in the Northeast, and My Place has been brought to my attention. High reviews on the food and cocktails are creating quite the buzz. You're a mixologist, correct? Are you the one who conceptualizes all the cocktails?"

"Yes, I'm the owner and I make all the drinks."

"From scratch? I'd like to focus not only on the unique look of your restaurant, but how your cocktails are making a name with a new breed of customers who want more than the normal wine and beer."

Raven ignored her beating heart and took a breath. "Everything is created and prepared by me. I work with fresh herbs, vegetables, fruits, and various liquors."

"Excellent. I'd love to set up an interview."

Raven tried to keep the excitement from leaking into her voice. The magazine was well known in the food industry, and was starting to gather steam from consumers of great cocktails. "Sounds like a wonderful opportunity," she responded smoothly. "What do you need from me?"

Papers shuffled in the background. "I'm interested in doing a feature for the September issue. I'd need to schedule a tour and in-depth interview within a month. Is this a possibility?"

"Of course. Let me check my schedule."

They went back and forth a few times and agreed on a date. Anastasia informed her there would also be a camera crew for the online digital version and social media pages. By the time Raven hung up the phone, her hands shook.

Good Food & Fine Spirits magazine.

It was big-time. A feature could change everything for her, and there was no way she was about to blow the opportunity of a lifetime. Squealing inside, she turned to run into the kitchen and share the news when a sudden realization halted her midstep.

The bar.

Her time had officially run out. She needed her bar restored in order to make an impression. She couldn't have pictures circulating without showing off the antique piece. And how could she keep the mismatched stools? They'd seemed funky and quirky when she opened, but now they just looked a bit sad. Wildly calculating in her mind the balance in her bank account, she decided it was a leap she needed to take sooner than later. She'd begin calling places and—

Ah, crap.

Dalton Pierce.

As if his words were hanging in front of her in a balloon from an old comic, she squeezed her eyes shut in pure misery. She could not hire him. Would not. Besides being stuck with his presence on a constant basis, she'd be surrendering and letting him win. Plus, he was still the enemy. How could she allow him to save her?

No. She'd follow every other alternative before she gave the Pierce brothers her business.

Firming up her decision, she marched into the kitchen to share her good news with Al.

chapter six

———⟫ ◆ ⟪———

One week later, Raven paused in front of the office. Fighting the urge to climb back in her Jeep and forget the whole damn thing, she reminded herself that business came first. She could do this. Just because she needed them for a job didn't mean she wasn't in control. With the strict timeline to get the work completed, the few places she'd managed to contact had informed her they couldn't start in time, given her outrageous quotes, or seemed so sloppy regarding the work, she couldn't bear to hire them.

Which left her with Pierce Brothers Construction.

She pushed the door open.

A structured type of chaos swirled around her. Phones rang, the receptionist at the front desk juggled multiple calls and folders, and a handsome dark-haired man was involved in a lively discussion with Sydney, the executive assistant who frequented My Place with Morgan. Her magnificent red hair caught the light, making the strands shimmer. She was dressed in a structured black business suit and smart heels, and peered at the man over trendy glasses that gave off an air of arrogance.

"I told you if I didn't file the new plans with the zoning board we'd be delayed," the man said with a touch of frustration. "Tristan's going to have my ass in a sling."

Sydney puckered her lips as if she'd caught a bad taste. "*Tristan* didn't give you the right date," she clipped out. She uttered the name with bitterness. "Tristan got all crazy about securing the property, forged ahead without giving me the correct timeline for the renovation project, and now both of our asses are in a sling."

The man groaned. "For God's sake, why is every conversation between you two a battle of wills? Didn't he talk to you?"

"He sent me an email with the wrong date."

"An email. We all work together and he can't go into your office and tell you what his plans are? I'm not getting caught in the middle anymore. You both need to work it out. I gotta go, I'm already late for my lunch appointment."

The man stormed away. Sydney grumbled something under her breath.

Trying not to be noticed, Raven tiptoed to the reception desk and waited. The receptionist looked in her sixties, with a smooth complexion, pale hair, and a serene smile. "May I help you?"

"I'm here to see Caleb."

"And you are?"

She tried to whisper. "Umm, Raven."

"First door to the right. I'll tell him you're on your way."

"Great, thanks so much, I—"

"Raven! What are you doing here?"

She winced at Sydney's enthusiastic greeting. So much for flying under the radar. She was desperate not to see Dalton, and was hoping he was out on a job site and not in the office. She offered a weak smile. "Hi, Sydney. I just wanted to speak to Cal about something."

"Oh, are you looking to do some renovation for the restaurant? I can track down Dalton for you, if you want."

"No! Umm, no, thanks, I want to speak to Cal."

"Okay, let me know if I can help you with anything. I'll see you tomorrow for dinner. Becca is in love with the chicken fingers, and I love that Al makes them with whole wheat flour and organic meat."

"I'll make sure I tell him. Thanks again."

Raven shot down the hallway and stepped into Cal's office. He looked up from his desk and gave an easy grin of welcome. "Raven, good to see you."

Though they knew each other casually from the bar, she stuck out her hand, and he took it with a firm grip. She studied his face in an honest assessment. There was a definite resemblance between the brothers, but Cal had inherited gunmetal-gray eyes instead of blue, and his hair was a deep hazelnut color and seemed thick and unruly. His face was an interesting mixture of sharp angles set off by a hooked nose and bushy brows. Not as pretty or classical as Tristan or Dalton, but no woman could easily look past him without thinking about him once or twice. He held a powerful presence that shimmered with authority, even in worn jeans and work boots. Thankfully, there was nothing that attracted her to Cal, or even Tristan. It seemed only the youngest in the crew had her like Ryan Gosling winking and uttering, "Hey, girl."

Pathetic.

She forced herself to focus. "Thanks for seeing me on short notice. I wanted to know if you'd take on a job for My Place."

His brow arched. He motioned for her to sit, and he fell easily into the chair across from her. "What are you looking to do?"

"I want to have the bar completely restored. I also need new stools. And I need it all complete within three weeks."

An odd tension simmered between them. She frowned, trying to sort it out, but why did it seem like he was suddenly studying her with a hawklike stare, as if he suspected she was up to something? "I'm sorry, but I can't do it," he finally said bluntly.

She blinked. Never once had she imagined Pierce Brothers would turn down the job. She expected them to be happy she was giving them her precious business. Her tummy tightened. "Is there something I can do to change your mind?"

A faint smile ghosted across his lips. "Not me. I'd be happy to take on the job, but any type of wood restoration is handled by Dalton."

She tried hard not to wince. "Oh. Well, is there any way someone else can do it?"

"Got a problem with Dalton? Has he made you uncomfortable in some way?"

"No. Well, he's made his interest well known, but he's always been respectful."

"Good. I can promise you he takes his jobs seriously. I can talk to him if you want. Warn him to back off."

She tapped her finger against the arm of the chair, her thoughts furiously scrambling. "No, I can handle myself. He's never put me in an un-comfortable position. I just think it may be easier to discuss the details of the job with you. I'm in a serious time crunch."

Cal crossed his arms in front of his chest, leaning

back. "Sorry, like I said, this is Dalton's territory. I'm sure he'll be flexible if you tell him what you need. But you'll have to ask him directly."

The memory of their conversation floated in her ears, reminding her of wants and needs of a different kind. Swallowing, she knew she had a choice. She could forget the whole idea of restoration and take on the interview anyway. She could tell *Good Food & Fine Spirits* the bar would be restored over the summer. Buy herself time. It could work.

But the idea of having such an important source photographing her beloved bar in broken-down condition hurt her heart. No. This was her chance to show the world what My Place was about. Damned if she couldn't put on her big-girl panties and ask Dalton to do what he wanted to do in the first place.

"Then I'll need to talk to Dalton now, won't I?"

Cal nodded and stood up. "I'll text him and have him meet you at My Place later this afternoon. Will that work?"

"Yes, thanks."

They exchanged good-byes and she headed back to her restaurant to wait.

Dalton got the text just as he was climbing into his truck. He read it three times, then once more to be sure.

Raven had gone to Cal about her bar?

Pure male temper flooded his system. He punched in the numbers and heard his brother's clipped voice come over the line. "Thought that would get your attention. What the hell did you do to her? Oh, you're on speaker. Tristan's here."

Great. His brothers were about to witness his humiliation as a tag team. And no one did it better than his siblings. Tristan's smooth, cultured voice rose in his ears. Dalton pictured him elegantly perched in the chair, suit and tie pressed to perfection. "Talk about crash and burn, bro. Has a woman ever rejected you? Losing your mojo in your older age?"

Muttering a foul curse, Dalton barked at the phone. "Can we save the witty banter for later, dude? I need to know exactly what she said to Cal."

"Said she needed the bar redone with matching stools, and she wants it within three weeks. I told her you were the one she needed to talk to."

"And?"

Amusement laced his voice. "And she said she preferred to deal with me. Did you come on too strong and scare her off? I know you've been begging to do her bar for a while."

Had he? Hell no. That woman shut down men with pure glee and seemed to savor every moment. For some reason, she was afraid to deal with him directly. That told him one thing.

She wanted him. She just didn't *want* to want him.

Dalton knew every hidden aspect of the mating game, and she was playing to its potential. By asking his brother, she had issued him both an insult and a challenge. His temper settled while he analyzed the best way to approach the situation. "Nah, it's not about that at all. It's hard for a woman to admit she wants someone that doesn't check all her boxes. She's just in denial. I'll take care of it."

A short silence came over the line. "Not if it involves a lawsuit, dude. Maybe you should let this one go," Tristan advised.

"Don't let your ego get you into any more trouble. You have enough jobs to keep you busy," Cal said.

"I'd never do anything to jeopardize Pierce Brothers. There must be a good reason she wants the restaurant redone so fast, and I intend to find out. Either way, the job will be good for the company. Plenty of exposure."

"What are you gonna do?" Cal asked.

Dalton tightened his lips. "What I do best."

"Seduce her until she's smitten, then break up with her?" Tristan piped up.

"No, asshat. Get the job *and* the girl. Then we both win."

Cal sighed over the line. "Famous last words."

Dalton hung up on his brothers and started the ignition. Satisfaction hit as he imagined Raven waiting for him to contact her. Though he was tempted to drive over right now for their meeting, he knew it was best to let the tension build. Linger. Settle.

It always made the surrender so much sweeter.

Raven waited the rest of the day, but Dalton never contacted her.

Dammit, she was running out of time and needed an answer today. Maybe she'd made a big mistake going to Cal first. Dalton was probably insulted. Would he refuse the job out of spite? Well, that would prove what type of man he really was, right? She didn't need him or Pierce Brothers. She'd find someone else, and maybe the work wouldn't be as pristine but it would do.

She finished closing up and heard a tap at the door.

Ignoring her wild heartbeat, she called out, "Who is it?"

"Dalton Pierce."

His rich, smoky voice rolled out his name with deliberate precision, as if to remind her who he was. Like she needed a reminder. Bracing herself, she unlocked the door and stepped aside.

He walked in.

No, more like swaggered. The delicious roll of his hips and his staggering height gave her the impression of confidence without arrogance, sexual assertiveness without aggression, grace without delicacy. He smelled of lemon and varnish and a smoky type of wood that reminded her of tangled sheets and musky sex. His jeans were ripped at the knees, his work boots scarred, and his shirt dirty. That glorious hair was pulled back from his face, emphasizing his carved features.

She tried hard not to drool or look affected as she locked the door again behind them and turned to face him.

"Thanks for finally showing up."

His brow lifted. His hip cocked out, and she tried not to lower her gaze to admire the way the denim stretched to accommodate him. "Didn't know we had an appointment."

"Cal said you'd be over this afternoon."

"Cal's not my keeper," he said mildly. "In fact, Cal only runs one third of the business. He builds the houses. Do you need a house built?"

Oh, he was here to torture her. No anger marred his face or leaked through his voice. That would've been easier to deal with. Instead, he intended to toy with her until he made his point. She thought about the prestigious magazine article that could take her restaurant to the next level, gritted her teeth, and decided to play the game. "No."

"Ah. Wait, maybe you needed Tristan? Do you need to sell a house or redesign one? Flip one?"

If she weren't so pissed, she could've laughed. This man was a master at the game. "No."

"Then what do you want, Raven?"

"I think you know already. I apologize if I made some type of error asking the wrong person, but all I need right now is a yes or no. Do you want the job or not?"

It was her best play, but damned if he didn't smile real slow and sexy. "Not going to be that easy, darlin'. You took the time to explain everything to Cal, so now I'll need you to repeat the specifics of the job and exactly what you need. It would also be nice to know why you refused to ask me."

She tried not to squirm under his hot stare. Her tummy was doing that weird flip thing that made her a bit light-headed. How did a simple conversation with him turn into a feast of verbal foreplay? "I thought it would be better to keep it simple," she clipped out. "You've made it well known you're interested in more than my bar."

His eyes darkened. "I am. But when I take a job on, I don't disrespect the client or my company. When I work at your place, there's a trust between us I refuse to break. I give you my word, I won't lay a hand on you or make any advances that would make you uncomfortable." He paused, his gaze sweeping over her face. "Unless you ask nicely, of course."

She swallowed hard. "Fine."

"I need to know you believe me, Raven."

She did. And though she was tempted to lie, she couldn't. It wouldn't be fair. "I believe you."

His muscles relaxed. "Good. Why do you need such an extensive job done so quickly?"

"*Good Food and Fine Spirits* magazine wants to do a feature article on My Place. I need it ready for the photographers."

A genuine smile curved his lips. "That's wonderful news; congratulations. You've really done amazing things here in such a short time."

Raven smiled back. She loved talking about her business. "This could lift the restaurant to the next level. But I've been neglecting the cosmetics until I had the guts solid."

Dalton nodded. "Makes sense. Your menu and cocktails are stellar, and your staff is amazing. You did the right thing waiting. I know how much money a new business sucks out."

She sighed and glanced at the mighty bar that sagged with age. "Yes, but it's time. The investment will be worth it. Can it be completed within the time period?"

He scrunched up his face in thought. "It's tight but doable. I'd have to delay another job, but I don't think that will be a problem. How many stools?"

"A dozen. I'm open to ideas."

He walked over, studying the motley scarred stools lining the bar. Then ran his hand gently over the surface, caressing the cheap gold rails with the lightest touch. Shivers raced down her spine as she imagined that hand on her body, on her naked skin. His fingers would be the slightest bit rough, but skillful. Would he be able to play her body as deftly as he stroked a piece of wood to glory? "I think I know what will work. I have a variety of samples to show you, and I'll sketch out my ideas tonight. I can come by again tomorrow, around closing."

He drew his hand away and she let out a relieved breath. Already her skin felt hot and stretched over her bones way too tight. She took a step back for more air. "Good."

"I'll also have a schedule, but you'll need to close the place for a while."

"How long?"

"A week to do the main parts of the job. The rest I can finish off-site."

"Okay. I'll take care of it."

"Good." A short silence fell between them, pulsing with crackling energy. "How many places did you try before settling on Pierce Brothers?"

She jerked back. How did he know? His

shrewd gaze told her his bluff had worked perfectly. Damn. "A few."

He stalked her, closing in on her precious distance and taking up her air. "Why?"

Because your family destroyed mine. Because your presence makes me feel like I'm betraying my father.

"I thought it would be easier."

The words were the truth. He seemed to accept her response, nodding slowly, his gaze shredding her barriers and probing too deep for comfort. "Yes, I can see why," he murmured. "I can take the job, Raven. I'll make your bar so damn beautiful everyone who sees it will compare every other one out there to it." His poetic words tugged at her soul, but she fought back. "You just have to do one thing for me."

"What?"

"Ask me nicely."

She stared at him. He made no move toward her. Still, his aura wrapped tight around her with pure demand. The knowledge of what he wanted to take from her might seem ridiculous to someone else. After all, it was a simple admission.

But to her, it was so much more.

He was forcing her to ask for something she wanted. Something only he could give her. The demand bristled with connotations and a seething intensity that stole her breath. Long moments passed. He kept still, waiting for her to take the first tiny step in surrender.

Bastard.

"Why?"

He smiled. "You know why," he said softly.

Her fists clenched. She fought the mental battle as fiercely as she did the physical. Oh, she wanted to walk away from it all and tell him to go to hell. Him and his massive ego and talent and complications. She didn't want him in her bar or her life, but she was trapped. To get what she really wanted for her business, she needed him—the very devil she'd hated since she buried her father.

When she took the fall, she refused to do it halfway. Throwing her head back, she straightened to full height and faced him. The few inches between them crackled with tension. Her voice seethed with resentment and the surrender he required.

"Will you take the job, Dalton?"

For one moment, something transformed between them. As if caught in a raging undertow, she drowned in a tsunami of pure emotion, tangled with lust and hate, need and desire, want and desperation. His eyes widened in acknowledgment, and he took a tiny step back, as if battered by his own wave.

In seconds, the room was once again calm,

and Raven wondered if she had imagined the whole thing.

"Yes. Yes, I'll take the job, Raven. I'll also make sure you don't regret it." He turned and walked to the door. "See you tomorrow."

Raven closed her eyes and wondered if she'd just played a very dangerous game with fate.

chapter seven

———→ ◆ ←———

Dalton showed up right before closing.

All day, he'd been anticipating seeing her again. She was never far from his mind, the image of last night replaying again and again. He'd forced her to concede, but it was he who was rocked by the encounter. He'd expected her to get a bit bitchy, or even lie before asking him to take on the job. Dalton admitted it was a power play, and he'd intended to pull back if she got upset.

Instead, she'd refused to back down. She might have been the one asking, but she did it with such power and pride, he'd been the one humbled.

Another intriguing piece to the puzzle. The woman was full of angles and edges that he longed to explore. Being able to work in her presence and get answers to those questions was just another perk of the job. Maybe after this week, he'd be able to figure out why things were so explosive when the two of them were with each other.

He took a seat at one of the tables, laying out his sketches and plans. Her voice echoed from the kitchen, along with the sound of laughing, chatter, and good-natured ribbing. Finally three females and a man built like a truck trudged out. The girls gave him a friendly wave of acknowledgment, but the man shot him a warning look. With his shaved head and staggering muscles, he looked . . . mean. Who the hell was that? The cook? Raven couldn't be involved with him, right? She'd said there was no one in her life at the moment, but damned if that guy wasn't trying to tell Dalton to back off.

Raven came out, hips swinging with an unconscious grace he loved to watch. "One more second?"

"Take your time." He enjoyed the view while she leaned over the bar with her MacBook Air and punched furiously at the keys. The lights were dim, and the bar was quiet. He wondered if she spent most nights here, alone, in the place she now called hers. Questions crowded his mind regarding her past and how she got here. There was a deep satisfaction that radiated around her, telling him she was happy with her life and choices. Not too many people he'd met along the way had gotten to that place. This past year had brought a lot of changes, but Dalton was a hell of a lot happier. He'd worked through issues with his brothers and gotten to concentrate on what made him happy: woodworking.

She shut her laptop, walked over, and dropped in the chair across from him. Sticking her jean-clad legs straight in front of her, she gave a little groan. "Sorry. Being on your feet all day is sometimes a bitch."

He grinned. "Understood. Here." He pushed another chair over, scooped up her feet, and dropped them gently down so she was completely stretched out. "You should wear flats, like your servers."

She shrugged. "I like heels. They make me taller than most of the men."

"You like to try to intimidate men?"

Her inky eyes glinted with mischief. "No, I just like to be tall. If they're intimidated by that, it's their problem. Would you like a beer?"

Damn, she was quick. He caught the wild scent of her, a mix of spices and cinnamon, like musk and earth. "No, thanks, I consider this a work meeting." He paused. "Are you involved with that guy who works in your kitchen?"

Her eyes widened. Then a laugh escaped her lips and she shook her head. "Al? No. Not that it's your business, but he looks after me and everyone else who works here. He's the chef, actually. He's good people. Why?"

"Shot me a look like he'd cut off my balls if I made a move on you."

Her eyes sparkled. Little flecks of pure gold shimmered in their depths. "Oh, he would. And trust me, he knows how to do it."

"Good to know."

"Not that I'd need the help."

He raised a brow. "Self-defense?"

She scoffed with disgust. "Child's play. Boxing and karate."

"Now you're just turning me on."

Her lips twitched with the need to smile, and a warm glow settled over him. He wished he could sit with her all night. "Whatcha got for me, Slick?"

He pulled out three samples and a few rough sketches. "First off, we strip down the whole bar. I'll take away the dents and scratches, sand it down, and restain it in a darker mahogany. I brought some samples I thought would go well with the other woodwork in the place." She studied them one at a time, her fingers caressing the wood in gentle motions. Her nails were short and square, but her fingers were long and tapered, like a musician's. He wondered what they'd feel like gliding over his naked skin. Dalton swallowed and prayed away his growing erection. "I'll remove the glass top and replace it with new wood, take away the cheap gold bars and replace them with bronze rope rails. I'd do a handrail and foot rail. This will enhance the new stain and give it a touch of arrogance. Elegance. An antique bar should have a bit of a wow factor. Here, I printed out a picture for you to take a look."

He waited for her to look at the pictures while he shuffled through the other papers and continued. "Now, the stools should match the wood of the bar, and I think a carved back will bring comfort for eating and still retain the atmosphere of My Place." He pointed to the stool on the paper. "I'd put in some suspension so they'd swivel, and use the bronze hardware from the railings so it looks like a set."

She was silent for a while, sifting through the papers and occasionally glancing at the bar to compare. "It's the exact look I was hoping for. And I like this wood." She gave him the sample he also preferred, and excitement ran through his veins. God, he loved starting a new project, especially one that would satisfy his soul. It wasn't often he was able to restore an antique bar.

"I agree. It works best with the brick wall background. Then I found these antique-looking booths from—"

"Booths? Wait a minute, I don't have money to renovate the entire restaurant. I still need a new roof and to fix the porch before this upcoming winter."

"Sorry, it's just I have my hands on these wooden

booths and if we stained them, they'd look amazing. It's easy to rip out these right here"—he pointed to the row of six booths lined up on the right side—"and replace them. You get rid of the cheap red vinyl and it's an investment. Low maintenance, and it will last. Here's the pictures."

She studied the photos. "Wow, you're really good at this. I suck at decorating. I don't seem to have the vision like so many other women have."

"I doubt many women can make a Bloody Mary like you can."

"You're right. That's a better talent."

Dalton figured he'd save the ideas for restripping the floors for another time. Yes, the floors could wait, but he had to convince her to do the booths. "I brought up two estimates. I can give you a discount on the booths because of the bulk of the job."

"What about the time restrictions? Can you really get all this done?"

"Yes. The booths will only add two days, which will still give you plenty of time."

She tapped a fingernail against the table while she flipped through the estimates and pictures. "I love the idea. Just don't know if it's smart to lay out the extra chunk of money right now."

"I'm happy to put you on a monthly payment plan. I just think this is a move you won't regret."

A ghost of a smile touched her lips. "Why do I feel you've used that line many times before?"

"Because I have."

"Did it work?"

This time, he gave her a playful wink. "Every time," he drawled.

She dropped the papers back onto the table and studied him. Dalton felt that touch of connection buzz through the room again. Like they'd known each other before, in another life. Not that he believed in that silly stuff. "Well, I guess your line worked again. I'll do the booths, too."

"You won't regret it. I'll make it so good for you."

This time she laughed out loud. The deep, husky sound made him shift uncomfortably in his chair with raw hunger. A sense of pride zapped through him. He wished he could make this woman laugh more often.

"How soon can you start?" she asked.

"I've cleared my schedule. I'll pick up the supplies tomorrow and start in two days. I'll need one full week for the pub to be closed."

She nodded. "I'll post it on Facebook and put out signs tomorrow so everyone knows we'll be closed. I already spoke to my staff. I've decided to do a grand reopening once the work is done. It'll draw more crowds and press, and I'll be able to unveil some special cocktails I've been working on."

"Great idea." Curiosity burned through him. "Have you always wanted your own restaurant?"

"God, no. I was going to be a movie star. I always felt like I was meant for big things."

"So your family doesn't own a chain of restaurants and begged you to run the dynasty?"

It was meant as a teasing remark, but Dalton noticed the raw grief that flickered over her face before she settled back into the familiar, distant chill. "No. My father was an artist. My aunt is an actress on Broadway. I never really knew my mother."

"Amazing gene pool. No wonder you longed for Hollywood. Do I know any of your father's work?"

"He's dead."

Dalton jerked back. Suddenly her dark eyes burned with a tinge of raw emotion and something he couldn't define. Almost as if she blamed him for asking the question. "I'm so sorry." She didn't answer, just stared at him, unblinking. "My parents are gone, too," he offered.

She dropped her gaze and studied the floor. "How?"

Now he was the one who stiffened. "Heart attack."

"Both of them?"

The lid on the memory gaped open. He slammed it closed. "Lost my father to a heart attack last year. Lost my mother a while ago in a car accident."

"I'm sorry." Her tone held . . . mockery? Anger? "Were you close to your mother?"

Oh, hell no. He never went there with anyone

other than his brothers, and he planned to keep it that way. He reached into the pocket of his jeans and popped out two mini Hershey bars, deliberately closing the subject. "Want one?"

"No, thanks."

He unwrapped the foil and popped one in his mouth. Immediately, the creamy morsel melted on his tongue and gave him a tiny sugar bump, soothing his nerves. He got the second one ready to go. Time to direct the conversation back to its original roots. "What made you want to buy this place, then? Movie star never worked out?"

She paused, as if recognizing his deliberate attempt to avoid the subject of his family, but then she seemed to relax. "Nah, I liked the idea of being a star, but I didn't want to actually take acting lessons, voice lessons, dance lessons, and spend my youth waiting in audition lines while I waitressed. I was a bit of a hobo. Traveled, took odd jobs, bummed places to live."

He popped the second Hershey bar into his mouth. "Not many people have the guts to do that. We're too tied to a college education and a job so we can raise our two-point-four kids with a BMW in the driveway."

She wrinkled her nose. "I was never interested in having children young, and I despise BMWs. Unless it's a convertible, of course."

"Of course. Where'd you travel?"

She gave a little sigh. "Italy. Spain. Paris. Amsterdam. I did a cross-country trip from California to New York, hitting every hidden spot I could possibly find. I wasn't tied to anything but the thought of what was around the next corner."

A woman after his own heart. He'd been ruthlessly trained to be a part of Pierce Brothers Construction since he was two years old. He'd rarely questioned it because there had been no other option, and thank God he liked the work. But heading out to California for five years had soothed his wild soul. Imagining a trip across the United States and the world was a dream for the very brave who rolled the dice and took the gamble. Raven was a rare breed of woman. Why did she want to ruin her freedom by getting married? Wouldn't a husband crush the beauty of her need to be free? He wanted to ask but figured she'd retreat back to her iciness, and he was enjoying her openness too much.

"It sounds amazing. Are you originally from Harrington?"

She shook her heeled foot, then abruptly stopped. Funny, she definitely wasn't one to be chatty about herself. It only made him want more facts about her past. "A few towns over," she finally said.

"What made you stop traveling?"

"I needed to stop running," she said simply.

Her answer shook him to the core. Needing more, he leaned forward, locking his gaze with hers. "Why?"

Too late. Obviously spooked from what she had shared, Raven jumped up from the chair in a flurry of activity. "I have to go. We're good here?"

"Yeah. We're good." Dismissed, Dalton rose, filing his papers back into the organized folders. "I'll see you Tuesday morning. Text or call if you have any questions. My private cell number is on here." He plucked a card from his wallet and pressed it into her outstretched palm.

A shock bolted right through him the moment his fingers brushed hers.

WTF?

She jerked back, eyes wide as a strange energy enveloped both of them in an almost misty fog. His dick roared to life, aching hard, and Dalton gripped her hand as he tried to figure out why his heart twisted in a longing ache for something he didn't know.

"Raven?"

Her name ripped from his lips as a question.

Pure fear flickered over her face. She snatched her hand from his, cradling it tight to her chest, and whirled away from him. "See you Tuesday."

He opened his mouth to call out for her, but she'd already disappeared.

chapter eight

Raven woke up with test stomach.

Holding back a groan, she tried to breathe past it. It was a condition that had plagued her all through school, even though she'd never been a nerd or obsessed with perfect grades. It was more like being at the mercy of a lousy number. One wrong answer, even though she knew the material, could skew an entire letter grade. Her father used to make her plain toast with a touch of marmalade to help soothe her stomach. He'd always known test days and anticipated her needs.

God, she missed him.

Fighting back a sigh, she checked the mirror before she headed out to the bar. She donned her usual outfit: jeans, tank, and Skechers sneakers with high wedges. She left her hair loose and messy, since she wasn't serving food, and deliberately veered away from makeup. No need to impress the man. They were both there for business, and maybe she'd gain more traction on his past. The image of his face turning cold and hard when he told her about the car accident haunted her. She'd been so intent on digging for information, she hadn't prepared for the emotion behind it. He was someone who understood what it felt like to lose a parent in an accident. Somehow, she'd kept her idea of him separate from any feelings, as if his accusations against her father had numbed him to the power of grief. She was just beginning to realize it was going to be harder than she thought to revisit the past.

She'd be more confident in her abilities to handle Dalton Pierce if he hadn't done the worst thing possible and touched her.

A shiver raced down her spine. The moment their skin had met, a jolt of pure feeling shook her body. She wished she could compare it to the unpleasant sensation of being shocked when her fur glove hit metal, but it was deeper than that. A hungry need pushed through her blood and burrowed into her gut, urging her to move closer to him, screaming for her to let the touch linger.

Hell no.

Instead, she'd jumped back and run away. Raven didn't even care if she looked like a coward, she only knew it was key to her survival that she get far away from him.

But today, there'd be no touching. She was ready, dressed in armor, and focused on gaining information without being vulnerable.

She drove to the pub, unlocking the doors and flipping on the lights. The vast space was quiet and hummed with the energy of people endlessly rushing in and out, now ghostly on this Tuesday. Brewing a pot of coffee, she got ready, making sure she'd moved everything off and away from the bar. Setting up her workstation at a table mid-way back, she sorted inventory files and made her agenda for the day.

The warm breeze blew in as the door opened. She looked up.

Damn him for being so hot.

There was something about men who worked with their hands that had always turned her on. She had a tendency to attract the starving artist types or bad boy rockers, but Dalton's craft was just as swoonworthy. The simple white T-shirt molded to his carved chest, and the jeans were faded and worn to cup his ass in exactly the right places. His golden hair was tied back in a short ponytail. He looked like Matthew McConaughey, one of her fave celebrity crushes. The longish nose and deep voice that dripped sex. The powerful aura and big hands that gripped tool cases and beams of wood. Even the work boots made her drool. Yep, large feet, too. Why was she surprised?

"Morning." He set down the materials and gave her a smile. "Got a lot of stuff to bring in."

"Need help?"

"No, ma'am. Part of the contract. I take care of everything."

He dropped his gaze to her breasts, sweeping lower, then back up. Her skin tingled. She cleared her throat, hating how virginal she was acting around him. For God's sake, she'd been around the proverbial block or two! She deliberately headed toward the bar. "Good. I made coffee. Want some?"

He chewed at his lip, looking a bit fearful. "Don't know. Did you use the whole coffee tree this time?"

"I like my coffee strong."

"Like your men?"

This time, she tossed him a careless smile. "Nope. I like my men one way only: committed."

She appreciated his deep laugh. She could handle a lot of missing qualities in men, but a guy without a sense of humor left her cold. "I can do committed."

Raven crossed her arms and tilted her head. "For the night?"

That slow, wicked grin hit all the right places in her girly bits. "The night, the weekend, the month. For as long as we're happy. Isn't that what life is about?"

"For you, maybe. For me, not so much. I can't

wait to start buying bridal magazines and talking about dresses and favors and cakes."

He actually blanched, causing her to almost break the farce and giggle. She wasn't wedding crazy, but it was the perfect weapon to use on him. "You sound like my future sister-in-law," he grumbled, shaking his head. "Even my brother is caught up in wedding chaos. Building a house and planning a wedding in the same year isn't a smart move, but hell, no one listened to me."

"Morgan, right? She designed the Rosenthals' estate. Can't believe a pair of Hollywood celebrities live right in our midst." The Academy Award–nominated super couple had bought property in Harrington while shooting a film, then decided to stay. Morgan had been all over the news regarding her talent in building the perfect house for celebrity clients, and was now highly sought after by Tinseltown. Raven considered her a casual friend, since she frequented the bar regularly, though her relationship with Cal made Raven keep up her defenses.

"That's her. The house Morgan and Cal are building to live in will be better. She's finally able to see her own personal vision come to life instead of designing around everyone else's tastes." He paused, regarding her intently. "Maybe you need the same freedom."

"How so?"

"Society tells us marriage is the only way to prove a relationship is real. Don't you think you may be bowing down to these constrictions in order to fit in?" His eyes suddenly blazed like a brilliant blue sky. "Wouldn't you rather have something real and good for a little while, rather than fake for eternity?"

Again, that connection between them rose up and practically strangled her with intensity. Oh, this man was a true master. He had every line memorized, and knew exactly how to charm a woman out of her panties. She turned her back on him, reaching for a mug and pouring him a cup of coffee. "I don't intend to choose, Slick." She slid it across the stripped bar with a flick of her wrist, not spilling a drop. "But maybe one day, you'll have to."

His slow grin gained her respect. He took her jabs with a sense of play, proving he'd be an interesting companion. Accepting the challenge, he took a healthy swallow of the bitter brew, shuddered, and put the mug down like he'd tossed back a one-hundred-proof whiskey shot. "This coffee doesn't get any better with time, does it?"

She laughed as he made his way back outside to bring in the rest of his supplies. He organized the setup with a ruthless precision that surprised her. For some reason, she'd pictured him as a sloppy worker, but he examined every piece of his equipment, from brushes to sander, and created a kind of assembly line. She scooped up her coffee and headed toward her table.

"Gonna hang out with me today?" he asked.

"If that's not a problem, yes. I have a ton of work to do and won't get in your way."

"I'd love company. Just one problem."

She prepped for a flirty, meaning-laden comment. "What's that?"

"I need music."

"Oh. Well, that's okay, I can put on the jukebox or Pandora radio."

"No, you don't understand." Why was his face turning a light shade of pink? "I have particular music I like listening to while I work, and not everyone appreciates it."

She tilted her head in consideration. "Is it, like, blackmail material?"

"My brother Cal would say so, but he's always lacked true taste."

A smile tugged at her lips. "Do your worst. I won't say a word."

"You swear?"

"Yes, I swear."

He considered her words, then nodded. "You're now in the circle of trust. Once you're in, you can never be released."

"Kind of like marriage?"

"Smart-ass."

She laughed again and sat down. He took his

phone out, swiped at the screen, and the strains of NSync belted out in high-energy, poppy form. Her eyes widened in surprise, but Raven didn't say a word. He cut her one warning glance, then focused on his work.

Raven decided to do the same.

Problem was, she couldn't.

A strange thing happened during the Backstreet Boys' greatest hits—had they really actually had enough songs to do a greatest hits album? Her attention kept getting tugged away from inventory and upcoming work shifts and toward Dalton Pierce's ass.

He leaned over the bar, denim stretched tight, powerful hands stroking the wood like a lover. Fascinated, she watched him walk slowly down the length of the massive mahogany front, palms coasting, lips moving in a whisper of sound she couldn't hear, as if he was speaking to the wood. Face set in concentration, he seemed in another world, a look of blissful peace radiating from his eyes. At one point, she let herself stare, wondering why he seemed like more of a puzzle than she'd originally thought. Each movement was coordinated with grace and an odd sort of poetry, whether he was sanding down the surface, scraping and chiseling out the bumps, or soothing the wood with soft strokes.

The scents of sawdust and varnish and oils

filled the air. She didn't even realize it was past lunchtime until she forced herself out of her voyeuristic daze and looked at the clock.

He'd never even taken a break.

Rising, she rotated her stiff neck and walked toward him. "You missed lunch."

He startled at the sound of her voice, blinking. "Huh?"

"Lunch. You haven't eaten."

"I'm good. In the zone."

She shifted on her feet. "Oh. Well, I brought sandwiches for us already. You can join me. To eat. For lunch."

Pure interest flashed in his gaze. "A lunch date, huh?"

Raven blew out a breath. "It's a roast beef hero, dude. Don't get excited."

"That's my favorite sandwich ever!"

She rolled her eyes and walked into the kitchen. Retrieving the subs, she took out some potato salad and chips, arranged them on plates, and brought them back out to the table. "Soda or water?"

"Water, please."

She grabbed two bottles of Fiji, put them on the bar, and reached for glasses.

When she turned back around, he stared at her with an open look of horror. "What? What happened?"

He lunged for the bottles and tore them off

the bar, studying the two wet rings on the surface. Uh-oh. A fine sheen of sweat gleamed on his forehead, and his golden hair was all mussed, looking like he'd just tumbled out of bed. His voice dropped to a sexy growl of sound. "Did you just place water bottles on my bar?"

His bar? She blinked. He'd turned from a relaxed, easy-mannered flirt into a man with a hard expression and buckets of arrogant dominance. Like when he was working on something it belonged to him, and he was deliciously possessive and in charge. Her nipples twisted into hard points under her tank in an instant. "Yeah. Sorry."

He flicked his gaze from the wet surface back to her. "Forgot to tell you about the number one rule."

Her mouth went dry. "You have rules?"

"That's right. When I'm working on a piece, no touching. Only I get to touch."

His eyes darkened with intensity, as if he was talking about something more than the bar. She struggled to ward off the sparks of sexual chemistry thrown from his figure. Holy Lord, this man was hot when he got all grumpy and OCD. No intelligent answer came to her brain, so she went with the only word she could remember. "Okay."

"This includes my tools."

Oh. My. God.

Had her gaze dropped to his crotch? Had he caught it? The flared light in his eye said maybe.

"My tools are sacred, and they can be dangerous if misused. I also have a careful system, and I dislike when things are out of order. I like to know exactly where my tools are at all times so they can be used to benefit everyone involved. Understood?"

Was he playing her? Raven snapped her teeth together and decided she wasn't brave enough to find out. She took a step back and threw up her hands. "Fine! I won't touch the bar or your tools, crazy man. Can we take it down a notch and eat now?"

"Yes. As long as we understand each other."

She fought a shudder and marched back to the table, sliding into her seat. He washed his hands and joined her there. He switched back to his easygoing way again. "This is really nice of you," he said. "Not many clients offer up lunch. I usually bring my own, but I rushed out this morning and forgot."

Shame burned. She'd only done it to have an opportunity to grill him, and now he made her feel bad. Dammit. "It's no big deal, I own a restaurant. You made a lot of progress already."

He dug into his sandwich, groaning with ecstasy. "Why does food taste so much better when someone else makes it?"

"That's why I make a profit."

"Your bar is magnificent."

She chuckled at the haze of lust in his eyes as he uttered the words. "Bet you say that to all the girls."

"I don't fool around with wood."

"God, there's so many things I can do with that statement."

His gaze flashed with humor. "The mahogany is pristine; it's only the surface that's stripped, I don't have to go down too many layers. There's a solidness and bulk to the piece that's known with antiques, but this is by far one of the best I've ever worked on."

She watched his face light up with excitement and took a few more bites of her sandwich. "You really love what you do," she said quietly. "The way you work is quite beautiful."

"You were watching me?"

Ah, shit. Raven tried not to back off too fast or she'd slide right off the cliff. "I watch every worker I contract," she retorted. "Especially in my restaurant."

He could have challenged her, but he chose to retreat. "Fair enough."

Her breath released. "When did you know woodworking was your career path?"

"My future was Pierce Brothers Construction—there was no getting away from that. My grandfather was well known as a master of woodwork. He carved out a name for himself in Harrington, and I seemed to have picked up his skill. I was always tinkering with stuff, even when I was little. It was kind of funny, actually. Cal would build the house,

I would work the wood, and Tristan would decorate the damn thing and try to sell it for a profit."

"Grandfather on your mother or father's side?" she asked casually.

"Mother."

"But the business was your father's, right?"

He reached for his water, taking a few long sips. "No, it was passed down from my great-great-great-grandfather on my mother's side. When she became pregnant with Cal, she changed the legal name to Pierce Brothers Construction. Guess she had a premonition she'd have more boys."

Raven tried to ignore her pounding heart. "Sounds like you had a close-knit family. Your parents must have made a great team."

He shut down. The light in his eyes disappeared, and his face grew tight and expressionless. "Not really," he said shortly. "I've learned not to trust surface images anymore."

"What do you mean?"

His grin was quick and held a bit of cruelty. "Marriages don't mean happily ever after, Raven. In my opinion, love has a certain death the moment you put rules on it."

Startled, she drew back, filing the hint away in her mental computer. His parents hadn't been happy. Was that why Diane Pierce stalked her father? Got him to fall for her so she didn't have to deal with her husband? Whatever had happened,

Dalton still held a ton of resentment. Was that where he'd gotten all his cynical ideas about love?

Maybe they weren't so different after all.

She lightened the tone. "You seem to be happy about your brother getting married."

He scrunched up his face as if thinking hard. "I guess you're right. Cal seems suited for marriage, though, and Morgan is his other half."

"Are you doing all the cabinetry for the new house?"

He nodded. "Got some amazing exotic snakewood I want to work with. And wait till I get my hands on the deck. People will be coming from miles away just to see it. It'll be shaped like an oval rather than square, with a loft-type roof and fitted benches. And the table is my present to them. I've got it stashed in the shed, and I spend most of my spare time working on it so it'll be finished in time. It's huge."

She smiled, propping her face up in her palm. "I get like that when I'm trying to create a perfect cocktail. Ingredients are key, but sometimes it takes a while to find the right mix of sweet and tart, or to achieve the subtle lingering effect on the tongue. It's a lost art nowadays. Everyone seems to want to wine or beer it."

He scratched his head. "I never considered it, but you're right. Bars just don't cater to the cocktail crowd any longer, and other than the standard classics, people don't seem interested in trying exotic mixed drinks."

"That's why I'm going to change things." Her plan was long term, and she intended to grow the cocktail crowd organically. She aimed to fill a niche no one even knew was empty. "I'm going to implement a cocktail night. I was thinking of combining it with some targeted activities or events."

"Like karaoke?"

She shuddered. "Overdone. I'm thinking more like poker."

His brow shot up. "You kidding?"

"No. Poker is hugely popular, but many people don't get to play because games occur in private houses or custom-made groups. I'd set up some casual tables—some mixed, some just men, others just women. Would love to set up a training class for women. I want to get away from the usual pool and darts everyone expects."

He took another slug of water and studied her. She tried not to squirm under the stinging blue of his gaze. "You keep surprising me."

"Why? 'Cause I have a big old brain?" She fluttered her lashes in mockery.

"I already knew that the first moment I spoke with you. No, you surprise me because you look at the world differently from anyone I've ever met. And I like it."

Raven stilled. A swirling tension filled the air.

His compliment should've been dismissed with a laugh or a wave of a hand. He was probably just flirting and trying to get into her pants. Right? But it didn't feel that way. He meant every word, and the sincerity of his confession hit her exactly where she tried to protect.

Her heart.

Stop being stupid. It's only a game. He plays his, and I play mine.

The disgusted voice shook her out of the odd trance, and she was able to pull herself up to sit straight in the chair. "Nice play, Slick," she said deliberately. "So, tell me a bit about California. Did you like it out there?"

A flash of disappointment flickered over his features, but it was gone so quickly she wondered if she'd imagined it. He took his final bite and wiped his hands. "Yep. Kind of difficult not to like sun, surf, and a laid-back attitude. It was good for me to experience, but Harrington must've gotten under my skin. Even though the winters suck and the people are still too rushed and way too high maintenance, I belong here. Those years away were key to figure it out."

"Yeah." She nodded slowly, thinking of the exotic sights she'd seen, along with sleeping on the ground next to strangers, looking up at the stars. Being back home and having something solid underneath her satisfied her more deeply than she'd imagined. "I get it."

"Course you do. You're a wanderer, like me. We're very alike, you know."

She let out a laugh. "Trust me, I'm nothing like you."

"I disagree. Name one quality you have that you don't think I do."

He leaned back in the chair and crossed his arms in front of his chest. She refused to stare at the bunched muscles underneath soft cotton. Why hadn't she ever seen him at the gym? His biceps were delicious. Did he have a lot of hair on his chest or a little? Was it blond or a bit darker? How far down did the line go—what had he asked? "Umm, what?"

His lip ticked up in amusement. "I told you to name me one quality you have that I don't."

"I'm a total control freak. I like to do it all by myself, and if someone tries to help, I get all crazy. Very annoying."

"I'm the same way."

She tilted her head and snorted. "You seem to be the type to go with the flow. Your brothers are more tightly wound than you."

"Until you touch my tools."

She sucked in her breath. He was right. He'd just demonstrated his irritation in pure peacock form. "You got me there. Unless it's just the bar that got your panties in a tangle?"

His lips twitched. "I've always been like that. My brothers know not to interrupt me or move a thing out of place. I have a system, and I'd never be able to work with an assistant. I like being in charge. I like dictating the terms. What I am able to do is balance that obsession with a more easy-going view of other life elements. Next."

She blinked. The rich tone of his voice washed over her in hypnotic waves. He spoke beautifully, like a highly educated nerd rather than a blue-collar worker. Not that she understood any of that class crap anyway. In her view, it was just society trying to pigeonhole people and personalities so they would be easier to manage.

She tamped down her lust, squeezing her thighs in punishment, and tried to focus. "I have a temper."

"No. You think?"

"Funny."

He flashed a grin. "So do I. I'm somewhat of a hothead."

She squinted with suspicion. He'd been nothing but laid-back with his brothers, and charming to everyone else. She couldn't even imagine him angry. "I don't believe you."

He threw back his head and laughed in delight. "Don't forget to put down suspicious on your list, too. No, really. I'm the youngest. You know the shit I've had to take in my life? My brothers know how to yank my chains, so to speak. And I always got into fights at school when I was younger." He scratched his head again, in deep thought. "Got into fights when I was older, too. Usually regarding a woman."

"You get jealous?"

"Nah, it was the other men who got jealous of me." She couldn't even be mad at his inflated ego because she suspected he was just telling the truth. "Come on, give me one more before I go back to work."

Raven blew out a breath and considered. It was ridiculous to be enjoying this conversation so much. "Fine. I'm very emotional. I teeter-totter from high to low, and sometimes it's hard to keep a delicate balance. Drives men crazy, and not in a good way. Bet you're cool as a cucumber, Slick, with no highs or lows. Now you know all my secrets."

She'd finished with a joke wrapped in truth. She wanted to end the encounter with a flourish, go back to work, and analyze what she'd learned so far. Instead, that glittering peacock gaze drilled into hers and she was done.

Blistering blue, as hot as flame, shot at her from across the table. Her breath left her lungs, and she tried to pull back, but he wouldn't let her. No, he kept her locked in a ruthless, intimate embrace, diving into her soul and trying to steal precious artifacts she kept hidden. Her body shook, and the air crackled like the beginning of a storm.

"You're wrong," he said simply. "Emotion means passion. It means you're alive, and you're not sorry for it. I can take that a hell of a lot more than I can your cold distance, Raven. I can match that type of passion, too. Just try me."

He slid his hands across the table, stopping just short of touching her fingers. Keeping his promise. Her fingers burned, curling into tight fists, seeking refuge. Fighting the need to touch his skin just once. She didn't know why the space between them had suddenly become so intimate, but if she didn't push back, she was lost.

The image of her father's face floated before her.

As if she'd been dealt an icy slap, she jerked away, her voice chilling. "You know one of my most important secrets already, Dalton," she said. "I'm looking for real, not a brief fantasy that will go up in smoke once the sun comes up. Remember that. Now, I think it's time we got back to work."

Frustration simmered in his aura, but he nodded, accepting the hit. "Thank you for lunch."

"Welcome."

He scooped up the plate and his drink, placed them in the sink, and headed to the bar.

chapter nine

———>◆<———

Dalton came home with sore muscles and blue balls.

Striding wearily toward the Pierce mansion's front porch, he groaned when he saw Fric and Frac hanging out waiting for him.

"So, we're dying to hear," Cal rumbled into the darkness. As Dalton got nearer, he saw that his oldest brother clutched a beer in one hand and had his feet propped up on an ancient, torn-up wicker table that was a complete eyesore—and one he refused to get rid of. "Did you sleep with her?"

Tristan held a glass of his expensive red wine, swishing the liquid around as if he held the secrets to the universe. His red-brown hair glinted in the moonlight, and his amber eyes reflected calm, but with a teasing glint reserved for his younger brother. "I bet yes, but Cal said no. The bartender has been your Achilles' heel and Kryptonite rolled into one, but I said not to underestimate the power of your charm. And the dimples. What is it about dimples anyway?"

Cal snorted. "It's a pretty-boy surfer thing. Hooks 'em in. But this one doesn't strike me as a dimple chick."

Dalton dropped his toolbox and sank into the third wicker rocker. "Why did I get stuck with assholes for brothers? Is there another beer out here somewhere?"

Cal passed over a bottle of his IPA. Dalton popped off the cap and took a long swallow. His brothers waited him out, like they always had. And as always, he broke. "We didn't sleep together," he mumbled. "For God's sake, I just got the job. Give me some damn time."

Cal slapped his hands together while Tristan shook his head. "Pay up," Cal demanded. "Twenty bucks."

"Morgan would kill you if she knew you placed bets on my sleeping with Raven."

Cal squinted with a warning flash in his eyes. "Do you like when Morgan cooks for you, Dalton? 'Cause I can get her to stop. Watch me."

Dalton rolled his eyes but stayed quiet. He really couldn't afford to lose his future sister-in-law's dinners. He had a limited amount of time left before she'd be moving into her own house, and then bye-bye shrimp and grits, and meat loaf, and pot roast. Good-bye.

"Couldn't close?" Tristan asked curiously. He rotated his glass once more.

"I was working! You may not respect the lines of employment, but I sure do."

Tristan and Caleb shared a look. Then burst into hysterical laughter.

Dalton brooded and drank his beer.

"Oh, please, say it again," Cal said. "Better yet, let me record you for the next time we have an inspection problem, or a supplier problem, or anything that entails a woman who is even the slightest bit hot."

"There haven't been any problems in months, and I resent you not taking my professional ethics seriously. Besides, we're getting to know each other better."

"Yeah, we know how you want to get to know her. BTW, I found another pair of pink panties in the laundry room last week. Tell your women to take their underwear home, please. I don't want Morgan doing their laundry."

Dalton shook his head. "I haven't slept with someone in a while. Must be old."

Tristan grinned. "Yeah, last weekend, right?"

Dalton gave him the finger.

"How long is the job going to take?" Cal asked.

"Three weeks, but I convinced her to go with

new booths. The place is going to look incredible. She's being featured in *Good Food and Fine Spirits* magazine, so that means—"

"Pierce Brothers will have some solid, free publicity," Cal finished.

"Exactly. She's also doing a big grand reopening party to show off the new look."

Cal nodded. "Nice work, bro. But my original advice stands. Don't mess with her. We like to hang out there, and you could ruin it for all of us."

Dalton stared out into the night. A cloud of depression settled over him. He knew his brothers loved him and respected his work. But sometimes they treated him like he was a clueless, insensitive asshole desperate to stick his dick in any female who moved. Hadn't they learned more about him this past year? Or was he fooling himself? Maybe they'd just see what they wanted to see, believing him to be the weakest link.

He'd worked his ass off to prove himself and his worth and thought he'd gotten there. Now?

Not so much.

He rose from the chair and headed in. "Thanks for the beer."

"Hey! I was just kidding." Cal's voice held confusion.

"Come back and finish your beer," Tristan called out.

He ignored them both and shut the handmade

wood door behind him. He remembered his grandfather carving it years ago. Dalton had watched him piece together segments of rare wood, from redwood to mahogany, creating a masterpiece. Dalton had sat every day by his side, handing him tools, watching the door transform into a legacy that would welcome people into their home long after his grandfather had passed. It was another thing he loved about woodworking. It was a form of art that not only thrived, but lasted.

Nothing much else did.

He was just turning when he caught the heavy breathing. Moving real slow, he lifted his hands in a warning and lowered his voice. "Gandalf. Balin. Down."

The two massive mastiffs shook with fervor and banked joy at his arrival. Since they both came to shoulder height, their enthusiasm usually knocked him over, covered him with hair, and dripped saliva on his clothes. Their mottled fur held tinges of dirt and mud from exploring the woods and chasing squirrels.

"I mean it, guys. Stay down or you go back to training. I—ah, shit!"

They leapt.

He had just enough time to block the attack, but the force of their love staggered him backward against the door. Half laughing, he dodged licking tongues and furiously wagging tails. At least the dogs didn't give him crap about his sexual choices or his work methods. They thought he was perfect.

Dalton gave them a few scratches and pushed his way through the wriggling fur. He headed up the spiral staircase, noting the quiet of the house. Morgan must be out with Sydney for girls' night. Funny how the absence of a female changed the atmosphere. Morgan had brought back a zest and joy they'd all been sorely lacking since—

A raw pang hit his chest. Damn, he missed his mother. He remembered how she used to sit on the edge of his bed, ruffle his hair, and just talk. She didn't even care when he got moody or didn't respond. She had a lightness of spirit that cloaked him and made him feel okay again. As if she filled an empty part of him inside that he didn't recognize until she was gone.

Memories hit. Oh, how she loved to tell him his birth story. Within a few hours of his birth, he'd come down with severe jaundice. But even after time spent under the therapy lights, he'd grown worse, until the doctor said the jaundice had reached such a dangerous level they needed to conduct a blood transfusion.

The process took hours, and he'd been in the NICU for seven days afterward to heal. He remembered how his mother described sitting by his side every day, watching him through the plastic bubble, unable to hold him for long periods of time. When he was finally brought home, he'd cried every night for over six months, refusing to sleep unless rocked in his mother's arms.

Oh, how his brothers teased him for that. His father had blamed Diane Pierce for babying him and making him a sissy. But his mother always said the needed touch and snuggling those first precious days had been ripped from both of them, and they spent the rest of their time trying to make up for it.

Even years afterward, his mother's soft voice always managed to settle that aching place inside and let him know it would all be okay. It was odd to have such a deep connection with one parent and feel completely ostracized from the other. His father had spent most of his time with Cal and Tristan, leaving Dalton behind. What Dalton rarely admitted to anyone was how much he enjoyed spending time with his mother alone. She was always telling him adventurous stories or making up elaborate games. She'd bake cookies with him in the kitchen, build pillow forts in his parents' king-size bed, or share her love of old musicals while she sang along in her off-key voice. She taught him to enjoy every moment of life and make the most of it. She taught him about being happy with who you were.

Until she left. And he realized she'd been lying to him the entire time.

Because he hadn't been important enough to her.

His feet hit the top step and his eyes stung.

Silly. A grown man missing his damn mommy.

He buried the emotions deep and walked into his room. The mansion could easily hold twenty guests without anyone ever bumping into someone else, so when the terms of the will had been satisfied, Dalton had decided to keep staying in the family home. No need to get a crap apartment when he usually enjoyed his brothers' company and got home-cooked meals from Morgan. He loved the goofball dogs, too, and the brothers had gotten into a habit of inviting Sydney and Brady, the company architect, over on Sunday afternoons for dinner.

Dalton's room was decorated in navy and earth tones, with simple, masculine furnishings that showed off an array of treasures he'd carved out. From the handmade trunk at the foot of the bed to the chest of drawers and burl wood poster bed, he'd filled it with major pieces that soothed him. Old basketball trophies, a signed Mets baseball including a signature from Mike Piazza, an old prom picture with his first real crush, Andrea Bellows, dressed in red satin with her boobs hanging out in magnificent glory. A tattered, thin volume of Walt Whitman's *Leaves of Grass*. There was a remnant of the first surfboard he'd finished and varnished on his own under the tutelage of a surfer god in California.

The walls were filled with photography, including a bunch of family pics that were his favorites. His maternal grandfather and grandmother on their wedding day, dressed in vintage clothes and staring solemnly at the camera. His mom sitting at a pre-K table during his first Mother's Day tea, holding up a plastic cup and a lopsided cupcake while he grinned toothlessly beside her. The official family picture every Easter, with his brothers miserable in their stiff new suits.

The en suite bathroom had a spa shower, a TV, and a sauna, and was finished with rich Italian marble. But his true private oasis called to him.

He opened the French doors and stepped outside onto the balcony. The quiet of the night folded around him, and he lifted his head up to the sky with a smile. Since his room was located on the upper level, he felt removed from the rest of the house and closer to the stars. The temperature had dropped, and the air hung ripe and still. The clarity of the night struck him full force, a dark wave of inkiness streaked with hundreds of bright points scattered messily across the sky.

He walked around the two Adirondack chairs toward the telescope. The tension in his shoulders drifted away as he set up the lens and swiveled the scope to do an overview. He'd always had a fascination with stargazing, but his lighthearted hobby had become more serious as he got older. Something connected him to the bigger world when he stared out at the universe, and the idea of so many galaxies looking over him made him feel at peace. Kind of like when he worked with wood on a project he loved. Energy buzzed within him, warming his blood. His Orion SpaceProbe telescope was top-of-the-line, and since it was a perfect late spring evening, he easily found Rigel, the brightest star of Orion, and then traced the Horsehead Nebula, located at the east end of the belt. Dalton got lost for the next half hour, enjoying the clarity of the sky and allowing his thoughts to wander like a shooting star.

Working around Raven was a constant, taunting reminder of how much he wanted her. Oh, sure, he'd always wanted to drag her into his bed, from the moment he first saw her. He recognized lust and figured he'd be able to scratch his itch or he'd move on. But this was becoming more than he'd originally planned. Their conversation was more satisfying than some of his sexual encounters. The way she both challenged and teased him was better than physical foreplay. She made him ache to know more and plumb those secrets that glittered in her eyes.

He respected her limits and her pronouncement that she only wanted a serious relationship. But her body screamed a different song, one he longed to play. He'd never felt so attuned to a woman's physical and mental presence. Sure, he'd experienced similar feelings on a lighter scale, especially during some more serious affairs, but not on this level.

Not like if he didn't kiss her, he'd die.

His brothers' teasing words simmered in his brain again. They were right, of course. He never held back when he wanted a woman. Problem was, nothing ever lasted past a few nights. Maybe a week or two.

Maybe his brothers had been right all along. Maybe he didn't have the emotional capacity to love like they did. Maybe he'd killed all those feelings after his mother died and he realized she'd been having an affair. Maybe all those awful fights and cold silences between his parents had sunk into his DNA and he was stunted. Who got to his age without falling in love at least once?

Something had broken with his mother's death. He'd always known his emotions were a bit fragile—like he was born with a vulnerable part he needed to protect at all costs. That was the primary reason he avoided love. His gut screamed that he wasn't the type to handle it and would eventually either screw it up or blow it up. Why invest everything in an ideal that didn't last?

The thoughts pounded and caused a slight headache. No, he was just living his life. Why on earth would he want to settle down to eventually get trapped in a hurtful relationship? It could lead to a disaster. His way was easier. No one got hurt because he refused to allow deeper feelings to blossom before it was too late.

But this thing with Raven needed to be explored. She haunted him, and until he delved deeper into the mystery, he wouldn't be able to move on.

Maybe she just needed more time with him. Maybe if he opened up a bit to her probing, she'd trust him a little more. He'd take it slow and easy, making sure he respected the boundaries of their working relationship. For now. Denying themselves this type of connection due to an imaginary future husband she hadn't yet met was ridiculous.

He didn't give up easy, and he wanted Raven. Not only in his bed, but he wanted her laugh, her banter, her passion. Wanted to see those inky eyes fog up when he touched her. When he made her come.

His trained eye settled on the gorgeous curve of the constellation Andromeda, named for the mythical princess caught in chains.

Yeah, he had just the lure he needed to get her on his turf.

Dalton smiled, turned from his telescope, and went inside.

chapter ten

—➤ ◆ ◄—

Raven didn't trust him.

Dalton had been extra sugary sweet to her this morning. Needing some distance after their last intimate conversation, she'd headed back to her house to finish up some work but finally lost the battle around lunchtime. She was too curious about his progress and the possibility of learning more from him.

He was whistling in tune to "What Makes You Beautiful" and varnishing the bar. She was amazed at how different the pub looked already. The old, sad wood was gone, and now the bar was shiny and new, with a gorgeous dark polish and rich undertones. The gold had been ripped off and replaced with bronze rope foot rails and handrails. The scratched glass top was gone, replaced with a smooth finish that complemented the varying shades of brick from the back wall.

He kept up a stream of casual chatter as she made her way around the pub, doing some light cleaning and prepping supplies. It was as if he'd lulled her into a state of relaxation for a reason, and her radar was pinging quite loudly with a warning that he had some master plan ready to reveal.

Or maybe not. She was also paranoid, another element that would make a terrible impression on a future husband. Experience had taught her trust was earned, not given.

Yeah, she was just a real fun package, wasn't she?

"When are you thinking of doing the party?" he asked, brushing slow, steady strokes with the grain.

"Depends on when all the work will be finished. I'm sure you don't just whip up customized stuff in twenty-four hours or do ready-made."

He gave a mock shudder. "I keep telling clients Target is not a store to buy actual furniture as an investment. Then they have that junk place on Marble Street that boasts clearance prices for wood. Last consult I had, the guy showed me his entertainment console he bought there. It had cracked and split in two pieces, and it wasn't even real wood."

"Hey, I love Target."

"So do I, but for soap, socks, or chips. Not

furniture." He shot her a suspicious look. "You don't have that stuff in your apartment, do you?"

She grinned. "No. I happen to enjoy antiques. And I live in a house. The log cabin down the road."

He stopped brushing and stared. "No way. The one with the huge front porch on that nice lot? With all the gorgeous maple? I bet the inside is amazing."

"It is."

"You don't give tours, do you?"

His question was all innocence, but his blue eyes were all danger. She kept her tone light. "Hadn't thought of selling tickets, but if My Place doesn't work out, maybe I'll give it a shot."

"I'll be first in line."

"Bet you will."

His lip twitched in a half smirk. "I'll be done by the time your interview is scheduled."

"So I'll throw the party the week after."

"Am I invited?"

"You did the work. I'll be happy to proudly advertise it to all the customers, including *Good Food and Fine Spirits* magazine. You'll probably get a ton of extra work from the deal."

"Sounds good. I'll need to swing back to finish the polishing. I'll start working on the stools while the bar dries."

"Great."

"Oh, and I need you to come with me some-place later."

She frowned. "Huh?"

He never paused in his work, as if his request weren't earth-shattering. "I've got something you'll want to see. If you like it, we can negotiate."

She waited for more, but it seemed he was done. A half laugh escaped her lips. Was he kidding? "Are you trying to proposition me?"

"Yes. But strictly for business. Of course, if you want to have sex, I'm a sure thing. But what I'd like to show you has to do with the bar and a product you may want to purchase."

Oh, this man was way too smart. For someone ridiculously good-looking, it was impressive that he was also an intellectual. She opened her mouth to refuse the offer. "Why can't you just bring it here? Or show me a picture?"

"You need to see it in person, and it's too heavy to bring over."

"Where is this product?"

He looked up with a contrived innocent expression. "My house. Actually, on the property of my house."

Unbelievable. She cocked her head in curiosity. "Do you really think I'm going to agree to come to your house to see some unknown product after you've made it quite clear you would like to get me into bed?"

He didn't even take a moment. "Yep."

Damned if he wasn't offering her a challenge.

The idea of seeing where he lived was also tempting. She could handle his advances. She could just start spouting about bridesmaid dresses and spring weddings. That would keep him far enough away. "Okay."

He didn't even look surprised at her agreement. He was like a sorcerer who spun a weird type of fog into her brain and made her do stupid things. "Good. I'll be finished around five."

"Fine." She waited, but he went back to his brushwork, humming to the pop music filling the air. "I'll be back."

"Cool."

He never even turned around. Raven tamped down an irritated sigh and headed to the kitchen to check supplies. It was probably a trap. A silly thing he'd constructed to lure her to his lair. No matter. She'd use the time to probe a bit more into his family and once again confirm to him she wasn't interested in his luscious body or ocean-blue eyes or rippling pec muscles.

Nope.

Not at all.

Dalton wasn't sure why it was so easy to get her to agree to accompany him back to his house, but he wasn't about to go looking for reasons.

He finished almost exactly at five, and when he

stepped back to survey the result, pride rippled through him. The bar was stunning. Restored to its old luster, the piece practically begged for attention—from the newly furnished bronze rope rails to the deep grains of polished wood with the perfect red stain and the clean, smooth lines relieved of bumps and bruises.

The memory of his mother's words drifted in the air, as if a ghost whispered in his ear.

You have a gift, my darling. Restoring something old to new brings beauty into the world. But always remember where each piece came from—its history, its legend. Only then can you make the past and present whole . . .

Goose bumps broke out over his skin. He looked around, feeling as if he'd catch her presence, but the place was empty.

The sound of Raven's footsteps broke his daze, and he turned to gauge her reaction.

Her slight gasp told him what he wanted to know, but her face was an even bigger present. Pleasure shone in her dark eyes, and almost in reverence, she walked around the bar, examining each inch, even kneeling down to get close to the newly installed foot rails. He waited patiently as the minutes stretched by, and finally she faced him.

"It's everything I always wanted it to be," she said simply. "You made it beautiful again. Thank you."

Dalton had done hundreds of jobs. He'd created

customized furniture that cost a fortune for people who never looked twice and rarely thanked him. He'd done multitier decks and carved designs out of precious, rare wood shipped from Africa. He'd felt pride, irritation, resignation, and frustration. But not once had he come close to the deep satisfaction and joy he got from Raven's words and honest gratitude.

Her face reflected a pleasure that was completely transparent. She didn't try to play games, or barter price, or ignore him. And in that moment, he fell a bit harder for her than he had for a woman in a long, long time.

He cleared his throat, feeling a bit ridiculous from the emotion. "Thanks. I'm glad you like it."

"I do. And I'm glad you were the one to restore it."

Her words popped out and surprised both of them. The widening of her eyes told him she hadn't planned on saying it aloud, so he gave her space and let her pull back. After all, he had all night. "Ready to go?"

"Sure. How far away do you live?"

"Twenty minutes, give or take."

She locked up the bar and climbed into his Bronco. He noticed she hadn't changed, which was probably a deliberate act on her part. Too bad she didn't know he loved women in their natural environment, with messy hair, casual clothes, and faces scrubbed free of makeup. It made them more real, and to him, more appealing.

He'd keep that to himself, though.

She cranked down her window, which gave her more points, and they drove in comfortable silence with the hot wind tearing through their hair. When he pulled into the marina, he braced himself for the explosion.

"Where are we?"

He played dumb, but he figured it would only buy him a bit of time. "At Harry's. I figured you liked seafood, right?"

She pulled herself up to full height in the seat and squinted those magnificent eyes at him. "Oh, you are not even pretending to act like a Twinkie, are you?"

"A what?"

"Twinkie. Hot man with no brain. Cream stuffing in his head. Because I know different, and I know this was planned."

He grinned with delight. "I'm hot, huh?"

"Don't even start. I agreed to come to your house and look at this item you seem to believe I need. I did not agree to dinner."

He rubbed his head in deliberate confusion. "But we need to eat. We're just sharing a harmless meal together before I show you the items and take you back home. No need to panic."

Sheer feminine temper shot at him in ragged

waves. His dick wept at the sensual assault she unconsciously wrapped around him. Oh, to experience that power in bed could break him with pleasure. "I'm not panicking, I'm just pissed at being manipulated."

He threw up his hands in mock surrender. "Forgive me for wanting to feed you. It's been a long day, it's dinnertime, and I really wanted some oysters. Shall we leave?"

She fumed, and he knew he had the upper hand. She'd rather die than admit sharing a meal with him would be challenging, so she'd bully her way through. It was a win-win.

"No. But I'm paying my share."

"No problem." He'd deal with that obstacle later. She stalked out of the car and marched ahead, giving him the perfect view of her swinging hips and ass. He almost bashed into the glass door due to the distraction. The satisfied look she shot him spoke volumes.

They were seated immediately at a table out on the expansive deck, overlooking the marina. Harry's was a staple in Harrington, known for its seafood but also crowded with tourists and people who liked to be seen eating in the center of town. Boats bobbed up and down, seagulls screeched, white umbrellas flapped in the breeze. Dalton didn't bother to check the menu, as he was a regular.

He noticed she went straight to the cocktail

menu, perusing it as if it were the Bible and she a good Catholic girl.

"Liquid dinner?" he teased.

"Hell no. I'm a woman who likes to eat. Just checking out the competition."

The waiter stopped by their table to take their order. "Do you need a few minutes, or would you like to start with a cocktail?"

Raven smiled and tapped the menu. "I have a few questions, please. I see you're featuring a watermelon martini."

The waiter nodded. "Yes, ma'am. Very popular. Delicious."

"You use fresh watermelon, right? And do you heat the sugar first or not?"

The poor man blinked. Looked behind him as if someone were going to give him the answers. Dalton sat back in his chair to watch the entertainment. "Umm, yes, we use fresh watermelon. I'm almost sure. I can check with the bartender."

"I'd appreciate that." Her finger jabbed the second item on the list. "The Malibu cocktail. It looks like you're making it with peach schnapps, but would you make it with melon liqueur instead and switch out the cranberry juice to sparkling?"

The waiter swallowed, scratching notes in his pad. "Yes, of course. Umm, do you want to order any appetizers?"

"Not yet. The red berry sangria. Do you use

Cabernet or Merlot? Is the base made with blackberries or currants or another berry—the menu doesn't seem to specify?"

"I, umm, let me get the bartender to check on this."

"Thank you, you're being so helpful." Raven gave him a knee-buckling smile that caused the poor guy's brain to short-circuit. He just stared at her, happy to be basking in the compliment. "Once those questions are answered, I can make my decision on a cocktail. In the meantime, can you bring me an order of crab cakes—is the aioli sauce house-made?"

Relief crossed his features. "Yes!"

"Wonderful. I'll also have a shrimp cocktail. What about the sauce for that?"

He scrunched up his face. "House-made, too."

"Excellent. And water, please."

Dalton lifted his finger. "One Raging Bitch and a bucket of oysters. That's it for me."

"Thank you, sir."

The waiter hurried away. Dalton shook his head slowly and gave a long sigh.

"What?" Her voice dripped with accusation. "Do you have a problem with me making sure I get what I like?"

He leaned in and growled. "No, darlin'. I'm a big advocate of you getting exactly what you like. Any time. Any place."

This time, he was prepared for the lightning-quick heat that surged between them. She stiffened as if trying to fight it but didn't drop her gaze. He was kinda crazy about her. "Glad to hear it. 'Cause what I want is a good cocktail that surprises me. Right here. Right now."

"You just let me know if there's anything else you want, and I'll make sure you get it."

She snorted.

The bartender came over, and Dalton watched while she peppered him with knowledgeable questions, and he looked like he had no idea he'd be grilled with a bartending final exam. Finally she seemed satisfied, and he asked her what she'd like to drink.

"All of them."

The bartender stared at her. "You'd like three cocktails?"

"Yes. Oh, and throw in a champagne cocktail, please."

"Well, we don't have those on the menu."

She cocked her head in challenge. "Then make one yourself and surprise me. You can do that, right?"

He stuttered, nodded, and left as quickly as the waiter had.

Dalton tapped his finger on the table. "I'm assuming you don't come here much?" he asked.

"No. I think they're overpriced and too crowded,

but it's probably a good time to test out their food and drinks."

His lip twitched. "You know they'll probably put your picture up like a most wanted sign and refuse you future entry?"

Her smile was nasty and he loved every part of it. "I don't think they're smart enough."

He laughed. "I like your style."

He kept up casual chatter until the waiter returned with a platter full of cocktails and Dalton's sole beer. She lined all the cocktails up before her and began a series of taste tests. Closing her eyes, she let each flavor linger on her tongue and then slowly slide down her throat. Depending on the result, her face revealed either a slight frown, a pucker of her lips, or a serene satisfaction. Dalton's jeans tightened around his growing erection, imagining how those lips would wrap around his own anatomy. Imagining how he'd dive deep into her and wrest that expression of sublime pleasure just for him.

"Sweet Hot Chris is so much better," she declared, popping her eyes open. Her fingers clasped the stem of the champagne cocktail glass.

"That sounds pornographic. A former lover?" he asked. He tried to act nonchalant, but the image of her with another guy bothered him, which was completely ridiculous and out of character.

"Oh, I wish." She sighed, licking her lips. "I named it on behalf of all the Chrises. Chris Pine, Chris Pratt, Chris Hemsworth, Chris Evans . . ."

"Ah, I get it. But I don't think they're the marrying kind."

Her dark eyes filled with laughter at his pointed jab. "I can make an exception," she drawled.

He swept his gaze over her body, then settled back on her face. He didn't need to see her nipples tightening under her thin tank or smell her arousal. It was becoming the norm between them—the underlying heat simmering every minute. "Good to know."

She was saved from responding by the delivery of their food. He dove into the sharp scent and taste of oysters, squeezing lemon and enjoying the salty flavor. "So, I've been dying to ask you a question."

"No, I won't sleep with you."

"What if we got married?" She choked on her crab cake, and Dalton laughed. Oh, her face was priceless and worth the impulse. "Is that a no?"

She wiped her mouth and glared. "Very funny. I doubt you'd marry someone just to score. What freaked you out about long-term relationships, anyway? Were your parents divorced?"

Of course, the question was casual, but it was like a missile launched into too much hidden pain. Many times he'd believed his parents should have divorced. He'd known for a long time his mother had been unhappy, and that his father had changed into a cold, domineering man swept up in all aspects of the business and success. Was that why she'd run away? Hadn't she known her sons would stand by her if she had decided to divorce? Was she so desperate to be free she considered them her captors, too?

"Dalton?"

His name fell from her lips whisper soft. Goose bumps broke out on his arms. "Sorry. No, my parents weren't divorced. But they weren't happy." He dragged in a breath. "In my opinion, things would've been better if they had split up."

"Did they fight a lot?"

He expected to shut down at the small probe. Instead, he found himself answering. "Yes, but it was more than that. I think the silence was the worst. Maybe if they'd fought more, there'd have been communication. My father wasn't an easy person to live with. After a while, I could tell my mother got tired of trying to make him happy. When she stopped, he shut down even more, and they just became roommates raising three sons."

"Were you close to your brothers?"

"Very. Sure, we fought and competed, but underneath it all we were tight."

"And your mom? Were you—were you close to her?"

The question was phrased tentatively, as if she wasn't sure she wanted to know his answer. Was she thinking about losing her own mother? Again, the truth came out before he could think about it. "Yes. We were very close. She was . . . everything."

Pain flashed in her eyes, and then she nodded, dropping her head. They ate without speaking, and once again, he respected the way she didn't need to fill silence with inane chatter. She was a woman who appreciated the impact of quiet.

"My parents were happy," she finally said. "I was young when we lost Mom to breast cancer. Don't remember much about her, except her scent. Papa said she liked to bake cookies. The smell of cookie dough and sugar makes me happy."

He knew how hard it was for him. Was it worse to never even have known your mother? To only rely on other people's stories or pictures to create a world you never got to share? "My mom liked to cook, too. Used to let me help in the kitchen a lot, and didn't care about the mess I made. Unfortunately, I inherited no skill."

Raven smiled and wrinkled her nose. "Yeah, I suck at baking, too. My cakes fall flat, and my cookies are always underdone."

"I'd eat your cookies any time."

His naughty wink had the desired effect and lightened the mood. She shook her head in exasperation, but her eyes twinkled. "You're incorrigible."

"Back to my original question. Your tat. It's beautiful."

She reached up and touched her arm. His nerve endings rippled with the craving to intermingle his fingers with hers, stroke her smooth skin, trace the lines of the ink. "Thanks."

"But it's brutal. A bit raw. Not your usual peace sign or rose. A sword reeks of symbolism. Why'd you pick it?"

The grief and flare of anger in her eyes made him pause. For one moment she was unguarded, and he delved deep and found a seething array of secrets. A caveman instinct rose up and strangled him with the need to protect this woman, to tear through each barrier until she was open and vulnerable to him. Shocked to the core at his response, he gripped the neck of his beer bottle in a stranglehold. What the hell was happening to him? It was like he was becoming someone he didn't recognize when he was around her, yet he wanted more.

"I had it done as a reminder on my twenty-first birthday."

The truth shimmered around her, but he was still too far away. "A reminder of what?"

A second dragged by. A minute. Two.

"Justice."

"Ma'am, would you like any more cocktails?"

The waiter chirped brightly, looking at her half-full glasses. "The bartender was quite impressed with your knowledge and wanted feedback on the champagne cocktail. How did you like it?"

Dalton cursed the man's appearance as Raven visibly pulled back from the brink of confessing something important. Justice? What could have possibly happened in her past to make her ink her arm with a symbol of justice?

"Thank you, I enjoyed them. Please tell the bartender the cocktail would pop better if he used a higher quality brut champagne and Angostura bitters instead of Peychaud's. I'll take the bill now, please."

"Right away."

She avoided his gaze as she took out her purse and fished for her credit card. Like he'd ever let her pay. "I don't mean to rush," she said, "but I think we'd better get going. It's getting late."

"Of course. I'll be right back—bathroom."

On his way, he grabbed the waiter and paid the bill. The whole time, the same word repeated over and over in his head, leading him toward a mystery he intended to solve.

Justice.

chapter eleven

Stupid. She'd been so stupid to tell him about the tat.

He swung onto a dead-end road, driving past the main office for Pierce Brothers Construction, and kept going. Not only had he paid the dinner bill, he'd snatched a piece of personal information she had never shared before, except with her best friend, Izzy, and Aunt Penny.

Then why had she told him?

Because something deep inside had sprung open, wanting the connection. She was beginning to realize the danger of getting close to Dalton Pierce. She could handle his gorgeous looks and killer charm. She could fight his dimples, and his droolworthy, rock-hard body, and his wicked sense of humor. She could even deal with his intelligence and woodworking skill.

What really demolished her was his vulnerability and the way he had given her his own truth. Those peacock-blue eyes flared with such raw emotion, she ached to put her hand in his and comfort him.

"Our family house is right down the road from the office," he said.

Massive oak and maple trees lined the roadway, bending forth as if to greet them. Following the winding lane upward, they passed through elaborate gates and the house came into full view.

Raven gasped. She couldn't help it.

House her ass. This was a mansion.

She sucked at identifying architectural styles, but it didn't matter. Struck mute by the huge multitiered home, she took in the fat columns, the wraparound porch, and a mix of colored stone, terra-cotta, and blinding white paint. Arched windows and a massive carved door that would rival the White House's gave off a stuffy dignity that was softened by vivid green trees and bushes and neon yellow and pink flowers hugging the pathways and lining the porch. She caught a hint of turquoise water from the infinity pool. Thick woods circled the structure as if hiding it from the world. "How big is the property?"

"Twenty acres, give or take." He pulled up and cut the engine. "What do you think?"

Her eyes were still bugging out. Yeah. The

Pierces were very, very rich. A tiny spark of resentment flamed within her. Not about the money. Raven didn't care that her father had been poor, because they'd lived big and been relatively happy. No, it was just that Diane hadn't wanted for anything, yet she'd pulled Raven's father into her crazy plans and ruined everything.

They got out of the car and she stared up at the house. "It's beautiful. Who lives here?"

"My brothers, me, and Morgan. She and Cal will be moving out once their house is built, but the place is so big, I rarely see Tristan. Want a tour?"

Yes. "No, thank you. Can you just show me the item you have for me?"

He studied her face, catching her stiff tone. She forced a polite smile and tried to avoid his gaze. Being here was more challenging than she'd thought. She felt as if she was betraying her father, or on enemy property. "Sure. It's in the shed down the path. A bit of a walk. We can go this way and—oh, no. Stay still. Just don't move."

Raven froze. "What's the matter?" she whispered. "You're freaking me out. A bug? I'm not afraid of bugs."

"Worse." His voice took on a hard, disciplined tone. "Stay. I mean it, guys. I said stay."

She swiveled her head slowly around and came face-to-face with two giant dogs.

They were covered in mud. Mottled brown, with perked up ears and chocolate eyes, they watched her and Dalton with a shaking excitement that told her they were about to launch. The tails began to wag furiously in rhythm. Damn, they were almost as tall as Dalton. Large canine teeth flashed in twin doggy smiles, and saliva dripped in small rivers to pool at their feet.

"Balin. Gandalf. Stay. Or I swear I'll put you back in military doggy school and this time I won't rescue you."

His firm tone only increased their shaking. She sensed the battle was already lost.

"I mean it! I am not joking around—stay right there—oh, shit!"

They leapt.

Dalton tried to protect her by stepping in front, but the dogs moved like a flash, flying through the air with abandon and knocking into them so hard they both staggered back. Laughter ripped from her throat as they licked her furiously, bumping hard against her legs and acting as if they were Chihuahuas rather than canine giants. Dalton tugged at their collars to drag them off, but she finally caught her breath and managed to stand straight. Oh, they were adorable, but playtime was over. Time to teach them to obey.

She whipped out the command. "Gandalf, Balin, down!"

Without hesitation, they slammed their asses to the ground. They managed to be still enough that she nodded and smiled. "Good doggies. Good boys," she crooned. "You just need some discipline, don't you?" One began to rise again, and she firmed her voice. "I said down."

He plunked back down.

Dalton's mouth fell open. He blinked in astonishment. "Wait a minute. How did you do that?"

She patted their heads. They wriggled with pleasure but managed to keep their butts on the ground. "Huh? Oh, they just need to know who the alpha is. They're still young, right? How old?"

"Two."

"Oh, they should be listening better by now. Are they yours?"

"Cal's, but we've all claimed them now. What do you mean alpha? Cal has always been firm with them. They flunked out of obedience school twice. We got blacklisted. They never listen."

"Which one is this?" She pointed to the dog on the right. He had mud in his ears and a slightly bigger snout than the other one.

"That's Balin."

"Balin, down." She lifted her hand and made the gesture to drop. "Lay down."

Balin slid to the ground. Gandalf remained sitting.

"Good dog. Good Balin. Stay." She turned her

attention to Gandalf and made the same gesture and command. The second dog slid down to the ground, panting with happiness. "Good Gandalf. Stay."

Raven smiled and turned to Dalton. His mouth was still hanging open like a guppy's. "They want to listen, but it's hard for them. Cal probably spoiled them as puppies and they never learned," she said.

"Yeah, he found them chained to a tree in the woods. They almost didn't survive."

"Poor little guys. Makes sense."

"Raven? How the hell did you do that?"

She shrugged. "My father used to call me the dog whisperer. Not sure. Something in my voice, maybe? I've just always been able to get them to listen."

"I am so turned on right now."

She couldn't help the laugh that broke out. He was such an intriguing mix of sexy, brainy, and funny as hell. "Then Cesar Millan must be orgasmic to you."

"He would if I swung that way."

They stared at each other, smiling. Why did she feel so comfortable with this man? He had the amazing ability to calm her usual tightly wound energy and sharpness. As if he softened her some way.

She cleared her throat and broke the spell. "Do you want them to come with us?"

The dogs gave slight matching whimpers, as if they understood the conversation. "Sure. It's getting dark and the woods are scary at night."

"I'm not scared of the bogeyman, Dalton."

"I'm talking about me."

She shook her head, released the dogs, and watched them bound happily around her and Dalton. The sun was sinking over the horizon, scattering bursts of orange fire, shadowing the woods. The rich scents of earth and wood rose up to cloak them. Their feet were soundless over the pine-needled ground, other than the occasional crack of a twig or the dogs' panting.

His fingers brushed hers. Lingered. Their pinkies intertwined. A simmer of heat hummed between them, reminding her that touching him was dangerous and not part of the plan. If he would've grasped her hand or made a sudden move, it would've been easy to pull away. But this seemed so natural, his touch just a whisper, giving her the option to break contact if she wished as they walked together through the woods.

Raven didn't pull away.

A large shed came into view. A simple structure, with no fancy windows or trim. Suspicion formed as he tugged open the lock on the red double doors and began slowly opening them.

"Holy crap."

The large space was filled with stuff. Tables,

chairs, mirrors, clocks, cushions, artwork, rugs, and headboards. It was garage sale and antique heaven. She let out a breath as she stood in the doorway, taking in the glorious clutter that would happily fill hours of adventurous exploring.

When she'd lived with her father, they'd go up to the attic together and rummage through her mother's things. She still remembered the musty scent of her dresses and scarves, the thrill of trying on the shoes and piling herself with jewelry. They'd flip through photo albums and she'd read while her father painted, the creaky floorboards and dusty windows an enchanted palace to her younger self. She'd felt sorry for girls who dreamed about being trapped in towers and rescued by princes, because her father was already her prince, and her tower was an old attic full of wonderful memories and magic where she wanted to live forever.

Raven swallowed back the raw emotion. Their fingers drifted apart.

"What is all this stuff?"

He cocked out a hip and studied the space. "Everything. When we do a project, there's always a mishmash that doesn't get used, so we put it in here. We just call it the shed. Morgan snagged a lot of pieces from here when she was designing the Rosenthals' home, and Tristan loves to pillage it when he's flipping houses. I like to grab pieces of wood or restore an antique I know will fit a certain person."

"It's amazing. This place is like a treasure trove."

"I found something specifically for My Place. After you talked about instituting a poker night, I remembered we had something I know you'll want."

The dogs seemed to know the shed well enough that they didn't need another foray. They bounded off on their own adventure, the sound of their paws fading away.

Dalton took a few steps inside, maneuvering down a path he'd walked before, and dug out two large game tables. Propping them up against the wall, he wiped off the dust and a few cobwebs and stepped back. "What do you think?" he asked.

She sank to her knees, examining the worn wood. The tables had six sides, with torn, faded red leather in the center. Built-in ashtrays and chip holders were carved into the surfaces. Elegant curved legs held each table with the ageless grace of an aristocrat who stubbornly held her dignity. Pockmarks were scattered throughout the finish, but the wood was magnificent.

"What type of wood?" she asked.

"Oak. I'd keep the original wood, but bring back its glory. A light varnish, I think, and nothing to hide the grain. I could replace the leather, too. Tell me you don't want that cheap green felt."

"I don't want the cheap green felt."

He practically shimmered with joy. "Good. The legs are solid, just need a bit of sanding. What do you think?"

Excitement nipped at her nerves. She tried to be casual. "I'll take them."

He chuckled and propped his arm against the door. "Thought you'd want them."

She straightened up and studied him. The lure of a good old-fashioned barter sang in her blood. "What do you want?"

His lips twitched with delight. He scratched his head, pretending to consider. "Hmm, that's hard to say. How bad you want them?"

"Not that bad."

"Ouch." His blue eyes sparkled. "What do you want to give me?"

She tapped her foot and considered. "A hundred each."

"Fifty each, and I restore them. Shouldn't take long to get them into shape."

Raven hated owing people favors, and being pitied. Didn't he know the rules of a deal? Dammit, she could hold her own. Her jaw tightened. "That's not enough money. I can pay."

His face softened, but he didn't look like he was humoring her. "Oh, you'll pay. That's just for the ownership, darlin'. We didn't decide on the price for the work of refinishing them."

Crap, she'd lost her temper too soon and tipped

her hand. Worse, he looked completely delighted at throwing her off. She backed up and regrouped. "Oh, well then you're already asking for too much," she said coolly. "I could get Jack the Stripper to do it for practically nothing."

He narrowed his gaze. "That guy is an insult to my profession. Not only his name but the cheap way he restores. Don't belittle me or yourself by mentioning him."

Now she was the one delighted by his irritation. Raven shrugged. "Fine. I'm just making my point not to think you can highball me. I have options."

"Not if you want my tables," he said.

Her lips pursed in a fake pout. "Fine. How much?"

He stroked his jaw with deliberate provocation. "It'll take three more days of work to get them perfectly in shape. I can work weekends, which'll cost you extra."

She tried not to fume.

"Two hundred for the restoration."

"Ridiculous. Highway robbery. Maybe I'll call Jack and see if he can get his hands on some other game tables."

He emitted a low growl in warning. "One seventy-five."

"One twenty-five and I get them before the interview."

"One fifty."

"One thirty," she shot back.

"Done."

Her breath came in short bursts from the high of their banter. The warm air spun around her like wispy cotton, lending to the intimate atmosphere. God, why did she feel on the verge of some sexual, delicious combustion? The man was dangerous as hell. She needed to stay away from him.

He nodded. "Good. I can load them in my truck tomorrow and bring them over before you open."

"Thanks." Her thoughts shifted. Yeah, he was getting extra work and she was paying him, but this seemed like more than just a good business deal. He'd found these tables for her. He'd bought her dinner. He seemed like he wanted to please her. Was he being this nice just to get her into bed? Why didn't it feel like a carefully constructed seduction, but more real? She did what she always did when she got confused. She asked. "Why are you doing all this for me?"

He jerked back. Those blue eyes met hers and buried deep. "Doing what? You're paying me to do a fair job. I haven't done anything."

She wasn't an idiot. He may have bargained, but she knew he was giving her the tables and the work at a huge discount. "Giving me a break on prices. Allowing me to pay in installments. And you bought me dinner." She couldn't help the way the words felt like an accusation.

"Crap, you're right. Why would I buy you dinner when you're not only beautiful, but great company? Why would I give you a break on my services when I'll be reaping the benefits of free advertising for Pierce Brothers once everyone sees my work? Darlin', if these are your high standards in a husband, I better rescue you right now. Let me give you some sound advice." He leaned in, each word punctuated with smoky, toe-curling heat. "Aim higher."

Sexual tension rippled around them. She mentally fought her treacherous body with clawing hands and desperate kicks. Then took a step back for safety. Raven was rarely nervous around men. There was nothing left of the once shy or broken girl who chased after an array of boys to prove something or slay the demons. She experienced sexual interest and enjoyed kissing. She liked the press of hard muscles against her soft curves, and the scratch of scruff against her lips. She was confident in her sexuality, comfortable with what she wanted, and rarely wasted time on head games or wordplay.

But Dalton affected her in a way that dragged the past and present together and merged them into one delicious chemistry. Her tummy tumbled, and her nipples hardened, and her mouth trembled, and he hadn't done a damn thing but just stand there, leaning against the shed door, fingers hooked in the loops of his jeans, blistering heat in his blue eyes.

She blurted out the first thing that came to her mind.

"I like it out here."

His gaze narrowed, assessed. Feeling ridiculously foolish, Raven cleared her throat and kept talking, scrambling for balance. "It's quiet, I mean. My cabin is also by the woods, but I don't have the same clear views you do of the night sky. I like looking at the stars."

Now, why the hell had she told him that? She needed to get her act together; this was getting embarrassing. He hadn't responded yet, just stared at her with that intense expression, making her more heated and uncomfortable.

"What did you just say?" He flicked out the question with a touch of demand.

She forced a laugh and waved her hand in the air. "Nothing, I'm babbling for no reason. Really tired. I'd like to head back now."

She turned on her heel, but his hand shot out and stopped her. Five fingers blazed into the skin of her upper arm. Her tat tingled under his touch.

"Wait. What did you say about the stars?"

"I like looking at the stars. Kind of a hobby of mine, that's all. Your house is elevated perfectly, with the eastern horizon on display. I bet you could catch Boötes tonight around eleven. Boötes is a constellation in the summer, it has this bright star called Arcturus and it's pretty cool to trace it. You can find it if you follow the Big Dipper." He looked so shocked, Raven shook her head. "Sorry, not many people are into stargazing. Can we go?"

"Not yet." He didn't release her, but the move still didn't feel aggressive. It felt more . . . solid. Right. "I know what Boötes is. I know Arcturus, too. I happen to have a telescope set up on my balcony. Stargazing is one of my hobbies, too."

She squinted with pure suspicion. "Dude, don't play me. You don't have to make up hobbies just to get an inroad. I told you we won't be sleeping together."

"God, you're a pain in the ass." He moved into her space, stopping inches away. She fought a shudder as the waves of male energy struck her like Zeus with his thunderbolts. "I don't lie, Raven. I don't pretend to be someone I'm not just to make a play. That insults me *and* you. I'm kind of obsessed with astronomy, and I've never met someone else with the same interest."

Her eyes widened with the knowledge. He was a closet nerd, just like she was. Suddenly there was too much between them. At his physical nearness, her barriers quivered in warning, and she was desperate to get away.

Yet she didn't move.

His eyes darkened to a gorgeous ocean blue with a bit of storm. His head dipped another inch, and his warm breath struck her mouth. She trembled.

"I'm in trouble."

She tried to focus on his words, but those carved lips fascinated her. His features were beautiful, from his square jaw touched with scruff to the arrogant blade of his nose and his perfectly arched brows. His gaze delved so deep, she felt trapped in a hypnotic state.

"Wh-what are you talking about?" Oh, my God, had she stuttered? Why weren't her limbs working?

He upped his game. His other hand reached out and he ran a finger lightly over her cheek. The slightest brush of skin-to-skin contact left a trail of fire. She tried to step out of the web of sensation, but the threads were strong and sticky, and she couldn't move. Didn't want to move. What was happening? She was always in control of her sexuality and what she would or wouldn't do. But right now, Dalton held all the power. Yet she didn't feel threatened. Only felt the need to move closer; breathe in his scent; touch the lean, muscled length of his body.

"I didn't plan on this. Wasn't going to push or make you uncomfortable in my territory. I respect what you're looking for, Raven. But you were able to discipline the dogs. You're passionate about your work and wicked smart. You're interested in the stars." He tipped her chin up, tangled his gaze with hers, and slowly lowered his head. "I don't want to think about the future, or why we're wrong for each other. I just want to claim this moment and kiss you in the moonlight, because you're so fucking beautiful my heart hurts." He paused. "But I promised not to push you while we're working together. Promised not to make a move you didn't want. So here's what I'm going to do. I'm going to kiss you. Right now. And if that's not okay with you, all you have to do is move back." He stopped an inch from her lips, allowing her one last opportunity to run.

She stayed.

His mouth closed over hers.

The kiss was pure and sweet. She swayed and needed to wrap her arms around his shoulders for balance. Soft, firm lips sipped, treasured, worshipped. A tiny moan escaped her throat and he swallowed it, his tongue pushing in for more and exploring every last inch of her mouth.

Her fingers slid into the thick strands of hair at his nape and held tight. She opened wider to his demands, and the sweetness sparked into something more, a wild craving that forced her to her tiptoes in an effort to slake her own hunger. She met his tongue thrust for thrust as heat surged in her blood and turned her limbs loose and weak.

Suddenly they were pressed tight together, his hands cupping her cheeks as the kiss deepened, and the spark that always hummed between them raged into an inferno. She clutched at him, trembling from the force of raw hunger demanding satisfaction, drowning in the taste of male need. He kissed her like she was the answer to his prayers, the queen to his king, and Raven was helpless to fight.

She gave him what he wanted.

His lips tore from hers. His eyes were wild, stinging blue and fierce. "Why is it like this between us?" he whispered. His hands were a gentle contradiction to the hardness in his voice. "Why do I crave you like my very breath?"

His scent surrounded her. Her chin tingled from his stubble. Her lips felt wet and swollen. Her body shook with a need for more. His head dipped again, and the reality of the situation slammed into her.

Oh, God, what was she doing?

Raven stumbled back, pressing her fist against her mouth. "Don't say things like that." She grasped at the tendrils of anger and pulled them tight. "This was a mistake."

His jaw tightened. "Don't pretend you didn't feel it, too. Are you really willing to walk away from exploring this connection? I've never had a kiss like that before, okay? Crazy, yes, but true. It may not be what we wanted, or expected, but it's real."

"Real? You're not ready for real, Dalton. You're a game player. I'm not denying the kiss was amazing, but I'm past jumping into bed to scratch an itch. We may have physical chemistry, nothing more. If you can't accept my decision, I don't think we should work together anymore. Now, I think it's time to go."

He didn't answer. Stubbornness shone in his eyes. Moonlight highlighted the glory of his thick, tawny hair. Her fingers still tingled from sliding through the soft strands. His scent wafted in the air, musky male, citrusy lemon, and the sweetness of chocolate. She waited for his temper, ready to walk away and cut her losses. It would be better not to see him again. It would be better to dump the entire plan, move on with her life, and forget that damn kiss.

"I'll finish the job you're paying me for," he ground out. "And I'll keep my hands to myself. But I'll tell you this. Physical chemistry is damn important in a relationship, especially long term. Passion is the foundation. Without it, the structure eventually sinks. Be sure you want to walk away from this for some fantasy husband who may not exist."

She shivered from his warning. Something shifted in her gut, a bone-deep knowledge that this man was offering a rare gift worth exploring, even with all the obstacles.

Raven ignored it. "I'm sure."

Dalton dragged in a breath and nodded. "Let's go."

This time, their fingers didn't brush. They walked back in silence. Desperate to get home to safety, she picked up the pace. The dogs shot out of the woods to accompany them, leading them back toward the light of the front porch.

"Raven? Is that you?"

Ah, shit.

The feminine voice carried in the air, and heels tapped over to her. Morgan and Cal appeared, trapping her halfway to escape. The blond Southern woman closed the distance, a welcoming smile on her face. Dressed in her usual chic white business suit even at this late hour, she was the image of sleek polish, from her silver bob to her smart heels. The surface didn't do her justice. Raven had learned over the past year that she had a big heart, a wicked sense of humor, and a steely exterior that refused to take crap from any of the Pierce brothers. How could you *not* like a woman like that? She knelt down and kissed Gandalf and Balin like they were babies, not seeming to care about the flying fur or lapping tongues. "Dalton, what are you doing dragging her into the woods? Didn't you offer her a proper drink first?"

A faint flush hit his cheeks. Raven prayed they didn't look as guilty as she felt. "Just showing her the poker tables in the shed. Raven's looking to start up a poker night at My Place."

Morgan rose, watching the dogs take off again after a sound. Cal hooked his hand around his fiancée's hips, tucking her close with an easy intimacy. "Poker, huh? Great idea. I know a bunch of guys who'd love to be in on that."

"I was actually thinking of starting a women's poker group," she said.

Morgan laughed and clapped her hands. "I love it! I'm in. About time we get something more interesting than knitting and book clubs."

"Even erotic book clubs?" Cal pointed out, his eyes teasing.

"Oh, hush. Will you be featuring cocktails, too?"

"Definitely. I plan to keep them on the lighter side and use some of the Skinnygirl products to balance the calories. When Dalton is done with the stools and tables, I'll set up an introductory class so everyone who doesn't already know how to play can learn."

Cal groaned. "I just lost my woman on a weekly basis, and maybe my money."

Morgan tossed her head. "Charming, I make my own money, and I'll win or lose it of my own accord, thank you very much."

Raven laughed at his chastised look. It was fun to see her plans for the bar garner the excitement she'd dreamed of. She hoped others would be as enthusiastic, or she'd be hanging out with just Morgan on poker night.

"Cal and I were going to sit on the porch for a bit. Why don't you join us?"

"Oh, no, thanks. I have to get back. Long day tomorrow."

"Of course, we understand. We'd love to have you for dinner next week if you're free."

She tried not to react. She'd be inside the Pierce house. See where their mother had lived. Gather more clues.

Be with Dalton.

Her thoughts whirled, and she forced a smile. "That's nice of you, but I'm sure I'll be slammed with the renovations and party planning."

Morgan sighed. "I need more girls around here. I'm overwhelmed by testosterone. But I understand; let me know if your schedule clears up."

"I will." She moved back toward the truck for her escape. "Have a good night."

Dalton watched her with the quiet of a predator but finally tipped his head to his brother and slid into the driver's seat. Halfway to her house, he spoke. "Morgan likes you. Don't punish her because you don't want to be around me."

She gasped. "I'm not punishing her for anything! I happen to like Morgan, but I told the truth. I'm busy with work right now, and that's my priority. Why would you care anyway?"

"Because Morgan brought back a joy in our lives we'd been missing for a long time." His hands clenched around the steering wheel. "Because I love her and want her to be happy."

She sucked in her breath. Stared at his profile. He kept his gaze on the road while his confession rolled through her like rollicking waves drenching the sand.

He loved her. Said so simply, so honestly, it cut right into her heart. This was a man who could love and had no problem saying it aloud. This was a man who treasured and cared about his family. This was a man with the potential to surprise her and destroy all her safe, manageable barriers.

He pulled into her driveway.

"Thanks. See you tomorrow." Frantic to escape, she practically fell out of the passenger seat, and hit the ground running.

She didn't look back.

chapter twelve

He was back to fucking square one.

Dalton brooded and tried to concentrate on the stools in front of him. It had only been a few days since the earth-shattering, rocket-blasting, volcano-exploding kiss.

Unfortunately, she was pretending it had never happened.

Even worse, she avoided his company and was unfailingly *polite*. No more veiled insults or sarcastic comments or withering glances. It was the worst type of rejection possible. She wanted to forget not only the kiss, but the budding relationship they'd begun to seed in the past week.

He wasn't sure what to do. His brain told him to forget her and move on. Was this really worth it? She didn't want him, whether or not they shared a red-hot chemistry. She was stuck on marrying some faceless guy who'd offer her stability, a low-APR mortgage, and exciting nights revolving around the DVR.

She'd die a slow, painful, boring death in a matter of months.

The blare of happy pop music didn't pick up his mood. He gritted his teeth and finished sanding the stools, admiring the curved backs he'd done with horizontal spokes rather than vertical. He'd mixed up the tones to give a beautiful impression of light and dark, blending in with the bar and the brick. The hinges were installed and they swiveled around to a perfect one-hundred-eighty-degree arc. He'd done the bulk of the work in his studio but decided to finish up at the bar in some adolescent hope she'd pay a bit of attention to him.

Instead, she'd been noticeably absent during the day, and dealing with a revolving array of people when she was there. She was definitely avoiding him. He only had a few more days before the place reopened, and the rest of the work could be done off premises.

Time to up the ante.

He hadn't been able to stop thinking about the kiss. How many kisses had he experienced in his lifetime? Thousands. Some had ranked higher than others. None had caused his entire insides to shift with a yearning so raw and pure, it shook him to the core. He lay awake at night, reliving each moment and imagining her naked and open under him, begging to be filled, until his cock ached and he was left with only one way to dispel the images for a little while.

He hadn't used his hand in a damn long time.

Yet he didn't feel like taking another woman to bed. It was sexually frustrating, but he needed more than a physical release. He wanted . . . more.

With Raven.

More. The term made little sense because he never figured on a future when it came to sleeping with women, but he was willing to try. If she'd give him an opportunity.

As if answering his thoughts, she strode out of the kitchen, refusing to glance his way. She threw some stuff into a bag and looked around the bar like she was packing up for the night. He walked over, stretching his arms behind his back in an attempt to work out the knots. "Going somewhere?"

She stiffened, then treated him to a polite glance. "Yes. Are you almost finished up here?"

"I'd like to get one more stool done before end of day."

A frown creased her brow. "Fine. I need to run out for a few hours."

"Oh, I'm not comfortable being in your bar without supervision. You should probably stay here with me."

She was kind of adorable when she got mad. Her mouth half opened, then slammed shut. "Excuse me? I've left you alone in the bar before!"

He rocked back on his heels, as if trying to remember. "Yeah, but that was different."

Her face flushed. "How was it different?"

"We were talking then. I felt like you trusted me more. Since we had that kiss—"

"I don't want to talk about the kiss!"

"Okay. Since we had that encounter, you've been all grumpy and mad. Stomping around and glaring at me. I'm afraid if you left me alone, you'd accuse me of doing something and that would mar our business relationship."

"What could I possibly accuse you of doing, Dalton?" She threw her hands up to encompass the deserted bar. "The cash register is empty. The kitchen is shut down. I'll lock the doors behind me. You gonna vandalize my dartboard?"

He shook his head. "You're the one who needs this work done in a short amount of time. I'm telling you I can't finish the last stool unless I have someone with me."

She practically seethed, making her even sexier. "Why don't you finish the stool at your workshop?" she asked reasonably.

"I already have two drying here, and one more to go. If I go back and forth, I'll be losing valuable time, and time is your money."

She glared, frustration simmering in a cloud around her. He wished he could walk over, yank her into his arms, and kiss the mad off her face, but she'd probably chop off his balls for such a move. Another reason he was so nuts about her.

"Fine. I'll babysit you so we can get this work finished and be out of each other's hair. One minute." She grabbed her phone and stomped into the kitchen. Dalton waited, doing a few more stretches and then heading back to his work. If he lingered, maybe he'd have a good hour to force her to converse with him.

God, if his brothers knew how low he'd fallen he'd never live it down. Practically blackmailing a woman for her damn company.

Pathetic.

The structure of the stool had already been cut, and sanded, so he was ready to apply the varnish. Raven came back in a few minutes later, her scent curling around his nostrils in mouthwatering anticipation. He felt like Balin and Gandalf and tried not to sloppily drool.

"Tell me this isn't Menudo."

He refused to blush. He never listened to Menudo if there was anyone around. "Of course not. You should give me some respect."

"For chaining me here to watch you work just because you're getting bored?" she challenged. "I had to reschedule my gym appointment."

"Personal trainer, huh? Some are pretty decent at giving you a workout. Too many have been disappointments. No vision or creativity."

She snorted. "Not my personal trainer. Unfortunately," she muttered.

"Good for you. Anyway, I figured you'd like being in charge of me. Telling me what to do. What not to do. How to do it."

"Is that how you like your women?"

"I like my women to be themselves. I like my women comfortable in their own skin, open to possibilities, and unafraid of who they are. I think too many bend themselves to what they think a man wants, and forget what they want."

Her startled gaze told him he'd managed to surprise her. He concentrated on smoothing the rough wood, evening the grain, bringing out the beauty. Waited for her response.

"That's quite insightful of you," she commented. "Seems like the perfect thing to say to a woman you still want to sleep with."

A smile touched his lips. "Maybe. But I'm not saying it to get you to like me. I'm saying it 'cause it's the truth."

"Do you like the truth, Dalton?"

"Absolutely."

"Then why do you concentrate so much on what a woman wants, and not what you really want?"

His hand stilled. He looked up, and their eyes locked. The familiar tension buzzed from a low hum to a slight simmer. "What do you mean?"

She hesitated, as if unsure whether she should dive in. "Never mind."

"Tell me."

She tilted her chin up in pure challenge. "I hear a lot about how you like to embrace the future, and the power of women being themselves, and how you're open to all of it. But you know what? Not once have you told me what you're really looking for. What type of woman would you like in your life? What sacrifices are you willing to make for her? How open are you to risks? Because I think, deep inside, you may be a bit of a coward, and just like to wrap words around grand gestures and ideas that keep you safe and alone in your bed at night. But that's just my opinion."

Struck mute, he stared at her, unable to form any words. He figured by being up front about his limitations, he was being fair. Hell, at times he called himself enlightened—a man who cited truth as his excuse not to get entangled. He thought he was one of the decent ones out there.

But Raven called him out as a coward.

He opened his mouth to deny, and reject, and challenge every word she uttered. Her phone buzzed and she jumped up with a smile.

"This is NSync, isn't it?"

He shook his head, confused. "Yeah."

"Funny, I haven't been able to get a particular song out of my head. Keeps playing over and over."

"Raven, I think—"

"It's called 'Bye Bye Bye.' So bye-bye, Dalton. See you tomorrow. Enjoy your new babysitter."

With glee, she threw the door open. Al stood there with a grumpy expression on his face. "How long do I have to be here?" he grunted.

"Until Dalton is done. Thanks, Al, I appreciate it."

He waved her off and trudged inside, shooting Dalton a nice glare. "Yeah, yeah, go to your workout. See ya later."

She kissed his cheek and bounced out of the bar, leaving Dalton with the overly muscled tank of a chef, who looked mightily pissed off at him.

Ah, fuck.

The chef took in the stool at his feet and shook his head. Plucked a battered pack of American Spirits out of his pocket. Then glared at him again. "I'm gonna have a cigarette."

Dalton sighed. "Fine."

The chef paused. "I don't like tattletales."

Dalton raised his brow. "You mean, you don't want Raven to know you smoke."

"Right."

"I got your back. But you know, smoking causes

some nasty shit, Al. I'd advise you to think seriously about quitting."

The chef shook his head in disgust and headed out the back door. "Just keep your mouth shut and we'll get along fine."

Dalton surrendered and got back to work. After a while, Al joined him inside the bar, and the sound of newspaper pages flipping echoed in the air along with the music, which he'd significantly lowered in volume. "The bar looks great," Al said.

"Thanks."

"I like the stools, too."

"They'll make a big difference. I'm gonna rip out these crappy booths and replace those, too. And wait till you see the game tables for poker night."

"Yep. Raven's happy."

"She said that?"

A grunt.

"Did she talk about the bar? Or the stools? Or me?"

"Want me to pass her a note? She can check a box: 'I like you' or 'I don't like you.'"

A flush crept up his cheeks. "Forget it."

A hearty laugh, then a cough. "Just fucking with ya, man. I know you have the hots for her. Funny thing is, she seems to like you, too, but you piss her off. Not sure what that's about."

"Me either. Maybe you can put in a good word?"

Al snorted. "Nope. Don't know you well enough, buddy."

"Understood."

Al read the paper and Dalton worked in silence. After a few minutes he asked, "You work for Raven long?"

"Almost two years now. You know she hired me out of prison?"

Dalton looked up. His respect for Raven hitched up a notch. "No, I didn't."

"Yeah, she gave me a chance right away. Especially when she heard I'd attended the CIA."

"In for something bad?"

"Losing my temper and trying to protect someone I once loved."

Dalton concentrated on the sanding. "Sounds square to me."

"Yeah, it was square. Raven's good people. She took a chance on me, and I'll never forget it."

"Only reason you're still here is you're good at your job and she respects you. Raven strikes me as rewarding people who are worthy."

Al grunted. "Maybe."

Dalton hid a smile. Yeah, Al was a softy underneath all that girth and muscle. "Doesn't hurt to have some protection around here, too."

Al squinted in confusion. "Protection?"

"Yeah. You're the only male in the restaurant.

Figured you watch out for the women if there's trouble. Right?"

The man gave a deep laugh. Dalton frowned. "You have no idea, do you? I'm not needed. Trust me, I'll kick anyone's ass that calls for it, but Raven handles everything herself."

A touch of annoyance hit him. The guy let Raven deal with trouble on her own? Dalton had been in his fair share of bar fights, and none of them were pretty. The idea of her getting hurt made him step forward, glaring at the cook. "I thought you were a decent guy. She's here alone at night and early mornings. Probably deals with a number of assholes who figure she comes with their orders. And you don't even help her out?"

Al's laugh got louder. "I've seen that woman almost break a guy's wrist who tried to grab her ass. She hauls out the drunkards with her own hands and keeps a clean house."

"How? I mean, she told me she does some boxing and karate, and works out with a personal trainer, but she never claimed to be an expert."

"She trains at the gym with some guy, Xavier, three times a week. That's where she was going today. Raven is fierce. I've seen her take down men twice her size with one damn punch, and they don't even see her coming. Trust me, she can take care of herself, and she likes doing it."

"Xavier from *American Ninja Warrior* trains her? Holy shit."

Al nodded. "Yep. Holy shit is right. Let me give you a golden piece of advice if you're still trying to date her. She's not the type of woman you protect, or coddle, or smother. If you want that, go get a dog instead, or some pretty, pampered Southern princess."

He made a mental note to introduce Al to Morgan. She'd wipe away any of his preconceptions of Southern hothouse flowers, and Dalton would enjoy watching it. But for now, he was still reeling from another punch.

The list of Raven's awe-inspiring traits kept growing. She was the most fascinating woman he'd ever met, and he kept craving more. More knowledge. More time. More . . . touch.

The problem was trying to convince her to want the same.

"Thanks for the tip, Al."

The chef raised his hand in acknowledgment and went back to reading.

Dalton liked to frequent the gym now and then for weight training, but he preferred outdoor activities. Running, hiking, swimming, anything that put his feet on the ground and offered fresh rather than recycled air. His architect, Brady, was a real gym rat and had mentioned his friendship with Xavier. Brady had even attended the filming of *American Ninja Warrior* to root him on. Xavier didn't take on just any client, and he was picky as hell about who he trained.

Another fascinating piece of the woman fell into place.

She might not talk to him at her bar, but maybe she'd talk to him somewhere else.

Maybe it was time to tweak his schedule.

chapter thirteen

Raven retied her Nike sneakers, grabbed her water bottle, and headed toward the second-floor workout room. She was looking forward to beating the punching bag and dreamed of a sparring partner she could take down hard. It had been a while since her emotions had teetered on such a razor-sharp edge between civil and primitive, but that damn kiss was beginning to piss her off.

She kept thinking about it. Before she fell asleep. When she woke up in the morning. Driving in the Jeep. Serving cocktails.

Why couldn't she just forget?

Because it was the best kiss she'd ever had, and she hated to admit it. She wasn't a hormonal teenager, yet she was acting like one. In her dreams, they hadn't stopped at a kiss. Each night, behind her closed lids, she ripped off his clothes and feasted on his golden skin, sank her teeth into his muscles, climbed on top of him and rode him with a searing intensity that tumbled her into orgasm in a matter of seconds. In her dreams, he held her and stroked back her hair, combining a primitive sexual ferocity with a shattering tenderness that destroyed her.

She'd been brutal these past few days about keeping her distance. Of course, he'd almost charmed his way past her defenses the other day, before Al had saved her. Being in the same space as him was too challenging, and she didn't trust her ever-weakening body.

So she'd changed her plan of attack. Instead of her usual snarky, teasing behavior, she'd been polite. Formal. She stayed in the kitchen when he was working, and made sure to schedule back-to-back meetings so they were never alone. After the work was finished and she did her interview, she wouldn't have to deal with her confused emotions any longer. Sure, she'd serve him drinks, but she wouldn't have to interact with him or his brothers. She'd scrap the entire stupid plan of learning about their shared past and move on with her life.

Xavier waited for her with a welcoming smile. "You have that look in your eyes, sweet pea."

"What look?"

"Like you're pissed off and ready to make someone pay."

She grinned back and set her water bottle down on the bench. The punching bag made her practically drool with anticipation. A good workout always cleaned out her head and drained her of all the negative emotions. It was the best form of therapy she'd ever invested in. "Maybe I am. Whatcha got for me?"

"We're doing drills."

She couldn't help the groan. "I hate drills! I'd rather work on my uppercuts and kicks."

"Tough shit. We're doing drills, and you're gonna smile through every set or I'll give you extra."

Oh, she despised Xavier when he was in beast mode. Her body trembled slightly at the thought of what lay ahead. Raven gritted her teeth and forced a grisly smile. "Good enough for you?"

His laughter rang out as he shook his head. "You're such a brat. We have company today. He's at your level of fitness, so I've decided to combine the sessions. You cool with that?"

"As long as he holds his own."

"Here he is. Hey, man, good to see you again."

"I appreciate you fitting me in last minute."

Raven froze. No. No, no, no, no.

She turned around slowly. Then almost swallowed her tongue.

It was him. Dalton. And he was dressed in clothes that should be illegal, even if it was the gym.

The gray tank with large cutouts barely covered him, showing off the corded lengths of gleaming muscles. He stretched, lifting the tank, and revealed the ultimate eight-pack. He actually towered over Xavier, but his thighs and calves were still thick and powerful, dusted with golden hair. He wore his lion mane in a man bun that showed off his sharp cheekbones and scruff-covered jaw and highlighted his dimples, which were currently flashing at her in an innocent gesture that reeked of duplicity.

Her heart stuttered, stopped, and then raced on. She ignored the little drop in her tummy and glared at him.

"Raven, this is Dalton."

"We've met." She practically snarled the words, her fingers curling into claws.

Dalton looked delighted at her response. "Raven, what a surprise! I'd heard you worked out here but didn't realize it was with Xavier. Thanks for allowing me into your session."

"Yeah, this is such a *coincidence*, isn't it?"

"It certainly is. Almost fated to be, right?"

"Yeah, like one of those epic disasters that destroys the planet."

"Or one of those chick movies like *Serendipity*."

She glared. He grinned wider.

Xavier glanced back and forth between them, his brow slightly raised. The tension cranked a notch tighter.

"Huh. Okay, enough chitchat. Let's head to the obstacle course and warm up."

Raven took up the rear, which afforded her an unobstructed view of Dalton's perfect ass, framed in tight gray shorts. She imagined gripping that ass while he pumped in and out of her, like he had so many times in her dreams.

She guzzled more water.

The course had been personally constructed by Xavier for the ultimate in cross-training, which combined strength training, flexibility, cardio, and endurance. Each stop had a specific exercise with a timer, and if she failed one, Xavier forced her to repeat it. She usually got through it by imagining her trainer experiencing a torturous death.

"Okay, children. Let's warm up." They completed a series of stretches, some tai chi, and a closed-eye meditation.

"This is not a competition; go at your own speed." A nasty grin curled Xavier's lips. "But bragging rights are afforded to the person still standing at the end." Raven glanced at Dalton, who seemed relaxed and at ease. Oh, yeah, she planned to demolish him. "Begin."

Raven didn't really remember at what point her limbs began to shake, or her heart to gallop so fast she could've won the Kentucky Derby. She realized faintly that she'd become a dripping river of sweat and every muscle begged for surrender, but then she caught Dalton's figure in her peripheral vision and pressed harder.

Xavier's voice was a whiplash of command, not allowing them to rest in between intervals, yet also the driving force behind her need to continue. She scaled the dreaded wall and the rope of doom, pushed and rolled weights, climbed on her hands and knees over and under a long obstacle course, and jumped on and off chairs that she wanted to rip apart with her bare hands.

The intensity was sparked deeper by Dalton's presence. With grunts and growls, he kept pace. They were evenly matched going into the final round, a timed sprint that tested endurance and the mental will needed to not only survive but flourish.

Her body felt like an overcooked noodle, but her mind refused to buckle, especially next to the man who was causing havoc in her life. Reaching deep, she shot forward through the laps, her heels pounding and echoing in perfect rhythm with Dalton's, until the sound of the bell rang in the air and they both collapsed on the floor in a heap of victory.

Somehow, some way, their legs tangled together. She pressed her cheek to the floor and closed her eyes, trying to find the strength to rise. His ragged breaths were close to her left ear, and she listened as they began to even out. She matched her breathing to his, her body slowly calming, and opened her eyes.

His face lay next to hers. His gaze drilled deep, demanding his own answers, and she didn't have the will to fight him in that instant. Lips trembling, she stared right back and let him see her. Naked. Open. Vulnerable.

"You're magnificent," he whispered.

His words might be pretty, and his lines well rehearsed, but the truth shimmered in all its glory. He was just as helpless to fight as her, and his smile came slow, and full, and so bright it dazzled.

Raven smiled back.

"I'm impressed, children, quite impressed. Not only did you both keep pace with each other, but, Raven, you broke your own personal record. Congratulations."

She didn't even bother to try to crawl off the floor yet. Xavier's workouts were legendary. "I'd feel better if I didn't want to kill you right now."

"Just part of the job I love," he said cheerfully. "You can hit the showers."

"Can you just take my hands and drag me there?" she asked.

Dalton gave a groan, tried to roll up, then stayed put. "You're a real asshole, Xavier," he threw out. "You couldn't pay me a million dollars to have another appointment with you."

"Now you're just flattering me. Say hi to Brady

for me. If you want another round, you can join Raven and me if she agrees. You seem to inspire her."

Her arm trembled, but she managed to lift it and give him the finger.

"Oh, and for God's sake, do everyone a favor, will you? Just sleep together and get it over with. It's like watching a fucking TV series with sexual tension that never ends."

The sound of his retreating steps echoed in the air.

They didn't respond for a while. Finally Dalton spoke.

"Can I buy you a juice at the health bar?"

She couldn't help it.

She laughed.

"How the hell did you find out my schedule?"

She fiddled with the straw in her organic blueberry smoothie, but her voice didn't hold its usual sting. Probably the workout. Other than a heady buzzing feeling from the exercise high, Dalton felt clearheaded and light. Hard to hold on to anything worrisome or bad after wringing out the body like a sopping washcloth. His mind felt bone dry and beautifully quiet.

"Al told me you train with Xavier. My architect, Brady, is a good friend of his."

"Smart move. Figured you had enough of me at the bar."

"You don't talk to me at the bar." He sipped at his chocolate peanut butter protein shake. "You haven't talked to me since the kiss. And you sicced Al on me."

She winced. He studied the high arch of her brow and the stray tendrils of hair that escaped her clip. She had the type of face a man would never get tired of looking at because her expressions were so bold. "I didn't want you to get the wrong impression. I figured I'd back off."

"I get it." She tilted her head as if trying to believe him. "No, I do. I'm not the type of man you want to get involved with. The problem is, I enjoy your company. I wondered if we could manage a compromise?"

"What type of compromise?"

"I'd like to try being friends." She tilted her head back and laughed, long and true and hard. He grinned. "It's not that funny, is it?"

"Have you ever been friends with a girl?"

"Sure, plenty of times."

"Before or after you slept with them?"

He scratched his head. "Mostly after."

"Exactly. Dalton, look, I actually like you. I don't know why or how, but you managed to charm me like you do every other woman. But I'm not getting involved with you."

"I know. I may not like it, but I accept it." He took a deep breath and struggled to tell her the truth. It would be easy to keep manipulating circumstances to gain her company, but it wasn't the way he wanted things between them. "I'd like to hang out. Talk. Try to be friends—not the phony type all those stupid movies are made of, but the real stuff."

"I can't believe we're having this conversation," she muttered, sucking on her straw.

Dalton made sure not to watch her lips purse in case he had very nonfriendly thoughts.

"I can't promise I won't want to kiss you or want more, Raven. There's this thing between us I can't seem to understand. But I want to get to know you better. If the only way to be around you is by friendship, then I can do that."

Her features softened. Wariness blazed in those inky eyes, but Dalton suspected it was more than fear of him breaking his word not to come on to her. No, there was another worry he hadn't figured out yet. He needed more time with her. Maybe he could turn this intense attraction into a solid friendship. After all, he'd slept with many women in his past and been able to become friends with them. It was possible.

He wanted to try.

"I don't want us to hurt each other," she said softly.

He jerked back. Emotion poured through him. He ached to reach out and take her hand, pull her into his embrace just for a few minutes. But he hadn't earned the right, and she needed to feel she could trust his intention for friendship.

"I don't, either. So let's not."

She ducked her head. He waited as she struggled with something he didn't understand. Finally she met his gaze and nodded. "Okay. Let's try."

Joy flooded through him. He clinked his cup to hers. "To trying. To friendship. And to kicking Xavier's ass."

She laughed. "You wanna continue training with me?"

"Maybe. As much as I hated him, I've never been pushed like that. It made me reach a higher level."

"Yeah, that's exactly how I feel. I carried around a lot of anger before. Most of us do; I'm not special. I tried plenty of ways to get rid of it, but most of them were pretty negative. These past few years, I feel like I've really grown up. Almost as if I needed to self-destruct in order to get here. Does that sound stupid?"

Her admission humbled him. It took him a while before he could smother his emotions about how well she had spoken to his own faults. The crap with his brothers. Kissing Cal's fiancée in an effort to prove his brother was marrying the wrong woman. The endless affairs with women he didn't care about, and fights with his father, and the way he'd run off with a big fuck-you, determined to never lose his pride, though he'd lost his brothers along the way.

"Not stupid at all. Sounds like my own life. I thought I was happy before, you know? But I wasn't even close."

"Why?"

He pondered the question. "I wanted to open my own business and prove my father was wrong for denying me my voice. See, we all had certain roles in the business back when my mom was alive. I wanted to expand the woodworking separately and target customized clients, but my dad always believed I was a fuckup. Sometimes I think he enjoyed making me feel useless. He was closest to Cal, who was the most like him. I was closest to my mother. When she died, I got lost, and everything at home fell apart. I made some mistakes and broke away from my brothers."

She didn't try to jump in with a soothing comment or pretend to know how he felt. She just nodded. Listened. Waited.

"When I bolted to California, I thought I was the man. I ran my own business, did what I wanted, and was finally away from my family. But looking back, I realize it was empty. I was trying to prove myself to everybody, but there was no one there. I had left it all back home. Then my father passed, and I came back here. My brothers and I began rebuilding something that was important once, and I realized this was where I belonged. And I didn't have to prove anything to anyone but myself. Suddenly I wasn't empty anymore."

Her gaze was transfixed on his, as if he held the answers to all the questions she had. "You said you weren't happy before." She paused. "Are you now?"

He smiled, enjoying the softer way she looked at him. "I'm getting closer."

A current of understanding passed between them. He rarely opened up to women, choosing to keep his private life and past to himself. But with Raven, the words spilled from his lips in a natural manner that didn't seem to spook him.

At least not yet.

She finished her smoothie and rose. "I gotta go."

"Will you talk to me tomorrow?"

She rolled her eyes, but her attitude had lost the edge and distance he'd hated. "Yes, I'll talk to you. You have my stools hostage."

"Good to know. If I keep to the schedule, I'll be able to tear out the booths this weekend, and you can reopen My Place. I can do the rest after hours or work on the back deck."

"Sounds good." She paused. "See ya."

"See ya."

He grinned like an idiot and didn't even care. He headed out shortly after, whistling while he drove home. At least they'd reached a compromise. It was going to be hell keeping his hands off her, but he wanted her company. Besides, friendship could lead to something more down the road, when she'd worked out her issues. He just prayed Mr. Right didn't walk into the bar and claim her first.

The light on the porch was on, and both his brothers' vehicles were parked in the drive. He walked inside and found them in the kitchen, platters of cold turkey, bread, and a bunch of condiments spilled over the counter. Suddenly the shake didn't seem enough.

He tried to grab a platter. "Hey, where'd you get the turkey?"

Cal slapped his hand back. "Me first. Morgan picked it up for us. She's out with Sydney."

Tristan finished stacking the meat on his bread, adding the perfect measured amount of mayo. He'd set aside his potato salad on a separate plate. The guy was a bit OCD when it came to his food. Mom had told them that as a toddler, Tristan used to scream when different foods touched on his plate. He denied it, of course.

"Haven't seen you in a bit. How are things going?" Tristan asked.

The leftover turkey was finally passed to him.

He'd always gotten screwed at dinner because he was the youngest. By the time it was his turn, most of the food was gone.

The memory of his mother hiding pieces of garlic bread and whipping them out just for him made him smile. It was still a pang, but he liked to think of the good things, rather than the ending.

Anything but the ending.

"Been busy working on the job at My Place. I'll be able to do the cabinetry you need for the Cummingses' place. Did they decide on the materials?"

Cal shoved his sandwich in his mouth and chewed with joy. "Walnut. They decided to make the cabinets larger, though, which threw off all our figures. Brady was pissed, but not as much as me."

Dalton shook his head. "They signed off on the final contract."

Tristan gave a snort. Even rude noises sounded elegant coming from the middle Pierce brother. He still wore his three-piece suit and sharp red tie, and smelled like he'd just showered and shaved instead of spending the day in the office or running around to sites. Unbelievable. "Problem is we want them to be completely satisfied. As long as they know it'll cost more, we're smart to accommodate the additions or changes."

"Spoken like a true company man." Dalton

took a seat on a bar stool and stretched his legs out. "I like to give them as few choices as possible because I always know best."

"Spoken like a true egotist," Tristan said.

"Don't forget to get Sydney the invoices for the job at My Place—that's a nice profit."

"Sure. I told Raven she could pay in installments, though."

Tristan and Cal stared at him. *Ah, crap, here we go.* "You allowed her to finance?" Tristan asked in astonishment.

Cal raised his voice. "First off, you know that's the number one rule we rarely break. Once we deliver the product, we get the money. Lesser companies have gone bankrupt. I swear, Dalton, keep your fucking love life out of Pierce Brothers."

Dalton half rose from the stool and choked on his temper. "Don't treat me like some lackey rather than a full partner," he shot back. "Think I'd offer that if I thought for one second she wouldn't pay? I pushed her for more work, knowing I could get both the money and the marketing from her bar. She's too damn proud to miss a payment, and already said she'd pay it off early."

Slamming his ass back on the stool, he glared at both of them. "Now, don't piss me off any more than you have."

Silence descended. He brooded, ate his turkey, and the tension finally calmed.

"Fine. I'm sorry," Cal offered. Tristan nodded in agreement.

"Let's forget it," Dalton said. He fought fiercely with his brothers, but in the past year there had been one unwritten rule they all abided by: no more grudges. Their tempers might burn hot, but they forgave easily. It worked for all of them.

"How's Raven?" Cal asked. "Morgan really wants her to come to dinner. I think she has a girl crush. She's always saying Raven this or Raven that. It may be the cocktails. Or the tat."

Dalton grinned. "I have my own crush, and I don't need any competition."

"Still no play?"

His grin disappeared at Tristan's question. "It's not like that. She's different."

"Didn't look any different when I caught you walking from the shed. You both had guilty looks plastered all over your faces."

"Just a kiss." The memory of her lips opening under his shot a bolt of electricity through his body. "I've never felt like that before."

Cal regarded him steadily. "Meaning you want her long term?"

He blew out a breath. "She wants long term, but that's not my thing. Doesn't mean we can't have a deep, satisfying relationship for however long we're both happy. For now, I'm trying to be her friend. Learn more about her. Figure it out."

"Good luck with that," Tristan said. "I've never been able to figure a woman out, so now I don't even try."

"Dude, if she wants a future, why don't you just leave her alone? Why torture the both of you? It's not cool. You'll end up screwing her over like you always do."

He stared at Cal, ignoring the twinge of hurt. Dalton knew he was the player in the group, and he usually had no issues with his brothers' opinions. Cal was now getting married, and Tristan was into sophisticated women who weren't emotionally messy. He'd said multiple times he'd be ready to settle down if he met the right one. But just because Dalton didn't see wedding dresses and rings didn't mean he felt nothing.

In fact, the big problem was how much he felt with Raven.

"Thanks for the support," he muttered, finishing up his turkey. "I don't plan to hurt her, Cal. I care about her."

Cal let out a breath. "Sorry, didn't mean to step in your business. I'm just warning you to be careful. Friendship breeds closeness and trust. Mix that with sex and you have a combustion ready to happen. I don't want to see Raven as the casualty. That's all."

Dalton gave a jerky nod, still not happy with the sweeping assumptions that he'd walk away undamaged. Looking back, there was no one he'd ever wanted past a few weeks. The buzz and emotional high always drained away. Crap, probably not many almost-thirty-year-olds admitted they'd never been in love before.

He fought off the depression and tried to change the subject. "I hear you. Tristan, did you buy the house on Bay Street?"

His brother grinned with pride. "Damn right, I did. Got it for a bargain, and the inspection came back sound. I think I'll turn it into an artist's loft type and change things up a bit. Next weekend I'm heading to Manhattan to get some supplies."

"Clear next Saturday," Cal said. "We have to clean out Dad's room. And the attic. It's past time."

Crap. The year after Christian Pierce had died had been taken up with trying to adhere to the terms of the will. They'd scrambled for jobs, moved into the mansion, and tried to find a way to not kill each other. Sorting their dad's stuff had been the last item on the list. Dalton winced, sharing a glance with his brothers. "Not sure I'm up for that."

Tristan gave a sigh. "Me neither, but Cal's right. It's overdue. We tackled the office, but no one's been in his personal space since he passed."

"Fine. I'll deal with the room, but forget the attic. Leave it."

"Dalton, we have Mom's stuff up there, too.

It's not something I wanted to do myself, so I kept it untouched after you left. I think we should do it together."

His gut churned, and he pushed off the bar stool. "Not interested. If you guys want to, go ahead. I'm heading to bed."

He threw out the trash and walked to his bedroom, feeling the weight of his brothers' sympathetic stares on his back. He refused to be dragged down memory lane. Hell, most of his memories were false anyway. Had they ever been truly happy, or was his whole life a hoax? Who was the real Diane Pierce? The woman who laughed with joy and encouraged him to follow his dreams? The woman who taught him not to lie and told him every damn day that she loved him, whether or not he wanted to hear it?

Or the woman who threw it all away for a man she wanted to chase across the world?

He'd blamed that son of a bitch for the first few years after her loss. Blamed him for seducing her and convincing her to leave. But as more time passed, he'd tried to bury the rage and move on. There was no point. Those unresolved emotions came out in one way now—in his sleep.

The image of his recurring nightmare flashed before his eyes.

He was running down the road with his mother, laughing while she chased him, her daisy-yellow dress blowing in the wind. He heard the car ahead but ignored it, too intent on the game he adored. When he realized she'd stopped chasing him, Dalton looked back.

A strange man stepped out of the car and held out his hand. His mother paused in front of the man, glancing once toward Dalton. He waited for her to tell the man to go away and keep chasing him, but she didn't. Instead, she smiled at the man, climbed into the car, and disappeared down the road.

In shock, Dalton began running after her, wondering if this was a brand-new game and she was just teasing him. He saw the taillights flash, and he ran faster, closing the distance. The shriek of brakes echoed in the air, followed by the crash of metal hitting metal. He screamed and ran faster, and faster, and faster . . .

The car was in flames. His mother cried, trapped behind the shattering glass, imprisoned by the strange man who held her captive. In that one final moment, their gazes met and she mouthed the last two words she'd ever utter.

I'm sorry.

The car exploded.

Dalton shook his head hard. The nightmare had haunted him for the first year after his mother's death, then receded for a while. But it was always there, like the bogeyman in the closet, ready to pounce after a stressful or emotional day. He'd had it again last week for the first time in months, as if it was a sign of something to come.

Opening up the balcony door, he took a calming breath and cradled his hands around the telescope. The stars glittered and beckoned, a million different stories and possibilities tangled together, full of pure and blinding light.

Even happy endings.

Dalton studied the stars.

chapter fourteen

Raven looked around the bar.

It was perfect.

Pride and joy mixed together and rushed through her system. Mahogany and bronze gleamed with high polish. The magnificent blended wood of the stools perfectly accented the brick wall behind. The old, ripped vinyl booths had been torn out and replaced by sturdy blocked tables and dark leather, blending into the walls instead of standing out, allowing the bar to shine as the main feature. The two game tables were strategically placed across from the pool table and dartboard, allowing a bit of separation to offset the balance of gaming and show off the antique beauty. Dalton had helped with the layout, able to envision what an onlooker focused on and how to get the most bang for her visual dollar.

He'd worked an insane schedule this past week in order to deliver everything in time for the interview. The crew would be here within the hour and she was so nervous, her tummy was jumping around in a wild dance. Dalton had checked in with her this morning to make sure she had everything she needed, and then they'd shared this strange silence that held more emotional undertones than she could handle. Finally he'd wished her luck and hung up.

So he was officially out of her life. Kind of. The work was complete, and the only time she had to see him was at her bar to serve him drinks and food. Sure, she wanted more information about his parents, but being around him was getting a bit too dangerous.

Raven might have to back off.

Her cell jumped. When she glanced at the caller ID, a relieved smile curved her lips. She pressed the button. "About time you called to check in with me. What's going on with hot cop?"

Her best friend, Izzy, gave a husky laugh. "He's still hot and all mine. Wanted to wish you luck on the interview. Of course, you're gonna kick ass and become famous, and travelers all over the world will flock to My Place just to get a taste of your exotic cocktails. Make sure you don't forget about the little people, babe."

"You could never be little if you tried."

She'd met Isabelle MacKenzie at a party in up-state New York, and they'd immediately bonded. Like two halves of a whole, they were both on the search to forget the past, bury their pain, and exploit every pleasure. They'd gotten their tattoos together, commiserated over sleeping with all the wrong guys together, and traveled with only a backpack to places young girls should avoid. Izzy was her soul sister, fellow mischief maker, and best friend in the world.

Unfortunately, when Izzy had gotten hooked on drugs, their friendship had become strained, but Raven was there to not only push her into rehab but hold her when she finally broke. Izzy had a twin sister, but there'd been a falling-out, so she'd turned to Raven to help get her life back on track. Izzy was doing well now, living in Ver-ily, New York, with her sister and working at the local matchmaking agency, Kinnections. She'd also met a hot cop who seemed to be her perfect match. Izzy was finally happy, clean, and sober, and they'd both stopped chasing disaster around every corner.

They'd finally grown up.

"I'm nervous I'll say something stupid and they'll print it and no one will come back to the restaurant," Raven admitted.

Izzy seemed to consider. "Could happen. But if you said something stupid, it would probably have the opposite effect. It will go viral, and everyone will want to come check you out to see why you said something that stupid."

Raven laughed and shook her head. "You're probably right. I miss you. Can you come visit soon?"

"Definitely. I'll bring Liam with me so you can get to know each other. Anyone I should be meeting?"

Raven hesitated. "Maybe."

"You don't want to tell yet?"

She blew out a breath. "He's been doing work on the bar for me. He's sexy as hell, smart, charming, and we have a crazy connection."

"Problem?"

"His mother is the one who ran off with my father. His name is Dalton Pierce."

Shocked silence settled over the line. Izzy whistled. "Umm, okay. Wow, didn't see that coming. Coincidence isn't a big enough word for this."

"I know."

"How do you feel about him?"

The question was too direct. She closed her eyes, trying to avoid her friend's probing. "I'm not ready to explore it yet. I think it may be better to stay away."

"Did you tell him?"

"No, and I don't want to. Maybe it will go away. Maybe it's just a passing sexual connection and when he moves on, we won't even think of each other again."

"Or maybe it's bigger than you think and you're meant to face your past, babe."

Her throat tightened. "Stop throwing the therapy stuff on me. You know it freaks me out."

"Sorry, all this evolved thinking and life philosophy can't be untaught. I'll stop pushing. Keep me updated—I'm here if you want to talk more."

"Thanks. I think I hear the camera crew outside."

"Go. Good luck. Peace out."

"Peace out."

She clicked off, pushing Izzy's words to the back of her brain. No time to be thinking about boys. Her big moment was about to arrive, and she wanted to focus on every detail.

Hours later, Raven locked up the bar, a silly grin tugging at her lips. She'd rocked the interview. The photographers loved the bar and had taken a bunch of pictures, and the reporter was super cool and chill. Al had joined them to talk about his background, not afraid to tell the truth about his prison stint, and had even whipped up a few of his choice appetizers for the crew. The feature would appear in the September issue, and could even get a blurb on the cover.

They dubbed her the "Cocktail Queen." Though it was a bit embarrassing, she admitted the title had clickbait power and would probably be great at drawing in more crowds.

Her phone registered a text. She picked it up.

How did it go?

Dalton. His words made her sigh a bit with girly pleasure. One of the things she'd missed most was telling her father when something wonderful happened. She had Izzy, and Aunt Penny, but she'd been mostly a loner these past years. Why did it feel so good to have a man check on her? She tapped out the response. **Went great. They loved the bar and setup. You can now call me the cocktail queen.**

A smiley face popped up. **Not surprised at the praise or the title. Congrats, darlin'. You deserve everything good to happen.**

Her heart squeezed. Her finger paused on the keyboard. He sounded like a . . . boyfriend. A lover. Someone in her life who cared about her and took her successes seriously.

No. This had to stop. Now.

Thanks again for all your work. See you around.

Raven turned off her phone and drove home. When she pulled into her driveway, something flashed in the light. What was on her porch?

She cut the engine and walked over. A dozen

bloodred roses lay before her. Reaching out, she touched one satiny, smooth petal, running her finger over the rich velvety texture, then down to the wicked, sharp thorn hiding behind the vivid green leaves.

There was no card, but she already knew who had sent them.

She shivered and looked up at the sky, wondering what she was going to do.

chapter fifteen

———➤ ✦ ◄———

I need another Sweet Hot Chris!"

Raven grinned and stuck up her thumb. "Nice choice, ladies." She grabbed a bottle of champagne and got to work. With lightning speed she combined the simple syrup, fresh clementine juice, lemon vodka, champagne, and aromatic bitters. The first batch had gone in record time, and she'd even had extra requests for her new mint-infused cocktail that put a twist on the mojito. Hmm, she needed to come up with a name for it.

She lined up four glasses, added sprigs of rosemary, and slid them down the bar.

"Two Bass on tap!"

"Can I get a Chardonnay?"

"Three frozen margaritas with salt, please!"

The requests shot at her like a firing squad.

The music pumped, countless people pressed together to grab appetizers and check out the new poker tables, and the alcohol flowed like molten gold.

God, this was a good day.

She'd decided to hold the party Saturday night for full effect. Her promos included showing off not only the restaurant's brand-new look, but the implementation of both cocktail night and poker night. For the past week, she'd worked nonstop to put it together, and she hadn't seen such a record crowd walk through her doors in months.

And this was even before the magazine released.

But the real hidden star had just walked in trailed by his brothers, bringing a healthy round of applause in his wake. She'd told everyone that Dalton Pierce had done the work for Pierce Brothers Construction, and she'd left out a stack of his business cards at the end of the bar.

It was fair. His work was stellar and beautiful, and he deserved success as much as she did. It was hard to think of his company in those terms, since for so many years she'd hated the Pierce brothers with a passion. But somehow, by giving him the praise he deserved, something inside her had loosened a few notches.

He put up his hand, laughing and waving off the applause with a good-natured roll of his eyes.

The adorable flush in his cheeks was sexy as hell.

Dalton Pierce was sexy as hell.

He'd cleaned up for the party, and wore a white button-down shirt, dark jeans, and leather shoes. His hair was loose and freshly washed, tawny strands brushing his shoulders. His jaw was clean shaven. When she went to greet him, the scent of lemon varnish and a touch of Hershey's chocolate drifted around him.

She wanted to devour him whole.

That's when the irony struck. She was hot for a Pierce brother. Her father should be here right now. Helping behind the bar. Laughing with Al. Hanging his paintings on the walls.

Instead, he was dead, and it was Diane Pierce's fault. Dalton's brothers had spread lies about her father, ruined his reputation, and gotten away with it. Could she leave the past alone and try to move on without answers?

Oh, she'd been trying. The odd relationship with Dalton was growing stronger, and this past week she'd tried to keep her distance, especially after she'd rudely dismissed him via her last text. But he'd sent her the damn roses. And he made a point to drop by the bar every single day, just to grab a drink and converse for a while. He was offering friendship, but she knew he wanted more, and each time she began to soften, the past roared up again. In order to allow him closer, she needed to know the whole truth, or it would haunt her forever. Somehow, some way, she had to get Dalton to tell her what he knew about the events leading up to the car crash.

It might be time to tell him the truth about who she was, too.

Raven didn't have time to brood or ponder her thoughts, and refused to ruin such a great night by replaying the past. She went back to work and the crowds doubled, so she had little time for chit-chat. If tonight was any indication of future traffic, the refurbishment had paid for itself already.

The party was a huge success.

Halfway through, she realized it was a little bit too successful.

Al ran the kitchen with military precision, and the waitstaff seemed enthusiastic about the crowds, but she was dying at the bar. The cocktails were such a hit, and she hadn't made enough batches, so the line kept growing. Damn, she should've hired an assistant bartender, but of course, with her control issues, she hadn't even considered it.

She hated denying someone a drink, but it might be time to shut down the cocktail station and just deal with beer and wine. Frustrated at her glitch in planning, Raven put her fingers in her mouth to blow a wolf whistle, then stopped cold.

"Hey."

She blinked. Dalton had come behind the bar and was calmly tucking a bottle opener into his pocket and grabbing a dishrag. "What are you doing?" she demanded.

"Helping you out. You're slammed."

Her mouth fell open. "You can't come back here! You're not a bartender!"

His dimples flashed. Her knees weakened just a tad from the laugh lines around his mouth. Why were his teeth so white? Did he use a whitener or were they naturally that beautiful, like the rest of him? "Actually, I am. Or was. I bartended as a second job in California." Those blue eyes tugged at her, filled with male mischief. "I kinda sucked, but I can certainly manage beer and wine. I'll leave the more exotic drinks to you. Deal?"

She shook her head stubbornly. "No, this is a party and you've done enough. This is not your job. Go have fun with your brothers."

He didn't move, just as stubborn as her. "I see my brothers every day. I'd love to help you out; I found bartending to be kind of fun."

"No, it's not right. Go talk to some women."

His grin was pure delight. Damn this man. "Already checked them out. Not interested in anyone. Besides, I'd like to help my friend." He gave a meaningful pause. "Unless you didn't mean it? About trying to be more friendly?"

Why did she even bother? She slammed a corkscrew on the bar and jabbed a finger at his chest. "Fine. You get twenty per hour and split the tips with the kitchen crew." She grabbed the jar that was halfway stuffed and plopped a brand-new shiny one on the bar. "This one's yours. Let's see what you got."

"If I let a woman touch my butt, do my tips go up?"

She rolled her eyes and opened the mini fridge. "Al will kick her ass. Now for God's sake, go pour that guy a Sam Adams."

"Yes, ma'am."

He turned to walk down the bar.

She couldn't help it. She checked out his ass.

Two hours later, she admitted he'd been right. She would've died without the help. Besides taking the pressure off her, he flourished behind the bar. Charming both males and females, he poured drinks, remembered names, joked good-naturedly, and up-sold her cocktails. His jar was overflowing and the curvy blonde at the end kept stuffing dollar bills into it like he was her own personal stripper.

The man was too much.

"He's something, ain't he?"

She looked up. Cal jerked his head at his brother, then regarded her with a curious stare. The first time she'd met the Pierce brothers,

Cal had stood out to her as the leader. He had a strong, quiet presence that commanded, and each motion seemed economical, as if he hated wasting energy on either inane conversation or action. Cal seemed completely solid, trustworthy, and low-key.

Completely different from Dalton.

"Yeah, he is." A smile curved her lips. "He kinda saved me."

"He likes you."

She pulled back, uncomfortable. "Umm, well, we got to know each other better when he was restoring the bar and stuff. Seems like a good guy."

"So I guess it all worked out for you. Restoring the bar, I mean. You were pretty stubborn about not working with him."

Damn. She lifted her chin. "I was wrong."

"Yeah. Maybe we both were." She frowned, not understanding. Cal shifted his weight, as if measuring whether to tell her something. She held her breath, wondering if he would warn her away or have his brother's back.

"He likes you," Cal repeated. "More so than I've seen before with other women."

"Yeah, he's a player. There've been many women, I've heard."

His gaze narrowed. Assessed. "He'll be honest about who he is and what he can give. That's not my concern."

"Then what is?" she asked curiously.

"You. The way he looks at you. The way he . . . is with you. Just don't hurt him."

She swallowed back a gasp at the stark words. Cal was worried about her? Every time Dalton's name was mentioned, she was warned about his reputation. About his womanizing, and inability to commit, and his expertise at charming the panties right off any female he desired. Never, ever had she imagined his brother would be concerned about her being some type of enchantress ready to break his heart.

"It's just an act," she insisted. "I'm a challenge to him, and we happen to have this strange chemistry. Believe me, it won't be long before he's moving on to the next woman who intrigues him."

"Don't be too sure. And don't judge him, Raven. Dalton's more of a romantic than any of us. He's gotten his heart shattered before and still hasn't recovered. When he loves someone, he doesn't hold back."

She pulled in a breath, leaning forward. The music and the laughter and the chatter drifted away as she hung on Cal's words, which gave her a glimpse into the man who was beginning to haunt her. "I didn't know he had a long-term relationship," she murmured. "Who was she?"

Raw pain flickered in his eyes, but it was gone so quickly she could have imagined it.

"Our mother."

Raven had no time to answer. Cal lifted his beer, nodded his head, and walked away.

Stunned, she took a few minutes to snap back into action. And in that moment, she wondered if fate was stepping in, entangling her with a sworn enemy from the past whom she was beginning to care about.

He wasn't even the enemy any longer. Just a man who may have experienced the same rage and pain she did and was learning to live with it. Maybe they were more similar than she'd originally thought.

"Daydreaming on the job?"

She jerked around at the teasing voice. He grinned down at her with the usual charm, but she wondered what really hid behind his walls. When she'd lost her father, the years afterward were filled with her own personal therapy. Dalton had run to California, but had he ever tamed the need to self-destruct? Wasn't blocking himself from ever thinking of a long-term relationship a way to punish and get revenge in a different way?

Holy crap, she was becoming a professional therapist. She needed to get it together and stop thinking about him so much.

Raven shook her head hard to clear it. "Just creating my next great cocktail."

He motioned toward the jar that held an endless array of singles. "I think they like me."

"Especially the perky blonde."

He didn't even deign to glance back. If he had, he would've caught the lustful gleam in her eye and the shiny, parted red lips that said *I'm yours*. "Think if I peeled off my shirt I'd get some fives?"

She had to clamp down on the smile threatening to break out. "Think this is Coyote Ugly, Slick? Not that type of bar."

He leaned in. "Damn, I'd pay a million to see you dance on the bar."

"Don't make promises you can't keep. I may do it for a million."

"How about my tip jar? The whole thing."

The connection tightened, crackled. She struggled for breath amid the short-circuiting of her body, which practically wept to experience one more kiss. Why was the forbidden so hard to fight? "Not worth a hundred bucks. Think I'm cheap?"

He gasped in affronted shock. "There's got to be over two hundred in there!"

She shrugged. "Maybe. Maybe it's all singles and mine are all fivers. Let's announce last call— it's later than I'd originally planned."

"Bet I got some tens," he muttered, grabbing glasses and refilling drafts. She watched as the perfect amount of head foamed up, and nodded with approval as he pushed them toward the customers. Not bad. "Maybe even a twenty!"

Why did he have to be so damn adorable?

They fell into perfect rhythm, as if they'd worked together before. She hated bumping into another bartender. Despised clumsiness and sloppiness. Not only did he clean up as he worked, he moved with the grace of a dancer, even with his staggering height. The crowds began to thin. His brothers popped over to say good-bye and rib him, which he took with his usual grin, and finally the bar was empty.

Amanda and Sheila came out of the kitchen groaning. "That was hard-core!" Sheila announced.

"But worth the tips," Amanda chirped. The two women slid onto bar stools, and Raven filled two cups of seltzer with lemon, sliding them over. She never served them alcoholic drinks in her bar, and they'd never bitched about the rules.

Dalton joined them in their familiar circle and groaned. "My feet hurt."

Sheila snorted. "Ever do catering? Come back to me after that and tell me your feet don't feel like you danced the ballet at Lincoln Center."

Raven smiled. "Beer?" she asked him.

He shook his head. "Seltzer sounds good to me."

Her respect for him went up another notch. He knew how to follow and how to lead. A solid combination of skills.

"So Raven and I are having a contest of who got the most tips. Who do you think won?" he asked.

The girls glanced at each other. "Raven," they said in unison.

He clutched his hands over his heart in mock hurt. "What? I had it going on! You're going to regret those words."

Amanda giggled. "Raven is a badass. Besides her drinks, she's just kinda hot. Girls and guys love her."

Raven tugged on the waitress's blond locks. "Thanks, babe."

Sheila snorted. "Dump the jars and let's find out."

Al trudged out of the kitchen, slid onto a stool, and grabbed his seltzer. "Bettin' on Raven," he rumbled.

"Don't dudes stick together?" Dalton challenged.

Al shrugged. "She always kills the tips."

Amanda squinted and took a long sniff. "I smell smoke, Al. Seriously?"

He gave Dalton a suffering look. "Told ya to stick to my team," Dalton said.

Raven sighed. "I'm disappointed, Al, but we're not ruining tonight by sharing details of lung cancer. Did you see the commercial where the guy loses his voice and has to talk through a machine?"

Al turned a bit green. "Cut it out."

"Sorry. Count 'em up."

The fun of the night was always totaling the tips, and with her team, distribution was a breeze. There was no fighting or egotism, just a sense of hard work and getting a fair share. "Two hundred and twenty-five dollars," she announced.

Al whistled. "Nice."

Amanda clapped her hands. "Hard to beat," she said merrily.

Dalton gave an annoyed frown that seemed mostly for show. "Thanks to all of you for your belief and support of my bartending abilities. Now stand back and watch me win."

When he counted past two hundred dollars, Raven was concerned. Even when she'd served at other bars, she'd always raked in double the tips her coworkers did. Many times she'd had to quit because the staff got pissy and thought she was stealing from them. Now she was able to give all her tips to her own crew, but she had a reputation to protect. Crap, two hundred ten? No. Way.

"He's going to win!" Sheila announced. "History may be made tonight."

"Not gonna happen," Al said.

Finally he reached the last dollar.

Two hundred twenty-one dollars and seventy-five cents.

Whew.

"Nice try, Slick. No one has ever gotten close. You're a good bartender."

The others agreed, giving him high fives and complimenting him on the restaurant updates. When Dalton gave away all the money, they tried to protest, but he insisted. He also made sure her offered twenty-dollars-per-hour base pay went into the tip jar for them. With bulging pockets and light spirits, they drank seltzer and bullshitted to come down from the energy of the night. Then Sheila, Amanda, and Al took off, leaving her alone with Dalton.

"So."

She took a casual step away from him. "So. Thanks for helping out tonight."

"What are friends for?"

He took a casual step forward. Oh, no way was she playing this game. She was no cringing virgin, and she wasn't going to allow him to play his stalking predator game. Pulling herself up to full height, she tilted her chin and claimed her space. "I hope you get a lot of work. I left your business cards at the front for everyone tonight."

"Thanks."

"It's the friendly thing to do."

His lips tipped up. Her palms began to sweat. Her nipples tightened into hard nubs against the black lace of her bra. A burning ache rested between her thighs, an ache she hadn't experienced in way too long. Sex had become routine and rarely exciting. She'd felt as if there was nothing left to explore.

She bet Dalton would prove her wrong.

"You amaze me." She lifted a brow at his

comment and he laughed. "No, seriously. I love watching you here. The way you handle the customers and the staff. The way you look when you're making someone a special cocktail, like you get just as much pleasure when they enjoy it. You've found your place. It's a beautiful thing to watch."

The way he expressed himself contained a hint of poetry. Maybe Cal was right. Dalton might be more of a closet romantic than she'd ever believed. Thing was, a bullshit artist was easy to dismiss, but his words rang with truth. And that was impossible to fight.

She shifted her weight. Her voice came out ragged. "Thanks."

"How do you decide to create a new drink? Is there a process?"

Leaning her hip against the bar, she thought about his question. "I always had a great palate, but I was at this dingy pub and the guy behind the bar was like the mixologist god. He was putting all these new spins on classic drinks, and they were taken to a new level. I was intrigued, so I began studying mixology. It's basically the science of combining different flavors to create a unique cocktail. I studied a ton of books, worked the bar with some interesting people, and practiced consistently. I figured out what tastes good together, and loved the art of surprising someone. I love the look on someone's face when they notice an unusual flavor that works perfectly."

"I've never heard you call yourself a mixologist. You always use the term *bartender*."

She shrugged. "I don't need a fancy word to impress people. Bartender; mixologist; you still serve drinks to the public and hope they like them."

"Yet you take it to the next level." He cocked his head, studying her thoughtfully. Once again, his gaze delved deep, patiently searching for something. "You take everything to the next level."

The surge of energy strengthened, rose up, and threatened to suck them both under. Her fingers clenched. "Not everything." She struggled with her next words. "I'm sorry I never thanked you for the flowers."

"Didn't need thanks. That's why I decided not to leave a card."

She tilted her head. "Why? Didn't you want the credit? Another of your seduction attempts?"

"Let me ask you a question, then. How did you know I sent them?"

She shivered. Because already she felt as if she knew a part of him. A part that spoke to her on a scale where words weren't needed. "I just sensed it."

"Exactly. You can hang up on me, refuse to talk at the bar, and avoid every single one of my advances, but there's something between us, Raven. Something bigger than us. I can't stop thinking about you. Fantasizing. You're like a fever in my damn blood."

"Sounds unhealthy."

He laughed without humor. "Maybe. But I want to get one thing straight. Sending you those roses had nothing to do with trying to get you in my bed. That was about admiring the woman you are and wanting to give you a little bit of pleasure. Because when you smile, you pretty much wreck me."

Oh, God. No. He couldn't say such things to her. Things that ripped into her heart and made her want him so badly she shook with pure need. His nostrils flared as if catching her scent. He growled low in his throat and stepped closer. "I promised myself I wouldn't touch you again unless you asked me."

She locked her thighs together, praying she looked like she was in control. "Good plan."

"But I want to touch you. Real bad." He took another step. His body heat licked at her, teasing. His masculine scent danced in her nostrils. "I keep imagining you naked. I'm obsessed with knowing how you taste. I fantasize about stripping off your clothes, parting your thighs, and licking you till you come. I can almost hear the sound of your screams and feel the bite of your nails."

A rush of wetness dampened her panties. Her

heart slammed against her ribs. "D-doesn't sound very friendly."

His eyes glittered with a fierce hunger. "No, it doesn't. But I made you a damn promise, and even though we're not working together anymore, I don't want to push when I'm not wanted. Am I?"

Her voice pitched to a high half shriek. "Are you what?"

"Wanted."

The silence roared with unspoken possibilities and dark cravings. What was wrong with her? She was acting like a yo-yo, back and forth, giving him enough mixed signals to confuse both of them. The truth of their shared past haunted her, but her body didn't care, slamming through the obstacle in a mad dash for another touch, another taste.

"I want you." The stark words fell between them. "But it doesn't matter. It won't work. We want different things."

"We want each other. We want to figure out what this thing is between us that's haunting me day and night. You're in every breath I take, Raven. It's driving me mad."

"I'm trying to be smart," she said desperately. "I don't need this complication now. You're not good for me."

"Do you seriously think you'll be able to give your heart to some perfect husband figure when your body is weeping for mine? Is that fair to anybody?"

Did he move closer, or was it her imagination? The perfect curves of his lips were inches away. She ached to slide her hands inside his crisp white shirt and stroke the sleek muscles beneath. Grab on to his rock-hard shoulders. Press her mouth to his and give her own demands.

"Let's slake the thirst we have for each other. Give each other pleasure. Maybe it'll take away this driving need I have for you and convince us both we're bad together."

She gave a shaky laugh. "Oh, God, that's such a line. Do you know how many movies and books use that excuse? It usually gets worse. More intense."

"Maybe. Maybe not." His breath caressed her cheek. His hands hovered by her hips. If she leaned forward, just a bit, they'd be pressed together and it would all be over. "We can find out. But you have to make the move. Say no and I'll walk." In that moment, his eyes blazed with raw intensity. "I don't want to hurt you, Raven."

She didn't respond.

The image of red roses floated through her mind. Of restoring her restaurant to something beautiful. Of that one perfect, glorious, soul-stirring kiss in the moonlight.

And in that moment, Raven surrendered to the

one thing she wanted most in the world. Just for tonight.

She reached out and pulled him into her arms.

This time, there was no buildup or teasing seduction. Her lips opened under his hungry growl, and he pulled her in tight, twisting his fingers in her hair as he devoured her mouth. She arched up for more, and he picked her up without breaking the kiss, setting her back down on top of the bar. Dragging her thighs apart, he stepped between her legs.

Drunk on his taste, she tore at the buttons of his shirt, sliding the fabric off his shoulders. She only got halfway before he pressed her back on the bar, yanking her tank up to cover her breast with his large hand. He flicked the hard tip of her nipple through the lace, ripping his mouth from her lips to press tiny bites down the length of her neck, licking the hurt away with his tongue. His hips slowly rocked back and forth, pressing his erection against the notch of her thighs. Shivers raced down her spine, and her toes curled in her sandals. She tried to finish the job of removing his shirt, but he pressed her down with his weight, forcing her to take the pleasure.

Oh, God, so much pleasure.

"Take the damn shirt off." Her nails dug into his shoulders. She tried to twist, but his mouth had found her breast, and oh, yes, his teeth tugged at her hard nipple, dragging the scratchy lace back and forth against her swollen bud as if he were conducting a scientific experiment in arousal rather than taking her hard like she wanted.

His low laugh shot warm breath over her other nipple, which now demanded the same attention. "First you."

"No way, Slick. This an equal opportunity encounter. Strip."

"You're so damn bossy." In one swift motion, he unclasped her bra and snapped open the button on her jeans. She sucked in a breath as his mouth dipped once again to suck on her nipple. The delicious, wicked heat of his mouth and sharp bite of his teeth ripped out a moan, and she frantically wriggled to get closer. He tugged the snug denim over her hips and bared her black bikini underwear. The material was already soaked with her arousal, and Raven panted, trying to tug at his belt buckle.

"Play fair or I'm gonna get mad," Raven warned.

His mouth moved down her tummy, licking a line of fire to the elastic waistband. He pressed his palm against the damp material, and her hips bucked up, begging for more. He spread her legs wider until she was completely open. "Yeah? Tell you what. You be a good girl and come first, and then you can touch me all you want."

"You bastard! You're not running the show here—oh, God!" His fingers hooked under the material and dove deep, moving in and out of her pussy while his thumb lightly played with her clit, rotating in the faintest brushes. She practically clawed at him to get closer.

He overwhelmed her, dominated her, claimed her. While he played his wicked games with her pussy, his tongue thrust into her mouth, fucking her with a fierce possession, pressing his thumb to her throbbing clit a bit harder with each rotation. She writhed and moaned and scratched with savage need until he finally gave her what she craved.

His fingers plunged deep, his thumb flicked her clit, and he bit down on her lower lip.

She came hard, giving in to the brutal waves that wracked her body. His name rose from her lips in a scream, and he helped her ride out the orgasm with his talented mouth and fingers until she lay splayed beneath him, sated.

Slowly, he raised his head and gave her a wolfish grin.

"*Now* it's your turn."

chapter sixteen

Dalton took one look at the woman half-naked on the bar, satisfied by his own hand, and wanted to throw back his head and roar.

Primitive waves of possession and victory beat within him. Something inside told him he'd be happy making Raven come for an endless period of time. Not hours. Days, weeks, months. He was already addicted to the way she surrendered so completely to her pleasure. Her skin smelled of sandalwood and sex. She tasted like forbidden apples and dark Hershey's chocolate and the smooth, honeyed bourbon Cal liked to drink. Her small breasts were perfectly formed to fit in his hand, and her raspberry nipples were extra sensitive to his touch. He wanted to steep himself in the study of her body, explore the slopes and planes of her curves, her sweet, tight pussy, her muscled arms and legs.

He knew in that moment Raven had been right.

She wouldn't be wrung out of his system tonight. A taste of her had only teased the beast inside, who was now already demanding more of her.

"You cheated."

The sexy pout made his dick hurt. He'd never been this ready to come in his jeans before. He was almost afraid to have her touch him. "Couldn't play fair this time, darlin'. You're too fucking beautiful." He brought his fingers up to his nose and breathed in her scent. His knees almost buckled with lust. "How can I make it up to you? Another orgasm?"

He loved her smoke-curling, rich laugh. She rose from the bar, hooked her index finger in the waist of his jeans, and pulled him close. Her voice lowered to a witchy whisper. "Definitely. But it is my turn, and I want to play. Keep your hands to yourself." She nipped at his bottom lip, tugged off his shirt, and touched him.

Dalton gritted his teeth at the feel of her hands coasting over his skin. She stroked every inch of his chest, raked her nails down his arms, licked his nipples. He groaned and let her take charge, keeping his hands fisted because if he touched her just once, he'd bury himself between her thighs in record time.

Those same legs he dreamed about suddenly wrapped around his hips. He jerked forward, and then she plunged her hand down the front of his jeans, found his dick, and squeezed tight.

Ah, shit. It was too good. It was too much. It was too . . . perfect.

Her satisfied laugh only stoked the fire. "I love a man who doesn't wear underwear," she murmured. "And I love the way you feel—hot and silky and so damn big."

Sweat broke out on his forehead. He was known for his stamina. It wasn't an ego thing, he'd just never had a problem giving a woman release numerous times, not needing it as much for himself. For him, sex was a journey, not the culmination most men believed it to be. But right now, he was about to explode, and she'd only given him a half-assed hand job.

"Raven." He grated out her name as she managed to cup his balls, stroke, then massage back up his shaft. "You feel too good. Can I move my hands now?"

"No."

The zipper rasped in the air, and she pulled down his pants. Those firm hands continued playing, this time giving him more needed pressure and a steady stroking that would tip him over the edge. Without the constraints of his jeans, he jerked freely in her hands, eyes half-shut, filthy curses dropping from his lips along with her name. Rocketing toward orgasm, he grabbed her hands, pushed her back on the bar, and lowered his head.

Fuck this.

Her panties ripped with one good pull. She squeaked and tried to fight him, but he had a grip on her inner thighs and managed to keep her firmly in place as he took his first delicious taste of her.

She cried out his name. *Yes.* This was what he'd dreamed of—hearing her whimper with pleasure from the stroke of his tongue. Drunk on the musky taste of her arousal, he took his time, watching her swell and tighten, nibbling on her clit, her smooth bare skin like heaven against his lips. She twisted, begging, ready, and he sucked hard, flicking her with the tip of his tongue with the perfect pressure.

She fell apart.

Fumbling for the condom in his pocket, he sheathed himself quickly and dragged her body to the edge of the bar. Dazed, pupils dilated, she tried to reach up for him, but he didn't wait. Placing her feet over his shoulders, he reared up and speared her with his gaze.

He waited a second. Two. The acknowledgment of what they were about to do hit her full force, judging by the parting of her lips, the loss of her breath, the need in her eyes.

He drove into her with one thrust.

Something crashed over him, under him, through him. A swirl of emotions washed into his head, and voices seemed to echo from a long distance away. What the hell was happening? He fought for control, but it was already gone, given to this woman the moment he first saw her.

She's the one.

Fear tugged at his gut and he tried to pull back, but it was too late.

She squeezed him, tight and hot and wet. Gripping her hips, he moved, her body welcoming him like an old lover he'd returned to. He drank in the beautiful lines of her face, caught up in her drive for orgasm, her swollen red lips, hard nipples, tumbling inky hair. But most of all, her eyes, pulling him in as tight as her body, wrapped around him in comfort and heat.

Dalton was lost. In her body, her gaze, her voice. She chanted his name, arched up for more, and his hand slipped between their bodies to rub her slow and easy, building her back up, staggered by the battering of sensations wracking him at once.

He exploded.

Her sobs confirmed she was right with him, but Dalton was too caught up in the power of his orgasm, shooting through his body like lightning. He jerked, emptying himself, and felt a strange burning behind his eyelids, almost like the threat of tears.

What the hell was going on?

Her body shook underneath him, and he quickly pulled her up, gathering her in a tight embrace. She laid her head against his chest, and they remained still for a while. Would she panic? Freak out? Get angry? Declare it a mistake?

The questions rushed in his head, but he swore he wouldn't let her walk away from this. Not yet. Something had happened between them, and he needed to figure it out.

"I didn't want this to happen on the bar, you know." A touch of shame hit him. His real dream had been to spread her out on her bed and dedicate hours to servicing her, pleasuring her, wringing out every last moan and scream and cry she had trapped in her body. Instead, he'd practically taken her with all his clothes on. "You deserved more than a quickie the first time. I'm sorry."

Her soft laugh vibrated against his chest. "You keep forgetting you're not the only one in charge here, Slick. I wanted it this way. I made this choice, and if I had wanted a damn bed, I would've demanded it. Besides, it was hot."

Some of the tightness around his heart eased. This woman took responsibility for her own needs and sexuality. It was one of the elements he adored about her. But what was next for them?

Could he convince her not to walk away now that she'd scratched her itch?

"Can I ask you a question that's been bothering me for a while?"

He tried not to stiffen. Head whirling with the possibilities, he swore to tell her the truth, no matter how difficult. "Absolutely."

"Do you whiten your teeth, or are they natural?"

He pulled back and stared down at her. The dancing glint of mischief in her dark eyes soothed him, promising she wasn't ready to walk away, either. For now.

He shook his head, a smile tugging at his lips. "You're a real brat."

"So is that yes or no?"

He grabbed her and lifted her up in his arms, tickling her under her armpits until she yelled for mercy, half laughing and struggling for escape. He stopped it by kissing her deep and long. She clung to him and he was hard again in seconds.

"Did you wring me out of your system yet?" he asked.

She bit down on his earlobe. "Not yet. One more round?"

"I'm sure that will do it."

chapter seventeen

> ◇ <

She'd slept with Dalton Pierce.

Her once sworn enemy. The man she'd planned to spy on to retrieve information to better understand why her father had left. A man who was a well-known womanizer, noncommitter, and overall perfect antithesis of anyone she'd choose to get involved with.

God, it had been so damn good.

She tried to stop smiling as she prepped for poker night. After she'd spoken with numerous women inquiring about poker, one thing had become clear: most had no idea how to play. Though that shocked her to the core, since her father taught her cards when she was about eight years old and the stakes were Oreos, it didn't make sense to open the games to everyone until the women knew how to play. She'd changed her original plan and decided to hold a training night on Monday, when the bar was officially closed. Over a dozen women signed up to learn, and Raven had whipped up a few different cocktails she needed feedback on. Once the women felt comfortable, she'd unveil regular poker nights on Wednesdays and be able to recruit more ladies. Then she'd open it up to mixed groups. Her vision included almost a Zootopia of perfection—men and women playing poker together in perfect harmony.

She'd always dreamed big.

Raven belted out a stanza by Nick Jonas, a familiar song from her time with Dalton. Her new appreciation for boy bands must remain a secret, but she was gloriously alone at My Place and could sing like no one was listening.

She wiped down the bar, and the images hit full force.

Dalton pressing her back, spreading her legs, thrusting in to fill her completely. The intense expression on his face as he claimed her, the bruising grip on her hips as he took what he needed, demanding she give him her orgasm again, and again, and again . . .

Ah, crap. He'd seared that memory into her brain forever. This bar would always carry the delicious secret of surrender, the shattering of her multiple climaxes, the aching tenderness when he held her afterward, worried she'd walk away.

She couldn't. Not yet. Something had been forged between them. It had only been two nights ago, and they hadn't seen each other since. He'd called and said Morgan needed him to track down a certain supplier, so he was in Vermont for a couple of days, trying to score a special order of Douglas fir at the warehouse. He spoke like he was making a billion-dollar deal, his voice hushed with respect for the material. He asked to see her after poker night, and she agreed. A man who disappeared the day after having sex for the first time was highly suspect. Raven waited for the slap of betrayal or anger to hit. Nothing did. Simply put, she believed him and didn't need any special coddling or reassurances. She'd never experienced this rightness before with a man—as if they completely understood each other on a deeper level and didn't need to steep themselves in endless analysis of each other's moves.

Weird.

Though this thing between them was a mess of complications, she didn't want to break it off yet. Soon. After all, their odd relationship had no future, and continuing it could just lead to disaster. He was also owed the truth, and she needed to tell him eventually.

Later.

The door pushed open. Morgan came in, dressed in her usual white, her blond bob swinging neatly above her shoulders. Sydney was at her side, a complete contrast with her fiery red curls and bright yellow shirt, green eyes sparkling with what seemed like anticipation. Raven had liked them from the very first night she'd served them, almost a year ago. They were fun, smart, and strong, the three ingredients Raven sought in a female friendship. She'd kept her distance only because of Morgan's relationship with Cal, but time began eroding the barriers. She didn't get to see Izzy much, since they were both so busy. It would be nice to make some new friends and hang out with Morgan and Sydney. Sometimes she just needed some girl time.

"Thank you for setting this up, Raven," Morgan said, her white Chanel purse swinging on her arm. "I swear, y'all, I needed to get away from the buckets of testosterone. Tristan and Cal had a fight and began wrestling on the ground like toddlers, and knocked over the Waterford vase. I stomped out and swore there'd be no dinner for the next week, and then I had to deal with the puppy-dog eyes and the promises that they were only kidding."

Sydney laughed. "I'm thrilled to escape watching *Frozen* for the billionth time. And I brought tons of singles!"

Sydney not only worked at Pierce Brothers and ran the offices with an iron fist, but also had a five-year-old daughter whom she adored and doted on. Raven gave her a lot of credit for being such a dedicated single mom. "Sweets, there's no strippers here. You buy in with chips, and I happily take twenty-dollar bills."

Her face fell with disappointment. "Oh. You know, the bank teller looked at me with suspicion when I asked for fifty singles. Should've known." ·

Morgan ripped out a hundred-dollar bill with glee. "I brought a hundred!"

Raven pressed her hand over her mouth, holding back her mirth. "This is a training session, ladies. I don't think we'll be playing for such high stakes yet."

Now Morgan looked disappointed. "Oh. Maybe next time?"

"Definitely. I made some new cocktails for you to try out. Come over to the bar and I'll show you."

"The place looks amazing," Morgan commented. Her gaze swept over the restored bar, new stools, and the rearranged tables and decor. "Dalton is a master with woodworking, isn't he?"

And so many other things . . .

"He is." She refused to let anyone know they were sleeping together. It would only raise further complications. "This is a twist on a key lime martini I've been playing with. I made it with Skinnygirl products, so calories are manageable." She poured two martini glasses rimmed with graham cracker crumbs, added a slice of lime, and plopped them in front of the women. Then she set out glasses of water with lemon. "I won't serve you another drink until you hydrate with one full glass of water in between. Limit is three per person, but you have to blow into this before I let you go home." She pulled out her Breathalyzer. "Can't be too careful, now."

Sydney sighed. "Is it okay to have a girl crush? 'Cause I have one on you."

"Aww, I'm flattered, sweets."

Morgan burst into laughter. "I love it! I swear, you're like my heroine."

Raven leaned her elbows on the bar. "I heard you have a pink hammer," she said. "And a pink hard hat with matching boots. It doesn't get any better than that."

Morgan tilted her head, considering. "Yeah, you're right. I guess I have a bit of cool in me, too."

"And, Sydney, you're raising a daughter, who you show every day by example that you can have anything you want if you work hard enough. That's as badass as it gets."

Sydney stared at her, gratitude gleaming in her green eyes. "Thanks. Sometimes I really need to hear that."

Morgan grabbed her friend's hand and squeezed. "Not supposed to be easy, is it? At times I feel like women have all this stuff inside that trips us up, more than men. Thoughts and emotions and worries. Expectations and analysis. It's exhausting."

"Men are so much simpler," Sydney agreed with a sigh. "Food. Beer. Money. Work. Sex. That's it."

"I know. But then after I met Cal, something shifted inside me, and all that junk rotating in my head became less important." Morgan's face softened, and her eyes glowed with a light that made Raven's heart ache. "It was almost like, because he loved me, he took on half of the load, giving me this beautiful air and space inside I never had before." She bit her lip. "Sorry, it's silly."

Raven smiled. "No, I think it's . . . nice."

"Me too," Sydney said. "The only time I ever felt like that was with—" She broke off, as if realizing the name she was about to drop like a nuclear bomb.

"With . . . ?" Morgan prodded.

A flush hit her cheeks. She waved a hand in the air. "Nobody. Not important. Someone I loved when I was very young and very naive."

Raven wanted to ask more questions, but she respected Sydney's secrets like her own. Some things weren't meant to be shared.

The door swung open, and a trail of women came through, giggling and excited about a night out for themselves. Raven set everyone up with drinks, noting that the key lime martinis were the most requested, and led them over to the tables. She dispersed chips, completed a round of introductions, and gave everyone cheat sheets to begin.

Most of the women had played some form of cards before, so it was easier than Raven thought. Within an hour, they were able to play a decent game with a big enough pot to get interesting.

Morgan threw a chip in the pot, her face cool and politely distant. She was definitely the best bluffer in the group. "I'll raise a dollar."

Susan, a sweet, doe-eyed pastry chef, batted her lashes like she was flirting. "I think you're bluffing," she announced. Her silver bracelets jangled as she threw a bunch of chips in the pot. "I raise five dollars."

A hush fell upon the table. It was the biggest raise of the night. Sydney quickly threw her cards in. "I fold."

Victoria stared at her cards, then back and forth between Susan and Morgan. She was a young blonde with animated gestures and seemed to have trouble keeping still. "I'm in. Five to stay."

Two more dropped out, including Raven, and there was another raise. When it came back to Morgan, a strange expression gleamed in her eyes. Almost like a predator sensing prey.

Uh-oh.

With a sharklike smile, she pushed all her chips into the center of the table. "All in."

The group broke into excited chatter and gasps. "You can't do that!" Susan said. "Can she?"

Raven nodded. "Since someone else raised, she could either meet the raise or raise again herself. We didn't put a limit on the raise, just the ante. So, yes, she can do that. But Morgan has fifteen left, and you only have ten, so you'd need five more to stay in."

"Fine. I'm all in, too." She pushed her chips into the center and turned to her friend Lindsey. "I need to borrow five dollars."

"Done," Lindsey said.

"Umm, guys, why don't we agree we've reached our limit at fifteen and everyone show their cards?" Raven suggested.

The quietest woman in the group—the librarian, for goodness' sake—practically stood up to make her announcement. "I raise by fifty dollars!"

And then it became a bloodbath.

The rush of adrenaline combined with key lime martinis turned them feral. Victoria grabbed more money from her purse, buying more chips, and friends borrowed from friends. Morgan shoved her hundred-dollar bill at Raven with the mad expression of a gambler on track to win a big pot. Voices raised in a fury, and when Raven finally halted the madness, there was five hundred dollars in the pot and almost all the chips were gone from her stash.

She'd have to buy more chips. She had seriously underestimated her students.

Tension settled over the group. Cards were gripped with deathly tightness, drinks drained, and everyone stared at the colorful pile of chips in the center of the happy red table.

Raven cleared her throat. "Susan, you go first, since you were the last to raise. Show your cards."

"Three of a kind. Jacks."

"Nice hand. Next."

They went around. There were two people who showed two pairs, one with three deuces, and two bluffers, including the librarian, who'd just gotten caught up in the excitement of the moment. Victoria bounced up and down in her chair when it was her turn and flipped over a straight with eight high.

"Sorry, Susan, straight beats three of a kind."

"Fuck!"

Raven pressed her lips together, trying not to laugh. Damn, she liked this group. "Morgan, show your cards. This is it."

Morgan's French-manicured hands flashed as she flipped them over. Raven figured she'd lost, since there wasn't a shred of emotion in her face. Five hearts stared up at her.

"Flush. I win."

Raven's mouth dropped open. Sydney screamed, the ladies cursed and congratulated in varying degrees, and Morgan finally broke out in a big, satisfied smile.

That woman had balls.

Everyone began taking out more money to play another round, but Raven held up her hand. "Sorry, ladies, we're done. It's almost ten and I have to work tomorrow."

Sydney gasped and shot up. "Oh, my God, my poor sitter! How did it get to be this late?"

"I'm sorry I didn't keep my eye on the time," Morgan said, tucking her hair behind her ear. "Things got a bit crazy."

Raven grabbed the wad of cash, quickly wrapping it in a rubber band and putting it in an envelope. "There's your winnings," she said. "I can't wait to see you hustle Cal. You're really good."

A frown creased her brow. "Yeah, but I get the feeling he was humoring me about poker. Almost patting my head, like I was some lamebrained blonde who couldn't play a man's game. Isn't that a bit archaic?"

Susan came over. "I agree! My husband laughed and said, 'Enjoy your cute poker game.' Cute? Screw him."

Lindsey agreed. "My boyfriend said you wouldn't be able to teach me right, Raven. Told me he'd teach me the right way."

Raven tilted her head, considering. "Got it. Well, it'll take a few more game nights to increase your skills, but I'll show you some simple ways to make sure you beat them when we finally combine male and female poker night."

"How?" Sydney asked.

Raven smiled slowly. "I'm going to teach you to cheat."

Sydney sighed. "I really love you."

Raven laughed, made sure each of them blew into the Breathalyzer, then watched them disappear one by one until the bar was finally silent.

Damn, that was fun.

She began cleaning up, wondering when Dalton would show. Maybe she'd text him to cancel. Or maybe he'd texted her already—she needed to check her phone. It was already late, and though she ached to see him, her emotions were still complicated. Another day to clear her head might not be a bad idea.

She was headed to the sink with the glasses, figuring she'd load them in the dishwasher for tomorrow, when the door swung open. Damn, she'd forgotten to lock it. Maybe one of the women had forgotten something, or Dalton was here.

Raven exited the kitchen and froze.

A strange man stood before her. Even though it was a hot night, he had a gray hoodie pulled over his head, with baggy jeans and dirty sneakers. A scruffy beard hid the lower half of his face. He was short—only about five foot six maximum, and his brown eyes were small and overbright, as if he was on something. He swayed back and forth, glancing wildly around the bar.

He held a gun in his right hand.

In that instant, her mind stopped. She stared at him with a touch of confusion, then began realizing she was in big trouble and had better get her shit together. Her palms sweat, and her heart pounded so hard, there was a roaring in her ears. For an instant, her vision blurred with panic and choking terror. She had no alarm system—the cost had been astronomical and she'd figured she'd revisit it later. Her gun was in a locked drawer in the kitchen, and right now it was completely useless. No time to run back there and get it; it would take too long to fumble with the key. Why hadn't she locked the door? She always locked the door—it was a habit completely ingrained. What was she going to do?

Be calm. Wait for your opportunity.

Years of boxing and karate and self-defense training suddenly burst inside her brain in trickling snippets of advice. She swallowed back the crippling fear and remained still.

"You alone?" His voice was slightly cracked, as if he was on the edge.

"No, there's people in the kitchen who are calling the police. I think you should leave."

The gun rose, wobbled. "Fucking liar. No one's

in there, I watched everyone leave. There's only one car left. I need money, bitch. Get it."

She glanced at the cash register behind the bar, trying to plot, trying to be calm. Her phone lay right in front of her, close to the register. But the gun was a game changer.

Act weak.

"P-please don't hurt me," she whimpered. "I'll get you the money. Anything you want."

The gun lowered. "That's right, I need the money now." Sweat and body odor stank from his skin. "Get it!" he yelled.

She jumped and headed behind the bar, arms raised in surrender. He walked further into the room, still looking around, his hands shaking. There wasn't much in the register—she kept the rest locked up in the back in a safe, and made regular deposits. Cash in a bar was necessary but dangerous. What the hell was she going to do?

"Hurry!"

She grabbed all the cash from the register and deliberately knocked over a glass. "I'm sorry, I'm sorry," she blabbered. "You can have it all, here, let me get it for you." She bent down as if to clear the glass, palmed her phone, and stuck it in the back of her shorts. There was no time to swipe it open and call 911 yet.

"Stop playing games with me!" he roared. "Get out from there!"

The tears that leaked from her eyes were genuine now, and didn't have to be forced. Gaze trained on the gun, she lowered her head in sheer meekness, hands outstretched with the cash grasped in her fingers, and slowly walked out from behind the bar.

"I know you have a safe, and I want that, too. Hurry up, bitch! Give me that money now. You hear me?"

If she went into the kitchen to the safe with him, she might not come out. In the open main area, she had more options, but the doors were already locked up in the back. Could she get past him and run out the front?

Distract.

"Yes, anything, please just don't hurt me. Here, here's the money."

The gun was now trained on her, and she eased forward, her hands shaking. He went to grab the cash, and she dropped a few of the bills onto the floor. He cursed viciously. "Pick it up!" he screamed.

She bent her knees, scooped up the bills, and stuck her shaking hand out again, offering the money.

The gun lowered, pointing to the ground.

He reached for the cash.

Act.

The rest seemed to happen in slow motion,

though Raven was sure it was only a few lightning seconds. Shifting her weight, she launched into a side kick, aiming directly for his face. The small square heel of her sandal caught him dead center, and the sound of his high scream shattered in the air.

He staggered back, the gun still in his hand, and without pause, she gathered all her strength and aimed her next kick right at his groin. He screamed again.

The gun hit the floor.

Her whole body quivering in fear, Raven dove for the gun, pointing it at him while she scrambled for her phone. It took her three tries to open it up and dial 911.

"I'll kill you, bitch! I'll kill you!"

"Stay back! I have the gun!" she yelled.

"Nine-one-one, what is your emergency?"

"Help me!" she babbled into the phone, trying to catch her breath. "There's a guy with a gun trying to rob me. My Place restaurant, Thirty-Three Hatsfield Place."

"Dispatching police. Are you hurt, ma'am? Is the gunman still there?"

"I'm okay, I have his gun and I'm pointing it at him right now. Please hurry!"

"I have a five-minute window for the Harrington Police Department. Stay on the phone with me."

She stayed on the phone with dispatch, watching the guy crawl on the floor while blood pooled from his nose. She kept the gun pointed in front of her, ready to shoot near his leg if he got too close. A strange calm began to settle over her as soothing words poured into her ear from her phone, and her fingers wrapped around the solid, cold metal of the gun. She was a decent shot, and if he got up, she could hold him off.

He wasn't going to hurt her.

When the police came, she released the gun. The guy was arrested. Someone wrapped her in a blanket and took her statement. She watched the whirling red and white lights flash round and round through the window and answered everything with a slow, deliberate precision. Raven was proud of the controlled way she was able to handle the aftermath, and when officers lectured her on trying to tangle with a gunman and told her that she was very lucky, she just nodded and agreed with them. Someone gave her a glass of water. The police seemed like they were wrapping up and about to leave.

And then she heard her name being called out from across the room. Funny, it sounded familiar. Panicked, though, and not the charming, mischievous drawl she was used to. Blinking, she watched as Dalton appeared before her, saying her name, stroking back her hair, frantically patting down her body like he needed to confirm she wasn't sporting a bullet hole.

"Raven? Raven, sweetheart, look at me. Are you okay? Are you hurt?"

"I'm fine."

Her voice sounded weird. Like it came from far, far away. Definitely shock. Too bad, she'd been doing so well.

He pulled her tight into his embrace, and the cold blob in her stomach began to melt, causing her to start to shake. "I'm fine," she said again. Her teeth chattered but she wasn't cold anymore. "He tried to rob me, but I wouldn't let him."

His hands cupped her face, and those blue eyes gleamed with a fierce protection and need that she hadn't seen from anyone since her father so many years ago.

"I know you didn't, sweetheart. He had no clue who he was dealing with. I'm so sorry I was late, I'm so sorry."

"Dalton?"

"Yeah?"

She tried to tell him it was okay, and she could take care of herself, and everything was just fine. But then she did something she hadn't done since the funeral.

She let go and burst into tears.

And Dalton caught her.

chapter eighteen

Dalton stepped through the door of Raven's house and wished to God he were here for a different reason.

The events of the night were still unreal. She had faced down a drugged-up gunman on her own. She'd kicked him in the face, grabbed the gun, and called 911, just like in a movie. And then she'd collapsed in his arms.

Now she was deadly quiet. He figured she was about to crash from the adrenaline high and needed to be in a safe place. He made the plan to bring her to her home and stay there. He'd sleep on a couch, but there was no fucking way he'd leave her alone.

"You don't have to stay."

He smiled at her, knowing she needed him to keep a lighthearted tone. "You're doing me a favor.

I'm exhausted and would rather crash than drive home."

She tilted her head, considering. Her clothes were wrinkled. Exhaustion gleamed in her cat-slanted dark eyes, and her tangled hair fell over her shoulders. Her eye makeup was streaked from tears.

She was earth-shatteringly, heartbreakingly beautiful.

"I love your place."

She looked around as if seeing it for the first time. His fingers itched to touch all the gorgeous, sleek carved wood, from the beamed ceilings and pine floors to the tables and cabinetry to the built-ins that held her television and an array of artwork. Braided rugs added a touch of color and broke up the expanse of natural wood. The open room was decorated with simplicity and an earthy sensuality, like its owner. Magazines and books were stacked neatly on table surfaces, and in one corner a canvas cloth covered up what could be artwork. The stone fireplace added warmth. The leather furniture looked roomy and touchable. It reflected a house well lived in and enjoyed.

"Thanks. Want coffee?"

"Yeah. Can I make it? I don't want to be up on a caffeine high till next week."

A smile touched her lips. She led him into the kitchen, which was open to the living room and contained a cute nook with two tables and a bench overlooking a nicely sized window. She pointed out the pot and filters.

"No Keurig?"

She sat down on the bench. "Can't get your coffee strong using a Keurig."

"Remind me to get you one for your birthday."

"It passed. February third."

"Remind me to get you one anyway."

He made the coffee in comfortable silence, until the familiar dripping sounds filled the air. He took out two mugs and sat down next to her. "Want to talk about it?"

"Yes. No. I don't know."

He reached out and snagged her hand. She instantly tangled her fingers in his, and something within him calmed. "I'm not trying to sound like a shrink or push. I just think sharing exactly what happened before it has time to fester is a good idea. I'd also like to know, so I'm asking for me."

She nodded slowly. "Yeah, you may be right. Thing is, I'm really okay, Dalton. It was scary as hell, and I hated myself for making the stupid mistake of not locking the door. I got sloppy."

"Happens to all of us. You just finished your poker night, right?"

"Yes. We had about a dozen women, and it was a lot of fun. They stayed later than I anticipated, so I had decided to load the dishwasher, and I was going to my phone to text you and cancel tonight."

He winced. Would he ever forgive himself for not getting there sooner? Then again, would walking in on a gunman have been worse? She'd managed to save herself and needed no prince on horseback. He waited to see if he'd feel an ego bite, but there was nothing but pumped-up pride for his woman.

His woman.

He pushed that thought to the side, for now. "I got held up. I had texted you, but when you didn't answer, I figured I'd just show up. What did the asshole do?"

She took a deep breath and told him the whole story. He let her pour it out, not interrupting her, just squeezing her hand when she paused. Her bravery under crippling fear was extraordinary, but now was not the time to tell her how proud he was. He handed her a mug of steaming coffee, and she drank it slowly. "I need an alarm now."

"I can recommend the guy who did one for Pierce. He's reasonable and does a lot of the local businesses."

"Great. I'll call him tomorrow. I don't want to go back and be afraid in my second home. I refuse to let him take that from me."

"He won't. The police will have him behind bars. You can get cameras installed also, with central monitoring. It will be okay."

She looked him straight in the eye, pure emotion seeping into her words. "Yeah, I'll be okay." They sipped their coffee. "The police told me I was reckless because he had a gun."

Dalton sensed she wanted his opinion. "The police don't see too many women like you, Raven. You kept a clear head even though you were scared shitless. You jumped for the opening you had, and you knew going in the back would have lessened your chances of escape."

"Yes, exactly. It wasn't about ego or being reckless. I've trained with Xavier for a while, and we've gone over various scenarios. I went with my gut, and that's what I've always been taught." She propped her elbows on the table and stared out the window into the darkness. "I told you I traveled a lot. I also partied with strangers, bunked in odd places, and saw a lot of stuff. I didn't have a college degree, but I had street smarts. I was lucky. I have no bad stories to tell, though something crappy happened to my best friend during our exploration days. She had to learn to live with it."

"We're supposed to make a lot of mistakes, or we're not really living."

She squeezed his hand. "Yeah. I don't regret jumping on my opportunity to take down that asshole, and I won't apologize for it."

"Agreed. You have the heart of a warrior. Like Xena."

She wrinkled her nose. "Like Xena? The warrior princess from back in the day?"

"Hell yeah. In that tight black leather, riding her horse. H-O-T."

A genuine laugh escaped her lips. Dalton smiled back. "I can sleep on your couch tonight."

The statement was really a question. He ached to fall asleep with her wrapped in his arms, safe and secure. Sex had nothing to do with it. But even though they'd been intimate, Raven might need her space after the highs and lows of the night.

She seemed torn, but then made her decision. "I'd appreciate that. Just for tonight."

"You got it."

She left the room and returned with blankets and a pillow. He set himself up on the leather recliner. "Do you need anything?"

"No, I'm perfect. Get some rest, Raven. I'm right here if you need me."

"Thanks."

She disappeared down the hall. Dalton shucked off his T-shirt and shoes, leaving his jeans on since he was naked underneath, and lay down.

It was a good hour of tossing and turning before he realized he wasn't going to be able to sleep and finally gave up. Rolling to his feet, he stretched and quietly went outside to the deck.

He admired the smooth cedar and rustic wrap-around. It was obvious Raven spent a lot of time out here. An oversize rattan couch plumped with multicolored cushions brought a sense of feminine fun. The low mosaic table held a Chinese lantern and various scented candles. The two matching chairs and porch swing added to the sense of comfort and peace.

The sky had exploded with light from the stars. Crickets screeched in varying musical tones, and the night was quiet and thick. He dropped onto the couch and stretched out, looking up. No clouds marred the sharp horizon. The humidity had finally passed, leaving a cooler waft of air to float and rise, bringing the heavy scents of earth mixed with smoke and touches of hydrangea. Twigs snapped in the distance, and a long, sad howl rose in the air to linger.

He didn't know how long he was out there before he heard the scrape of the screen door. "Want some company?"

She shifted back and forth on bare feet. She was wrapped in a thick white comforter that trailed behind her, clad in a black T-shirt with the My Place logo on the front. The fabric hit her knees and swallowed her whole. Her hair was a messy tumble around her face. His heart squeezed. "Always."

He held out his hand. She opened her blanket

and climbed onto his lap like they were long-term lovers, easy with one another, two parts of a whole. She stretched out on top of him and cuddled against his chest, her long legs interweaved with his, her body warmth seeping into his bare skin. An aching tenderness sliced through him. He drew in a breath. Her scent made his head spin.

"What perfume do you use?" he asked.

"Huh? Oh, I don't like perfume. I use some type of sandalwood body lotion. Same with the shampoo. It's organic."

She was too fucking adorable.

Sandalwood. He'd never forget that scent as long as he lived. Arms wrapped tight around her body, he cuddled with her. "When I was young, I had a big fight with my father, who called me useless. My mother lit into him, but the damage was done. I always felt like the odd man out in the crew. Maybe because I was the youngest. Cal was the favorite, Tristan handled Dad in this controlled way that worked, but I was a bit of a hothead. Anyway, my mother came to my room while I was sulking and trying to lose myself in video game world, and gave me a telescope. Nothing big, it was just a simple handheld one."

The feminine body above him stiffened, but he kept talking.

"She said the world is bigger than my problems, and I needed to remember who I really was.

Inside. Not who I wanted to be for my father, or her, or anyone else. She took me outside and showed me the stars. Should have been boring, right? But not the way she taught me. She'd tell me stories of the constellations and the Greek myths. Each night, I'd look forward to more. I finally got a real telescope, and when I got stressed or pissed off, I'd go study the sky and this peace would come over me."

She didn't answer for a while, seemingly wrapped up in her own thoughts. Her voice was soft when she finally spoke. "My father loved the stars. He'd take me on these camping trips out in the mountains, and we'd pitch the tent together and look at the sky. He'd make up funny stories for me, and then he got me all these books that explained the constellations. I got hooked. I almost majored in astronomy, but ended up dropping out of college and hitting the road. Saw a lot of night skies in my travels, and though I was still pissed at him, I feel like he was watching out for me in those stars every evening."

He wanted to ask why she was mad at her father, but now wasn't the time. They shared so many things from their pasts. Maybe that's why he felt so close to her? She'd experienced the death of a parent. She'd lost herself for a while and rediscovered her footing. She loved the stars and liked to run her business her way, following her unique vision without compromise. Each quality was a mirror image of his own.

"Dalton?"

"Yeah?"

"Tell me a story."

Her voice was tinged with sadness and memory. He lifted a finger toward the night sky. She wasn't looking for a lesson, she was looking for comfort, and he intended to give it. "There's Scorpius, one of my favorite constellations." He traced the outline, which was right in the center of the Milky Way.

"Why is it your favorite?"

"Ah, I'll tell you the story. But first we must find Orion." He made a line to the opposite side of the sky. "Which is right here. There are mixed tales regarding what happened with Orion and Scorpius, but this was the one I was first told. Orion was known as the great hunter, so one day he was out hunting with the goddess Artemis and her mother, Leto. Seems he was feeling quite confident in himself, so he began boasting that he would kill every animal on Earth. Pleasant, isn't he?"

"Quite."

"Now, Artemis was a fine hunter herself, and challenged Orion's skill, but his threat against the creatures of Earth pissed her off. Don't piss off a goddess. Especially one who is a protector. To make her point and topple Orion from his pedestal forever, Artemis and Leto sent a scorpion to do battle with him, and after an epic fight, Orion was killed. Now, the gods enjoyed their entertainment, much like the Romans adored their Colosseum, and Zeus was so amused by the fight, he decided to raise the scorpion to heaven."

"Poor Orion."

"Yes, indeed. But Artemis wasn't done making her point. She asked Zeus to send Orion up to heaven along with the scorpion, and Zeus agreed. Now Orion is the warning to all peasants below to watch their foolish pride. A warning, I think, we all need. At opposite points of the sky, the constellation Scorpius rises in the east and Orion sets in the west, fleeing from the scorpion for all eternity in a visualization of tragedy."

A sigh released from her lips. "You tell a good story. Why is this your favorite constellation?"

The night squeezed around them in a lover's embrace. "Antares. The fifteenth brightest star in the night sky."

"Yes, of course. It gets confused with Mars a lot because it's red and a supergiant."

"The heart of the scorpion. Completely badass and destined for doom."

She twisted a bit to look up into his face. "Scientists say it'll soon run out of fuel to burn, right?"

He nodded. "It'll collapse and explode into a supernova. Whenever it happens, tomorrow or a hundred thousand years from now, it'll be a sight to see." Dalton gently stroked her hair away from her face. "You remind me of a Scorpio."

"Alas, I'm just a simple Aquarius."

"Bet if they did your chart you'd have Scorpio hidden everywhere."

Her dark eyes lit up with mischief. "Please don't tell me one of your lines to your many women is 'What's your sign, baby?'"

He winced. "Absolutely not. Do you think I'm an amateur?"

"No, you're a master."

"Exactly. I'd say something like this." He paused, waggled his eyebrows, and gave her a lustful look. "Hey, baby, why don't you let me read your chart so we can see if we're written in the stars?"

She collapsed into laughter, punching him in the shoulder. "I'd pay to hear you say that line."

"You just heard it for free. Plus, I don't have many women. I have one woman."

That statement shocked her just as much as him. They stared at each other, accepting the connection that tightened around them and demanded acquiescence. He cupped her cheeks, lowered his head, and pressed a gentle kiss to her lips. Tracing the lines of her face, he smiled with sheer pleasure.

"For now," she whispered.

He hesitated, struggling with his answer. "For now," he repeated. He tucked her back against his chest, and they sat in silence.

"Dalton?"

Her voice held the tinges of sleep. He dropped a kiss on the top of her head. "Yeah?"

"Thank you for being with me tonight."

"Welcome."

Her breath deepened, evened out, and she slept. He kept watch, holding her close, thinking about the future, staring up at the stars.

"My goodness. Don't men take you to bed any longer, or is that too old-fashioned?"

Raven jumped off the couch. Streams of sunlight had replaced the night sky, and she blinked, shielding her face as she stared at someone on her doorstep.

"Aunt Penny!"

She launched into her aunt's arms, hugging her with a fierce need that made Penny squeeze back just as hard. Her petite figure was deceiving—her aunt was solid and strong, and still lifted weights at the gym with the boys. Her signature scent of expensive floral perfume wrapped Raven in comfort.

Her gaze greedily took in the only family

member who'd stepped in after her father passed. Aunt Penny was a mother figure for her, taking on a troubled young woman and doing her best while she managed a thriving career as one of the most prolific theater actresses in New York. Even in her sixties, her face was smooth and unlined, her dark eyes filled with animation and a worldly charm that never bored. Her chestnut hair was styled in a short, classy bob, and she wore her trademark outfit of black on black—always preferring not to fuss with her wardrobe and waste precious hours. She adored jewelry, and even now, in the early-morning hour, she dripped with bling—from her diamond earrings to her silver bangles and the jumbo heart-shaped pendant around her neck.

Raven finally stepped back, swallowing the lump of emotion lodged in her throat.

Her aunt's gaze lasered in on the tall, muscled man who climbed off the couch and stretched. His bare chest was a work of art, the solid pec muscles, the gorgeous dusting of golden hair, and the tight eight-pack on display. They'd fallen asleep wrapped in a plush blanket and an embrace that shouldn't have been so easy and comfortable.

Yet she genuinely *liked* him. Last night, he hadn't tried to turn their encounter into sex, which was the easiest way to communicate.

Instead, he'd talked to her, held her close, and told her stories about the stars. She felt trapped in a John Green novel, but she wasn't sixteen and didn't believe that type of all-consuming, all-encompassing love really existed.

Dalton approached her aunt with an easy, welcoming smile, offering his hand. "Pleasure to meet you, ma'am. Seems we fell asleep stargazing last night. I'm Dalton."

Relieved he didn't state his last name, just in case her aunt remembered, Raven held her breath while Aunt Penny studied him with a thorough, assessing gaze. Then she broke into a delighted smile. "No 'ma'am' is needed. 'Penny' will be fine. And it's lovely to meet you, too, Dalton. It's nice to know Raven finally found someone who appreciates astronomy. To me, it's complete torture. Now, why don't we go in so you can make me one of those horrid cups of coffee?"

Dalton laughed. "I'll make it," he said. "Then I'm going to get going so you can have some time together. I need to get to work."

"Where do you work?" Aunt Penny asked.

"Construction," Raven burst out. She'd tell her aunt later about Pierce Brothers. Dalton nodded, allowing her to answer. He pulled on his T-shirt and began making a fresh pot of coffee.

"Ah, no wonder you look fit. Muscles like that don't come from a gym."

"Why didn't you call me?" Raven demanded, pulling out some fresh fruit and yogurt from the refrigerator. "I thought you were still in London."

"I'm doing a brief stint on Broadway and decided to come visit for a few days. I wanted to surprise you." Her dark eyes sparkled. "I guess I did."

Dalton laughed with ease. "Actually, I think Raven will appreciate the company. She had a bit of an episode last night."

"What do you mean? What happened?"

Raven set out some bowls and grabbed granola. "Just a gunman holding up the bar. It's fine."

"Didn't you warn me you were emotional and overdramatic?" he asked.

Raven shrugged. "I am. Just not when someone threatens me or my bar."

"Now you know why I'm kind of crazy about her," Dalton said to her aunt.

"A gunman! Are you okay? Why didn't you call? Oh, my Lord, are you okay?"

"Yes, Aunt Penny, everything's fine, I swear."

Dalton interrupted by pressing a short kiss to her mouth. Her lips tingled for more. His blue gaze delved deep. "Catch up with your aunt and I'll check in later."

"Okay." Her voice came out all soft and wispy, like a starstruck teen's. Ugh.

"It was nice to meet you, Penny."

"You too, Dalton."

The screen door banged behind him. Aunt Penny rested her index fingers together and regarded her with warning. "Sit down, young lady. Tell me everything and leave nothing out."

Raven sighed, sat down, and began to talk.

An hour later, breakfast was finished and her aunt had relaxed, assured her niece had not only survived but thrived. They moved to the living room, and Aunt Penny tucked her legs underneath her. "Now, I want to hear about the hot shirtless guy."

Raven laughed, curling up against a plump pillow across from her. "Funny you should ask. I kind of wanted to talk to you about him."

"Uh-oh. I've seen that face before." Her aunt shook her head. "Had that expression myself a few times. You falling for him?"

Raven squirmed. How was she going to explain such a complicated relationship? Still, she trusted Aunt Penny, who was one of the few who understood the heartbreak she'd suffered with her father's death. They'd also shared an open, truthful communication that was the key to surviving her wild youth. She owed her aunt the truth.

"Yes. But Dalton is not just any guy. His full name is Dalton Pierce."

Her aunt tilted her head, frowning. "Pierce? Wait a minute—why does that name seem familiar?"

Raven dragged in a lungful of air. "The Pierce

brothers. Their mother was Diane Pierce—the woman who ran off with Papa and got him killed."

Her aunt jerked back with shock. "No, that's impossible," she murmured. "He's one of the sons?"

"Yes, the youngest. There's Cal, the oldest, and Tristan, and Dalton. They came into my bar on the anniversary of Papa's death. I had no idea, they were in pain and got drunk on JD, and when I heard their last name, everything finally fell into place. I told them to get out—I never wanted to see them again."

"Oh, my darling girl, I'm so sorry. Why didn't you call me?"

"I needed to process it. I was doing so well. I'd gotten through the anger and revenge fantasies, and suddenly my past was sitting in my damn bar. Then Dalton ended up doing restoration on my restaurant so I could get ready for the feature in *Good Food and Fine Spirits* I told you about. For those few weeks, we ended up getting closer, which only got more confusing. I started having the nightmare again. I decided it was an opportunity to find out more about the Pierce brothers. About the mother."

Her aunt's eyes filled with sympathy. "You can't go back there, Raven," she said quietly. "It almost destroyed you. What do you expect to find by using Dalton?"

"I don't know! I thought I'd prove Diane Pierce

was using Papa, and that he never planned to run away with her. I figured I'd end up disliking Dalton and the rest of them and confirm what I've been feeling about them for years—that their mother was a spoiled, rich, manipulative woman who cared nothing about her children."

"Is that what you found?"

Raven glared. "No. No! So far, from the stories Dalton's told me, she sounds—nice. Like she cared about her boys. But that doesn't mean she didn't use Papa to get away from her husband. Dalton said his father was brutal. Maybe he hit her? Abused her? Maybe she needed Papa to help her escape?"

Aunt Penny rose and sat beside her, taking her hands. "Raven, do you see what you're doing? Torturing yourself about things we won't ever know. Are you sleeping with Dalton?"

She nodded, miserable. "Yes. I tried to fight it, but I was weak. But how can I do this, Aunt Penny? I'm betraying Papa, and I have these feelings I've never experienced before, which is ridiculous because he's a womanizer who will probably get bored in record time and leave me behind. Then I won't even have the truth!"

Her aunt gave a long sigh. "You need to tell Dalton the truth, especially now that you slept together. It's not fair to him."

"What about the way his family treated Papa?"

she asked. "They said horrible things. About how he just wanted money and tricked her into running away. Stores stopped selling his paintings because they ruined his reputation with no regard for the truth. I had no power back then, and I let them smear our name. I stood at his graveside and vowed revenge. Don't I deserve my turn at justice?"

"To do what, child? Hurt back? Justice doesn't bring back your father. Those boys were just like you—vulnerable and feeling betrayed. They were young and their beloved mother was killed. They struck out, but they were probably led by Christian Pierce. Listen to me, Raven. What happened to your father is a tragedy, but there were . . . things you didn't know about him. Things you didn't need to hear back then."

"What things?"

Her aunt ducked her head for a minute, considering. "He was completely devoted to you, like no other father I'd ever seen. He seemed to have no interest in bringing any female into his life after your mother passed, and was completely content. Of course, I was traveling a lot back then, but I remember when he called me in London. He said he'd met someone. Someone important. He said this woman had the capacity to change his existence, but he had to move carefully. He never talked like that before. There was a depth of emotion in his voice he only used for two people. You and your mother."

"You think it was her? Diane Pierce?"

"Yes, I do. I suspected then that this woman was married, but he wouldn't answer any of my questions."

The bitterness still brewed heavy in her gut. "He left me, Aunt Penny. He left me for this woman I didn't even know. I came home from school and he was gone forever. I thought we had something special, but he proved I wasn't even important enough to say good-bye to."

Her aunt snapped her voice like a whip. "Now, you listen to me, young lady. I've told you this over and over. Your father called me to stay with you for a few days. He wouldn't tell me why, but I know in my heart and soul that man would've never left you. You were his whole life. He was coming back for you, and it's time you finally believe this, because it's the only truth that makes sense."

Her mind spun. She didn't know what to believe any longer. Her aunt had never told her Diane Pierce might have been mentioned by her father. What was she going to do?

Aunt Penny's words flared inside her like a small flame, gaining heat. Maybe she hadn't been ready to hope he'd been coming back. Maybe it had been easier, in a way, to feel betrayed and blame Diane Pierce for everything falling apart. For his death. For his leaving her alone.

Her aunt softened her voice. "How do you feel about Dalton as a man? Not as a Pierce brother?"

She met her aunt's steady gaze. "There's this power between us. A connection I always feel when he's in my space. Like I'm drawn to him, no matter how much I try to fight it or ignore it."

Her face grew serious. "Destiny."

"I don't believe in destiny. Neither do you!"

Aunt Penny tapped her finger against her red lips. Her giant amethyst cocktail ring flashed in the light. "Of course I do. Your father did—he was a big believer in love and fate. It never happened to me, so it was something I couldn't personally confirm."

As if she heard Raven's thoughts, Aunt Penny stared at her with a touch of fierceness. "You're going to tell Dalton the truth. You're going to talk it through. Then see what there is between the two of you. Love is rarer than you think, Raven, and I believe there are different levels. This connection you speak of is too important to just throw away. You need to figure out what it is, or you'll regret letting it go."

The realization hit her full force. She was falling for Dalton, even within this short period of time. Her aunt was right—she owed them both a fresh start and the truth. Would their pasts shatter any type of hope for a future? Or was a future even possible between two people who blamed each other for their pain?

Raven didn't know anymore. But instead of playing endless games, it was time to find out.

"I'll tell him."

"Good. Now, I was hoping I could pull you away for a night. There's a production in previews on Broadway starring a close friend. I'd love to take you into the city. Can you close the bar tonight?"

Normally, nothing was important enough to close for a night, but since it was midweek, and she was still a bit shaken, she agreed. Besides, she hadn't seen her aunt in way too long. "Let me make some calls. I'll post on Facebook and I may need to go into the police station today for followup. I could use a night off."

Aunt Penny broke into a smile. "Excellent. You need to pack an overnight bag. We'll eat at Carmine's tonight. You need pasta. It's comforting."

Raven hugged her aunt, deciding to focus on the evening ahead.

chapter nineteen

Dalton headed into the Pierce Brothers head-quarters and shoved his phone back in his pocket. He had no right to be disappointed. He was glad Raven was going to spend time with her aunt. Even happier she'd decided to close My Place and take off for a fun evening in Manhattan. She needed some time to process the break-in and ease back into her schedule. One night away was perfect.

What bothered him was he wasn't the one with her.

He dragged his palms over his face, groaning. What was up with him? He was terrified she was going to announce that the experiment was over, thank him for the sex, and move on her way toward finding a husband. Yes, he wanted her back in his bed. But last night, just holding her with the stars overhead, he'd been at peace. Happier than he'd been for a long time.

He was falling for her. All of her.

The worst part?

He didn't care anymore what was happening. Since he'd claimed her on the bar, every waking thought revolved around when he could see her again. Hold her. Kiss her. *Talk*. In record time, it had become more than just physical. He knew every step needed to be carefully trod or she'd break it off, thinking he was just playing around.

He was in so much shit.

"Dude, you look awful." Tristan stopped on the way to his office. Shoes polished to a fine sheen, he cut an impressive figure in his charcoal suit and purple tie. He had on those gold-rimmed glasses he needed for reading, which gave him an even more authoritative look. No wonder clients trusted him with million-dollar renovations. "Everything okay?"

"Someone broke into My Place last night. Had a gun. Raven disarmed him."

Tristan's mouth fell open. "You're kidding me! Is she okay?"

"Yeah, she's fine. Just a bit shaken."

"How the hell did she disarm him?"

Pride radiated in his tone. "Gave him a vicious kick in the face, then in the groin."

"Holy shit."

"What are you two gossiping about now?" Cal held a cup of coffee as he walked in from the kitchen. "We need to reschcdule a date to go through Dad's belongings; you both keep canceling on me."

"Raven took down a gunman at My Place," Tristan said.

"Are you fucking kidding? When? Is she okay?"

Dalton groaned. His brothers loved gossip, no matter how they denied it. He started the story again. "She's okay. Some guy high on drugs broke into the bar after the ladies left poker night. Had a gun. Raven kicked him and took him down, grabbed the gun, and called 911. I got there when they were questioning her."

"Morgan and Sydney were there last night."

Morgan appeared, a stack of folders in her hands. "What about last night?"

Cal pulled her to him, as if reassuring himself she was okay. "Baby, did you know that Raven took down a gunman after you left?"

"What?" The papers and folders dropped to the floor. "Is she okay? What happened?"

Everyone looked frantically at Dalton. Ah, hell, this was ridiculous. He'd have to do this in one shot. "Sydney! Brady! Get over here!"

The architect and office manager came hurrying out of their offices. "What is it?" they asked in unison.

"Just so you all know the same exact story, something happened last night at My Place." He explained all the details, answering questions and slowly going over the events as he knew them. Morgan and Sydney looked sick. Cal immediately stroked his fiancée's back with soothing strokes, holding her against him. Tristan took a few steps toward Sydney, reaching out to gently place a hand on her shoulder. She flinched but didn't pull away, eventually leaning a few inches toward him.

"I'm calling her now," Morgan announced. "She can stay with us if she doesn't want to be alone."

"She's out with her aunt. She'll be back home tomorrow. When I left her this morning, she seemed in good spirits. Raven is tough."

Suddenly silence descended. They all stared at him like he'd gone ugly.

"What?" he asked in puzzlement.

Cal cleared his throat. "Umm, dude. You said you left her this morning. Meaning you spent the night. Right?"

Ah, shit.

They looked hungry for the dirt, but damned if he was telling them the details of his personal life. "I was just checking on her."

"Late at night after closing? Early morning, when you like to sleep till noon?"

"I don't sleep till noon! Not since I was sixteen."

Morgan jabbed a finger in the air. "You're deflecting. Look, Dalton, I adore you both and think you're an amazing couple, but, just . . . Well. Just—"

"What?" he demanded.

"Go slow," Tristan cut in. "You've been hot for her for a long time, and you jump into these relationships that seem to blow up, and we just don't want you to screw this one up. Like the rest."

"Or hurt her so she doesn't want to see us or make her cocktails. I'm getting good at poker, too," Sydney said.

Fuming, he glared at his family and friends, who were supposed to have his back. The only one who didn't seem to speak was Cal. He just studied Dalton's face thoughtfully, like he was trying to figure out a puzzle. Unbelievable. They still treated him like the big bad fucking wolf, ready to eat poor Little Red Riding Hood. Well, his Red could kick his ass just like she had the gunman's. If he tried to tell them she was holding all the power in this relationship, they wouldn't believe him.

"Thanks for looking out for me, but I got this. I won't ruin your poker or cocktails or break her heart. Okay? If anyone needs me, I'll be out at the Sullivans', building their new deck. Oh, and your snakewood came in, Morgan. I dropped it off at the house. Tristan, I took care of the supplier in Vermont. And here's the bill for My Place, Sydney. I put it on monthly installments." He thrust the papers into her hand, ignoring her guilty look. "Guess that's it for the screwup."

"Dalton—"

"Don't go—"

"Hey, dude—"

He walked out of the office and didn't look back.

He needed some damn air.

Dalton drove out to the Sullivans' place, looking forward to losing himself in his work. The colonial was bright yellow, with pretty white shutters and a small, manicured front yard. The older couple had saved for a while to finally install a deck, and Dalton was going to make sure the wait was worth it. The old screened porch had been badly constructed and was leaking air, so he'd ripped it down and was now replacing it with a half-covered open deck with benches. He'd decided to use Trex for the floor for easy maintenance, but the rest of the structure was a gorgeous cedar, one of his favorite materials for a deck.

He walked up the curved stone pathway toward the back. The job was halfway done, and he intended to spend next week finishing it up so the couple would be able to enjoy the deck for the rest of the summer. Art Sullivan raised a hand to him, riding on his mower, motioning at him to make himself at home.

Dalton walked the area, donning his safety gear while he powered up his band saw. Then jumped back.

"Hi." The woman stood a few feet from him, shielding her eyes from the sun. "Oh, I'm sorry. Didn't mean to scare you."

"No problem, I didn't see you." He frowned. The Sullivans had no children, so he wasn't sure what this woman was doing in their yard. "Can I help you?"

She laughed, and it sounded like wind chimes. Her hair was long and straight, and held streaks of cedar and honeycomb timber colors. She was on the short side, with killer curves and huge hazel eyes. Dressed in white shorts and a pink T-shirt that declared JUICY, she could've easily been eighteen. "No, I'm Charlie. I'm Art's niece. I'm staying here for a bit while I look for my own place. I just moved here."

"Oh, welcome to Harrington. Are you trying to stay in the dorms or closer to the campus?"

She tucked her hair behind her ear and grinned. "I'm done with college. Graduated a few years ago. I know, I look like I'm barely legal, right?"

"Sorry, you do look young."

"I get carded all the time. Everyone says I'll be happy twenty years from now, but it's a bit embarrassing when I'm looking for a job that requires leadership."

He grinned back. "I bet. What do you do?"

She jerked her head toward the deck. "That."

Dalton frowned. "Build decks?"

"Rehab. I'm an addict. Not the drugs, just construction. Kind of like that show on HGTV, actually. I like to tear down houses, or parts of houses, and rebuild them on a strict budget. I'm a bit of a miser, so I like to save lots of money. Another characteristic that's not too much fun. Umm, there I go again, telling my life story to a stranger 'cause I'm desperate for company."

"No, that's amazing. So how come you're not doing this deck?"

She motioned to her uncle on the mower. "I don't mix family with work. They've been supportive, but Uncle Art still can't wrap his head around the fact his only niece used to reject Barbies for a hammer and nails. It's better this way. I need to work on my résumé."

"Have you found a job yet?"

She shook her head. "Not yet. Thinking of taking on some projects myself and trying to build a name."

He scratched his head, his thoughts whirling. "I work for Pierce Brothers. Why don't you stop by the office and fill out an application? Tell Sydney I sent you. We'd probably only offer part-time to start."

Her face brightened, and he was struck again by the blast of animation from her figure. Almost like she was filled with light, and it poured out of her. Now where had that analogy come from? "Okay, I'm going to try real hard not to freak out with excitement or you will think I'm in high school. I appreciate it. I'll bring over my portfolio."

"If you have one of those, you're already ahead of the game."

"Thanks. Umm, can I ask you one more thing?"

"Sure."

"Would you like to grab a meal together sometime? Lunch, or dinner, or even coffee?" A touch of pink hit her cheeks, and she shifted from foot to foot as the words flew out of her mouth. "God, don't think I'm trying to ask you out on a date or something, it's just I don't know too many people and I'd love to learn more about your company and just the layout of Harrington. Are you scared of me yet?"

He chuckled. "You'll have to work a lot harder to scare me. Sure." He took a card out of his pocket and handed it to her. "Here. Call me next week."

"Thanks! I'm going to get out of your way now."

She bounded down the stone path, waving madly to her uncle, and disappeared.

Oh, yeah. Morgan was probably going to like her.

chapter twenty

———— ⟩ ◆ ⟨ ————

ey, Raven. I've been a bad boy. Come give
me an ass whoopin'!"

The guy turned around, flashed his naked ass,
and fell into hysterical hoots of laughter with his
college friends.

Here we go again . . .

Without pause, she flashed her best come-
hither smile, leaned over the bar, and crooked her
finger. "Come over here, gorgeous," she purred.

Awestruck that he could score, he covered his
ass back up and stuck his face over the bar. She
thought about throwing him out for the nudity,
but he was harmless and friends with the regular
crew who haunted her bar. She'd take care of it
her way.

"I'm here. Whatcha got for me?"

He practically licked his lips in anticipation.

So did Raven.

"How about an ass coolin' instead, baby?"

She dumped half a glass of ice water over his head.

The bar erupted in supportive shouts and laughter. The guy spluttered and stared in shock, caught between male temper and embarrassment. In her usual move, she took the sting away by pushing a shot glass of her full-powered whiskey at him.

"Show your ass again in here and you won't be back." She flashed another smile. "Here, this one's on the house."

His friends clapped him on the shoulders as if welcoming him into the rejection club, and his shoulders relaxed. They knew the drill and easily filled him in, and in seconds he flicked back the whiskey and gave her a thumbs-up, his wet hair still dripping in his face.

Just a typical Wednesday night.

Raven worked her way down the bar. The crowd had easily doubled since everyone heard about her tussle with the gunman. It might be a bit awkward to be hailed as a heroine from that scary night, but she was raking in the money. A few more nights at this rate, and she'd easily be able to afford the high-tech alarm system that was being installed tomorrow.

Not a bad bargain.

She headed into the kitchen, checking in quickly with the servers, and called out to Al.

He didn't answer. Back stiff, he kept flipping burgers and working his station with a half-mad fury. Something had changed between them. When she'd called him about closing Tuesday and told him about the gunman, he'd freaked out but seemed supportive. Now there was a brewing distance she couldn't seem to breach. After briefly looking her over as if to confirm she wasn't hurt, he'd refused to talk or meet her gaze. It was almost like he was mad at her, but she knew that was impossible.

"Al!"

"Yeah?"

"Dude, why aren't you listening to me? I want to check if you need anything from supply."

"Don't need nothing."

"Al, are you mad at me for something?"

"Nope."

She let out an aggravated breath but had no time to press him. Already Amanda was rushing in, pinning more tickets to the pass and grabbing plates to serve. Raven swore to push him for an answer later and hurried back to the bar.

Then stopped short as her gaze hit ocean-blue eyes full force. Oh, he was smoking hot tonight. There was something deliciously dangerous about his aura, set off by a black tank top that left his sculpted arms and chest available for drooling purposes and tight jeans that told a woman exactly what he was packing. His tawny hair was loose but slicked back from his forehead, emphasizing the sweep of his brow and the long line of his nose. His dimples flashed as he gave her a slow, purposeful smile, full of wicked meaning.

God, she hoped he wasn't just a big tease.

She'd had a wonderful time with her aunt. The play was amazing, and they'd dined at Carmine's, feasting on Italian food served family style. Three of Aunt Penny's friends had joined them, and she'd loved talking about theater and the behind-the-scenes politics that made her laugh so hard her ribs hurt. She and her aunt had spent the night at the Waldorf Astoria and ordered room service for breakfast that cost a billion dollars, and she'd arrived back home more settled, and ready to attack work that day with a clear mind.

Problem was, she missed Dalton.

Bad.

She'd dreamed of him last night. Dreamed he'd snuck into her room, climbed into her bed, and stripped her naked while she slept. Dreamed he'd pushed her thighs apart and buried his mouth at the heart of her, licking and sucking until she came hard against his tongue. Dreamed he'd pushed inside of her, pinned her wrists to the mattress, and fucked her like he owned her.

Her skin tingled as she leaned her elbows on the bar and gave him a smile back. "Hey, Slick."

His eyes darkened, and he got that hungry look on his face. His voice was a touch ragged. "Hey, darlin'." They stared at each other, not needing words, as if they each knew the other's intimate language. "Another busy night. How was your big city outing with your aunt?"

She smiled. "It was nice to spend some quality time with her. She's leaving tomorrow, though. Rehearsals begin on Broadway."

"I like her. She cares about you."

Raven nodded. "She does. Took care of me after my father passed. Put up with my crap. Still loved me."

He reached out and ran a finger down her arm, as if he couldn't stand to not touch her. "Not surprised. You're easy to love."

She sucked in a breath. He snatched his hand back, shock reflecting in those baby blues.

"Can we get another round down here?" someone shouted.

The spell broke, and Raven hurried away. It didn't mean anything. She knew how easily words spilled from lips with no action or intention behind them. She also knew the psychology of a traumatic event increasing bonding hormones, especially between a male and a female. It was textbook.

The night flew by as she took care of the customers, kept up a light banter with Dalton, and sold a crapload of her special raspberry-mint cocktail. Amanda sailed past her, a frustrated expression on her face. Raven reached out and touched her arm.

"You okay? Anyone giving you trouble?"

She blew out a breath. "Yeah, Al. He's out smoking again, and got snippy with me. What's up with him?"

"I don't know. He refuses to talk to me."

Dalton rose from his stool. "I need some air myself. Let me check on him. Could be guy stuff."

Raven nodded. "Okay, maybe you'll have better luck. I'm worried about him."

"Us men are complicated creatures. Sometimes we need some space to work things out."

He winked, then strode out to the back, tight denim cupping his perfect ass.

Amanda gave a dreamy sigh. "He's so hot."

Raven sighed with her. "Yeah, I know."

"So is he, like, your boyfriend?"

The question was simple coming from Amanda's lips. Of course, she was a college student, boy crazy, and looked at the world with a touch of shiny-eyed optimism. Raven wished for one moment she could just say yes. Dalton would be her boyfriend, and they'd go on dates together, sleep together, and head toward something beautiful and maybe permanent.

But it wasn't that simple. And even if they managed to get past their family history, he didn't want anything longer than a few beautiful weeks or months.

"No," she said with a touch of regret.

"Too bad. You guys seem to fit together."

Amanda disappeared, leaving Raven in surprised silence.

Dalton followed the trail of smoke outside. Al leaned against the back wall in his usual spot, puffing away. His white uniform was splattered with grease, one of his sneakers had a hole in the side, and his clean-shaven head shone in the trickle of moonlight. He stared into the darkness like he was planning to kick someone's ass.

Dalton thanked God that someone wasn't him.

He hoped.

"Hey, Al. What's up?"

The cook didn't answer. His fingers tightened around the cigarette.

Dalton kept talking as if they were having a two-way conversation. "Amanda's worried about you. So is Raven. Seems you're not your usual sunny, chatty self."

That got him a grunt.

"Funny, this attitude started after Raven tangled with the gunman. Would've thought you'd be a bit more protective instead of shutting her out. Would've thought you'd be threatening to kill that asshole if you ever laid eyes on him."

That did it.

Al spun around, temper glinting in his eyes. With a low growl, he practically spit out the words. "She doesn't need me around here to protect her! She proved that to all of us, didn't she? You know, I asked her if she wanted me to stay and work the kitchen on poker night, but she insisted she didn't need me. And she was right. Stupid to think an ex-con could do anything around here to help."

Whoa. The rage shaking Al's body was mixed with a frustration Dalton recognized well. Al hadn't been there to help Raven. In his own code of chivalry, he'd failed her, and he couldn't stand living with it.

"Yeah, you're right." Dalton leaned back against the wall and shook his head. "That's why I'm not going to see her anymore."

Al narrowed his gaze with suspicion. "What are you talking about?"

"You know how crazy I've been about her, right? She was finally giving me a chance, but then after she proved she didn't need me, I realized I wasn't good for her. Let's be honest. It's humiliating for me to admit she kicked some jacked-up criminal around with her bare hands. What if I had been there? Maybe I wouldn't have been able to save her as well as she did herself."

"That's the most asinine thing I've ever heard!" Al yelled. "I told you she's not looking for some guy to take care of her or fight her battles. She can do that on her own! She needs someone to stand beside her. Support her."

"Huh. You're saying just because she takes care of herself doesn't mean she has no need for me in her life? Or you? Right?"

Al jerked back, shock on his face. The psychological twist seemed to hit him like an uppercut, and he looked disgusted with himself for not catching on. "Son of a bitch. I'm embarrassed for falling for that crap. My situation is not the same. I look out for my crew, and I let them down. Pisses me off." Al threw down his cigarette. The butt glowed bright in the dark.

Dalton nodded. Oh, yeah, he got it. Being a guy who wanted to protect the women he cared about was hard today. Al had probably seen a lot in prison. If the gunman had hurt Raven, he wouldn't have forgiven himself.

Neither would Dalton.

But he'd learned the hard way there were no guarantees when you loved someone. One day they just got in a car and never came back. One day they just went to work and confronted an asshole with a gun.

A shudder wracked his body. He understood Al better than he'd thought. And that was why it was so much better not to get involved forever. He couldn't imagine not being able to take care of a wife, or a child. Caleb was the bravest in the crew, choosing to let Morgan into his life when the future was unknown.

Yet Raven proved she walked her own path, on her own terms. Al was right when he said she couldn't be with a man who coddled or tried to shield her. She just wanted a man to accompany her on the journey.

The idea that it wouldn't be him burned through his gut like acid, rotting it away.

"Pissed me off, too," Dalton offered. "I came in after the police were here. Felt helpless, and that's not an emotion I do well with." He shook his head, trapped in his own thoughts. "I don't know what the answer is. All I know is, those women inside care about you, and if you happened to be there, you would've given your life for her. I think she knows that already. No need to punish her for our own insecurities. Right?"

Al rubbed his head and shot him a look. "What are you, anyway? A woodworker who moonlights as a shrink? Or a wannabe talk show host?"

"Just a guy who wants to go back in and drink my Raging Bitch in peace, Al."

The cook laughed and clapped him on the shoulder. "You're all right."

"Thanks."

"I'm glad you didn't take no for an answer. You two just fit together."

Uneasiness trickled down his spine, but he ignored it, walking back in with Al. He headed to the bar, took his place on the stool to the far left, and lifted a finger. "Can I have a beer, please?"

She had the bottle in front of him, uncapped and frosty cold, in a matter of seconds. Damn, she was amazing. "How'd it go?"

Al took that moment to pop his head out of the kitchen. "Raven! I need more sweet potatoes, rosemary, bacon, and olive oil. And I want the hickory-smoked bacon this time, none of that fancy crap they try to sell you. Understand?"

She grinned. "Understood, Al."

"Good."

He disappeared again, and she practically clapped her hands with happiness. "He's yelling at me again! You fixed it!"

Dalton laughed. What the hell was he going to do with her? He was certifiably nuts about this woman. "Yeah, I told you, he just needed some space."

"He's still smoking, though."

"Give him time, sweetheart."

"Okay."

"Can we go back to your place tonight?"

Her eyes widened. It was a bold proposition, dragging their intense sex sessions from the bar to her house. It meant they were consciously making a choice to sleep with each other, rather than chalking it up to one impulsive encounter. His palms sweat, and his gut lurched with nausea. She could say no. Then he'd try to persuade her, but he wanted her to want him as crazily as he did her. He wanted to stretch her out on the mattress where she slept, strip her, worship her, and make her fall apart. He wanted his head next to hers on the pillow. He wanted to wake up in the morning and drink her godawful coffee and see her with the morning light shining on her skin.

"Okay."

He tried not to break into a happy, sloppy, joyous grin. "Cool."

He drank his beer, content.

chapter twenty-one

———— ⟩ ◆ ⟨ ————

She was nervous.

The door closed behind her, and Raven wished she had two dogs bounding out to greet her, distracting them both from the outcome of their decision.

To sleep together. In her bed. Deliberately.

She should've said no. She should've grabbed the opportunity to tell him about their parents and stop this before it got too messy. One time on the bar was impulse. Bringing him to her home was planning.

Instead, her greedy body stole her voice and heartily disagreed. One more night together couldn't possibly hurt, right?

"Ah, to hear the thoughts in your head right now would be fascinating."

She stilled, turning around to face him. He leaned against the door, arms crossed in front, that cocky smile on his face that curled her toes and made her breathless. The cut muscles revealed by his tank made her think of two words.

Arm. Porn.

She raised a brow. "Why?"

"Women get tangled up in their thoughts. What they should do or shouldn't. What are the consequences of an action and how will it play out. Rarely do they just do what they want because it feels really good."

"You're a real female connoisseur, huh, Slick?" She knew he'd been with a long line of women, but tonight she didn't want to think about it. A touch of temper blew through her. She was being stupid. This was nothing but sex, no matter how strong their connection, or that they'd slept together under the stars, or that he looked at her like she was the one who'd save him. God knows she'd been down this road multiple times. Why did she think this was different? "Maybe because if everyone did what felt good without thought, we'd live in a broken, chaotic society. We can't all live by the call of the id."

"You're angry." His gaze narrowed, assessing. "You think I'm here just to fuck you until you're out of my system and I can walk away."

She shrugged, pretending she didn't care. "Sounds good to me. Maybe we should get on with it and stop the babbling."

"That's what I intended, you know." He acted like he hadn't heard her last words. "I thought a few naked sessions together would finally calm this crazed need I have for you. I don't like feeling this way."

Frustration welled up inside and ran over. "Neither do I. So why are we here? Let's walk away before this gets more complicated. We want different things. We're courting disaster."

"Don't care." His eyes blazed with a fierce, glowing heat, like blue flames erupting from a gas stove. He pushed away from the door and stalked toward her, his features set with pure intention. "You've crawled under my skin. Torn away every damn barrier I've built over the years. Your name sings in my head, your touch is burned in my fingertips, your scent is imprinted in my memory. You are completely tearing me apart, Raven, and there's nothing I can do about it. So I'm taking you to bed, where we can even the score."

He reached her, pulled her in, and lowered his mouth to hers.

Oh, yes.

This. This was what she yearned for and craved, the drugging, blistering, aching need to be swallowed whole by this man. His taste swamped her, his tongue thrusting between her lips to drink and ravage, and she wrapped her arms tight around him and kissed him back with everything she had.

He nipped her bottom lip, picked her up, and headed to her bedroom.

Kicking the door open, never breaking the kiss, he laid her down on the sage-green quilt and slowly pulled back. "You like pillows."

She laughed, noting the numerous throw pillows in soothing greens and earthy browns littering her mattress. "I like comfort."

"Those are going to come in handy soon." Intensity and male hunger beat from him in waves. Her nipples hardened and pushed for freedom. "I'm going to try very hard not to rip off your clothes like a savage tonight, but I'm already at the edge."

She twisted under him, tugging at his tank. "I've been at the edge since you walked into the bar. Been dreaming of doing this." She lifted herself halfway and bit into his upper arm. His muscles jumped under her teeth, and when she flicked out her tongue to lick the hurt, he muttered something dirty under his breath.

"Savage it is."

He moved lightning quick. Her cropped T-shirt was over her head, and her black lace bra gone in seconds. With a low growl, he pushed her back on the bed, making quick work of her jeans and tiny black panties, until she lay naked, breathing hard, and totally turned on.

He smiled real slow. "Now I can take my time."

Her eyes widened. "No way! We'll slow down later. Get your ass out of those clothes and do me."

"God, you're hot. Gorgeous." His gaze ate her up. "Perfect."

He peeled off his shirt, and she relaxed, licking her lips, reaching up, and—

With expert skill, he flipped her over on her stomach, pressing his jean-clad legs to the backs of her thighs, holding her pinned to the mattress. "Now, be a good girl and shush up."

She opened her mouth to yell his name, but her cry turned into a long moan at the feel of his hot, wet tongue licking down the length of her spine. His fingers tangled within hers, fisting tight as he worked his way down her back, nipping and tasting, his breath hotly caressing her goose-bump-peppered flesh. He stopped at the swell of her buttocks, tracing the vulnerable line between her cheeks, then slowly parted her legs.

"Oh, God."

His wicked chuckle made her squirm against the bed, her wet pussy throbbing for contact. "You have the most beautiful ass I've ever seen."

Her words were muffled as she tried not to scream into the covers. "No, *you* do."

She sucked in her breath as he dipped his

tongue in the center, nibbling over the full curves. "Stop arguing. You do. I can smell you. Musky and spicy, all for me."

Removing his fingers from hers, he pushed the weight of her hair to the side, caressing her shoulders, her back, her hips. Long, smooth strokes that relaxed as much as they tightened the tension within her gut to a hard ball, ready to burst. He massaged her backside, then slipped between her legs to slowly tease her hard clit with light circles that drove her to insanity.

"You're dripping."

"You're gonna pay," she muttered, arching up for more contact.

"Oh, I love a bad girl. But if you're still able to speak, I need to work harder."

"Bastard."

He plunged two fingers inside her.

She cried out as he stretched her, his thumb strumming her clit, and she gave up and begged right then, right there. Her entire body tightened in anticipation, but he was ruthless as he used his hand to pleasure her while he licked and kissed her buttocks, driving her to a place of physical madness . . .

"More. Come for me, Raven. Scream for me."

He added another finger, curling toward the right, and dove deep. At the same time, his thumb flicked and rubbed her throbbing clit.

She came.

She screamed.

Shuddering as the tension shattered and broke her into a thousand pieces, she heard his curse and the sound of a belt buckle behind her. A wrapper tore. Then he was grabbing her legs, pushing her onto her knees and spreading her wide. Scooping up two pillows, he shoved them under her hips and then pushed inside her in one long, slow, full stroke.

"Dalton!"

His fingers twisted in her hair, guiding her head to the side so his mouth could take hers. Somehow, this time was different. Every inch of him covered her, pressing, demanding. There wasn't a part of her body that wasn't claimed by him: his tongue in her mouth; his cock buried deep in her pussy; thighs entwined with her legs. For a few seconds she struggled against the overwhelming male power of possession, trying to break free, but he gentled his kiss, murmuring her name over and over, completely still as her body adjusted to his.

The bond between them switched from the usual hum to a live, crackling explosion of heat. Her body shook as if in a fever, and something within uncurled and loosened, like a ray of light transforms from a speck of sparkle to a powerful beam.

She opened, blossomed, accepted. There was nothing left to do but make her own demands, so Raven pushed back, sending him as deep as he could go, and kissed him with a warrior fierceness.

He broke.

He claimed her, his hips jerking with each thrust, taking her back to the cliff, his fingers twisting her hard nipples, adding a touch of pain to push her closer to the edge. That magic spot deep within shimmered with each thrust, and then his hands traveled down her belly to rub her clit, and Raven was coming again.

With a roar, he joined her. Head thrown back, he let himself go, holding her close as he reached his release.

Raven collapsed.

He rose up behind her, disappearing into the bathroom, then rejoined her on the bed. Moving the pillows, he cuddled her close, stroking her dampened skin, kissing her neck. She melted into his delicious body warmth.

"Tell me something you've never told anyone else," he said, his voice husky with male satisfaction.

She brought his hand to her lips and nipped at him playfully. "Chatty after sex, huh? What if I just want to roll over and sleep?"

"Indulge me first."

"Secrets in the dark?"

"Maybe."

Her heart pounded. This was the time to do it. She just needed to take a deep breath and say it. Instead, she bought time. "You first."

"My brothers and I created a boy band when we were young. Cal played the drums and Tristan played the guitar. I was the singer."

She relaxed again. This type of secret was easier to share. "Is this how your love for the Backstreet Boys and NSync sprouted?"

"Yes. We were going to be rich and famous. We tried to send in a video to MTV but never heard back."

Giggles burst from her like tiny bubbles. The picture of three young boys trying to rock out and film themselves for an audience was priceless. "What type of songs did you sing?"

"Stop laughing. This is serious stuff."

She bit her lip. "Sorry."

"We wrote our own songs. Some of them were pretty good, too. Not sure why we never took off."

"I'm impressed. You did more than some groups who go viral. What was your name?"

"The Builder Brothers."

That did it. The laughter burst back up and escaped. "Oh, my God," she squealed in mirth. "Priceless. No wonder you got no response! Who came up with that?"

"I did. I'm not feeling very inspired to share any more secrets with you, darlin'. I entrusted you with a secret my brothers would deny to the very grave."

She twisted around to press a kiss to his lush lips. "I apologize. I suck. I'll do better next time."

He wrapped his legs around her and took the kiss deeper, punishing her in the most pleasant way possible until she surrendered to the embrace. "Your turn," he growled against her ear. "And it better be good after mine."

She scrunched up her face and thought hard. "Well, remember when I told you I wanted to be a movie star when I was younger?"

"Yep. I still think you missed your calling."

"Many wouldn't agree with you. Well, in third grade we were putting on the play *Cinderella* and I was positive I'd get the lead. I practiced every night, and then the day came when our teacher assigned our roles."

"Why do I have a bad feeling?"

"I got cast as a wicked stepsister. Judy Filly got the lead role, and I was pissed."

"I hope she changed her name for the billboards."

"I know! And she was a real brat about it. She knew I wanted the part and that I dreamed of being a famous actress, so she took every opportunity to brag. Each day I got madder and madder until the day of the play."

"I'm getting nervous here. Put me out of my misery."

"I found the princess dress she was supposed to change into and sprinkled itching powder in it."

He sucked in his breath, pausing. "Wait a minute. They actually make real itching powder?"

"Haven't you ever seen the *Brady Bunch* episode?"

He began laughing. "I had no idea you were so ruthless. I'm also sad I didn't know I could get that type of stuff. Would've loved to put that in my brothers' underwear."

"It was terrible. She started twisting around and couldn't sing the song and they had to yank her offstage before she got to meet the prince. Then I felt horribly guilty, but I was afraid to tell my father, so I kept it my secret."

"Until now."

She sighed. "Until now. Huh. You know what? I feel better that I confessed."

"See? I won't tell a soul. But if I was a bartender at Harry's, I'd be real worried."

Raven chuckled. "Yeah, I forgot to add that to my long list of bad attributes. I'm a terrible loser."

"Luckily I don't mind putting up with you."

They fell quiet for a few moments. The next time he spoke, something had shifted in his voice. "I'm sorry you lost your parents."

"I'm sorry you lost yours," she whispered.

A pause. "It's my mother's death that haunts me. Even after all this time, I still keep going over the pieces, wondering what would've changed if I'd known more."

Nerves danced in her tummy. She tried to keep her voice even. "You said it was a car accident?" she prodded.

She waited, not expecting him to answer.

But he did.

"My mother was running away, Raven. I knew she was unhappy with my father, but she never indicated there was someone else in her life. The day of the accident, she was with another man. We found one-way tickets to Paris, and she hadn't told anyone. She just intended to disappear from our lives forever."

Raven closed her eyes. Hearing the story from his lips was a different experience than she'd imagined. It was more real, hearing the pain in his voice, the obvious confusion she'd felt herself for so many years. The constant questions of why barraging her thoughts. Her hand slid into his and he gripped it tight.

"You don't think she was coming back?"

"I want to believe she was. But we found something that says the opposite. She took our baby teeth."

"I don't understand."

"My mother had a thing about our baby teeth.

She kept them in this box. We used to tease her all the time that it was icky, but she said they made her feel close to us and reminded her of our childhood. She said they made her happy. She was taking the box of baby teeth with her to Paris. Wouldn't she have left it if she planned to return?"

Raven's head spun with more questions. Would she? Or was it possible she'd taken them only to feel close to her sons while she made her own leap for love? Did it really prove they weren't coming back? And when had Raven begun thinking of this story in a different light? When had Dalton's hurt become hers?

"She didn't leave a note? A message with your father or a relative or friend?"

"Nothing. She left nothing."

She dropped her gaze. Confusion swamped her. He was finally giving her the true information, but she didn't feel good about it. "Maybe she didn't say anything to you because she was coming back," Raven said softly.

"No, she would've told me. We were close. We talked every day, about everything. She listened with an open mind and she . . . got me. She made me laugh and helped me look at the world in a better way. I loved her. I loved her so fucking much, and she left, and I have to live with that fact every day."

Her heart broke open and oozed the raw, angry wounds of the past. This didn't sound like a woman who'd manipulate a man or leave behind her family. This sounded like a woman who adored her sons and was trapped.

"I'm so sorry, Dalton," she whispered.

"I can't believe I told you that," he said. "I've never told anyone the whole story before." The warmth of his hand wrapped around hers. "I don't know what's happening to me," he confessed, as if he realized the secrets murmured tonight would go no further. "I don't know what's happening with us. But I've never felt like this. With anyone."

Raven didn't answer, too terrified of what confession would spill from her lips.

Her eyes stung with tears. They lay in the quiet, in the dark, for a long while. Finally Raven knew it was time. She couldn't listen to his truths and not give her own. This thing between them was too big, and right then, right there, she came to a shattering, awful, splintering conclusion.

She was falling in love with Dalton Pierce.

The words formed in her mind, and she tried desperately to focus so she could communicate all of her feelings. She dragged in a shuddering breath. "Dalton, I have to tell you something. I know you're going to have a lot of questions, but first I owe you the truth. I'm falling for you just as hard, and I'm scared to death. Because my father was the one who ran away with your mother. I've wanted to tell you for a while, but I was confused and trying to work out this whole thing in my mind. God, I'm probably telling you this all wrong, but I think they fell in love with each other and I think they were coming back. I believe it. My father wouldn't have left me, and now I know your mother wouldn't have left you. Do you understand? I'm so sorry . . . Please answer me."

Silence.

"Dalton?"

A low snore rose up behind her.

She turned slowly around to look at his face. Eyes closed, brow smooth in sleep, those gorgeous lips parted halfway to allow his breath to escape, he hadn't heard a word of her own confession.

She watched him for a while, biting her lip as she struggled to decide if she should wake him.

No. She'd tell him tomorrow.

It had to be done.

chapter twenty-two

D alton lay awake and stared up at the ceiling. The early-morning light snuck in through the blinds and scattered dancing patterns on the honey-brown walls.

She was a cuddler. She managed to surprise him again. He'd expected her to be more like Amy Schumer's character from the movie *Trainwreck*. He'd prepared himself for a quick embrace after sex, then for her to roll over and fall asleep, making sure there was plenty of space and distance between them.

Instead, her arm was flung over his chest, as if imprisoning him during the night. Her face smooshed against his shoulder, and her thigh wedged firmly in between his legs, urging a morning erection. Glorious waves of gypsy hair sprung in all directions, covering him in a silky blanket.

His skin felt wet, which confirmed she drooled in her sleep. Why did he find that so damn charming? Was he nuts?

She trusted him on an instinctual level that soothed the wild beast inside. It was difficult to sleep soundly with a partner, especially in the beginning of a relationship. Natural slumber required a deep innate trust and willingness to be vulnerable. He'd rarely been able to grab an hour of light rest with other women. But last night, not only had he shared an integral part of his past, he'd collapsed afterward into a deep sleep.

He stared at her relaxed form. Damn, he ached to wake her up by spreading her thighs and pushing slowly inside her. Watch her orgasm between the delicate line of slumber and wakefulness. But she needed rest.

Moving slowly, he slipped out of bed and padded naked into the kitchen. He made a pot of coffee, deciding to take a quick shower while it brewed. Pulling on his jeans afterward and leaving them unzipped, he poured a mug and stood by the window to watch the day bound into existence with joyful abandon. The sun streamed through the windows, and birds flew back and forth, playing hide-and-go-seek within the tree branches. He sipped the steaming brew and wondered what he was going to do.

He'd practically confessed his deepest emotions and been met with . . . silence.

How many times had a woman spilled intimate thoughts that bordered on the L word to him? Numerous? He was honored and humbled but had never felt even a hint of the same. Even with the few women he'd begun strong with, the spark that he hoped would turn brighter always sputtered and died like a birthday candle blown out. He'd never passed more than a hard like for another.

Not with Raven. He'd never shared the circumstances of his mother's death before. Never wanted to. But last night, something had broken inside him, and for the first time he felt right about telling her everything. He wanted her to know more about him.

He wanted her to trust him.

The initial spark between them not only burned brighter but turned into a raging forest fire, crashing through each of his barriers until he was left with a devastated landscape, completely vulnerable. Everything inside him turned from gray to neon. With her, he was completely alive, his nerve endings tingling, his heart galloping, his dick aching. It was so much more than like. So much more than lust.

Was this what falling in love was?

Yet she hadn't responded to his admission. Was she scared because he didn't fit in with her planned future of marriage and kids? Was she protecting herself? Did she still think he played games with her? Or even worse, did she just not feel the same way and not know how to tell him?

Dalton groaned, squeezing his eyes shut. He was a lovesick pup begging at her feet. He hated it, but he didn't know what else to do. He needed to explore and push further, to possibly see what else could blossom between them. Morgan insisted he convince Raven to come to dinner. Maybe getting her on his own turf, around his family, would help her see him in his own element.

He loved the idea of having her eat at his table, surrounded by his family. He pictured her as part of his noisy, dysfunctional, loving circle and had no desire to run. Maybe Raven needed more time with him so he could convince her she was different. He still didn't intend to make long-term promises, but God, he craved her like a drug, every minute of every day.

And it was getting worse.

"Morning."

He turned. She smiled, walking into the kitchen to pour a cup of coffee, clad in a short, silky scarlet robe. He admired the way the fabric emphasized her tight nipples, the flare of her hips, and showed off the bare curve of leg down to her pretty red toenails. She didn't seem freaked out or concerned about last night. In fact, she seemed at ease in her kitchen, walking over to him with her coffee and pressing a kiss to his mouth.

"Morning," he said gruffly.

She sipped her coffee and made a face. "Too weak. Where's the punch?"

He tugged at a stray tendril of hair, then tucked it tenderly behind her ear. "Coffee shouldn't be a wham-bam-thank-you-ma'am experience. It should be a journey, a slow slide upward, a buzz of energy that warms the blood."

Her pupils dilated. Her nipples poked out, begging for attention. His dick strained against his jeans, and he savored the discomfort, knowing she was as aroused as he was, though they'd feasted on each other for hours last night.

Her voice came out husky. "Nothing wrong with a good, hard bang now and then. Gives you the energy you need quick. No long-drawn-out, complicated waiting."

Oh, she was a bad girl. Her tongue slid over her lower lip in a deliberate teasing gesture. "You like your coffee quick and hard?" he murmured in warning.

"Oh, yeah." She took a sip and gave a throaty, catlike moan. "And hot. Really, really hot."

He almost came in his damn pants. She was gonna pay.

Dalton put his mug on the table. Then reached out, snagging hers, and slowly placed it next to his. He bet if he snuck his fingers under that robe and slipped them inside her tight pussy, she'd be soaking wet. Good, because he wasn't going to last.

"Maybe I should give my woman the coffee she really wants."

He paused, taking in the quick flare of wariness on her face, the hidden lust in her inky eyes.

He grabbed her around the waist and lifted her high. Pivoting on his bare heel, he slammed her against the wall, pinning her there while he worked his jeans down over his hips. She was panting hard, her thighs squeezed around his hips, her robe falling open to reveal her small, naked breasts.

"I'm on the pill," she burst out.

His head jerked up, teeth gritted against the surging pull of sexual need pumping between them. "I'm clean. I get tested regularly."

"I am, too."

"You sure?"

"Yes."

He needed no other words. In one quick movement, he slid her up higher against the wall, then slammed her down on his cock.

She screamed his name. He lowered his head, sucking on her hard nipples, encased in drenching heat that hugged him tight and sent him to heaven. Without the barrier of the condom, he relished the amazing feel of her surrounding him. She grabbed his shoulders, digging her nails hard into his flesh, and never easing his grip, he kept control of her body, forcing her to ride him.

Her head hit the back of the wall as he drove himself deeper, harder, licking and biting her nipples until she shattered around him and he felt her come all over him. His name echoed from her lips in a prayer, and he kept up the brutal pace, making her continue riding him until another mini orgasm clenched her muscles and he came hard inside her.

Shuddering, the scent of sandalwood and sex rising to his nostrils, he gentled his embrace, slowly letting her down inch by inch. He pulled her into his arms, stroking her back, and pressed a kiss to the top of her head. God, why did he feel whole when he held her? Made love to her?

"Now, that's the way I like my coffee," she finally said.

He laughed, looking down into her beautiful face. "It's a good thing I have a weakness for brats. What time do you have to go in today?"

"I need to prep and do a bunch of paperwork. Around nine. What about you?"

His phone beeped as if in answer. He grabbed it from the table and read the text. "Have to head to the office, then work on the deck. Listen,

Morgan wants you to come to dinner tomorrow night. And so do I."

She hesitated, her gaze jerking away. He pushed down the sliver of pain, sensing she didn't want to be with his family. Usually he was the one dodging offers of parental dinners and sibling meet-ups. He didn't like the uncertainty and hope twisting inside him. "I'm not sure I can make it."

Dalton turned his back on her. Damn, it hurt. Maybe she just wanted him for sex. "I understand. I don't want to push. I know you may not feel the same way I do, so—"

"Dalton, I want to go." She grabbed his arm and made him face her. Misery etched the features on her face. "I just—I just need to talk to you about a few things. Important things."

He sensed the breakup speech hovering in the air. For the very first time in his life, he gave in to panic. "No, you're right, we should talk. I want to talk. But I have to get going, and I'd like to continue this later."

She chewed on her lip, seemingly hesitant about his quick escape. "Okay. Tonight?"

"Yes, tonight. Will you think about coming to dinner, though? Morgan's been worried about you since the break-in, and she considers you a friend."

"Okay," she said again. "I'll come to dinner. But we'll talk tonight?"

"Absolutely." In record time, he threw on his shirt and shoes, took one last sip of coffee, and kissed her. "I'll call you later."

He headed out the door, running away from the shattering truth: the woman he was falling in love with just wasn't in love with him.

Raven watched him flee out the front door and slumped into a kitchen chair.

What was she going to do?

He'd wrung orgasm after orgasm from her body last night. She'd cried his name in the dark hours, but it had become so much more than physical. Her heart sang in ecstasy, and a deep peace seeped into her blood when he held her. It was as if every dark road she'd explored, every journey she'd embarked on in an effort to erase the pain of her loss had finally led her to the answer she sought.

Dalton Pierce.

She sipped her coffee, still reeling from his confession. Diane Pierce didn't seem like a selfish woman who had wanted to hurt her father. Unless Dalton was blind to the true characteristics of his mother. Would Raven be betraying her father's memory by falling in love with Dalton Pierce?

Tears stung her eyes. She looked over at the covered paintings and envisioned her father sitting with his art brushes, looking at something she couldn't see yet, a peaceful smile on his face. A conversation from long ago drifted in her memory like puffs of smoke, half-real, half-imaginary.

"Papa, I want to play."

"Not yet, Bella. I'm working now."

Frustrated at his lack of attention, she couldn't understand the other world he seemed caught in, someplace over the rainbow where she wasn't allowed to go. "But there's nothing there. What are you staring at?"

He turned to her, his dark eyes full of a creative zeal and joy he always exuded when he was around his easel. She loved art and enjoyed painting with her father, but she never experienced the drive and consistent need to create. "Sometimes you have to take a leap of faith. Believe in things you may not see, but sense."

She looked hard at the white canvas, but nothing came but blankness. "I still don't see anything," *she muttered.* "And I don't sense anything, either."

He laughed, pulling her into his arms for a quick hug. "That's because you're not looking hard enough. If you're very quiet inside your mind, inside your heart, answers will come. You need to be brave enough to follow them, though. Others may tell you it's impossible, but if you believe in yourself, you'll get the help you need, from this world or the next."

Papa liked to talk about mystical things like

angels and heaven, faith and hope. She enjoyed hearing his quiet, soothing voice, but now she just wanted to see a picture like he did. "Maybe I don't have what you do, Papa."

"You're not supposed to. I see it through art and color and pictures. You may see it a different way. There is no right or wrong way, just what makes you happy."

She scrunched up her face and thought real hard. "Maybe I'm meant to be a rock star?"

He never mocked her. Another reason why she loved him so fiercely. "Maybe. If music is your expression, you'll find answers through song."

"What happens when you find your way?"

He turned back to the easel, already slipping away again into that magic place he loved to visit. This time she swore not to get jealous, because it made him happy. "You treasure it. You protect it. Whether it's love or art or song. Don't ever be afraid, Bella. It may scare you, or not make sense. It may seem ridiculous or impossible or wrong. But if it's your road to follow, take it."

That was the end of his lecture. He smiled again, patted her head, and picked up his brush, listening only to his muse.

Raven walked over to the covered paintings. She stared at the canvas for a while, then slowly pulled it off. Propping up the paintings side by side, she gazed at the visual feast before her.

The first was of her as a child. Hair flying, head flung back, she was running through a mystical field of high grass. The blast of blue sky and streaks of yellow-gold caught the light. The expression on her face was one of pure joy, capturing the natural thirst for freedom and adventure contained within an innocent heart. A heart not yet broken by the world. Somehow he'd possessed the skill to show it all in her face.

The second was a starry night. Matching chairs faced away from the onlooker, and two people sat side by side, pinkies touching, staring up at the stars. Not seeing their faces made it more powerful. She caught the memory of the night Dalton first kissed her, their fingers just touching, the stars streaking overhead as if daring them to take a chance. Raven studied the painting, seeing what her father saw, and then moved to the last one.

A woman. Turned to the side, staring out a window, shrouded in partial shadow. The graceful arc of nose and slanted jaw; the fall of her golden hair over her shoulders; the clasped hands in front, as if she was trying to make an important decision. Grief and sadness touched her face with such delicacy, Raven moved closer, as if wanting to run her fingers over the woman's profile and catch her hidden tears.

This one had a title. Sometimes if an image

spoke to her father, he'd name it, saying it was an impulse that he committed to once the painting was finished. The scrawl of words stopped her heart.

The Road Not Taken . . .

She took her time, letting her father's art wash over her. She never had found the talent she always craved, but she believed her father would say mixing cocktails was its own art. She wondered what he'd think about Dalton the man—not the son of Diane Pierce, but of his own standing.

Her father had been right. Dalton had carved his way inside her heart, and she needed to follow the path put in front of her. It didn't make logical sense. He terrified her on many levels. Yet he fulfilled her in ways that should be fictional—a romantic love story of film or book only a lucky few were able to experience.

But if it's your road to follow, take it.

She had no other choice.

Raven went back to the kitchen and fished out the hammer and nails from the junk drawer.

Then she hung up her father's paintings.

chapter twenty-three

Raven stood before the massive carved door, feeling like she was going to be sick.

The plan had been simple: tell Dalton about their shared past and try to work things out. Instead, he'd texted her about some building emergency with Cal and Morgan's house and said he'd pick her up for dinner with his family.

She didn't want to tell him over the phone, so she'd insisted she'd drive over and meet him there. Raven came up with over a dozen excuses to cancel, but the thought of Dalton's pained face stopped her each time. This was important to him, and somehow it had become important to her, too. It was time to get to know the Pierce brothers on a deeper basis and see the place where Diane had made her home. She intended to invite him back to her house after dinner and confess the whole story then.

But her feet were still glued to the porch, unable to gather the courage to ring the bell.

"Is the bell not working? Sometimes that happens, you can just walk right in," a strange voice said behind her, with a touch of a Latin accent.

She spun around. A dark-haired man grinned at her. He held a bottle of wine and a white box tied with string, which looked like it was from the bakery. He was average height, with large, soot-colored eyes and gorgeous brown skin. "Oh, I'm sorry, I just got here. Didn't try the bell yet. I'm Raven."

"Nice to meet you, Raven. I'm Brady. I'm the architect at Pierce Brothers."

She shook his hand, liking his firm grip, and hoisted up her case of Raging Bitch. "Guess we should go in."

He gave a deep laugh and pushed the door open. "I better go first. Don't want the crazy mutts to topple you over with their enthusiasm. You're okay with dogs, right?"

"Yes, I love them."

"Good, don't be worried, they should-—Balin, Gandalf, down!"

Raven tried not to laugh at the elegant man ahead of her flailing his arms to stave off the licking tongues and scrabbling paws. Shifting her weight, she stepped from behind Brady and snapped her voice.

"Balin. Gandalf. Sit."

Joy flitting over their faces, they stopped mid-flight and slammed their asses to the floor, wriggling madly but staying put.

Brady's mouth dropped open. "You did not just do that. Oh, my God, are you from the Animal Planet channel? Did you come to finally train these goofballs?"

Dalton strode into the room, dressed in khaki shorts and a hunter-green T-shirt with the Pierce Brothers logo, with freshly damp hair and bare feet. Those delicious biceps flexed, as if tempting her to take a bite. Dear Lord, *Magic Mike* strippers had nothing on the man, who had the finest arms in the land. "Raven is a dog whisperer," he said, stopping in front of her to press a firm kiss to her lips. He greeted Brady and took the case of beer from her arms, his blue eyes twinkling with pleasure. "She's the only one they seem to listen to."

Raven dropped to her knees, watching the dogs shake with the exertion of being good. "Good boys," she crooned, rubbing their heads and bellies. "Such good, good boys."

"Does it work for men, too?" Morgan asked, trailing behind Dalton.

Brady groaned. "Men are easy. It's women who have so many layers they make onions seem one-dimensional."

"Kind of like Shrek, huh?" Raven tossed out.

Morgan burst into laughter at Brady's look. "Watch out, Mr. Dominant. You may have finally met the woman to put you in your place."

Brady scoffed. "Since Raven is definitely not my woman, she's completely safe. There's nothing wrong with wanting to take care of my lover, and I can do that much better if I set the rules. Women don't seem to know what they want anymore. Is it wrong to want a relationship with no stress, complications, or dishonesty?"

Raven shared a look with Morgan. Fascinating. Though his name didn't fit his obvious Latino heritage, Brady seemed quite focused on a submissive type of woman. She rose to her feet. "Well, since I'm nobody's woman but my own, I'd have to wish you luck on your hunt for the snipe."

Brady frowned. "What's a snipe?"

"The mysterious fictional creature from the movie *Up*."

Morgan giggled. "I love *Up*! I watched it with Sydney's daughter, Becca. I cried."

Cal strode into the room with Tristan. "She did. Also cried at *The Lion King*, *Inside Out*, and *The Good Dinosaur*. We don't allow Disney movies in this house any longer if anyone dies."

Brady shook his head. "See, I'm confused already by this change of topic. I think it's time for a beer."

"I think you're right," Cal agreed, linking his fingers with Morgan's.

"Make that wine and I agree," Tristan piped up.

"Let's head out to the deck. I set it up for cocktails and apps," Morgan said, leading the way past the massive kitchen and out the back. Raven tried not to gape. The foyer was impressive enough, with a magnificent circular staircase and vaulted ceilings. But when her gaze registered the rich teak deck with a view of the infinity pool, white latticed gazebo, gardens, and sprawl of woods, she kind of lost her voice.

The blinding colors of sky, grass, woods, and pool enwrapped guests in another world. A partial roof shielded the deck from any odd weather, but the open portion was huge, containing a hand-painted mosaic table to fit at least twenty people, with apple-green cushioned chairs. Carved benches in teak matched the deck, while brightly colored geraniums, poppies, and tulips burst from planters. She felt wrapped up in an old-world fantasy of elegance and glamour. Music played softly in the background. A fire pit, grill, and smoker lay to the right. A full bar made of mixed stones took up one corner, and she watched Tristan stride over to pour himself a glass of red.

"How are you, Raven?" Tristan asked. "Do you prefer red or white? Or can I make you a cocktail?"

She smiled. "White wine is perfect. And I'm doing well."

Morgan handed Tristan a bottle. "Here, let's try the Chardonnay. I just got it from the cellar."

Raven soaked up the view, enjoying the warm breeze scented sweetly with flowers. "Thank you so much for inviting me to dinner."

"We've been wanting to have you here for a long time," Morgan said. "But since we heard about the break-in, I've been sick with worry. How are you handling it?"

Raven had been asked about the encounter numerous times, occasionally with a touch of concern, but most people seemed greedy for details only to gossip. Not Morgan. Other than Dalton, Raven hadn't really told anyone how the scene affected her. "I got spooked a bit," she admitted. "Especially during closing, but damned if I was going to let him take my safe haven from me. Dalton was nice enough to stay with me a couple of nights. It helped."

Dalton grabbed her hand and squeezed. She noticed the deliberate looks and nudges from his brothers, as if they'd never seen him with a woman before. "You were really brave," Morgan said. "I think I would've frozen up. When I first met Gandalf and Balin and thought they were Cujos about to tear me to pieces, I couldn't even scream."

Cal laughed. "Trust me, I think you sensed those two beasts would love you to death. I've never known you to back off from fear. You tackled me head-on, didn't you, princess?"

She rolled her eyes and handed Raven a floral-painted wineglass. "I was never afraid of you, Charming. Just irritated."

He kissed her, and Tristan groaned. "Dudes, can't you keep your hands off each other for a minute?"

"No," Cal said.

"I saw the way you played poker," Raven commented. "She played like a badass. If you have balls in poker, you would've definitely taken that guy down."

Morgan puffed up with pride, and Cal grinned.

Brady grabbed a Raging Bitch and settled into one of the Adirondack chairs near the fire pit. "I heard you took him out with two kicks."

"Two kicks and a punch," she said.

"I talked to Xavier this week. He said he's never seen such a talented student. When he heard what you did, the man couldn't speak for a while. I think he was actually tearing up. Ever think about training for *American Ninja Warrior*?"

Raven laughed and took a sip of wine. Nice.

Crisp and dry with a touch of peach and lemon. Long finish. "God, no. I just want to run my bar without assholes bothering me."

"Then what are you doing here with Dalton?" Tristan asked, deadpan.

Dalton glowered. "Funny. As always."

Raven tried not to smile at the sibling jabs. She'd always wished for a sister or brother, and enjoyed watching them interact. Morgan seemed a core part of the family, as if she'd been with Cal longer than a year. A pang surprised her. She'd never craved belonging somewhere after her father died, because she hadn't believed it was possible to replace what she had.

Until now.

She refocused on the conversation. "Looks like Sydney's running late," Tristan said, swiping a cocktail shrimp from the iced platter. A bucket of oysters sat among mouthwatering treasures like crusty French bread with brie and figs, mini spinach quiches, and a tray of meatballs that looked perfectly browned. Raven loaded up a plate of food and fell into culinary heaven.

"Oh, I forgot to tell you. She can't come," Morgan said.

He frowned. "Why? Is Becca okay?"

"Yes, but Sydney came down with the flu. Poor thing sounded terrible. I told her I'd run over there after dinner, but she insisted she was fine.

Said she'd put Becca to bed early and just sleep it off."

In seconds, Tristan's easygoing features grew hard. His voice came out clipped. "And you believed her? Sydney is stubborn, she never wants to bother anyone. She's not going to be able to take care of a five-year-old if she can't even move. I'm going over there."

Morgan's mouth dropped open. "Tristan, I don't think that's a good idea, she probably wants to just stay in bed and sleep. We can check on her later."

Tristan ignored her. He put his glass on the bar and shot his cuffs. Even relaxing before dinner, he looked like he could easily attend a society function in his fitted charcoal suit. "I'll stop at Marty's Deli and get her some chicken soup."

Cal shook his head. "Dude, I don't think it's a good idea to surprise a woman when she's sick."

"I don't care. She needs someone to take care of her. God knows, she's not good at taking care of herself. Good to see you, Raven. Don't bother saving me dinner, Morgan, I'll grab something on the way."

He strode out.

Silence fell. Cal threw up his hands. "Let him go. He's just as stubborn as Sydney."

"Umm, are they friends or something?" Raven asked.

"Or something," Dalton answered. "They dated years back, but it ended badly. Not sure why."

Brady popped a meatball into his mouth. "He's still got it bad for her," he announced. "I hate being in the office with those two. Tension is so thick, you wish they'd just jump each other."

Morgan gasped. "Seriously? I always suspected there was something between them."

Dalton groaned. "Can we not talk about Tristan and Sydney banging, please? It hurts my head."

Raven laughed. "Why? Did you have a crush on her when you were young?"

Cal waved his hand in the air. "Hell no. Tristan was always possessive of Sydney. Besides, sleeping with my fiancée was bad enough—Dalton didn't need another problem on his head. We ready to eat?"

Raven choked on her wine. "What did you say?"

"I didn't sleep with her, man! I've told you over and over!"

"Sorry, I know. Habit."

Morgan patted Dalton's shoulder. "He knows you were doing it for his own good, Dalton, don't listen to him. He's just teasing. Okay, everyone, let's head to the dining room."

Raven turned her watering gaze to the man beside her. "You slept with your brother's fiancée?" she practically shrieked.

Dalton sighed. "No. It's a long story. I promise to tell you later. Let's go eat."

He grabbed her glass of wine and her hand and led her inside.

Hours later, Raven had to admit Southern cooking was her new favorite thing. Morgan had made biscuits with gravy, shrimp with vegetables, grits, and some sausage dish Raven kept scooping up portions of. Conversation flowed along with wine, and she relaxed into the easygoing atmosphere in the Pierce household.

The dining room reminded her of the foyer— elegant, aristocratic, and formal. A dripping crystal chandelier set off a mahogany table with high-backed chairs, and an array of expensive, antique furniture in various sizes and wood finishes. Even the wall hangings held a flavor of class, with scenic watercolors, tapestries, and beveled mirrors. The details were extraordinary, like the crystal knobs on the doors, the floor-to-ceiling windows, the hand-carved moldings, and the lush velvet drapes.

Raven clearly saw the value in each carefully picked detail, especially since the mansion was probably the spec house used to retain clients. She wished she had more information about Christian Pierce and the type of man he was.

Dalton had said many times he was hard, brutal, and held to his own vision of the company. Had he been a controlling husband? Had he made Diane so unhappy she'd clung to Matthew Hawthorne to save her?

There were no answers, just more questions. She hoped later tonight, when she shared the information with Dalton, they'd be able to talk and maybe figure more things out.

With dinner finished, they all pitched in and began clearing the table.

The kitchen felt so different from the rest of the house. The cabinetry was warm, and the room seemed set up for comfort, from the marble islands and high countertops to the cushioned chairs and brightly colored accents that brought a joyful zest to the classic surroundings. There was a distinct feminine touch to the kitchen that was lacking in the foyer and the living room she'd glimpsed. Had this been Diane's haven? The men chattered easily, loading the dishwasher without fuss and pouring a final round of cocktails.

She finally said yes to a limited line of apricot brandy, enjoying the feel of the snifter as she warmed it in her hands. Morgan suddenly appeared before her, a worried glint in her blue eyes. "Can I talk to you?"

Raven stilled. "Are you okay?"

"Yes, but I have to ask you something and you have to promise to tell me the truth. It's serious."

Raven tried to look cool, but her heart hammered against her chest and her palms sweat. Did Morgan know her secret somehow? Would she tell Dalton before Raven got the chance? "Sure," she said with fake calm. "What is it?"

"Not here. Let's go in the living room. Guys, give me and Raven a minute alone, please."

Dalton, Cal, and Tristan stilled. Then slowly turned. Cal was the one who finally spoke. Why did they look a touch panicked? "Umm, princess. Maybe you can talk to Raven tomorrow about girl stuff. I need some help putting out the pie."

"You know how to put out pie, Cal. I won't be long."

"But—"

Her stony glare halted the words on his lips. He finally nodded, looking a bit miserable, and turned back to the dishes. What the hell was going on?

She followed Morgan, noting the vaulted ceilings and the intricate marble sculpture in the foyer. Like the dining room, the formal living room boasted a French vintage-style decor, with lots of glass, antiques, and uncomfortable, stiff furniture she was afraid to sit on. My goodness, how did three boys manage to not trash the place?

The majority of the house was decorated with expert precision to show off expensive furniture, rich tapestries, and striking patterns all meant to impress and woo visitors. Yet the kitchen was pure warmth and simplicity, as if a different decorator had stepped in and claimed it as someone else's space. What type of woman had she been, really? Raven's father never would have felt comfortable in this stuffy living room, but would have sought out the kitchen and claimed his spot right at the marble kitchen island. Maybe even the deck.

Morgan picked up a thick, fabric-covered book that resembled a wedding album on crack. She sat down on the blinding-white claw-footed velvet couch and faced Raven. "Are you ready?"

Oh, God, what was in there? Proof about Raven's father? A biography of her? She couldn't stand it any longer. "Yes, please, Morgan, just show me."

Morgan dragged in a breath and slowly opened the book.

An array of fabrics fell from the pages. Raven blinked.

"I can't decide on the curtains for the master bedroom. They need to have an intimate, quiet feel, with a touch of femininity, but not so feminine Cal won't want to sleep there." Her voice was strained, and a frown creased her brow. "I've lost my touch, Raven. It's gone. I'm a high-priced, custom design artist and I can't make a decision about my own curtains. Cal refuses to listen to me and said the house and the wedding have begun to make me a bit bitchy. But he's not helping me at all. No one is. I need help."

Pure relief sagged her shoulders, softening the urge to strangle her new friend. "Are you kidding me right now? Just because I have a vagina, you assume I give a crap about curtains?"

Morgan sniffed in misery. "I know, but even Tristan won't deal with me any longer, and I swore I'd pick out the final choice myself." She tapped a finger against a sketch. "I'm going with a mix of silver and purple, matching various tones, but the crushed velvet curtains seem too heavy, and the sheers seem too feminine, and I don't like that color but I think it suits the room better, and I really, really need to make a decision."

Oh, hell no. She was not about to watch this strong, independent woman lose it over curtains. No. Way.

She grabbed the book, slammed it shut, and faced her. "Listen up. You will not fall apart on me and become one of those ridiculous women who gets so stressed about planning a wedding and building a house she collapses in tears, becomes Bridezilla, and loses her friends and fiancé. Not on my watch."

Morgan's eyes widened in shock. Good, she had her attention.

"When we get too caught up in our heads, we lose our gut instincts. When you design for other people, it's easier to follow your training, but this has become too important to you. You've lost your balls."

Morgan nodded. "Yes, yes, I have," she agreed. "I've lost my balls."

"Close your eyes. Think about each of the fabrics in the book and anything else that you've seen. Picture you and Cal in your bed, opening your eyes in the morning. The light is pouring through the windows, you're warm and happy, and you look at these damn curtains. What do you see?"

Morgan scrunched up her face. Seconds ticked by. Raven waited.

Her eyes flew open. "Hell and damnation. It's the sheers with an underlay of the storm-gray linen!"

"Umm, okay. Sounds perfect to me. Done."

Morgan threw herself at Raven, clasping her arms around her neck in a strangling hug. "Thank you! Oh, thank you, I think I know how to get my balls back!"

Raven laughed, hugging her in return, and felt something inside her shift, strengthen, connect. Dalton's family wasn't her enemy. No matter what had happened with his mother, he was a separate person, and he deserved to be given a chance without her chaining him to her past experience. Especially one seen from the view of a devastated young girl who had no concrete answers.

It was time to truly let go.

She pulled back from Morgan. Her chest loosened. Lightness flooded her body.

"I'm glad you came tonight," Morgan said with a smile. "Besides enjoying your company, I've never seen Dalton so happy." Raven caught the curiosity gleaming in her blue eyes, but her friend seemed to respect her privacy. "I hope I get to see more of you."

"I'm happy, too," she offered. Damned if a flush didn't heat her cheeks. "But we have some important things to talk about first."

Morgan nodded. "I know how that is. Cal and I had some obstacles to get through before we could really be together. I kept a secret from him for a while because I really wasn't ready to acknowledge our relationship could be anything more than a short affair."

Her heart galloped. "But you were able to work through it?" The hope in her voice must have given her away. Morgan reached over and patted her hand.

"Yes, we were. He needed some time, though. Facing the truth about love is harder than most think. It's raw and vulnerable and feels terrifying."

Raven sighed. "Yeah, it's sure not all roses and chocolates and heartfelt confessions, is it?"

Morgan laughed. "Nope. That stuff's not for us anyway. Way too easy. I'd rather have great sex, messy emotions, and real depth."

Raven laughed with her. "Damn, I like you."

"So do I," a familiar voice drawled from the doorway. Dalton strode over and swung Morgan up in his arms for a big hug, ignoring her squeal as her petite five-foot-three frame lifted easily in the air. "But it's dessert time, and I need some help."

"You just want me to do it," Morgan corrected.

"I can help. Want me to make the coffee?" Raven offered.

"No!" yelled Morgan and Dalton at the same time.

"Wimps, both of you," she muttered, rising from the stiff sofa.

They piled into the kitchen for banana cream pie and almond cookies, spending the rest of the evening in entertaining conversation. Finally Brady announced his departure. Cal stretched and gave a motion to Morgan. "We should probably go up now. You need your sleep."

Dalton groaned. "Real subtle, bro. And we both know you're not going up for sleep."

Morgan didn't even blush, just gave her fiancé a naughty wink.

"Good night, Raven. I hope we see more of you," Cal said.

"Thanks." She remembered his strange words at the bar, warning her about Dalton's heart. Almost as if he knew his brother was more vulnerable than anyone believed.

"Hey, Dalton, we still need to clean out Dad's stuff. I swear I'll kick your ass if you cancel on me again. This weekend. Okay?"

"Yeah, sure, absolutely."

"Good. I'll tell Tristan, too." Cal and Morgan headed up the circular staircase toward the left and disappeared.

Raven realized it was time for the big talk. "We should go. Do you want to come back to my house?"

He grinned and kissed her hard on the mouth. "Yes. But first, I want to show you the stars from my telescope. Come on." He tugged on her hand and they headed left down the hallway into the other half of the mansion. She passed about a dozen rooms and just kept walking.

"How many rooms do you have in this house?" she asked in disbelief.

"About forty, I think. Dad used it as a model house as the image of Pierce Brothers. My mom didn't like the highbrow decor, but she understood it was more of a business decision. Her domain was the kitchen and their master bedroom.

She liked things simpler, very different from my father."

Yes, she'd been right. Diane had claimed the kitchen as hers. Had Raven's father sat with her there, planning their escape? How had they met? How long had they been involved before they decided to run away together?

She tried to push the whirling thoughts out of her mind and concentrate on Dalton. He opened the door to his room and she tried hard not to gasp.

The masculine, almost rustic feel suited him. Navy-blue bedding covered a gorgeous hand-carved poster bed, and various woodworking pieces filled the space. Interesting treasures decorated the shelves and walls, from trophies and sports memorabilia to framed photos. She longed to have time to study every picture, learning more about his youth. Massive French doors opened up to a balcony, allowing an unmarred view of the night sky streaked with stars. The warm summer breeze blew in and cloaked them with the scent of wildflowers and pine. She walked outside, tilting her head up to take in the breathtaking view.

His hand slid into hers.

In that moment, she felt every road had led her here. Staring at the stars, hand in hand with a man she wanted to give her heart to. Had this been how her father felt? This loosening of breath and lightening of spirit as rightness poured into all the empty spaces and filled her up with meaning and purpose?

Was this real love?

And if so, would she have done anything to protect it, even at the expense of her family?

"Here, take a peek. Saturn is visible tonight."

She closed one eye and peered through the telescope. She located the constellation Scorpius and pinned down Antares. The red star was gorgeous close up.

"What are you viewing?"

"Antares. I love the reddish sheen through the scope. It's beautiful."

"Isn't it? Okay, so point west of Antares toward that flock of stars called—"

"The Crown of Scorpion."

"You are so turning me on right now."

"Slick, it doesn't take much."

His deep laughter cut through the night air. "Only with you. Saturn should be a golden light and easy to spot."

"I see it!" She let out a breath, enjoying the sheen of gold vibrating in the sky. She feasted on the vision, then motioned him over. "Come look."

They switched places and took turns studying the night sky, diving into astronomical talk she hadn't enjoyed since her father first taught her. Suddenly the air between them crackled to life, buzzing like an electrical charge that got hit by drops of water. She sucked in her breath, still overwhelmed by the connection that seemed to belt them both with its fierceness.

"You feel that?" he asked softly. He took her hand, raised it to his mouth, and kissed her palm. Bit gently. Placed her thumb between his lips and sucked hard, his tongue swirling around until her vision fogged and her body ached. "It's always there between us, ready to flare up. Like the universe is trying to tell us something."

She tried to protect her final barrier, flinging out the words in desperation. "Yeah, it wants us to fuck."

His eyes darkened with anger. He jerked her toward him, tangling his fingers in her hair. "It's more than that, and you know it. You don't get to lie about this. About us."

"What are we doing?" she asked softly. "What do you want?"

"You. I want you. I want to hear you say you're just as freaked out as I am because it's more than fucking. Isn't it?"

She fought back the tears and gave him the truth. "Yes. It is."

"Good."

His mouth slammed down on hers, demanding she give him more than the words. Demanding her body surrender to him completely. And she did, kissing him back, her fingers dragging off his clothes as they backed up toward the bed, desperate for each other. She pushed him down and climbed on top of him, her hands stroking his erection, loving the moans she pulled from his lips as he grew harder and longer under her fingers. Lowering down, she took him in her mouth, mad for the taste of him on her tongue. He fisted her hair and chanted her name as she sucked and licked, taking him deep until he cursed and grabbed her hard, flipping her back on the mattress and surging between her thighs.

She cried out. He cupped her face, stared into her eyes, and pressed his forehead to hers.

He moved.

The dance was graceful, shattering, pure. He loved her with his body, his eyes, his touch, taking her higher until she broke apart, held tight in his embrace by a promise to never let her go.

The energy swirled between them, growing stronger and fiercer, but he never took his gaze from hers, giving her the gift of his own release, his naked face twisting in ecstasy, and she drank in every expression with a greediness that shocked her.

Never had lovemaking been this personal, this intimate. Skin to skin, his cock deep within her, his mouth pressed to hers, they let go and joined together.

The drift back to earth was slow, like a mystical flight from another world. She lay in his arms, knowing her life had completely changed and her path was unknown.

"I think I love you," she whispered.

"I think I love you, too."

She smiled, blinking back the sting of tears. "I have to tell you something, Dalton. Something I've kept from you but don't want to hide anymore."

His arms tightened around her. He propped himself up on his elbow to look into her face. "You can tell me anything."

She took a deep breath. "There's something you don't know about me. About who I am. My father's name was Matthew Hawthorne."

He blinked. She watched a variety of expressions flicker over his face as the name jogged his memory. "Did I know your father? I know that name, why can't I—"

"My full name is Raven Bella Hawthorne. I was only nineteen when he died in a car crash."

Slowly, recognition seeped into his eyes. Heart pounding, she remained calm as he jerked back, shock slowly replacing the warm love she'd seen a few moments ago. "Wait a minute. The car crash. The name. Your father."

She swallowed and told the rest. "Yes. My father was with your mother when they died in the crash. They were running away together."

It took him a while to process. She waited, naked, in his bed, and hoped he'd let her explain. "Wait a minute. How long have you known about this?"

His voice was so cold, as if he were speaking with a stranger and not someone he'd just held like a precious gift. She pressed the sheet to her bare breasts and sat up. Oh, how she wanted to lie.

But she couldn't.

"I've known for the last year. Since the first time you came into my bar with your brothers."

Dalton got up from the bed. Refusing to look at her, he tugged his jeans on. She flung out words, desperate for him to understand. "Dalton, please listen to me. At first, I was in shock and angry when I found out who you were. I was going to tell you to never come back. For years I've been bitter and resentful over how my father died. I was young when I lost him, and I blamed your mother. I never knew what really happened and why he would've left."

"And you thought I had more information," he said tonelessly. "That's why you started finally talking to me. That's why you allowed me to do the work on the bar."

She nodded, miserable. "Yes, I'm not going to lie about that. You kept asking me out, and I thought I might be able to learn some crucial pieces to this puzzle that's haunted me for the last eight years."

He shook his head and laughed humorlessly. "And you think I know more about the accident than you? You don't think I've had my own shit storm to get through, knowing my mother was manipulated by your father to run off with him?"

"It wasn't like that," she said hotly. "This whole time, I thought your mother seduced him! But I think we're both terribly wrong, Dalton. This was more than a casual hookup or impulsive decision. I also know my father never would've left me for good. From what you've told me about your mother, it's the same way. I think there's much more to this story that we haven't figured out."

He rubbed his hands over his forehead, cursing viciously under his breath. "That would be convenient for you, wouldn't it? You'd feel better about lying to me and realizing your father broke up a marriage and a family."

"I'm not going to start trading insults about our parents," she said softly. "Aren't you tired of living your life blaming someone who won't ever be able to give you answers? I'm tired. Tired of the nightmares, and anger, and hate. Don't you realize you taught me there's so much more for us? We don't have to let our parents' past dictate our future. Yes, I started off wanting more information, but every day I spent with you, I fell deeper and deeper. Nothing between us was a lie, Dalton. I fell in love with you."

He just stared at her. She shifted under the sheets, almost wishing he'd be angry. Yelling would be so much better than this icy silence and calculating gaze as he assessed her. "Let me make sure I've got your story straight now," he said, his tone mocking. "You decide to do an undercover operation and spend time with me to gain knowledge about my mother. You try to gather information from my brothers and my family, using me and my interest in you as bait. Were you willing to sleep with me for it?"

She raised her chin, ignoring the cold, hard piece of ice lodged in her gut. He had every right to be angry and cruel. She owed him the truth with no excuses. "No, sleeping with you was never in the plan. You got the job for the bar because you asked for it and were the best. I decided the time we spent together could be useful."

"*Useful.* I like that word." His gaze flicked over her in disgust. "What were you going to do when you confirmed my mother was a lying, conniving bitch?"

She flinched. "At first, I wanted to restore my father's reputation. After the accident, your family ruined his name, spreading cruel rumors about him seducing and killing your mother. I was destroyed. I had no money or family name, like you did, and couldn't fight back. That's why I ran away all those years, to find myself and heal. I'd always wanted to get revenge by discovering the truth, proving my father was taken advantage of."

"But now you don't believe that."

"No, I don't. I think they were in love. I think there were other things between them we don't know about, but that neither of them wanted to hurt anyone."

"How generous of you to forgive them both. When did you decide your spy games were officially over? Last week? Tonight? A few moments ago?"

"The night of the break-in," she said quietly. "I realized there was much more between us, and I didn't want to sacrifice it for some strange sense of justified satisfaction. I wanted to get to know who you were, separate from your mother. And I did. Dalton, there were never any lies between us in bed, or with my emotions. I planned to tell you."

His jaw clenched, and he spoke from between gritted teeth. "You planned to tell me, huh? I lay beside you and told you everything about my mother and the accident. Stuff I never shared with anyone else, because I fucking trusted you. Why didn't you tell me that night, Raven?"

"I tried! I swear to God, I began talking, and then when I finished, I looked at you and you'd fallen asleep! So I promised myself I'd tell you the next morning, but you had to run out before we had a chance to talk."

"Convenient. At least you've gotten the answers you need, Raven. Is that your real name? Or is it Bella?"

"My father called me Bella, but I go by Raven."

"Good to know." His words were like jagged paper cuts against her bare skin. She tried not to jerk back from his cold mockery. "It's kind of funny that I played completely into your hands, isn't it? I pursued you. I originally asked for the job to restore your bar. I stayed late at closing and showed up at the gym. It really was my fault, you know. I had no idea this whole time you had another agenda." He began walking back and forth, tapping his finger to his mouth. "It makes sense now. The biting anger and sarcasm beneath your words. The way you looked at me sometimes with hatred. Studied my brothers and asked questions about my family. Convinced me to share secrets after sex. It was all for information gathering."

"No, it wasn't," she interrupted. "I wanted to know more about you and your family—for me. Because I was beginning to truly care about you, separate from our past. Don't you see we can move forward from this? We can even heal some of the rift between our families, and all these years of bitterness."

"Because you don't blame my mother anymore?"

"Yes. I don't know if we'll ever know what truly

happened, but I don't believe she was using my father."

"I'm glad you don't blame her anymore, Raven." He spun around and faced her. His next words came like slow, deliberate bullets, and tore through her. "But I do blame your father. My father thought he was a coldhearted, manipulative bastard who wanted my mother's money and saw an easy way to get it. And I do, too." His blue eyes blazed like fire, but it wasn't the warm kind that wrapped you in heat. No, this was the type that destroyed and broke, leaving nothing in its wake but devastation. "I think he was a liar, and I think you're just like him. You only care about yourself, and you're willing to hurt anyone else along the way to get what you want."

"You can't believe that." She forced back the tears, strengthening her voice. "You're angry and feel betrayed, and I understand. But I've never lied about my feelings for you. I know you feel the same way about me. You told me tonight."

"I was wrong. It was just fucking, after all. I look at you now and feel . . . nothing."

She shook her head. "Don't say that. Don't walk away from us."

"There was never an us, Raven, or Bella, or whoever you are. There was just pretty lies, and great sex, and a mystery that's now solved. Now I want you to get out of my house."

"Dalton—"

"Now."

He turned and walked out to the balcony, leaving her behind. Slowly, she rose from the bed and dressed, her movements numb. Heart shattering, she pushed through the raw pain and paused with her hand on the doorknob.

He needed time. With time, he'd calm down, they'd talk more, and they could fix this. He was in shock and needed some space to realize it was real between them.

Clutching that mantra to her heart, she left the room.

chapter twenty-four

The week passed in a fog.

He worked on the deck at the Sullivans'. He steered clear of the office and made sure to give constant excuses for why he wasn't at dinner or around Morgan and Cal's building site. He stayed away from My Place and ignored Raven's daily phone calls, refusing to listen to her voice mails. He buried himself early in his room with a bottle of Cal's whiskey and drank himself into a stupor. Then repeated the next day.

This was what he had feared. This was why he'd locked himself up so tight no woman before had been able to break him open. All those years he couldn't return a woman's affections, until now.

Maybe he was being punished. How many women had longed for him to return their feelings? Dozens? He'd wrapped himself in a bubble, and no one had ever busted in. Worse, he'd never felt like he was missing out on anything until Raven came into his life and made him . . . want.

Lies. All lies. From the moment they'd met till the last moment in his bed, when he said the words. Stupid. He'd been so stupid to think it could last, or be different. Sickness twisted inside him at the thought of her father haunting him even years later. The man had destroyed his family and killed his mother. If it weren't for him, she would've been safe at home that night. And Raven knew all along while she manipulated his emotions and made him fall for her. He couldn't stand the humiliation, and constantly analyzed each moment between them, picking apart the stories he'd shared with her and wondering if she'd been taking notes for the sole purpose of proving his mother was at fault.

He grew more and more haunted.

After a long, brutal day spent working until his body ached, his brothers finally confronted him, blocking his entry from the front porch. Tristan held a glass of wine, and Cal thrust a bottle of Raging Bitch in his hands. Normally, he'd sit back and let them help him sort through the mess, but it was still too raw. Telling his brothers would drag up the painful past. Hadn't they been through enough?

He tried to force a smile. "Thanks, dudes, but I gotta go up. Have some stuff to do."

"Sit, Dalton. We're worried about you."

"I can't—"

"Do you want me to bring Morgan out here for the inquisition, or do you want it to be just us? Because I know it's bad. Half of my whiskey stash is gone, and that shit has to be specially ordered."

Dalton smothered a curse and sat.

"Good choice," Tristan said, taking his place in the rocker to the right. "Now, I'm not a touchy-feely 'Kumbaya'-type guy, but lately you've been beyond miserable. Even scarier, you don't eat anymore. I haven't even seen Hershey wrappers around. What's going on?"

Cal remained silent. Dalton took a sip of beer. His breath strangled in his chest, and in that moment, he knew he needed his brothers.

"Raven's father was Matthew Hawthorne. The man who ran away with Mom."

Tristan jerked so hard, red wine sloshed over the rim of his glass and onto his pressed slacks. He didn't even notice. "You're fucking with me."

Dalton shook his head, rubbing his gritty eyes. "Wish I was. I just found out last week. The night she stayed for dinner."

Cal finally spoke up. "What did she say?"

Bitterness leaked through his words. "She was full of excuses. Said she's been haunted for years about her father and the way we talked about him back then. Said she realized who we were the first night in the bar, but she didn't say anything until she decided to use me to gain information."

"Wait. She what?" Tristan asked in shock. "You mean Raven was dating you to get information on Mom? What the hell!"

"What was her plan?" Cal asked quietly. "To confront us? Confront you? What did she expect to find?"

"She said at first she thought Mom was the one who manipulated her father, but now she thinks they were in love. She planned to confront us when she learned Mom was some type of seductress—such a bunch of crap. But then she decided she'd been wrong, and she doesn't believe Mom was at fault. I guess I told her shit along the way that she was filing in her head. I can't believe I didn't see this coming, or make any type of connection. Her father called her Bella—that's how she was listed in his obituary—so that probably threw me off. And to be honest, we were so shell-shocked we never really cared about who Matthew was leaving behind."

"Did she admit she slept with you to gather this information on Mom?" Cal asked gently.

His gut lurched. "No. But she was lying." He studied Cal's face, which reflected calm. "Why aren't you freaking out about this?"

Cal met his gaze head-on. "Because I knew."

His fingers gripped the beer bottle. Rage swept over him. "You knew she was lying and manipulating me and didn't say anything? Do you still hate me for what happened years ago and want some revenge?"

Cal cut his hand through the air. "Don't be stupid, it wasn't like that. When you started crushing on her so bad, and she kept treating you like she'd known you before, I got curious. So I Googled her. Figured out he was her father. I didn't want to tell you anything, because I was keeping watch, and you both seemed genuinely happy. I just got a feeling, Dalton, that she wasn't lying about how she felt. I planned on confronting her if she didn't tell you soon."

Dalton jumped up from the chair, glaring. "Are you fucking kidding me? How could you not tell me the woman I was hot for was the daughter of a man I despised? He killed Mom!"

"What were you thinking, Cal?" Tristan asked.

Cal remained steady, staring back with an innate calm. "Because I agree with Raven. I don't think this is about blame, or manipulation, or one of them seducing the other. I think they were truly in love and were trying to figure it out."

"But she left," Dalton said. "She took our baby teeth, remember? That proves she wasn't coming back."

"No, I thought that, too, but after this past year I changed my mind. I reconnected with you both, and it started me thinking about Mom again and what I knew about her. I think she took those teeth to keep us close with her, and I think she was coming back. Mom loved us too much. But she'd been miserable with Dad for so long, maybe when she met Raven's father, she found real love." He sighed and looked out into the dark, his voice sad. "Maybe I understand better because I now know what it's like to love someone so much."

"I can't believe it," Dalton muttered. His head throbbed. "You're defending her."

"No. What she did sucked, because it made you question if anything was real. But if she was like us, and obsessed with figuring out why her father left, don't you think you might have done the same?"

"No," Dalton said stubbornly. "I don't lie."

"What about when you decided not to tell me my fiancée was cheating on me? Instead, you kept the information to yourself and made this elaborate plan to prove it. That was a lie."

"I told you—I was young and stupid, I wasn't thinking."

Cal shrugged. "Maybe she got wrapped up in trying to defend her father's reputation. She was young when he died. Dad made sure he told everyone Hawthorne manipulated Mom, and gossip was fierce. Hell, stores wouldn't even sell his paintings anymore. We'd dragged his name through the mud. Must've stung."

His thoughts whirled, confused. "I don't understand why you kept this from me."

"Because I've never seen you so happy before," he said simply. "You changed. It was like you found a piece of yourself, and that's rare. I wanted her to tell you herself, in her own time, so you could both work it out."

Dalton backed up, shaking his head. "There's nothing to work out anymore. It's over. I can't trust her, and God help me, I don't feel like I can trust you, either. I'm going to bed."

He ignored his brother's calls and headed to his room, running from the ghosts of the present and the past.

Raven checked her phone. Nothing. It had been an entire week since their night together, and he refused to return any of her calls or texts. Panic was beginning to set in. She'd never imagined they wouldn't be able to work past their history, but now she realized her lies had damaged him on a deeper level. She'd broken his trust, and Raven wondered if he'd ever be able to give her another chance.

Sick at heart, she went through the motions serving drinks at the bar and keeping orders moving from the kitchen. Should she try to go to his house? Did he need more time? Her mind spun with possibilities. She'd thought about reaching out to Morgan or one of his brothers, but that felt cowardly. No, she needed to deal directly with Dalton, because he was the one she'd hurt.

Through spending time with him the past weeks, Raven had reached her own conclusions about their parents. But Dalton never had the chance. Maybe if she gave him an opportunity to talk about her father, he'd understand more. She needed to convince him the only reason she'd slept with him was her body's wracking demand and need for him to complete her.

The night was long. Al stayed while she locked up, refusing to budge, and finally she got in her Jeep and drove home.

Dalton's truck was parked in her driveway.

Swallowing down the raw urgency to reach him, she walked deliberately slowly, trying to clear her mind. *Please, God, let him be here to talk*. He sat on the steps, jean-clad legs stretched out in front of him, resting his arms on his knees. His hair caught the moonlight, turning to molten gold, and his face remained carved from stone when he finally looked at her.

Her heart sank.

"I want to talk."

She nodded, leading him inside. Heart pounding, she waited for him to accuse or fling angry insults, but he stood in front of the wall, staring at the paintings she'd put up. "Are these your father's?" he asked tightly.

"Yes. I had them covered up for a long time. But I think we've all been in the dark for too long."

"Poetic. Maybe if I'd seen these before, I would've known. Or asked questions."

"Maybe. I don't think it would have changed what happened between us, though. I put them up that morning, you know. I always planned to tell you."

He remained silent, studying the paintings. Then he turned his back on them and sat down on the couch.

Nerves attacked. "Do you want coffee?" she asked politely.

"No, thanks."

She sat in the opposite chair. The distance between them stretched as long and deep as the Grand Canyon, and there was a terrifying silence she didn't know how to breach. "Did you get my voice mails?"

"Yeah. I listened to them all today. When you were making excuses to not get involved with me, you said you wanted to get married. Was that a lie, too?"

"No. I may have emphasized it a bit more, because I needed some defenses against you. It was a way for me to make sure you kept your distance. But I do want long term. I've done my playing around and intended to look for a man who'd like to settle down. A man interested in marriage and a family."

He didn't answer for a while, seeming to process her statement. Vulnerability hit her. It was hard sharing things with a man who no longer acted like he cared about her. She kept telling herself the man she loved was still there, he was just buried underneath a mess of emotions and hurt right now.

"You said your tattoo was a symbol of justice. Care to elaborate now that all our skeletons are out?"

She refused to wince. Her fingers came up unconsciously to stroke the familiar lines. "I thought your mother had ruined my father. Your family forced me to question his love and loyalty, and it was easier to hate. I got the tat so I'd never forget the day I lost him. I wanted to be reminded that one day, justice would finally be served."

"Congratulations. How does it feel to scratch something off your bucket list?"

"I can't apologize for the girl I was and how I felt, Dalton. I won't even try. I can only say I see things more clearly now, and we owe it to ourselves to forgive. That's the real justice I was looking for all along."

He seemed to ponder her words, taking his time before asking another question. "What made you change your mind about my mother?"

She took a deep breath and clasped her hands in her lap. "The stories you told me. The way you loved her. The way she loved you. They didn't add up to the woman I'd imagined. Then my aunt Penny mentioned something to me recently. She said Papa told her about a woman he'd fallen in love with, but who needed time to sort things out. We both agreed it sounded like a married woman. I think it was your mom."

He flinched but kept talking. "You believe they were coming back?"

"I do. All this time, I was so angry and confused. But along the way, I'd forgotten how close I was with my father. What purpose would there be to fleeing to Paris on a weeknight, leaving families they loved behind? My aunt kept telling me the same thing, but I wasn't ready to accept it. Now I realize it doesn't make sense."

"People rarely do," he muttered. "Especially when sex is involved, which is too often mistaken for love."

She hugged her body tight against the sudden chill. "Love would've brought them back."

"Love made them leave and killed them both. You're being a romantic fool because it's easier to believe. You're still denying the idea of your father going after my family's money?"

"Papa wasn't interested in money—not that way. He lived for his art and everyday pleasures. We were poor, but it never felt like it. We were happy."

"Maybe that was a mirage, too."

"No. Just like I don't believe your mother hated your father so badly she decided to cut her sons loose. She loved you."

"You know nothing about my mother," he whipped out.

She fell silent, caught between words that couldn't reach him and the voice inside begging her to touch him and bring him back.

"Cal told me he knew who you were."

She blinked in surprise. "He knew about me?"

"He didn't tell me, though."

"Why?"

His face revealed a flicker of pain. Her heart swelled with the urge to reach for him, comfort him, but she kept still. "Guess he's come to the conclusion you have—that our parents fell in love and were coming back. He told me I looked so happy with you, he wanted you to tell me the truth yourself."

She choked back a sob. "Dalton, I never wanted

to hurt you. Never. This connection between us has always been there, and I've been fighting it from the very first day. But I don't want to any longer. I realize you're the man I was meant for, even though it's been a short time. There's an emptiness in my core that's filled when I'm around you. I've traveled the world and met a thousand people to try to slake that emptiness, but it all went away when I first saw you."

His jaw tightened. "I did, too. But what was real and what was a sick way to get closer to the memory of your father?"

She jerked back. "It wasn't like that!"

"Maybe. Maybe not."

The rage was back, shaking his body like a storm wind clutching a weak tree branch. Her body hurt, and she moved toward him, desperate to take away the pain and convince him of the truth. She knelt in front of him, her hands resting on his knees. "This is about you and me," she said. "This is about how you make me feel when you take me in your arms and make me yours."

"Then prove it." His eyes glittered like water droplets hitting stone, brilliant under the glare of the sun. "Prove it to me, Raven."

His challenge caused a wave of longing to crash through her, and there was nothing left to do but reach for him.

Still on her knees, she pulled his head toward

hers and kissed him, sinking her tongue deep into his mouth, drunk on the taste of chocolate and a touch of whiskey, his dark, male fragrance rising up to surround her. He dragged her onto his lap and she straddled him, pressing her breasts against his muscled chest. He yanked her tank top down with her bra and sucked on her breasts, his teeth rough, his tongue hot. She arched into the sting, opening his belt and freeing his erection, her hands squeezing and stroking until he groaned and jerked under her touch. He raised her up just enough to tug her jeans and underwear off, splaying her open to his plunging fingers. She gritted her teeth against the impending orgasm, needing him to be inside her, and scraped her nails down his chest, half-crazed.

"Take what you want," he commanded.

With an animal-like cry, she grasped his cock and pushed him inside her dripping entrance, then slammed down hard.

"Dalton!" She shuddered at the throbbing fullness of him; the feeling of rightness as they connected on the deepest level, and tears burned her eyes as she fought for more of him. He growled and tugged her head back hard, his lips fastened to the delicate line of her throat.

"Take what you want," he said again, his skin hot, his fingers brutal, his voice a primitive growl in her ear. "Now."

She moved, rising up as high as she could on her knees, then lowering so he was seated fully within her, riding him at a frantic pace that was more animal than human. She gave him everything she could, refusing to hold back, her hips working wildly to have more, always more of him.

"Now," he grated out, his teeth sinking in where her neck met her shoulder. "Now!"

She screamed and shattered around him, tears pouring down her face. He surrendered to his own release, still clutching her so hard Raven knew she'd wear his marks tomorrow. They rode out their climaxes until the last shudder wracked them, falling back together onto the couch.

Her head lolled on his shoulder. His hands stroked her back. She relaxed in the beautiful space between them, her heart so full she had an idea how the Grinch felt that Christmas day when his heart grew three sizes. It was all going to be okay.

"That was amazing," he said.

She smiled and pressed a kiss to his shoulder. "It certainly was."

"Thanks." He lifted her off his lap and placed her down to his right. Standing up, he stretched, zipped his jeans, and regarded her. "I better go. Maybe I'll see you around."

Ice slivered down her spine. "What?"

"Well, this isn't going to work on a regular

basis." He motioned between them with a humorless smile. "But the sex is incredible. I think I was clear from the beginning I'm not the marrying sort. Now that your secrets are out, we can be more honest with one another."

Her breath caught in her chest, and she fought to keep air in her lungs. A terrible premonition crawled into her brain, but she refused to believe it could be true. He wouldn't do that to her. Wouldn't hurt her so cruelly, not after what they'd just shared.

"Dalton, what are you trying to do? Punish me? Push me away? I'm not running anymore, and I've told you everything. Please don't let this destroy what we can have together."

His laugh was ice-cold. "There's nothing left to destroy, Raven. It was bound to end anyway; at least we can deal with it before we pretend we have something more than sex."

She stood up, shaking with fear and raw anger. "That was more than just sex! I gave you everything I had. I love you!"

She looked into his beloved face, searching for a glimpse of the tender, gentle, mischievous man who had so much love to give. All she saw staring back at her was a stranger.

"But I don't love you," he stated calmly.

"You said you did the other night," she whispered, hating the brokenness to her voice. Her insides were bleeding, raw and open wounds that tore her to pieces. "Don't do this to me. To us. You'll regret it, Dalton, we both will."

He stepped back, jerking his gaze from hers. "There's nothing to regret. You played your game, we enjoyed each other for a while, and now it's time to move on. I'm not punishing you, Raven. I'm just . . . leaving."

Then he did exactly what he promised.

He left.

Raven sank to the floor, leaning her face against her raised knees, and cried for the second greatest loss of her life.

chapter twenty-five

$\rightarrow\!\!\!\!\diamond\!\!\!\!\leftarrow$

It was done.

Dalton knew he wouldn't be able to continue a relationship with a woman who lied. A woman whose father had a direct responsibility for not only killing his mother, but manipulating her to leave. Both were unforgivable. He'd needed to hurt Raven so irrevocably, there'd be no coming back.

He drove back home, feeling curiously empty. Her scent drifted from his skin, the spicy musk of sandalwood. Her taste lingered on his tongue. His chest tingled from the scratch of her nails.

He drank the rest of the whiskey with the desperate intention of forgetting. Sickness formed inside him, but he wasn't sure if it was the result of his actions or of realizing he'd never hold her again. Finally he passed out, fully dressed on his bed, hand still clutching the bottle.

But he dreamed.

The familiar nightmare took hold, but this time it was different.

It began the same. His mother chased him playfully down the road, her yellow dress flapping in the breeze. Suddenly she stopped, gazing at the strange car parked before her. The man got out and held out his hand. She took it. Climbed into the car. And drove off.

Dalton chased her down the road, calling her name, and the car burst into flames. Screaming and crying, her familiar face pressed against the window amid the fire. Dalton waited for her to mouth the words in her final moments, caught halfway to wakefulness, forced to watch the last, devastating scene.

Suddenly, his mother faded away.

Raven was in the car.

Her beautiful, inky hair surrounded her face in messy waves. Those huge dark eyes begged him from behind the barrier of the glass, her palms pressed to the window in one last plea.

I'm sorry . . .

The car exploded.

Dalton woke up, gut twisted with nausea.

He ran to the bathroom, vomited violently, then crawled back into bed.

He didn't go back to sleep.

The nightmare came to Raven that night.

This time, when the car exploded and she tried to run, the woman's face was no longer there with her father, trapping him in a fiery death.

This time, Dalton blocked her from rescuing her father, a cold, distant look on his face while he watched him burn. Her screams ripped from her throat, echoing in the air, but he never turned or acknowledged her presence.

Raven woke up drenched in sweat, her cheeks wet.

She didn't go back to sleep.

chapter twenty-six

$$\Longrightarrow \diamond \Longleftarrow$$

Dalton turned off the band saw and examined the piece of wood. The grain had a deep color that would go well with Morgan's choice of cabinetry. He made some adjustments, sinking into the familiar rhythm of work, the scent of sawdust thick in the air, soothing his senses.

His workshop seemed the only place he felt at peace lately. Between the repeated nightmares wrecking his sleep and the constant memories of Raven during the day, he was poised on the edge of some strange breakdown. Two weeks had passed. He'd kept away from the bar, distanced himself from his family, and tried to bear down and deal with the fallout.

Problem was, he didn't seem able to move on. He was stuck, still unable to pry her from his mind and his heart. A wrenching emptiness sat in his gut, messing with his appetite. He got through the day, but nothing held a glimmer of happiness or satisfaction any longer. It was as if a piece of himself was now missing—a piece he'd never known existed before Raven.

He peeled off his glasses and gloves. Swigging some water, he wiped his forehead and went to change the song on his iPhone when a text came in. His breath caught, then held as he waited to see who it was from.

Busy tonight? Thinking of grabbing dinner— wanna join me?

His shoulders slumped. Charlie. After he'd finished the Sullivans' deck, they'd spoken a few times, but they hadn't gotten any further since he'd broken up with Raven. He stared at the phone for a while. Maybe it was time to force the issue. Get past these feelings that had no place in his life and move on with another woman. He'd never had trouble before. He'd been out of the game too long, and Charlie intrigued him. They had a more friendly vibe, but it wouldn't take much to cross over.

He quickly texted back. **Sure. Seven? Where?** The phone shook. **Great. My Place?**

He stilled. Pain clawed at his gut, but he fought it back, pissed off and frustrated. Morgan and Sydney still went there for drinks and poker night. Cal and Tristan never mentioned it, but he was sure they frequented the bar also. He couldn't avoid Raven forever. If he showed up with another woman, it might be the catalyst needed to prove he could move on, and confirm to her it was over.

Even though he'd driven that point home their last time together.

The memory of her ravaged face hit him like a sucker punch. The raw pain in her eyes as she realized he was walking away, treating her like some cheap whore. He regretted the cruelty of his actions, yet at the same time, Dalton had been convinced it was the best way to break it off. Brutal, yes. But final.

He tapped out his answer. **Ok.**

A smiley face popped up.

He kept himself busy all day, stopping only at the last minute to shower and change. When he pulled into the parking lot, he almost decided to turn around. Sheer stubbornness pushed him forward on legs that seemed a bit shaky.

He opened the saloon doors and stepped inside. The crowd had been steadily growing since the refurbishment of the bar and the initiation of poker night, so it was packed. The article in *Good Food & Fine Spirits* would hit next month, and he anticipated even more growth. His gaze went immediately to the bar, but Raven wasn't there. Swallowing back the lump in his throat, he caught sight of Charlie in one of the booths. She waved him over.

He slid in opposite her and forced a smile. "Hey. Good to see you."

"You too. I figured I wouldn't bug you till the deck was finished. It looks amazing, by the way. My aunt and uncle are really happy."

Pleasure cut through him. Knowing his work was enjoyed and appreciated always reminded him he was lucky to have found his calling. Glancing again at the bar, he admired the gorgeous lines and polished bronze. Remembered how she'd brought him lunch and they'd talked while he worked. He couldn't look at the poker tables, because all he thought about was their first kiss by the shed, under the stars.

"Dalton? You okay?"

"Sorry. Had a long day. You look great."

"Thanks."

She did look great. Her looks were all natural, from the streaky straight strands of hair that fell to her shoulders to her wide hazel eyes. Her lips were pale pink and perfectly formed. She wore a cropped purple top with ANGEL scrolled across her breasts, and ragged denim shorts that seemed extra short. On another woman, he'd say she was trying too hard, but there was something down-to-earth about Charlie he immediately liked. As she chattered animatedly, he began to relax and enjoy her conversation, realizing she seemed to know a lot about architecture and photography, along with renovating houses.

Amanda stopped by their table. "Hey, Dalton. How are you?"

Her gaze was full of curiosity but not hate. Had Raven told her what happened? Or did he not mean as much as he'd originally thought, so she hadn't even mentioned him to her staff? "Good. How about you? Al?"

"Same. We're getting busier, though. Must be your work on the bar."

Charlie swung her head around to study the bar. "I didn't know you renovated the bar! My God, it's an antique. I'm drooling."

Amanda looked at Charlie with a reserved expression. Her voice was clipped and not her usual friendly tone. "What can I get you?"

"Sweet potato fries and a veggie wrap, please," Charlie said. "Is Raven making those key lime martinis?"

"Yep."

"One of those, please."

Amanda turned to him. His stomach flipped, and he forced the words out. "Umm, just a beer with some chips and salsa."

"Raging Bitch, right?"

He winced. "Yeah."

"Got it."

She turned and walked away.

"So you know Raven? You did the matching stools for the bar, also?"

"Yeah."

"Nice. Her cocktails are a work of art."

He cleared his throat. "Yeah. So have you found a place yet?"

"I have. Renting a studio close to the harbor. It's a bit pricey but worth it. I can walk everywhere and get to know the residents. I think it's key to building a reputation in a community. Word of mouth is the best way to gain referrals."

"I agree."

"I also have an interview set up with Pierce Brothers next week, along with one for Stanton Builders."

"Stanton doesn't like their employees working on the side. If you like rehab, you'll want to be able to pick up jobs you're passionate about. Just a heads-up."

"Good to know."

Amanda came back with their drinks and food. A loud shout echoed from the bar, then a round of enthusiastic clapping. He froze, then slowly turned.

She was there.

Leaning over the bar, elbows propped up, she delivered a stinging rejection to the guy trying to hit on her. The men surrounding her went wild, and in her usual move, she offered him a shot of whiskey for having the guts to try to pick her up.

Dalton stared greedily, devouring her whole with his eyes. Her hair was clipped back—she must be serving tonight. The black tank emphasized the small curves of her breasts, and her jeans fell under her hips an inch lower than usual. Had she lost weight? She was smiling, but there were lines etched around her eyes, as if she hadn't slept in a while. The diamond nose ring caught the light as she turned her head. Her tat flashed past his vision—the droplets of blood from the sword reminding him of how his tongue would trace each individual dot, as if his kisses could ease the pain it symbolized. Her fingers flew in an elegant dance he knew so well as she poured and mixed and joked with her customers. The earthy sensuality was so much a part of her, she didn't notice the lustful, longing glances from every man seated at her bar.

But he did.

God, what was he doing here? This wasn't going to help him. Seeing her again just brought it all back, until he had to fight down his instinct to cross the room and go to her. Tell her it was a mistake. That he wanted her back.

But it was too late.

"You look like you got whacked in the head with a blunt object," Charlie interrupted. "Are you all right?"

Numbing loss crashed through him. "Yes. Sorry. Tell me about your new place."

She chattered through dinner. He listened with half an ear. Snuck glances at the bar. Raven never saw him, usually keeping her attention focused on the bar and letting her servers take care of the booths. By the time he paid the check, the emotional hurricane inside him had risen to a fury, confusing his brain.

Why was he being punished for falling in love with a woman who lied and betrayed him?

They walked to the door, but Dalton paused, his gaze locked on the woman behind the bar, who still held his heart.

She turned. Saw him. Stilled.

The connection surged, pumping through the air and distance to squeeze in a merciless vise. He lost his breath, and in moments he was hard and aching and empty. Shock and hunger swirled in her soot-colored eyes. Her fingers curled into fists. Her mouth made a tiny O.

He looked at her, digested the aching pain on her face, in her eyes. The room fell away, and it was only them, in a final, heartbreaking moment.

Then Dalton turned his back and pulled Charlie outside. Dragging in a breath, he fought for composure, trying to focus on his current companion. Suddenly Charlie lifted herself up on tiptoes and jabbed a finger hard in his chest. "Listen, dude, I don't like game playing. It's obvious you and Raven have something, and I don't appreciate being paraded around in an effort to piss her off or get her jealous."

He shook his head, trying to clear it. "We broke up."

"You still want her, she still wants you. Just leave me out of a love triangle—it's icky. Plus, I deserve a hell of a lot more than being used."

His eyes widened. The good-natured, sweet woman had turned into a tigress. Temper looked good on her, giving her a bit of an edge he hadn't seen before.

"I'm sorry," he said. Dalton dragged his palms over his face and told her the truth. "I'm a fucking wreck lately. I didn't mean to use you like that. I genuinely wanted to see you as a friend."

She crossed her arms in front of her chest and glared. But her voice softened a tad. "Okay. Are you trying to get back together with her?"

"Yes. No. I don't know. I think I made a mistake, but I'm confused."

"Love always makes us confused." Her face took on a faraway look of longing. She sighed, shaking her head. "Can you fix it?"

"I don't know."

"I've never been in love, so I'm not one to give advice. But I'd say if you know she's the one, do anything possible to fix it."

"This is more complicated."

She shot him a grin. "Isn't it always?" He managed to smile back. "See ya. And next time, just warn me if you have an ex-girlfriend at the place I suggest to eat. You're hot, but I'm just not that into you."

Dalton laughed. "That's the nicest thing anyone's ever said to me."

She winked. "Later."

He watched her walk away, in her too-short shorts and crop top, wondering at the hidden layers beneath. It would be nice to be friends with Charlie. There was no mess, or heartbreak, or deep emotion.

There was only one woman who had the power to touch his soul.

The one he'd crushed and sent away.

Raven smiled, poured drinks, and slowly died inside.

He'd brought another woman into her bar. Deliberately.

The gaping wound that had just begun to scab broke open and bled freely. The pain was excruciating, pounding in her bones and stomach and heart. She swore she'd never do this again. Love was too agonizing and ended badly too many times.

Dalton had been right all along.

She double-checked on all her customers, told Al she needed a quick break, and headed out the back. Gulping in deep breaths, she put her hands on her knees and let the hurt wash through her.

Two weeks. Not a word since that agonizing night when he'd walked out after making love to her, making her feel cheap. Somehow she still realized his intention to hurt her came from a twisted place inside he hadn't been able to deal with. The man who'd stolen her heart had turned to cruelty like a wolf caught in a trap, ready to gnaw off his own leg to escape.

But his reasons didn't make it any easier to accept. There'd been many roads to choose from, but Dalton had chosen to turn away from the precious seed beginning to grow between them. No amount of force or begging or even sex changed the result of a person's decision.

But why had he come back? Why throw another woman in her face? Was he still so enraged he needed to strike out? Prove a point? Was there nothing left of them he wanted to remember that was good?

Raven stood up, wiping the last tear from her cheek. She couldn't do this to herself any longer.

She'd been holding on to a false hope that with more time, he'd come see her. Tonight proved there was nothing left between them.

She owed it to herself to truly move on. Seeing Morgan and Dalton's brothers was hard, but they were kind to her, and she'd forged a friendship with Morgan and Sydney that was important. She wouldn't let him take that from her, too.

Reaching down for inner strength, she said a silent good-bye to the man she loved, knowing they both had to choose each other or there could never be a chance for either of them.

She wasn't going to be a martyr any longer. If he wanted to go back to his usual ways of seducing women, he could do it someplace else, not in her safe haven. She had a right to peace here, at least, until she healed.

Raven went back inside with a new determination.

chapter twenty-seven

The door banged open.

Dalton blinked and burrowed deeper under the covers. "Get out," he mumbled, smashing his face into the pillow.

"Fuck, man. It smells in here."

The clatter of a bottle hit his ears. Shuffling feet echoed. What time was it? Why was someone here in the middle of the night? He lifted his head a fraction, squinting, then retreated from the piercing sunlight streaming through his balcony doors. Hard hands shook him.

"Dalton, get up." Cal stood over him on the right, Tristan on the left. "We've left you alone for two days, but now you're freaking us out."

His mouth felt like a dirty cotton swab. His head pounded. "Fuck you. How'd you get in my room?"

"The skeleton key over the door. Ah, shit, he went through two bottles of your whiskey, Cal."

"I'm gonna kick his ass when he's better, I swear."

Dalton ignored them both, trying to remember what had happened. He'd gone to bed and drank a lot. Stumbled around the balcony. Had he cried looking at the stars? Why?

Raven.

The image of her face hit him, and the bed whirled. She was gone. He'd fucked it all up, like he did everything in his life, and he needed to stay in bed.

"Leave me alone." His voice was barely a whisper. "Just go away."

Cal sighed. "Gonna have to do this the hard way; he's in bad shape."

"Like the old days, right?"

"Yep, I'll get his arms, you do the legs."

"What the—are you nuts?" The covers were whipped off him and he was dragged to the side of the bed. "Get off me!"

"Shit, he's naked. Why does he always have to sleep naked? I'm not touching his balls."

"Shut up and get his feet."

Dalton tried to twist away from them, but their grips were steel. He had a flashback to when he was younger and got drunk at one of his friends' parties. His brothers had found him in bad shape, dragged him upstairs to hide him from Mom, and stuck him in a cold shower while he bellowed and threatened them.

Like now.

He heard the hiss of water hitting tile, and he cursed viciously, trying to slap Cal away. "I'll kill you both! You have no right to come in my room, so get the—agh, fuck!"

The icy spray hit him straight in the chest, and he howled. They kept him in there, forcing him to wash the stink of alcohol and heartbreak from his skin. When he was finally clean, they shoved a towel at him and marched out of the bathroom to wait.

More clearheaded, he took off after them in self-righteous fury. "I'm not a kid any longer, assholes. If I choose to sleep off a hangover in my room, you have no right to come in here."

"We do if it's been two full days. You haven't been to work. You don't answer your phone. Morgan's knocked plenty of times, and she got frantic. What if you had done something to yourself in here?" Cal shouted.

"I told you I was sick! I think I got the flu from Sydney."

"Bullshit," Tristan called out. "I've seen downward spirals before, but this one's epic. You broke up with Raven, realized you love her, and don't know how to handle it."

The anger drained away, leaving him empty again. "Doesn't matter anymore. It's over."

He walked out to the balcony. Looked up. The horizon shone a happy, bright blue, with fat, fluffy clouds floating past in a graceful dance of earth and sky. Bees hummed. The sun warmed his skin. And inside, his heart cried out for the woman who was his other half, even though he'd pushed her away in self-righteous pride and anger.

Tristan and Cal followed him out and flanked him. He pushed back his wet hair, and they all stared together at the view in silence.

"It does matter, Dalton. We tried to give you space, but now it's time to deal. Do you want Raven back?"

Yes. Somehow, over the past two days of trying to forget, he'd realized his heart wasn't as coldly clinical as his brain. He missed her. Needed her. The raw emotion in her inky eyes when she'd spotted him with Charlie told him the truth. She'd never wanted to hurt him. She wouldn't be able to fake such need and grief and pain, all nakedly revealed when their gazes locked. And sometime last night, he'd come to the only conclusion left.

He needed to make things right between them, because he couldn't let her go.

"Yes."

"You love her, don't you?" Cal asked. Dalton couldn't speak, so he just gave a ragged nod. "Why don't you try to talk to her?"

Dalton dropped his face into his hands. "Because I already did." He dumped out the whole story, including meeting Charlie at the bar. "Too much has happened now. I was so angry and sick at the idea she had played me. I wanted to hurt her like she did me. How screwed up am I?"

Tristan sighed. "You just made mistakes, like Raven did. Problem is you're so hotheaded, you do things without thinking them through sometimes."

"I hurt people."

Cal squeezed his shoulder. "We all do. I walked out on Morgan when she needed me the most. But she forgave me."

"I did something horrible to Sydney," Tristan finally said. "I never said I was sorry, either. It still haunts me."

"We fuck up. We're men. It's what we do about it afterward to try to make it right that counts. To try not to hurt the people we love again. Remember what Mom used to say?"

"'Forgiveness is so much stronger than hate,'" Dalton said slowly.

"Have you really forgiven her, Dalton?"

He thought about Raven. The way she'd confessed the truth with a raised chin and determination in her face. The way she'd loved him, and held him, and squeezed him into her body like she never wanted to let him go. She'd made mistakes, too, but had she truly lied about the way she felt about him? The agony on her face would haunt him forever. Didn't you have to love someone to allow them to hurt you that deeply?

The answer came up from within the deep, dark place inside. "Yes. I really have forgiven Raven."

"No. Not Raven. That's not where the real problem lies."

"What are you talking about?"

Cal gazed at him with worried, gentle eyes. "I'm asking if you can forgive Mom. For leaving you. For dying."

He flinched. The words slapped and bruised. He tried to bury it, but there was too much that had come to the surface.

Cal continued. "You were the youngest, and I think you were hit the hardest. Tristan and I were better established with who we were and what we wanted to do. You were still figuring things out. But I swear, you were her favorite. Sometimes I'd watch you together while you talked, and this peace would come over you, as if she was the only one who was able to reach you. I saw that again when you were with Raven."

Tristan's voice came from afar. "Cal's right. It took me a while to accept what happened with the accident, but I got there. Especially this past year. I feel like we found each other again."

"Raven forgave her father, and that's why she's able to really love you. You won't ever be free until you do the same."

Dalton stared at his brothers. The realization pierced through him like a sword, striking deep and true. He was right. It had been Mom all along. If he believed Raven, he'd have faith Mom had planned on coming back and would never have left him behind. Wasn't it time to allow that possibility to heal him? Hadn't he carried the secret guilt of anger and pain at her betrayal for way too long?

His brothers turned from the balcony. "Think about it. Come down for breakfast, please. Morgan wants to see you."

He nodded. "Thanks."

Tristan patted him on the shoulder, and his brothers left him to his own thoughts, their words still echoing in the air.

Raven launched herself at the bag. Her foot connected with a satisfying thump, and she spun into a round of tight jabs with a solid left hook. Sweat pooled in her eyes, and her heart galloped in her chest. She waited for Xavier's signal to stop, but his voice was a whiplash.

"Did I tell you to stop? Give me another round!" he demanded. Motherfucker.

She gathered up her last shreds of energy, pumping out all that pent-up anger from inside, and threw herself back at the bag. Over and over she punched, until her fists were sore and her legs were shaking and she didn't think she could stand for another moment.

"Time."

She stumbled toward her water bottle, drinking half of it in one gulp and pouring the rest over her head. His white teeth flashed at her in smug satisfaction. "I don't think this relationship between us is working for me anymore."

He chuckled. "Tough shit. You're my best student and I won't let you walk. That was intense. Got yourself some demons there, girl?"

She kept her silence and drank some more.

Xavier didn't seem to respect her space or her silence. "It's Dalton, right? Brady's friend? Unless you were picturing another cracked-up burglar? What happened with that guy, anyway? Is he locked up?"

"He got two years because of the gun."

"Good. Bastards don't seem to do time anymore unless they hurt or kill someone. You still spooked?"

She shook her head and wiped her mouth. "Not anymore. I have a brand-spanking-new alarm system, cameras, and two hot buttons that go to a central station. I feel much more secure."

"Excellent. You and Dalton broke up for good?"

This time she barely winced. Practice really did make perfect. "Yeah."

"I'm sorry, Raven." His face reflected a seriousness he rarely showed her unless he was training. "Want me to kick his ass? Take away his gym membership? Anything?"

She laughed. "No, I'm good. After a session with you, I'm so damn tired I pass out with barely a nightmare."

"We're opening up a new training team. Sure you're not interested? You have more talent than I've ever seen."

"For *American Ninja Warrior*? God, no. But thanks for the compliment."

"Last one you're gonna get for a while. I gotta keep you hungry. And a bit mean."

She grabbed her workout bag and shook her head. "And that is exactly why I can't handle the *Ninja* thing. It's too hard-core for me."

"See ya later, chickie."

She blew air kisses at him, ignoring the scattering of jealous looks she got from the girls watching her trainer. He reminded her of Dalton. The moment he walked in the room, he oozed charm and muscles, spinning a web no woman could resist.

She jumped in her Jeep and headed back

toward her house. It was poker night, so she'd get to hang out with Morgan and Sydney. They were getting so good, Raven suggested they open it up to mixed groups, since a crapload of men were dying to get into a game. She couldn't wait to see how much money Morgan swiped from them with her incredible poker face and sweet Southern charm. She swung into her driveway, cut the engine, and froze.

God, please, no.

Dalton stood on her front porch.

Panic reared. She sat in the Jeep, not wanting to get out. Her heart wept. Why was he torturing her? Drained from the energy of the workout and plain old sadness, she forced herself out of the car and walked toward him.

"I don't want you here," she said.

He held his hands out, palms up in a gesture of surrender. "I know. I don't blame you. I thought about coming to the bar, but I wanted to talk to you in private."

Fragments of white-hot anger whipped through her. "You didn't seem to care when you brought that girl into My Place," she tore out. "You wanted to make a point? Fine. You did. But it's still my damn bar, and I don't want you there any longer. Stay away from me."

His face looked ravaged. A mixture of misery and grief shone from his ocean-blue eyes. "I'm so sorry about that, Raven. You have no idea how sorry I am. I've been in a bad place these past few weeks. There's no excuse for what I did, except that I was a fucking asshole, and really mixed up. I convinced myself you manipulated and lied like your father. I've been stuck in the past, just like you accused me of, and all I wanted to do was strike out and hurt you like I was hurt."

"You did well," she said softly. "When you walked away from me that night, saying all we had was sex, I lost a piece of myself. Why? Do you hate me so much?"

His eyes shone with wetness. A muscle worked in his jaw. "No. I don't hate you. I love you. When you told me this whole thing was a setup, I panicked. I figured out a lot about myself these past weeks. I've been carrying around a bunch of crap that has no place in the present or my future. And that girl? She's a casual friend who means nothing. I was using her to convince myself I didn't love you."

She shook her head in disbelief. "Do you hear yourself, Dalton? Games. Lies. Fear. I'm tired of it, and I can't have it in my life anymore."

"I'm begging you for another chance."

She fell silent. The breeze whispered through the trees, and birds sang. She realized this was what she had wanted so badly since the night he'd left. But now, it had changed. Too many words and deeds. Too much hurt. The trust had been broken between them, and Raven didn't think they'd ever be able to recover.

"It's too late, Dalton." She raised her head and stared into his beloved eyes. His golden hair fell against his cheeks, emphasizing his square jaw, full lips, and scruff hugging the lines of his face. "I think we've managed to destroy everything good between us. Funny, it started with sex, didn't it? And that's exactly where it ended."

He took a step forward. "No, don't say that. It wasn't just sex. I loved you, but I was too fucked-up to see it and admit to myself I needed you. I needed you more than I needed to hate your father, or my mother, for running away. I'm asking for forgiveness. Another chance. Please."

Her chest tightened, but she already knew the answer. "I'm sorry. See, I can forgive you, Dalton, because I know the man you really are inside. The man I fell in love with. But I can't forget the cruelty. The way you deliberately tried to hurt me because you felt trapped. What if it happens again? I can't trust you anymore."

"It won't happen again. I'm not scared of what I feel for you any longer."

"I'd like to believe you, but I can't take that chance. You deserve my forgiveness, but not my trust. No longer." She paused. "I need you to leave, Dalton. Please."

Odd, how quiet it was. She expected to hear one of their hearts shattering like tinkling glass, but even the birds had hushed, respecting the moment.

"I understand. I won't bother you again." He walked to his pickup and drove away.

Raven went inside the house and told herself over and over she had done the right thing. The only thing.

It still tore her apart.

chapter twenty-eight

> ◇ ———

"Look at this! Remember this picture?"

Cal gave a long-suffering sigh. "Yes. And I remember the last thirty pictures you showed me. We're supposed to be boxing things up, not spending hours on the floor with old photo albums."

Tristan shot him a look and took a sip of coffee. "You're just pissed I found the evidence from that Halloween party."

Cal ground his teeth, cheeks flushed. "I did not fucking put on a Snow White costume. I was just fooling around with Dalton, trying to get him to laugh."

Dalton pressed his lips together. "Sure, Cal. Whatever you want to believe."

"Fuck you."

Dalton laughed, sharing a look with Tristan. It was rare that Cal was the butt of the jokes, being the oldest. Dalton had been the easiest target, always following his brothers around and trying to get their attention. The natural domino effect in the household always ruled. Cal tortured Tristan. Tristan tortured Dalton. And Dalton dealt.

He looked over Tristan's shoulder, sucking in his breath as he turned the page.

His parents' wedding photo.

He reached out to gently touch the images. His mom and dad looked so happy. Joyful smiles and unlined faces, hands clasped together like they were united against the world. So optimistic about the future that lay before them.

"Damn, they were a good-looking couple," Tristan muttered.

Cal stomped over, then knelt to peer closer. "Dad looks relaxed. And he's showing teeth when he smiles."

"Mom could've been a model."

They stared together in silence, each caught up in his separate memories. Dalton might never know what had happened between his parents to cause them to change, but somehow, falling in love with Raven showed him there were no guarantees. You took your shot with the person you loved, and sometimes it didn't work. Sometimes it did. Dalton realized in that moment he doubted his mother ever had regrets, because she'd gotten a beautiful family and she'd gambled on love.

It was more than he'd ever done.

Cal cleared his throat and stood up. "Dudes, I'm serious. We still have the closet and we've only gotten through half of the drawers."

"Fine, fine, stop the bitching." Tristan shut the photo album and pulled open the bottom drawer of the bureau. "It still feels weird going through Dad's stuff. He was so damn private. I feel like he's yelling at us from up in heaven. Or—"

"Don't say it," Cal said.

Dalton laughed. His father had been cold, but there were still memories he treasured. Not of the business owner who ran an empire or the disciplinarian who demanded obedience, but of the man who'd loved his sons and enjoyed his life before he grew bitter. The man who played catch in the yard with them, or made his famous omelets on Sunday mornings when he was feeling creative. The man who hung their drawings in his office and taught them to ride bikes and hugged them when they fell, even as he pushed them to try again. There were good times, and that's what Dalton intended to hang on to.

They worked for the next few hours with the occasional ribbing until Tristan yelled out both their names.

"Another stack of photos?" Cal teased. "Your senior prom, perhaps?"

"Guys, come over here."

They peered around his shoulder. Tristan held a letter in his shaking hand, along with a yellowed, crumpled envelope. Dalton caught the elegant lines of his mother's script. His breath stopped at the first words.

My darling boys. Caleb, Tristan, Dalton . . .

"Holy shit," Cal breathed out.

Tristan turned white. "I found it stuck in the back of Dad's drawer, under the Bible."

They sat down together and read the letter.

My darling boys. Caleb, Tristan, Dalton . . .
This is a difficult letter to write, but I need to have faith you will somehow understand. To do that, you will need to think of me not only as your mother, but as a woman who has to make choices in her life.
I loved your father. I always will. But there has been something broken between us for a long, long time. I have lived with this emptiness for so long, I began to stop questioning it, until I met someone else. Someone who not only recognized my lonely heart but healed it.
His name is Matthew Hawthorne. He's an artist. I met him when I took an art class at

the community center where he taught. At first, we recognized the connection between us but fought it. I was married, and he was respectful of your father. But as time went on, we became friends. I was able to tell him things and open up in a way that made me discover I still had time left—time to be happy again and enjoy life. He opened me up to possibilities of the woman I wanted to be, worthy of not only love but respect and kindness. Of acceptance.

I know this is hard for you to hear, my precious boys. No son wants to learn that his mother is more than a parent, or that she needs to leave in order to find herself again. But you are grown men now, with choices of your own to make. Your father and I have been unhappy for too long, and it's time to let go before we end up hating who we once loved.

I will be going away for a while. When I told your father about Matthew and our need to be together, he said he would destroy not only Pierce Brothers, but also your feelings for me. He convinced me you would never forgive me for my betrayal. For a long time, I stayed to protect you, thinking it was worth the sacrifice. But what would I have really taught you, my beautiful boys? To follow your head and not your heart? To survive rather than truly live? To be a coward rather than face your greatest fears? To search for perfection rather than what is real?

Pierce Brothers will always belong to you. My great-great-grandfather built a company based on family and blood, and changed the name to Pierce Brothers after you boys were born. You will run it together one day, strong in each other, and hopefully respecting each of your individual talents that will make it whole.

As for forgiveness, I must believe you will find it in your hearts to give me such a gift. When I return, I will be moving out and trying to build my own center of happiness. It will be hard for all of us, but you must understand one thing will never change. You are the loves of my life. I will never leave you, but you are old enough to make your own happiness, separate from both my and your father's expectations. Matthew has a teenage daughter, Bella, who will be going through her own struggles. She is his world, as you are mine, but it's time for us to take a leap together and hope that, one day, you all will understand.

We're flying to Paris tonight. We need the space to breathe, to be, to savor each other

for a little while before we return. I decided
writing this letter will not only give me the
time to explain, but give you time to process.
 I love you all.

    Mom

The world Dalton always knew shattered around him, for the second time in his life. All the questions and accusations . . . the fear and the pain . . . faded away with each word he read.

She'd been planning to come back.

He looked at his brothers and automatically reached out to hold their hands. They squeezed back.

"How? How did we never see this?" Tristan asked.

"Dad hid it from us." Cal's voice turned hard. "It makes sense. She left this letter for us, but he never wanted us to know. It was his own form of revenge."

The cruelty of the man his father had become shredded his insides, but once again, Diane Pierce healed him. Yes, she had been going to get a divorce, but hadn't they all known for years how miserable she'd been? If they had read this letter, wouldn't they have understood and encouraged her to be happy? She'd never intended to leave them behind. She'd only wanted to grab some time away to set her own intentions and prepare for a new future.

There was no blame there. There was nothing for him to forgive.

Head spinning, tears threatening, Dalton looked at his brothers and smiled.

"Now we know."

They nodded, hands still clasped together.

"Now we know," Cal repeated.

They sat together on the floor for a long, long time.

Raven pulled up to the mansion.

Dalton was on the front porch. When he'd first called her, she'd ignored the message, but after he'd tried to contact her numerous times, she'd finally picked up. He'd gotten straight to the point: A letter had been found. It had something to do with her father.

She'd told him she'd be right over.

Hardening her heart, she got out of the car and walked over, trying not to greedily devour his appearance. He looked the same, but different. Tired. Yet . . . stronger. Hair twisted up in a man bun, and his eyes burned clear and bright, with more focus. She swallowed the pain, realizing he was doing better without her. He'd gotten past her final rejection and moved on.

"Thanks for coming," he said. His deep voice stroked her everywhere, licking every hidden place on her body. "It's important."

She stiffened her muscles. "You said something about a letter?"

He nodded, motioning for her to sit down next to him. She lowered herself onto the rocker, curling herself up tight. "My brothers and I were cleaning out my father's room. He died over a year ago, but we never got around to really sorting and boxing his belongings. We found this letter hidden in the back of his drawer. It's from my mother."

A strange premonition swept over her. With hands that slightly trembled, she took the outstretched letter, shivering at the brush of his fingers against the back of her hand. Raven didn't question why he wanted her to read it. She sensed a piece of the big puzzle was about to slide into place.

She took her time with the words, noting Diane's graceful penmanship, savoring the sound of her father's name from the woman he'd fallen in love with. When she was done, tears stung her vision, but she read it again. Then again.

Finally she lifted her head and looked at Dalton.

"They were coming back."

"Yes. You were right all along. You knew who they were, even when I doubted."

The hard shell inside her cracked open and she began to shake. Dalton rose, tugging her into his arms, and wrapped her tight in his embrace. She allowed herself this one last time to take comfort in his strength, reveling in his spicy, masculine scent, the heat of his skin, the warm breath rushing past her ear. He rocked her like a child, and she cried as the past fell away and all the answers suddenly became clear.

She quieted but stayed in his arms, hating to leave.

"I'm sorry I hurt you, Raven."

Raven sighed. One more moment in his embrace and she'd pull away. For now, it felt so good. So . . . right. "I know."

"I made a lot of mistakes, but I see things more clearly now. And I understand why you don't feel like you can just open up again and give me a second chance. So I'm going to earn it."

Slowly, she pulled back. "I'm glad you called me. I needed to see the letter. I think there's some closure for both of us now, don't you? But there's nothing left of us. We need to move on."

His jaw tightened, but he nodded. "We do. But I don't think it's too late for us, Raven."

"Dalton—don't."

He tipped her chin up, smiling down at her. Resolution gleamed in his eyes, along with a peace she'd never really noticed before. "I gave you words.

But trust isn't won back with words. It's won back with actions. If I let you walk away without a fight, I'll spend the rest of my life with regrets."

She stepped away, tired all the way to her soul. "You need to move on. You've never wanted anything permanent anyway."

"No, I didn't. Because love is just a word until it's attached to a person. I didn't understand what it felt like to want to be with one person longer than a night or two. With you, I saw beyond. When I think about my future, I see you, sweetheart. Only you."

"I've got to go. I'm glad you found the answers you needed, but I can't do this anymore. I won't. Some things can't be fixed."

"Watch me."

His words should have sounded like a threat, but somehow, they were more like a promise. A promise she didn't believe any longer.

Raven left and swore not to think about it again.

Dalton stood on the porch and watched her drive away.

His insides hurt. Holding her in his arms again was like coming home. But he didn't expect her to believe him. He'd taken something precious she'd given him and destroyed it. She needed time to believe in him again and trust that he wouldn't hurt her. He needed to be in this for the long haul, even if it was possible she would never give him another chance.

It was a risk he had to take.

He heard his brothers' footsteps. They flanked him, watching Raven as she disappeared down the long drive.

"How'd she take it?" Cal asked.

"Good. She cried. I got to hold her."

Tristan nodded. "Will she forgive you?"

"I hope so. I need to prove myself again. It's going to take time."

"Think you should make some grand gesture? You know, like they do in those romance novels and stuff?" Tristan asked.

Dalton shook his head. "Nah, it's fiction for a reason. Women need long term. Small actions every day that make a difference. I'm fighting for something bigger here."

"You're probably right."

"I think she'll forgive you. Eventually," Cal said. "In the meantime, we're here for you. Whatever you need."

"Thanks."

"But you're still paying me for some new bottles of whiskey."

Dalton shot him a look, and they all burst into laughter.

chapter twenty-nine

What the hell was he doing?

Raven looked up. Perched on the bar stool to the far left, he sat quietly, iPhone in hand. Three weeks had passed, and he still continued the same behavior. The first night, she'd explained quietly that he needed to leave. He did, but he ended up sitting in his Bronco the entire time, waiting until she closed up. He followed her home, waited to make sure she got in, then drove away.

He repeated the same actions for the rest of the week, until she finally gave up and let him stay on the bar stool. She refused to serve him, hoping he'd get the hint and eventually go away.

He didn't. He just brought paperwork with him, or read on his phone, not even drinking water. After a few nights she realized he hadn't eaten. She allowed him to order from the menu and gave him a damn beer. But she refused to talk to him. She treated him like he was invisible, and it worked well for her. Kind of.

Raven knew what he was trying to do in this twisted plot to win her back. She also knew it was impossible, and with enough time, he'd tire of the game and move on. No man could continue in the same vein.

Until another week dragged by, and he kept sitting in her bar, night after night, happy to take whatever scraps she threw him.

It was driving her crazy.

Since it was a Tuesday, the crowd was a bit thinner than usual, so she took the opportunity to stomp over to his chair. He looked up, his expression happy, like he was grateful she noticed him. It reminded her of the first months after they'd met, when she'd given him a hard time. "Why are you doing this?" she demanded. "I don't want you here. You don't want to be here. Just move on, Slick, and pick up a pretty blonde who you can have fun with. Got it?"

His smile was pure joy. His dimples flashed. "Don't you get it, Raven? I'm happy just being around you. This is the first time you've called me Slick in weeks."

"It's not a compliment," she hissed.

"Okay."

"Stop agreeing with me."

"Okay." He paused. "Can I have some sweet potato fries, please?"

"No."

"Okay." He just stared at her with that hungry look in his eyes. Her stomach dropped to her toes, but she turned her back and refused to say another word to him for the rest of the night.

But she got him the fries.

Days and nights rolled by, and they got into a strange routine. He was there like clockwork every night till closing. He followed her home, made sure she got inside, then disappeared. He showed up at the gym on the days she trained with Xavier, keeping his distance and working out in the weight room by himself. But he always greeted her, watched over her, and made sure she got safely to her car after her workout.

He sent her flowers. Not expensive roses or lilacs, but daisies. Simple, happy flowers that showed up in small batches on her doorstep. She threw them away the first few weeks, then began keeping them. No reason to waste a living thing that looked so pretty in her kitchen.

When she opened up the bar one Tuesday morning, she realized the front steps had been fixed. It had been on her list for a while, but with the budget of restoring the bar, she'd decided to patch them up until winter closed in.

Now she noticed they had been completely redone and sealed, with no cracks or bumps that would cause liability. She almost called him to demand to know whether he'd done it, then decided ignoring him would be the better option. After all, the man would probably boast about helping her out to win brownie points.

He never said a word.

Slowly, like rock eroded by water and smoothed out over the span of years, her emotions began to soften. She became more used to his presence. He was never with another woman, and the few times she caught a female trying to pick him up, he politely told them he was in love with the bartender.

He'd begun to recruit the crowd in My Place. They cheered him on like they were watching a love story unfold. Like she was some prize for him to win.

It pissed her off.

Even Al went from threatening to throw him out to chatting with him during his breaks. She tried to keep the pain of the night he'd left her close to her heart so she wouldn't get tricked into believing this was real. Raven couldn't let herself be hurt like that again. The next time he took her to bed and casually walked away as if she meant nothing would destroy her.

Why did it feel different, though? Like he'd

made a decision to love her unconditionally and nothing would deter him? Not even her own stubbornness?

She finally snapped when she caught him leaving an envelope on her front porch early one Sunday morning. Not caring that she'd just rolled out of bed, she marched to the door, flung it open, and began yelling.

"What are you doing? Penance for your sins? They're forgiven, Dalton, now please go away!"

He straightened up and grinned at her. "Morning. You look beautiful."

Her mouth dropped open. She should've scared him with her crazy hair and no makeup and the baggy sweats she slept in when she needed extra comfort. "Are you kidding me? You cannot force your way back into my life just because you decide! I get to decide, do you hear me? I'm the commander of my ship! The queen of my castle!"

"Yes, you are. I don't want to piss you off, sweetheart. I want to prove something to both of us. We need to start over fresh. I've never fallen in love before, so I freaked and screwed it up, but I'm not going to do that again. I intend to show you every day, from now on. I enjoy watching you close up the bar, and having terrible coffee with you in the morning, and admiring how you try to kick Xavier's ass in the gym. All that time

I couldn't understand why I was so damn happy sitting in My Place, even when you'd just insult me. Now I know." He beamed, and that charming male beauty reminded her of Gabriel, an angel so stunning, poor mortals were helpless beneath his smile. "Because as long as I'm with you, I'm happy. I get it now. I was a bit slow, and now I need to convince you I won't make that terrible mistake again." He cocked his head as if thinking through an inner schedule. "You're stubborn. And prideful. So it may take weeks, maybe even months, but eventually you're going to look for me and I will be there."

Stunned, she listened to the words with a hope she needed to squash. She opened her mouth to say something terrible and awful and cruel. "What if it takes years?"

He rocked back on his heels. "That's okay. You're worth it." His eyes glittered. "We're worth it."

She stuck her chin up in the air, refusing to get lost in his pretty words. "I don't believe you. Now leave me alone so I can enjoy my coffee in peace."

He handed her the envelope. "This is for you. I told Cal no grand gestures, but this was different. I wanted to do this."

"You didn't have to fix my front steps," she grumbled.

"Yes, I did," he said softly. "Because I want to take care of you."

He left her on the porch, simmering with unresolved tension and rioting emotions. Damn him. Why couldn't he just go away like a normal man? She ripped open the envelope and took out the piece of paper.

A certificate.

A star has been chosen and named in your honor . . .

Raven Bella Hawthorne

Ah, shit. He'd named a star after her. It was the most romantic gesture a man had ever made to her, but like the enemy of Moses, she hardened her heart and refused to get all weak and soft and girly.

Absolutely refused.

Raven didn't know what to do.

She sat on the leather couch in her living room and tried to analyze the whirling array of emotions clutching her body. It had become more than a game now. Dalton had been seriously pursuing her for almost three months, with no signs of slowing down or getting frustrated. The open affection and love glowing from his ocean-blue eyes tempted her to give in and surrender. But the raw pain of his brutal rejection still ached.

He seemed different. More centered, as if he accepted his feelings with an ease he'd never shown before. There was no more fighting or pretending. He told her every day with actions and words what she meant to him, and that he didn't want to let her go.

Was it enough? Was it time to take another leap and hope he caught her?

Raven reached for her cell, dialed the familiar number, and prayed she'd get an answer. The voice that came on the line was one she both trusted and admired.

"'Bout time you surfaced." The sleepy feminine grumble reminded Raven of all the times she'd tried to rouse Izzy before noon, mostly so they could get into more mischief together.

"I'm in trouble."

She heard the rustle of movement, then Izzy spoke again, serious. "Tell me everything."

"It's a guy."

She gave a snort. "Duh. It's always a guy. Dalton? I thought it was over."

"I did, too."

"Tell me everything," she repeated.

Raven did. She spilled the whole story about the letter, Dalton's never-ending crusade to win back her heart, and her own struggles to trust again. Izzy did what she did best. She listened.

When Raven fell silent, her spirit lightened. Nothing like unloading on your best friend for a quick therapy appointment.

"I'm so glad you learned about your dad, babe. Do you feel better?"

"God, yes. I feel like I can finally close the door on a question that kept haunting me. But now I don't know if Dalton was meant to be mine for always, or just for a little while. Maybe we met to solve the mystery, but we're not fated for long term?"

Izzy snorted again. "What have I always told you?"

Raven laughed. "Don't leave anything to chance or fate. She's a real bitch."

"Exactly. Why aren't you listening? As I learned in rehab, everything is a choice. You choose to love or walk away. To forgive or keep resenting. To stay or leave. To be happy or miserable. It's time to make a choice, Raven. Now, maybe fate had a way of stepping in to make sure you met, but after that, it's all on you. Do you still love him?"

The truth rose up inside, refusing to be denied. "Yes."

"Can you take the leap again? I gotta give the guy credit; not many men would've stuck this long. He's not a crazy stalker, is he?"

"No! He's beautiful to look at, Izzy. Golden hair and blue eyes, and his arms—all I can say is *arm porn*."

"Niiiice."

"But he's gentle and kind. He's really funny,

and no matter how sarcastic I get, he just grins and teases me back."

"Good, 'cause you can be a real bitch."

"And he respects my job. He doesn't give me lip service, he really helped make the bar better, and he encourages me. Oh, and when I kicked the gunman that held up the bar, he didn't get all ego on me and insist I should've waited for help. He was proud and supportive."

"Dalton sounds like he's a good fit for you. Are you calling me to hear my opinion? To have me tell you what to do? Or to confirm the decision you were going to make anyway?"

The knowledge burst and shimmered around her. Her friend was so damn smart. Izzy knew her well; it was only a matter of time before she'd come to the one conclusion that was possible, since the first day she'd met him and he'd asked for a bottle of Jack.

"I don't want to give up on him. On me. On us."

"That's what I thought. Gonna make him suffer any longer? 'Cause if you need more time, make him work for it."

She took the phone and opened her door. The night sky exploded with stars, and Raven slowly smiled. "I think it's time I let him off the hook."

"Good for you. When are you coming to visit me in Verily?"

"Soon. I'll bring Dalton. You'll love him. Tell Liam

I said hello and that he has the smartest woman on earth in his arms."

"I'll make sure to relay the message. Take care of yourself, babe. Peace out."

"Peace out."

She ended the call. Watched the stars for a while. A faint voice drifted to her ears, whispering through the darkness.

But if it's your road to follow, take it.

She smiled and hugged herself. "Yes, Papa."

It was time to go see Dalton.

chapter thirty

Dalton heard the sound again, and frowned. Sitting up in bed, he strained his ears, listening in the silence.

Ping. Ping.

Something was hitting the windows.

He padded naked over to the balcony doors, which he'd closed to keep in the heat. Squinting, he peered through the glass. Was a bird hitting it? He doubted a robber would use a ladder that high. Escape wouldn't be too easy.

Ping. Ping.

He pushed open the doors and stepped outside.

Everything slowed, stopped, then restarted again with a lurch. Raven stood below the balcony, her hands full of rocks, and motioned for him to come down. In seconds, he flung on a pair of shorts, then raced down the stairs and past the dogs, who gave him a grumpy glare before plopping their giant heads back down in their beds to go to sleep.

He tore down the path and stopped in front of her. Dressed in jeans and a baby-blue T-shirt that emphasized the perfect swell of her breasts, she cocked a hip and studied him as if she were out for a casual evening stroll. Across town.

"Are you okay?" he huffed out, trying to calm his racing heart.

"Yes, I'm fine." Her heated gaze raked over his bare chest and legs. His skin tingled where she lingered, as if she'd run her hands over him. "Whatcha doing?"

His brow lifted. "Umm, sleeping. It's one a.m. What are you doing?"

"Having a revelation."

A mixture of nausea and excitement churned his gut. Was she here to finally tell him to go away forever? Was she tired of him following her around, trying to gain her forgiveness? Was she ready to move on with another man who hadn't been stupid enough to hurt her? He tried to swallow, but there was no spit left in his mouth. "Oh. I guess revelations are good for this time of night. Are you here to share it with me?"

"Yes."

He waited. She didn't say anything, just kept

looking at him with a hungry she-devil sort of gleam in her dark eyes. The moonlight played in her hair, which was wild and curly around her face. He didn't want to imagine his life without her, and at that moment, Dalton didn't know what he'd do if she announced it was completely, irrevocably, definitely over.

"Have you ever watched the movie *When Harry Met Sally*?" she asked.

He didn't even blink at the weird change of topic. "Not into chick flicks, but yes. Along the way I was forced to watch it. Wasn't too bad."

"Well, that's the reason I'm here. In the middle of the night."

He tried hard to understand, but he was too damn nervous and his brain wasn't working. He caught her scent on the breeze and almost groaned from pure lust. Sandalwood. So damn sexy. "Umm, you want to watch a movie? I can do that."

A hint of a smile tugged at her lips. "No. Remember the scene in the movie where Harry ran all the way through the city on New Year's Eve and finally found Sally, in the middle of this big holiday party around midnight, and she looked at him like he was nuts and asked him why the heck he was there?"

Damn, he wished he'd paid better attention. Dalton swore to study every chick flick in the future if he could pass this one test. But he'd promised no more lies. "No," he said sadly. "I don't remember."

"That's okay. Harry said when you realize you love someone and want to spend the rest of your life with that person, you want the rest of your life to start as soon as possible."

Dalton didn't move, didn't breathe. "What are you saying, Raven?"

This time she smiled fully and walked over, closing the distance between them. Reaching out, she slid her arms over his shoulders and pressed her forehead against his. "I'm saying I love you. I forgive you. I trust you. And I want the rest of our life to start right now."

His hands caressed her cheeks, her hair, her body, as if he was terrified she was an illusion ready to drift away in a puff of smoke. "You'll be mine?"

"I think I always was, Dalton Pierce," she whispered against his lips. "Now will you stop talking and kiss me?"

And he did. With a groan of delight, he took her lips and slid his tongue inside her mouth, fusing them together with pure intimacy. He kissed her like she was the most precious gift in the world—because she was. His hands stroked over her body, bringing her tight against him, reveling in the crackling energy that stole his breath.

"I love you so much," he said, finally breaking the kiss. "Today. Tomorrow. Always."

She ran her fingers gently over his lips, tracing his jaw. "You gonna take me to bed or what?"

"I'm gonna take you to bed."

He swept her up in his arms, cradling her close, and brought her inside. Up the stairs, into his room, onto his bed. He stripped her slowly, removed his shorts, and touched her. Loved her with his tongue and teeth, lips and fingers. Worshipped the gorgeous ink of her tat and paid homage to her slick, wet heat that closed around him and begged to be claimed. When he finally surged inside, clasping her fingers within his, their breath intermingling amid the whisper of sliding sheets and soft gasps, he made her forever his.

And when the sun came up, Dalton lay in her arms and realized he'd finally found home.

epilogue

———>◆<———

I'll raise you five bucks."

Cal gave a fierce frown, holding his cards close. He stared at her hard, taking his time, then threw his chips in the pile. "I'll see your raise. Now, don't be a bad loser, princess. Bluffing is something that's very hard to do, and you'll need a bit more practice. Time to show your cards."

Raven watched Morgan with satisfaction, waiting for the final attack.

She did it with her usual Southern style, a bit of a simper and an innocent smile. "Three of a kind and a pair is good, right?" she asked with fake innocence.

Cal's mouth fell open. He threw his straight on the table, shaking his head in disbelief. "You got a full house. Did you know that?"

"I remember something about a house, but

thanks for clarifying it. My goodness gracious, is this pot all for me?" She raked in the pile of chips and checked her fiancé's small heap. "Do you need to borrow any money, Charming?"

Cal glowered. "No. I'm fine. Who deals?"

Dalton stood up from the table, his lips twitching with the need to grin. "Gonna take a break and get a drink. This is getting way too intense for me."

Tristan scooped up the cards and began to shuffle. "Beginner's luck or something. You're doing real good, Morgan," he said, with obvious patronization. "Raven taught you well. You too, Syd."

Sydney looked at her towering chips and shared a meaningful glance with Morgan. "Those lady poker nights must've paid off," she chirped. She took another sip of her Sweet Hot Chris. "There's now a waiting list for the mixed group. Seems everyone wants to try to play us."

"Because you two seem to beat everyone at the table," Raven spoke up.

Tristan gave a snort. Cal forced a smile.

"Be right back." Raven headed to the bar for refills. A hard arm circled around her hips and pulled her in tight. She was barely able to breathe as Dalton kissed her with sheer possessiveness, forcing her lips open to take his tongue, thrusting his hips against her with demand. Arousal curled her toes and heated her blood. When he finally broke the kiss, she was practically panting and thinking about a quickie in the kitchen.

"What was that for?" she asked raggedly.

He pressed a thumb against her swollen lips. "You are the sexiest goddess to walk the earth. You taught them to count cards, didn't you?"

Raven blinked. "Of course not. I don't know how to count cards."

"Liar." He nipped at her jaw, then soothed with his tongue. "I know a con when I see one."

"Sorry, Slick. The only con going on right now is the one you're playing on me. Getting me all hot and bothered and doing nothing about it."

"Wait till your punishment tonight." Her tummy dipped in thrilling anticipation. His hot breath blew in her ear. "If you're lying to me, I'll be the one doing the counting. I'll demand a minimum of three orgasms before I even get inside you. Sound fun?"

Oh, it did. Bastard. Now she'd be thinking about her *punishment* for the rest of the night. "You'll have to prove I taught them to count cards."

"I will. Sydney's gonna show up with a flush next. Watch."

He forced her to watch the game unfold while his fingers stroked all the hidden parts of her, safely concealed behind the bar. By the time

Sydney showed her flush, Raven was about to explode with sexual tension. Arousal pounded between her thighs and tightened her nipples. The slightest touch elicited goose bumps and shivers over her skin.

"You've been a bad girl, Raven."

"Are you going to tell your brothers?" she asked breathlessly, rocking her hips back against his erection.

"Hell no. They deserve a good trouncing. Oh, and make that four."

"Four what?"

He winked and flashed his dimples. "Four orgasms before we even start." Then he walked away and sat back at the table, congratulating Sydney on her epic win. Raven grabbed a bottle of water and her gaze settled on the prestigious framed article from *Good Food & Fine Spirits*. The write-up with a full center spread of photos had made a huge splash in Harrington, and now most weekends were standing room only. Al had belted out a laugh when she told him they might need to start taking reservations. Cocktail night had exploded, and Dalton had been known to jump behind the bar to handle the overload.

God, she loved him.

Raven watched the crew ribbing one another with good-natured teasing and affection. Over the few weeks since she'd shown up at Dalton's door, they'd only grown closer, until Raven felt as if she had stepped into her own circle of adopted family. The nightmares had completely stopped, and a peace had settled over her.

For the first time, she felt completely whole.

It was odd how the crazy twists and turns of life could lead one to love.

Dalton crooked his finger, motioning for her to come over. She loved the path she'd chosen, and sometimes felt the soothing presence of her father stirring the air, as if he was happy, too.

Raven slid into the arms of the man who'd always been meant for her.

acknowledgments

Writers are only as good as the team that surrounds them. I have the best.

Thanks to the crew at Gallery/Pocket for everything they do. Lauren McKenna, my fab editor, I love writing books with you, lady! Thanks to my agent, Kevan Lyon; my assistant, Lisa Hamel-Soldano; and Jessica Estep at InkSlinger PR. A big shout-out to the Probst Posse—you guys rock!

Finally, thanks to all my amazing writing colleagues and friends who are always around when I need to bitch and who cheer me on or just remind me I'm not legally insane. I'm just a writer.

Keep reading for a sneak peek of the next book
in the Billionaire Builders series

all or
nothing
at all

Available from Gallery and Pocket Books this fall!

chapter one

———≻ ◇ ≺———

Sydney Greene rushed into the offices of Pierce Brothers Construction, madly calculating how she'd make up the twenty minutes she'd lost in morning madness. Her daughter, Becca, had insisted on wearing her hair in a French braid, then had raced back to her closet to change twice before school. If she acted like this at six years old, what would happen when she reached high school?

Sydney shuddered at the thought. Juggling her purse, laptop, and briefcase, she dug for the key, then realized someone was already in. She was a bit of a control freak when it came to running the office where she'd worked since she was eighteen years old and liked to arrive before everyone else started. Order was the key to dealing with chaos. Her life had been such a series of sharp turns and fear-inducing hills, her soul was soothed in the one place she could not only control but thrive in.

Her job.

The office was quiet, with only a few lights flickering, but the scent of brewed coffee drifted in the air. She sucked in a breath like a druggie smelling weed, quickly heading to her office to drop her stuff before darting toward the kitchen in a hunt for sanity.

Or at least some clarity.

The kitchen was high-tech, from the stainless steel refrigerator to the cappuccino maker, soda machine, and various vending booths. She grabbed her fave Muppets mug and filled it up, already mentally clicking her way through the day's activities. Brady needed to deliver the final architectural plans for the house on Tree Lane, and Dalton needed to get her invoices on the deck project so she could calculate the final-quarter profits. Numbers flashed in her mind in a precise, neat little row, and she muttered under her breath, wondering if they'd break last year's profit margin, which would prove they were finally back on top. If only—

"I brought in some blueberry muffins."

She jerked at the deep, cultured voice spilling into her thoughts. Coffee splashed over the edge of her mug onto her apple-green business suit. Cursing, she swiveled her head, her gaze crashing into whiskey-colored eyes that were as familiar as her own beating heart. Familiar yet deadly, to both her past and present. Why did he have to be the one who was here early?

Anyone else would've brought a smile and cheerful "good morning." But Tristan Pierce didn't talk to her. Not really. Oh, he lectured, and demanded, and judged, but he refused to actually have a conversation with her. Not that she cared. It was better for both of them to keep their distance.

"You scared me," she accused. "Why don't you ever make any noise when you walk into a room?"

Those carved lips twitched with the need to smile. Unfortunately, her presence rarely allowed the man to connect with any of his softer emotions, so he kept his expression grim. They'd been dancing around each other for over a year now and still struggled with discomfort when they were together. Well, he experienced discomfort in the form of awkwardness.

She experienced discomfort in the form of sexual torture.

"I'll work on it. Need help?"

"I got it." Her body wept at the thought of him touching her, even for a moment. *Down, girl.* She grabbed a napkin and ran it under water, then dabbed at her suit jacket. "Why are you here so early?"

"Working on a real estate flip. Can't seem to figure out if I should tear down the porch and turn it into a ranch, or fix it to keep it as a colonial. Been going over the plans but I may need to talk to Brady."

She swiped at the stain with the expertise of a mom used to last-minute disasters. "What's the address?"

"Rose Lane. Right outside of Harrington."

Her memory brought up the city street and its residents. Lots of rentals. Old architecture. It was a street once known for drug problems, but was slowly being rejuvenated by renovated houses and young families moving in.

"Take down the porch. A ranch fits better with the new population they're trying to attract. They'll want to keep their kids off the front of the property since it faces a main road. Build them a nice deck instead so they can hang out as a family in the back."

His face flickered with grudging admiration, which quickly vanished. Tristan didn't believe in complimenting her. Most of the time he barely tolerated her presence, and his only nice actions revolved around one strong emotion.

Guilt.

"I'll check into it."

She nodded and tried to ignore the masculine waves of energy that emanated from his figure.

He'd always been the quiet one of his brothers, but he'd never needed words or noise to make his presence known. When he walked into a room, everyone noticed—men and women. His demeanor conveyed competence and power in a whole different way than his brothers, Caleb and Dalton, did. As the middle child, he was a peacemaker, and able to make decisions with a confident quickness that most respected but never duplicated. His thoroughness was legendary. Tristan was able to see a problem at all angles and attack it with a single-minded intensity and level of control. Once he'd brought that same talent to the bedroom, concentrating on wringing pleasure from her body with a thoroughness that ruined her for other lovers.

She studied him from under heavy-lidded eyes. His suits were renowned—custom-made with the best fabrics and cuts that emphasized his powerful, lean body. Today he wore a charcoal-gray suit, snowy-white shirt, and a vivid-purple tie. Engraved gold cuff links. His shoes were polished to a high sheen and made of soft leather. He always reminded her of one of those jungle cats who prowled with grace, amber eyes lit with intention, taking their time before deciding what to do with their prey. His analytical mind was as drool-worthy as his body. Hard, supple muscles balanced with a beautiful grace most men could never pull off.

His hair was thick, perfectly groomed, and a deep reddish brown. His face was an artistry of elegance, from the sharp blade of his nose to the square jaw, full lips, and high cheekbones. Lush lashes set off eyes that practically glowed, darkening to an intensity that made a woman's heart beat madly. He was beauty incarnate, a feast for the senses a woman could never bore of, spending the rest of eternity studying every angle and curve and drowning in his cognac gaze.

Once she'd been that woman. Of course, that was centuries ago, before the ugliness between them sprouted from dark corners and swallowed them up whole.

Didn't matter. She only dealt with Tristan for work now, though the past year had been more difficult as she was forced to spend so much time in his presence. Those five years he'd moved to New York and had been away from Harrington were hard, but she'd finally grown up. Become a mother and made her own niche in life, rather than waiting for him to dictate her wants and needs.

If only she wasn't still attracted to the man.

Already, the room surged with the innate connection between them. Some things never disappeared. They'd always had chemistry. Now it was just a matter of accepting it as fact and ignoring it.

Most of the time she managed.

"Better get to work," she announced in a fake voice.

"Have a muffin."

"Maybe later." She threw out the napkin, grabbed her mug, and turned.

"Did you eat breakfast?"

Her nerves ruffled. He still treated her like a child. Or an annoying kid sister. "Not hungry."

"You skipped lunch the past few days. Do you think it's smart to go all day without eating?"

Sydney ground her teeth. His arrogance pissed her off, as if he consistently knew what was right for her. Not anymore. "I think I'm able to handle getting myself something to eat when I'm hungry."

He didn't move. That gaze drilled into hers, searching and finding the past and heating up all the secret corners of her body. Damn him for still turning her on.

Damn her for still letting him.

"Don't you owe it to Becca to keep yourself healthy?"

Her daughter's name on his lips broke her out of the trance. With a low growl, she took a few steps forward to close the distance. The scent of his aftershave drifted in the air, reminding her of the ocean, but she ignored the pull and let out her anger full force.

"Don't ever tell me what to do as a mother. I've

been taking care of both of us for a long time. And I don't want your damn muffin."

She turned on her heel and stalked out of the kitchen.

Tristan watched her leave and cursed under his breath.

Once again, after two minutes in her company, he'd screwed it up.

He grabbed a mug from the pine cabinets and poured himself a cup of coffee. Every conversation only proved how much she despised him. When he'd first come back to Harrington, he'd been tortured by thoughts of her. Their breakup had almost destroyed him, but after five long years, he'd ached to see her face again. How many nights in New York had he spent dreaming about her, twisted with rage and betrayal by her speedy replacement of him and what he thought they'd had together?

He'd always felt as if he led their relationship. He'd known Sydney had crushed on him for years, and he felt almost like a supergod around her. It was only when she turned eighteen that he began to regard her as a woman rather than an annoying younger sister. It was easy to take charge of the relationship, especially since he was four years older. He'd never expected such intensity from a teen crush, or that he'd react with a strange possessiveness around her. It was as if she brought out all his baser emotions, always contained right below the surface. But when they'd broken up and he came crawling back to her, ready to beg her to take him back, she'd proven how little he'd really meant.

And how she'd been in control the whole time.

The memory still stung, so he slapped it away like an annoying fly and pushed it aside. He'd tried, dammit. Tried to deal with her snippiness toward him even though he'd held out the olive branch many times. He hated the way she left a group conversation when he showed up. Hated how she ignored him when she came to dinner on Sundays, focusing her attention on Morgan and Cal, Dalton and Brady, and only offered him polite nods. He hated the way his gut lurched when he looked at her daughter, proof of her betrayal. But most of all, Tristan hated the way his dick hardened every time he caught her signature scent of orange blossoms, or heard her throaty voice say his name, or watched her ripe curves move toward him clad in those sexy designer suits and high heels.

She'd only gotten more beautiful with age. She walked with the power of a woman who knew how to get what she wanted. Her strawberry-colored hair now hung halfway down her back, still curly and wild as ever, like silk trapped in fire. Her face had always been a bit too round, her mouth and eyes a bit too wide, and she'd always despised the scattering of freckles across her nose and dotted generously over her white skin. Tristan used to kiss and lick them in an erotic game of connect the dots. She'd never been petite or small-boned—no, her body was all Eve, lush and curvy and ripe like the apple that had tempted her. In New York, he'd rarely met a woman over size 6. Their makeup was always flawless and they regularly visited blow-out salons to kill any curls, and they were all vegetarians who believed in saving the earth. They never looked at him with adoration and always paid their own check, and would instruct the bartender exactly how to make their Skinnygirl martini cocktail.

But he'd come back because he missed her. Wanted her. Was ready to commit for life.

The joke had been on him.

Yet she still haunted him, and it was driving him insane. He'd do anything to move on and move past these leftover emotions from their shared history. Somehow, he'd turned into the lovesick teen with a crush, and the humiliation of it burned through him.

Something had to be done.

The thought took hold, though it was rife with booby traps. She may treat him like shit, but he'd memorized every inch of skin on her body, every expression on her beautiful face. He knew she crinkled her brow when she lied, and tapped her index finger against her bottom lip when she was deep in thought, and shivered uncontrollably when he bit the place where her neck met shoulder.

She still wanted him.

Oh, she hated it as much as he did. It would've been so much easier between them to keep a business-type relationship or even a distant, casual friendship. The only reason they bantered and argued and tried to avoid each other was simple.

They wanted to drag each other to bed.

The memory of her naked and vulnerable drifted to his brain, then melted all thinking-cells. He'd been with other women, of course, but no one had given him what Sydney had. The way she'd reached for him with eagerness, her body melting and surrendering to any delicious thing he wanted to do to her, and the adoration in her sea-green eyes that pumped him up with adrenaline and power. No one had come close.

He wondered if any woman ever could.

Tristan rubbed his eyes, picked up his mug, and headed back to his office. They couldn't keep doing this. Eventually something was going to break. And the more he thought about dealing with all this built-up angst and frustration in bed, the better his new plan looked. Perhaps the only way to move forward was to revisit the past and close the book properly.

All clichés led to one road.

Seduce Sydney.

chapter two

———— >─◆─< ————

"Mama, it's almost my birthday! Can we get an ice cream cake?"

Sydney laughed, grabbing her daughter and pulling her onto her lap. "Of course, you know that's my favorite. What do you want to do, sweetheart? Have you decided?"

Her daughter tilted her face and scrunched up her nose. "Can we go to Chuck E. Cheese's?"

Sydney couldn't help wincing. It may be a kid's paradise, but it was a mother's nightmare. The loud, flashing games; the overexcited children hunting for prize tickets they'd only win enough of to get a spider ring; and the large mouse character who danced in a purple sweater. She always left with a headache.

Maybe she could sneak in a flask filled with wine.

"Sure. Just get me a list and we'll send out some invitations."

"Okay. And I want to see Uncle Cal and Morgan and Dalton and Tristan and Uncle Brady. Can they come to my party? 'Cause they're my family."

Her chest tightened but she managed a breath. The guilt was manageable this time. Practice did make perfect. "Yes, honey. But we'll have a cake for you at Uncle Cal's house, too, and Morgan said she's making your favorite dish."

"Spaghetti and meatballs?"

"Yep." She savored her daughter's soft body sprawled over her thighs and the scent of her coconut shampoo. Her pink T-shirt boasted her favorite Disney princess, Ariel, because they had the same hair color. Her jeans had pink sparkles and matched the glittery nail polish on her fingers and toes. Already Becca was moving away from her cuddling, demanding more alone time and independence to read, draw, or play on her Kindle. How had so much time flashed by without her realizing it? She used to laugh at mothers warning her to enjoy the toddler years, when she'd just prayed to be out of diapers and formula and sleepless nights. Now her daughter was reading on her own and had a group of friends she insisted on seeing at regular revolving playdates. She was going to be a powerhouse one day, but until Becca grew into that power, Sydney tried to keep her daughter's temper, and independence, in check. "I can't believe you're going to be seven," she murmured, stroking her daughter's hair.

"Was Matilda seven in the movie?" Becca asked. "'Cause I want to be like her."

"I think so. Wait a minute—you want to have terrible parents who lock you up, are mean, and don't let you go to school?"

Her daughter giggled. "No, but she gets to watch TV all the time. I'd like that part."

"Brat." Another giggle. Becca was always trying to finagle more television time. "For now, I need to get started on dinner. Sorry I've been working late this week."

"That's okay, Mama, but don't forget about my ballet recital."

"I'd never forget that. Are you nervous?"

"A little."

"I'll get there early so I can be in the front row, okay?"

Her daughter's smile was Sydney's heaven and earth, exploding her heart with a fierce emotion that still humbled her. From the moment Becca pushed her way into the world, wailing in pissed-off fury, Sydney tumbled into a love that knew no bounds.

The voice she'd shoved deep inside, trapped in

a locked box of her own making, slithered up to whisper.

She doesn't just belong to you . . .

Dear God, it was getting worse. Every day since the Pierce brothers came home, she'd struggled. Her peaceful, ordered existence was shredded to nonexistence. Now she was haunted every day. Every night. Haunted by the truth she'd sworn to hide when Becca was born.

Her thoughts broke off as her daughter shot off her lap, snuggling complete. "I'm hungry, Mama. Can I go play?"

"Yes, I'll call you when dinner's ready." She watched her daughter bound up the stairs, and with a sigh, Sydney headed to the kitchen. Her home was small but perfect for the two of them, a yellow-shingled bi-level on a dead-end road. With a small fenced-in yard and no worries about traffic, she felt safe and secure, tucked away from the world. She'd decorated the house with all the girly stuff she loved—throw pillows in bright teal, cozy afghans, and fuzzy throw rugs supersoft under bare feet. She liked her work ruthlessly organized and her house casually messy. A good thing, because Becca was a whirlwind of activity and she was constantly reminding her to pick up her toys so she didn't trip on Barbie dolls, DVDs, and books.

Sydney opened the refrigerator, removing the

thawed tilapia and slipping into mechanical mode. She still told Becca it was special chicken since her daughter gave her a hard time about eating fish. Dumping the fillet into a pan, she doctored it with citrus, dill and basil, olive oil, fresh garlic, and Himalayan salt. The potatoes were scrubbed and slid into the oven, and she grabbed a bag of frozen peas to steam—her child's only accommodation to green vegetables. She removed a bottle of Chardonnay from the refrigerator and poured herself half a cup, sighing with pleasure at the first cold, fruity sip.

As she moved around the kitchen in a dance she could complete with her eyes closed, she mentally ticked down the list of items to complete before the weekend. Running Pierce Brothers was a challenge, but she took pride in the way she was able to consistently multitask and keep the office running smoothly. When she'd first started there and Christian Pierce was alive, she was a simple receptionist, learning the business from the ground up. Funny, she always knew that was exactly what she wanted to do with her life. She had no dreams to attend college or leave Harrington. She was happy in the quaint Northeast town, working in a family corporation where she was not only valued, but admired.

It had been Tristan who'd wanted to leave.

The memory caught hold and played out. God,

how she'd loved him. Since she was twelve years old she'd been following him around like a lost puppy, thrilled at any type of attention he wished to throw her. She'd been like the annoying little sister to their crew of three, and though Cal and Dalton treated her more kindly, there were no burning, lustful feelings toward them.

Just Tristan.

As she struggled to finish high school, she was tortured by the long line of women Tristan brought home from college. How many times had she sat in his mother's kitchen with a poisonous envy wracking her body? He'd say hello in that arrogant way of his, tug at her hair like she was a toddler, then parade his newest squeeze right in front of her. Diane Pierce knew early on how much Sydney adored her son and advised patience.

You both need to grow up a bit, sweetheart. And you'll find each other if it's meant to be.

Diane Pierce had been a mother figure, and Sydney was always welcomed. Her own mother had gotten pregnant at sixteen and taken off the moment she left the hospital, choosing not to return. Sydney never mourned her. She'd been lucky to be raised by her grandparents, who took care of all of her needs and gave her the love her mother couldn't. But being a part of the Pierce family was something she'd always treasured.

When Diane was killed in a car crash years ago, the family had fragmented, spiraling into a series of events that ripped them apart. Since Diane had been discovered running away with another man, Christian Pierce had turned into a cold, empty father who treated his sons with harsh abuse. In the midst of grief and confusion, the brothers split up after a horrible fight. Dalton fled to California, Tristan headed to New York, and Cal remained behind to work beside his father.

They hadn't spoken for five long years until their father's death forced them to reconcile. The will had stated that the brothers needed to work together to run Pierce Brothers for a year or it would be sold off. After a rocky year of raw emotion, they had finally united as one, deciding to stay and run Pierce Brothers as the family business Diane had once dreamed of.

Sydney smiled as she thought of them now. Sure, they still ribbed one another like normal siblings, but there was a respect and love that hummed under the surface. They were finally healed and a real team. Over the past year, she'd watched both Caleb and Dalton fall in love with incredible women she now called friends. Morgan and Raven had become part of their family. This should have been one of the most satisfying times in her life.

If only she could stop thinking about Tristan.

The muffin incident was just one in a long stream of bad encounters. She tried to avoid him at all costs, hating the familiar sexual energy that surged between them and wrecked her concentration. They were barely able to have a polite exchange without one trying to attack the other. He refused to see her as a grown woman who'd made her own place in life. To him, she would always be the young girl he needed to guide and protect from the big bad world.

Even though in the end, he'd betrayed her.

She finished her wine, shaking her head to clear her thoughts. She'd just have to live with her lingering feelings. Keep avoiding him. Stick to business when they did converse. Be polite but distant. Eventually, she'd find a nice man to date and fall in love and leave Tristan Pierce behind for good.

Because he could never know.

Discover a new love with bestselling romance from Pocket Books!

Pick up or download your copies today!

XOXOAfterDark.com

POCKET BOOKS
An Imprint of Simon & Schuster
A CBS COMPANY

53880

Discover more bestselling romance from Pocket Books!

Pick up or download your copies today!

XOXOAfterDark.com

POCKET BOOKS
An Imprint of Simon & Schuster
A CBS COMPANY

50748

Because the best conversations happen after dark . . .

ANNOUNCING A BRAND-NEW SITE FOR ROMANCE AND URBAN FANTASY READERS JUST LIKE YOU!

 *Visit **XOXOAfterDark.com** for free reads, exclusive excerpts, bonus materials, author interviews and chats, and much, much more!*

XOXO**AFTERDARK**.COM